SUSAN WIGGS

TEXAS WILDFLOWER

ZEBRA

EAN

ISBN-13: 978-1-4201-2988-5
ISBN-10: 1-4201-2988-0

5 0 3 9 9

Books by Susan Wiggs

*Published by Kensington Publishing Corporation

TEXAS WILDFLOWER

SUSAN WIGGS

ZEBRA BOOKS
Kensington Publishing Corp.
http://www.kensingtonbooks.com

ZEBRA BOOKS are published by

Kensington Publishing Corp.
119 West 40th Street
New York, NY 10018

All Kensington titles, imprints, and distributed lines are available at special quantity discounts for bulk purchases for sales
promotion, premiums, fundraising, educational, or institu-
tional use.

Special book excerpts or customized printings can also be
created to fit specific needs. For details, write or phone the
office of the Kensington Special Sales Manager: Attn. Special
Sales Department. Kensington Publishing Corp., 119 West
40th Street, New York, NY 10018. Phone: 1-800-221-2647.

ISBN-13: 978-1-4201-2988-5
ISBN-10: 1-4201-2988-0

First Printing: April 1987

20 19 18 17 16 15 14 13

Printed in the United States of America

Dear Reader:

   Texas Wildflower is my first novel, originally published in 1987. Since that time, I've written another two dozen novels, changing and improving my craft along the way. I've made some minor editorial revisions to the text of this new edition, but the story retains the energy and passion that spurred me to write it in the first place. Revisiting this book reminded me of why I was so captivated by Justin, Shiloh, and the challenges they face when circumstances plunge them into a world of deception and temptation, and of the power of love to transform the lives of a driven man and a troubled woman. I hope you enjoy the romance and adventure of *Texas Wildflower* in this newly repackaged edition.

My very best wishes,
Susan Wiggs
www.susanwiggs.com

For Jay

PROLOGUE

Salado, Mexico
March 1843

Isabella's brown eyes blinked twice, very slowly. The incredibly long black lashes grazed her tawny cheeks. Her lovely face was immobile, but her lush, ample bosom rose and fell quickly.

Looking up from where he knelt in the dust, Justin McCord was struck—not for the first time—by her sultry beauty. She had the face of an angel and a body straight from heaven. Justin's gut tightened as he remembered the long, breezy nights he'd spent in her arms.

"You bitch." His voice was a soft snarl in the dusty afternoon quiet.

"Justin, *caro*, you do not understand—"

"Oh, I understand everything now, Isabella. 'Just one more night'—wasn't that what you asked me for? How sweet you were when you claimed my wound still needed your care, yet all along you were waiting, weren't you? Waiting for Huerto and the reward he'd give you for my capture."

"That is not true! Your shoulder has not healed properly—"

Justin laughed harshly. "I guess that doesn't matter much now, does it? Huerto will see to it that I die well before the wound has a chance to fester."

"You will not be killed. Domingo promised." She moistened her lips. "You'll be questioned, and then you can come back to me." She bent down and leaned close to him. Her tongue darted artfully into his ear. "You will come back, won't you, *caro*? We were happy together, were we not? No man has ever made love to me like—"

He pushed her into the dust. "Get out of my sight."

One of the guards stepped forward quickly. The butt of his rifle swung out, knocking Justin on the side of the head.

"*Diablo tejano!*" the soldier spat. "To your feet. I think it is time you joined your *compadres sangrientos.*"

Heat shimmered on the dusty white plains of Salado. The air was still, silent but for the incessant buzzing of flies. Justin was taken amid the other Texans, most of them even worse off than himself, having been marched from where they had been captured in the border town of Mier. Sweat coursed down Justin's face and drenched his shirt as he was shackled to the line. His shoulder throbbed and oozed from the bullet he'd taken. Through a haze of pain, he looked around at the walls of the Hacienda del Salado, which bristled with the tiny black eyes of dozens of muskets.

Colonel Domingo Huerto, the ranking Mexican officer, strode forward to explain the fate of the Texans with obvious relish. His eyes flickered over the group.

"Your sins against my people are many," he said loudly. "For the taking of Mier and the capture of its *alcalde,* you deserve to die like dogs."

Around him, the soldiers and subalterns nodded in agreement and nudged one another. Huerto continued. "However, I am told that British and American envoys in Mexico City have been begging for your miserable lives. Do not ask me why. You are a disgrace, storming villages and stealing from innocent people. But you will not all die. One in ten will face the firing squad. That is the Latino way, but I am told you Anglos have a fondness for gambling, too. So that is what we shall do. Gamble for your lives."

At his gesture, a subaltern scurried forward with an earthen crock. Over the opening was a folded scarf.

Huerto held the jug high. "There are one hundred seventy-six beans in here—one for each of you. Seventeen are black; the rest are white. Those who draw the black beans will die."

"Sweet Jesus," someone muttered. Justin looked to his left and saw that it was Edmund Katz, whose pockmarked face and trembling lip betrayed his adolescence. He couldn't have been more than sixteen.

On Justin's right was Thaddeus Stripling, who swayed and almost fainted from a gaping saber wound in his side. Discreetly Justin put his arm around the man to hold him steady, and wondered why Stripling, a political appointee, was among the scruffy men of the Mier expedition.

"You should've listened to me back in San Antone," Stripling wheezed.

"What do you mean by that?"

Stripling wiped the beads of sweat from his upper lip. "The Hernandez woman—Isabella. Isn't that where you first met her? I told you she wasn't just an ordinary whore. She's with the Accord, but I guess you know about that by now."

Justin drew in his breath with a soft hiss. How had Stripling known about the Accord?

Before he could ask, the crock of beans was put before him.

"Is this your idea of a game, Colonel?" he drawled.

"It is better than you deserve," snarled the Mexican officer. He looked over his shoulder at Isabella. "Well done," he told her. "We could not have afforded to let this one go."

Isabella only nodded, refusing to look up.

Huerto thrust the crock at Justin. "Draw."

With deliberate slowness, Justin reached in. His hand closed around a bean and he pulled it out. His eyes never left Huerto. The Texans around him were laughing and joking, characteristically full of bravado in the face of danger.

"Beats rafflin' all to hell," one of them said.

"Tallest gamblin' scrape I've ever been in," said another.

Finally Huerto grew impatient. "What are you waiting for, *tejano*? Show us your hand."

Justin held out his clenched fist and opened it slowly. The sunlight glinted across his palm. The bean sat there, deadly as a lead ball.

Isabella gasped aloud. "No—"

Huerto grinned. "Sorry, my friend. It is the luck of the draw, as they say."

As a cold feeling gripped Justin, so did an overwhelming hatred of Huerto and his kind. Texas had won its independence seven years before, but the defeated Mexicans persisted, trying to eat away at the borders, taking all the little villages and hamlets that would succumb. Justin was surprisingly calm about his fate; he only regretted that his passing would leave a lot of unfinished government business.

The lottery went on until all the black beans had been drawn. Cries of outrage, pleas for mercy, and curses of defiant bravado sounded among the Texans. Justin remained silent, refusing to think of what was to come.

Stripling swayed against Justin and pressed a white bean into his hand. "Give me the black bean," he rasped. "I'm going in your place."

Justin drew away. "I can't let you do that, Thad—"

"Just shut up and listen. There's not much time. I'm dying anyway, Justin. I wouldn't last the night."

"Thad—"

"Now, look, I'm not doing this out of any sense of brotherly love, although I'd be obliged if the Maker would believe that." He coughed and grinned crookedly, his dry lips cracking.

"I wasn't along on this raid as a regular, and I happen to know you weren't either. I'm a special agent of the government, like you. I've been charged with investigating the Accord, a group of Texans and British who mean to overthrow the government and sabotage plans for statehood. The ringleader is Harmon West, a Houston judge. You'll want to watch that one." He pushed a set of keys into Justin's back pocket. "I've got a farm near Houston. There's a strongbox in the library that has all the information you'll need. Use it, Justin."

"Damn it, Thad, I—"

"You've got a job to do, and I aim to see it gets done. Now, don't wait around for the Mexicans to set you free," Stripling rasped. "They'll kill the seventeen as promised, but the rest will be marched to Mexico City."

The doomed Texans were unshackled. A soldier prodded Justin with his bayonet. "Let's go."

Stripling staggered forward. "I'm going in his place."

The soldier shrugged and stepped aside for Stripling to pass.

"Don't fail us," Stripling whispered, and reeled ahead to the makeshift execution gallery.

Justin's heart pounded with relief, with dread, with agonizing wonder at the nobility of Thad Stripling's last act. The Texans were lined up and seated on a log some distance away. Blindfolds were given to those who requested them. The Mexican Red Cap company assembled, their muskets loaded.

There was no time to think. Justin took a step back, then another. He heard Huerto's shouted command.

"Ready . . ."

Two more steps. Justin was now behind the line of silent, appalled Texans.

"Aim . . ."

Suddenly, Justin felt the tingle of someone's gaze. Isabella was watching him with her sharp, bright eyes. His heart grew cold as her lips parted to cry out.

But she didn't. Giving him a look that begged forgiveness, she closed her mouth and looked away.

Justin ran, the dust flying under his boots. It was just a few steps to the crumbling wall of the hacienda, where a few horses were tethered to a rail. Hands flying, Justin unlashed a pair of reins.

"Fire!"

The discharge of forty guns masked the sound of hooves thundering off to the north.

ONE

Shiloh Mulvane slapped at a lazy fly that buzzed about her neck. She shifted her position slightly and lifted the hem of her scratchy wool serape to let in a small breath of hot, dry air. Sweat rolled in rivulets down the sides of her face, which was concealed by a wide-brimmed sombrero.

The waiting seemed interminable. Afternoon had lengthened into evening. Dust motes spun amid the amber shafts of light that slanted in through the window of Hatfield's saloon. A scruffy assortment of men, the members of Congress indistinguishable from the outlaws and gamblers, lounged at the bar, laughing raucously at coarse jokes and downing the sharp-edged whiskey that was served by an aging barman.

Shiloh ignored the jokes and gossip of the dusty frontier capital. Her shaded eyes were trained on one man, who leaned against the

back wall of the saloon. By now, she'd memo-
rized the shape of his black hat and the shock
of straight blond hair that fell across his brow.
For hours she'd watched that hard, angular
face, the eyes of flint that flicked watchfully
about the room. She knew every fold in his
snug-fitting trousers, every dust-lined crease in
his boots. She gazed with interest at the man's
hands. Tanned and rough, one of them held a
cheroot, and the other, which had a curious little ring on the fourth finger, rested with studied
nonchalance on the polished handle of his
Texas-model Colt's. Justin McCord had the look
of a dangerous man: strong, capable, and tense
as a coiled spring.

Judge West had warned her about him. Mc-
Cord wouldn't be an easy one to take; only the
element of surprise would give Shiloh an edge.

With studied casualness, McCord checked the
gold watch from his vest pocket, and frowned
slightly. Obviously, the person he'd come to meet
hadn't shown. Finally, as if in sudden decision, he
tossed back the last of his whiskey and stood to
his full height. He was well over six feet tall,
Shiloh noted, tensing a little. With swift, easy
movements he tossed some silver coins onto the
bar, lifted his hat, and strode out, leaving the
doors swinging lazily behind him.

Unremarked by anyone, Shiloh rose from her
position on the unswept wooden floor. Her stiff
legs screamed in protest as she crept along the
planks of the walkway, her soft knee-high moc-

casins making no sound. Main Street, so primitive that numerous stumps still marred it, was deserted. After his triumphant meeting with Indian tribal leaders in the spring, Sam Houston and his entourage had left Washington, taking the better part of the population with them. Grateful for the isolation, Shiloh advanced silently on her quarry. She was inches from McCord. Her hand closed around her six-gun. As she drew it out, a bead of sweat collected on the tip of her nose. McCord had reached his bay horse and was untying it.

Shiloh cocked her gun with a metallic click and shoved it hard into his back.

McCord froze.

Shiloh pressed harder, her eyes riveted to his hands. The fingers of his right hand twitched slightly, a sure sign that he was going for his gun.

But he didn't. With shocking speed, he spun about and swung his doubled fist into Shiloh's middle. She grunted, fell back against the building. Her sombrero fell askew, revealing a mass of tight, red-gold curls. Yet her well-trained hands hadn't betrayed her. She still held the gun fast and was ready for him when he lunged.

Quicker than McCord by a split second, she leveled the barrel at his face.

"You make me nervous." Her finger tightened meaningfully around the trigger. "I'd feel a whole lot better if you got rid of that gun."

McCord was practically smiling as he looked

at her. A dimple showed in his tanned cheek, and his eyes crinkled at the corners. "Aren't you a little young to be playing with a grownup weapon?"

Shiloh put still more pressure on the trigger and prayed that her nervousness didn't show. "I'm not playing," she replied. "Now, drop the gun."

It fell with a thud onto the planks. Eyes never leaving him, Shiloh stooped and picked it up, and shoved it into her belt.

She jerked her head toward the street. "Get in the wagon. And put those handcuffs on."

McCord's mouth tightened. "Now look—"

Shiloh thrust the gun closer. "Get in, McCord."

He studied her for a long, deliberating moment.

Reading his thoughts, she said, "No, Mr. McCord, I won't kill you. But if you don't cooperate, it could cost you some vital part of your anatomy."

She heard him swear under his breath, but he swung himself up into the wagon and fastened the cuff around his right wrist. The other ring of the cuffs was secured to an iron bolt on the wagon's side.

Shiloh nodded, satisfied, and holstered her gun. With a sigh of relief, she stripped off the stifling, musty serape and untied the oversized sombrero from where it hung about her neck. She felt McCord's eyes on her tight-fitting doeskin breeches and sweat-drenched cotton shirt. Despite the heat, a shiver went through her.

She reined his bay to the back of the cart and settled herself next to him. They left the tiny frontier town of Washington-on-the-Brazos in a cloud of dust, their departure remarked only by a large armadillo that scuttled out of the wagon's path.

McCord seemed surprisingly—maddeningly— unruffled by his capture. He even joked with the ferryman who took them across the river. As they turned eastward, he lounged against the side of the wagon.

"So tell me," he drawled, "to what do I owe this ride with a girl who masquerades as a Mexican?"

Shiloh glanced at him, a little surprised at the barely disguised overtones of culture in his speech.

"Not that it's any of your business, but I'm a grown woman of twenty. And to answer your question, you've got an appointment to keep, Mr. McCord. With Miss Jessamine West."

"Jessamine—" For the first time, a line of concern deepened his brow. "What the hell does she want with me?"

"You would know that better than I, Mr. McCord. Although I suspect it has something to do with marriage."

McCord gave a low whistle. "I'm not in any position to oblige."

"You should have thought of that when you

compromised the young lady." Shiloh made no effort to conceal her distaste. She had no respect for men who used women.

The flinty eyes narrowed. "So that's what this is all about." He chuckled. "A good old-fashioned shotgun wedding. But I must say, I always thought it was the offended damsel's daddy who brought the reluctant groom to the altar."

"I'm sure Judge West fully intends to deal with you when we reach Houston."

McCord nodded. An unpleasant look had crossed his face at the mention of Judge Harmon West. It was clear to Shiloh that he wanted nothing to do with the man or his daughter, although she wondered why he'd got involved with Jessamine in the first place. Apparently, McCord was like most men, allowing his head to be turned by the young lady's yellow ringlets and teasing, pouting red mouth. She shrugged. Jessamine's conquests were well known in Houston. She'd always wondered who the girl would finally settle down with, and wasn't surprised by the choice.

They rode along in silence for a while. The sun sank low behind them, gilding the gentle rises of pasture and the stands of post oak in the distance. A lone hawk wheeled overhead and dove for its prey. Somewhere far away, a coyote howled.

At length Justin asked, "Is she—Jessamine—with child?"

Shiloh shrugged. "It didn't occur to me to ask. But no mention was made of it."

McCord settled back then, seeming to grow more relaxed with each passing moment. He rested his free arm on his drawn-up knee and looked over at Shiloh.

"At this rate, it's three days to Houston."

Shiloh nodded and stared ahead.

"Don't you think I should know your name?"

Shiloh glanced at him, wondering if he was honestly trying to be friendly, and then doubting it.

"All you need to know about me is that I was sent to do a job, and I intend to see it through. To be honest, Mr. McCord, I find this whole business as distasteful as you seem to, but I wasn't in a position to turn it down." Anxiety tightened her throat as she had a sudden image of her father, sweating and feverish, abed with a dangerously festering leg.

She swallowed hard and forced herself to sound nonchalant. "I'm a reasonable person, Mr. McCord. There's no reason why you shouldn't know my name. I'm Shiloh Mulvane."

He let out another of his low whistles. "Nate Mulvane's daughter? Damn, I should've recognized that carroty hair, those green eyes, the freckles—"

"You know my father?"

"Anyone who's been in Texas for the past ten years has heard of Nate Mulvane. His reputation as a frontier detective is known pretty well in these parts."

Shiloh was proud of her father's accomplishments, even though his personal traits were something again. After distinguishing himself as a scout in the Texas Revolution, he'd gone into private service, bringing down criminals from every class: from cattle rustlers to murderers, bigamists to robbers.

Because her father was a master of his trade, Shiloh was able to live with his faults. Although he drank heavily and seemed to lack affection for his daughter, that had never interfered with his work. And though he managed his money with total ineptness, that didn't matter. Mulvane had little sense for anything other than his work. That was why this job was so important to Shiloh. If he couldn't love her as a daughter, at least she might win his respect.

She drove on, aware of her prisoner's eyes on her. Justin McCord was as wily as they came: smart, cautious, and self-assured. She knew the next few days would not be easy.

She chose a sheltered coppice in a quiet meander of a deep creek to pass the night. There was a wealth of salt grass for the team and a thick covering of long, reddish-brown pine needles to cushion their bedrolls. Jumping down from the wagon, Shiloh drew out a heavy length of chain and locked it around the base of a pine tree. The other end she clamped around McCord's ankle.

"Leg irons?" he questioned mildly. "How imaginative."

Shiloh shrugged, freed him from the handcuffs, and drew the wagon away. "I can't afford to take any chances with you, Mr. McCord—oh!"

She gasped as his hand closed around her wrist. His other arm encircled her waist and pulled her against him so that she was forced to look up at his angry face.

"Let's get this straight, Miss Mulvane. I'm not real happy about being dragged around by a money-grubbing female bounty hunter. I could break your neck right now with only the slightest effort."

She squirmed against him, equally angry. "A whole lot of good that would do you, McCord. You'd still be chained to this tree, and everything—guns, keys, team, and wagon—is out of your reach. No one is likely to pass this way for days. You'd die of exposure if you didn't starve first."

He grinned, his teeth glinting white in the starlight. He brought his face very close to Shiloh's and held her wrapped against him. His mouth began a slow, deliberate descent to hers. With a startled cry, Shiloh turned her head away. He might use his attractiveness to get what he wanted from some women, but not from her.

With an abrupt laugh, he relaxed his hold on her so quickly that she stumbled back.

"You've thought of everything, Miss Mulvane,"

he said, raising his hat in mock salute. "I concede to your superior wiles. I'm at your mercy."

More shaken by the encounter than she cared to admit, she went to unhitch the team and McCord's big bay, tethering them near the water. As McCord watched with almost patronizing amusement, she laid out two bedrolls. From the wagon she brought a hamper of bread, hard cheese, jerky, and a pair of soft, ripe peaches. For all his blustering and dickering over fees, Judge West had equipped her generously.

Both ate sparingly, sitting on the soft bed of pine needles. McCord watched her thoughtfully as he chewed on a piece of jerky.

"So tell me," he said, "how is it that you're in the business of pursuing hardened criminals? Hasn't your mother taught you that women don't do things like that?"

"My mother died when I was five. Father sent me east to a school for young ladies, but I never took to practicing inane conversation while pouring tea and fluttering a fan in front of my face."

McCord laughed. "I don't guess you would. I didn't think there was much of the woman in you."

Shiloh had bitten into a peach and was about to wipe away a trickle of juice with her sleeve. She stopped in midmotion and delicately dabbed at her lips with a napkin from the hamper.

"I don't give a damn what you think of me," she said. "But I'm not a complete oaf. I can behave properly if necessary."

"Touchy, aren't you?"

She turned away and tossed the half-eaten peach into the creek. Without looking at McCord again, she went to rub down the horses. She spoke softly to them as she worked.

"Damned outlaw," she muttered, pulling the currycomb down a sweat-dampened flank. "What would Jessamine West ever want with such a man? She must be more a fool than I thought to be taken in by his handsome looks. Lord knows, he doesn't have anything else to recommend him." The horse bobbed its head and snorted as if in agreement. Shiloh worked on with a satisfied air. This was the first job she'd done on her own, and it had gone without a hitch. It had been almost too easy. He seemed a cooperative captive, but Shiloh knew better than to let down her guard. She gave each horse a sack of oats and returned to the campsite.

McCord had fallen asleep on his bedroll, his long, lithe frame relaxed and his hat pulled down over his eyes. Still, Shiloh didn't trust him.

"McCord . . . ?"

No response. For a man being forcibly dragged to the altar, he was amazingly unperturbed. Shrugging, Shiloh went to her own bedroll some yards away. One by one, she removed her high moccasins and loosened the top buttons of her cotton shirt. Grimacing, she noted that nightfall had brought scant relief from the hot, dry heat of summer. She felt gritty and sticky with dust and sweat.

One glance at the slow, eddying waters of the creek convinced her to put off bedding down for the night. She gave one last look at McCord. He hadn't moved. Shiloh left her clothes in a heap and stepped soundlessly down to the creek's edge.

She waded in, sighing softly at the cool, silken feel of the water as it swirled about her thighs. She went deeper, her breasts tightening as the creek closed over them. Finally, she sank beneath the surface, glorying shamelessly in the cleansing, cooling sensations.

Stars sprayed across the night sky, silvering the tops of the pines. The sliver of a new moon cast an otherworldly, enchanting glow upon the water. Cicadas buzzed their endless night song. Shiloh's heart filled with love for the country called Texas, the country her father had fought for, the one that had given her the freedom to do as she pleased. Its rugged beauty daunted some, but Shiloh felt completely at home.

She went to the sandy edge and took up a cake of honeysuckle-scented soap, one of the few indulgences she'd brought along. Standing hip-deep, she lathered herself slowly, soaping her torso and arms, her tightly curling red hair. Then she plunged in for a last rinse.

Justin stared sleeplessly into the black inside of his hat. He'd ignored Shiloh when she'd spoken his name, preferring to use the time to mull over what was happening. The ridiculousness of it all was almost laughable. He'd survived every major battle of the Texas Revolution seven years before, and after that had cheated death in countless Indian raids and the Mexican army's forages into the Rio Grande Valley. More recently, he had avoided being killed on the Mier expedition. His superiors in Washington considered him one of the most discreet, elusive agents in Texas.

Yet a mere slip of a girl had managed to seize him. He wondered if the little spitfire was aware of the fiasco she'd caused. He'd been trying to make contact with Raúl Delgado, a Mexican operative who had vital information about the Accord. It was no accident that Harmon West had sent Shiloh to Washington-on-the-Brazos in time to foil the contact, but did she know that?

Probably not, Justin decided. As far as Shiloh knew, she was merely bringing him to Jessamine. Among Stripling's personal effects he'd found a scribbled note suggesting that Jessamine might be induced to shed some light on her father's scurrilous activities. So Justin had approached her, and found her more than willing to strike up an acquaintance. The sweet Southern-belle facade had rapidly fallen away to reveal the girl's healthy interest in fleshly delights. In addition to a few tidbits about Harmon West, Justin had been treated to a large dose of

Jessamine's charms. She'd been a mildly pleasant diversion.

The one thing Justin had underestimated was her possessiveness.

He groaned audibly as everything fell into place. Harmon had hit on a perfect solution for halting the United States' investigation. The judge intended to make the government's chief agent his son-in-law. That would neatly destroy Justin's credibility as an impartial operative.

If marrying the girl was personally unappealing to Justin, it was out of the question on a professional level. He hadn't left his native Virginia eight years earlier to pursue a life of obscurity in Texas. He meant to do something that counted, and Jessamine couldn't be included in his plans.

His father's angry words, spoken years ago at Justin's final parting from his Virginia plantation, came back, hauntingly clear in the quiet of Justin's mind.

"You'll regret going to that godforsaken frontier," Angus McCord had warned. "Texas will milk you dry, and if you aren't killed by a Mexican saber, you'll wind up beaten by the land itself. The day you were born I promised the Grangers you'd marry their daughter Ivy and our plantations would merge. I know how you feel about that, but believe me, you'll thank me for it one day."

Justin had rebelled against the arranged marriage, yet now a similar one seemed imminent.

Harmon West would be well within his rights to force a wedding. Laws in Texas tended to be an individual code, and many would admire the judge for protecting his daughter's honor.

There had to be a way out. Justin knew that with a little maneuvering, he could easily break free from Shiloh Mulvane. But that would only buy him a little time. The moment he showed his face in Houston, West would pounce. No, what Justin needed was a much more permanent solution.

A sudden splash startled him out of his musing. He swept his hat from his face and sat up, looking toward the creek. The sight that greeted him drove all thoughts of Harmon West's treachery away.

Shiloh's moon-silvered shoulders glistened as she bathed herself in the creek. She was rinsing soap from her hair, the foam being swept downstream. Justin caught sight of her profile: a high, clear forehead, a small, slightly upturned nose, a proudly angled chin.

At first he'd thought the girl plain, almost homely, but in this unguarded moment he recognized a subtle yet undeniable beauty. The revelation was confirmed when Shiloh emerged slowly from the water.

Her nude body, its contours shining, was perfection. Lean yet shapely, her legs carried her to the shore with unconscious grace. Her breasts were little more than rises of soft flesh, but the sight of her tight coral nipples sent a flood of liquid fire to Justin's loins. She had a tiny waist and flat belly, and barely rounded hips.

As she stooped to pick up a rough blanket and began drying herself off, Justin drew in his breath with a hiss. He steeled himself against the urge to tear his ankle from the leg iron and enfold the lovely body in his arms.

But he didn't. He relaxed onto his bedroll and let a slow smile spread across his face. Like the moon bursting from behind a bank of clouds, a plan began to take shape in his mind.

Feeling refreshed after her bath, Shiloh drew a wooden comb through her matted curls. Suddenly, a chill touched the base of her neck.

Glancing over at McCord, she gasped and dropped the comb. He was lying on his side, propped up on one elbow.

"I take back what I said earlier," he drawled, "about there not being much of the woman in you."

Shiloh dove for her Colt's, holding her shirt closed with her other hand. Her grasp wavered as she leveled the gun at him.

"Damn you!" she said. "How long were you— have you been—"

McCord grinned, his dimple making a dark impression on his face. "Long enough to know that you're every inch a woman."

A burning blush crept over Shiloh as she gritted her teeth. She raised the gun.

"Damn you," she said again.

McCord's laugh angered her further. "If I thought it would do any good, Miss Mulvane, I'd apologize. But I honestly didn't do anything wrong. *You* were the one who disturbed *me.*"

She cocked her gun. "Turn around, Mr. Mc-Cord."

"I doubt Judge West would be willing to pay for a corpse." But he turned obligingly, pulled his hat down again, and said no more.

Shiloh hurriedly donned her breeches and lay down, but sleep would not come. No amount of tossing and turning could dispel the image of McCord's flinty eyes, silvered by moonlight, watching her with a strange mixture of hunger and cold calculation.

During the next day's drive, she felt his eyes on her almost constantly, studying her profile or the curve of her breast, his hand brushing her thigh from time to time. The miles of red clay mounds and heat-shimmering yellow-green fields seemed to crawl by.

When they stopped at nightfall, some twenty miles west of Houston, Shiloh's nerves were stretched taut, dangerously close to the surface.

"I think you liked me better before I found you so damned attractive," McCord said.

Agitated, Shiloh fumbled with the leg irons. "It's not my place to like or dislike you, Mr. Mc-

Cord. My only concern is to deliver you to Houston."

He flexed his booted ankle slightly. "Oh, yes, to my wedding."

Shiloh finished with the leg iron and looked up. "It won't do you any good to try and get out of it."

He grinned charmingly. "Oh, I intend to be married, Miss Mulvane. Even sooner than you might think."

There was no warning. One moment McCord was lounging easily on the seat of the wagon, and the next he moved like a striking snake. He grasped Shiloh by the wrists and kicked off the leg iron, which hadn't latched properly. With one great, angry tug, he broke the handcuffs away from the wagon, splintering the dry wood.

He let go of Shiloh so abruptly that she fell. With an air of studied casualness, McCord ambled over to a live oak, where Shiloh had stowed the guns and keys out of his reach. He freed himself from the handcuffs, shaking them off in an annoyed manner. Then he bent and holstered his own gun and emptied hers, tossing the bullets into the nearby stream.

While McCord's back was turned, she scrambled to her feet and edged around to the back of the wagon, where a loaded rifle was stashed beneath some hopsacking.

"I wouldn't go for the rifle, Miss Mulvane. You'd never be quick enough to use it."

She backed against the wagon, her heart

thumping, her hands clutching at the rail. Mc-Cord walked toward her and didn't stop until they were inches from each other. Shiloh caught the scent of dust and cheroot. Absurdly, she found herself wondering how he'd got the small scar on his left cheekbone. It was very faint, shaped like a crescent.

"Let's get one thing straight, Miss Mulvane," he drawled, his breath warm on her face. "I'm not a man who takes to being chained up like a dog."

Shiloh's mouth felt dry as cotton. "What are you going to do?"

He smiled lazily. "I'm coming with you to Houston, if you don't mind my company. But I'm afraid we'll have to make a brief stop before seeing the judge."

He reached behind her. Shiloh tensed, thinking he was going to embrace her. But instead, he simply picked up the rifle, emptied it, and tossed the ball into the stream.

"Any coffee in there?" he inquired, jerking his head toward the hamper under the tree. He was as calm as if nothing had happened.

Shiloh nodded in a dazed manner. She watched as McCord made a small, crackling fire and set the coffee brewing. She considered running off, but she knew she wouldn't get far. McCord's feigned nonchalance masked a tense vigilance.

"Relax, Miss Mulvane. I'm not going to run out on you."

"That's the least of my worries, she retorted.

He drew a small flask from his boot. Shiloh noticed with alarm that he had a Bowie knife sheathed there, and cursed her own stupidity in overlooking it. She'd been so smug about having captured him, but now she realized all the mistakes she'd made.

When he offered her the flask, she took it and drank deeply. The fiery liquid nearly made her gag, but the second time she raised it to her lips it went down more smoothly. After a third drink, she passed it to McCord. He didn't drink.

At last she found her voice. "I don't understand you, Mr. McCord."

He shrugged and sipped his coffee. "If Judge West had taken the trouble to check, he'd've spared you this trip. I bought the Stripling farm outside Houston just six weeks ago. Planned to make it into a horse ranch. In fact, I was going to look at some livestock when I made your charming acquaintance."

"I didn't notice any horse traders in Washington-on-the-Brazos."

"I had other business as well." He didn't elaborate on that. "So you see, I'm quite willing to return to Houston. If Miss West is expecting a child, I'll make the necessary arrangements."

"But you won't marry her."

"Nope." He flicked the stub of his cheroot into the fire. "By the time we reach Houston, that will be quite impossible. Jessamine may find that I'm not the eligible bachelor she thought I was."

Shiloh reached for the flask again, wondering what heinous truth he would reveal about himself that would turn Jessamine away. "That won't sit well with the judge. Besides, won't you be needing a wife if you're starting up a ranch?"

"Could be." He looked at her squarely. "But if I do, it'll be on my own terms and not because I've been prodded into it. One of the reasons I left Virginia and came to Texas in the first place was that I resented my father's trying to pair me off."

Shiloh looked at him. She couldn't imagine a man like McCord even having a father, much less one who believed he could keep a son like Justin in line. She traced her finger in the dust, wondering what sort of life he'd left behind in Virginia.

"You could do worse than Jessamine," she suggested. Personally, she found the young woman cloyingly sweet, with a subtle streak of feline nastiness. But Jessamine had the plump, yellow-haired looks that brought men to their knees, and she knew how to simper and giggle expertly.

McCord chuckled. "Ah, the delectable Miss West. She has all the conversational interest of a mockingbird. No, I'm not prepared to spend my life gowning her in silks and escorting her to social functions."

In spite of everything, and because of the whiskey that warmed her veins, Shiloh laughed. For some reason it pleased her that McCord's impression of Jessamine matched her own.

"I'd say you're in a heap of trouble, Mr. Mc-Cord. Whatever made you take up with Jessamine if you don't even like her?"

He shrugged. "I like women. And Jessamine made no mention of future commitments when she threw herself at me."

Shiloh scowled. "That's a pretty arrogant thing to say."

"You asked." He shifted and was suddenly sitting closer to Shiloh. Again she caught his scent, and noticed the play of muscles in his thigh as he drew his knee up to his chest.

"I don't much fancy talking about myself, Shiloh. I'd rather hear about you."

It was the first time she'd heard him use her given name. He slid into using it easily, as easily as his arm moved behind her, barely touching her as he rested his hand on the ground. Shiloh drank some more of the whiskey.

"I live in Houston with my father. He brought me back there when I didn't do so well at the girls' school in the East. I've been working with him for two years."

"I could tell you were no amateur. You handle a gun pretty well. You'd've had me nailed if you hadn't been so softhearted with me."

She straightened up, frowning. "Softhearted? Me?"

"If you'd really meant business, you would have trussed me up like a spring turkey and thrown me in the back of the wagon. I'd've been none the worse for the wear."

Shiloh fumed. He was right, of course, although she'd never admit it to him. Privately, she vowed to follow his advice the next time . . . if there ever was a next time.

"Mc—Justin." She shifted, putting her shoulder against the tree to face him. A bird called, a yearning sound in the night. "I agreed to work for Judge West because my father and I need money—badly. But there's also another reason."

He gave her his full attention, looking at her intently.

"Father has never taken me seriously. When I wanted to work with him, he had me shuffling papers and poring over account books, occasionally writing a report.

"Four weeks ago, he was stabbed in the leg and the wound festered. He's been bedridden and doesn't know I took this job. He'll be furious when he finds out. He'll never trust me again when he learns that you—that I botched everything. But if I succeed—"

"You'll have proven yourself," McCord finished for her.

Shiloh nodded.

"And all I have to do is let you haul me into town, as if you'd dragged me, fighting and hollering, every inch of the way."

Shiloh gave him a dubious look. "I know it's a lot to ask—"

He touched her and she gasped. His long-fingered hand traveled ever so lightly up the side of her arm. Gently, he lifted the curls away from her neck and caressed the leaping pulse at her throat.

For a moment, Shiloh was fascinated by the wave of intense sensations that washed over her. The hard-planed face drew down to hers, closer . . . Shiloh could almost taste his lips on hers.

With his mouth poised just a whisper away, he said, "That's a mighty big favor you're asking of me, Shiloh. But I might consider it if you'd . . ."

A chill came over her, snuffing out the sudden hot longing that had seized her. She slapped his hand away.

"No deal, McCord."

He laughed. "A minute ago you wanted something badly enough to—"

"Not enough to warm your bedroll for a night, McCord." Shiloh jumped up and stalked over to the bubbling stream. She filled her cupped hands with cool water and bathed her flaming cheeks. She felt him come up behind her. He knelt and spoke intimately into her ear.

"No moonlit swim tonight, Miss Mulvane?"

She tossed her head in angry denial. "You've already shown that you can't be trusted."

"But you won't mind if *I* do," he said, a smile in his voice. "I'll want to look presentable for tomorrow."

"Do as you please." She whirled around, intending to brush past him. Instead, she found herself staring point-blank at his bare chest. Powerful bands of muscle stood out, tapering down to a flat belly. His skin glistened in the moonlight. There was a curious absence of hair, but that only served to heighten the image of unadorned masculinity. Shiloh had an urge to study him closely, from the deep, arrowhead-shaped scar on his right shoulder to the narrow waistline of his trouser tops, but she forced her disconcerted gaze away.

"Excuse me," she muttered, and hurried to her bedroll, where she buried her face in her arms and refused to look at him.

The wagon creaked over deep ruts in the clay road, jolting the two silent passengers. They passed by a small farm with a tiny log house and a few thrown-together outbuildings, all covered with a fine coating of reddish-brown dust. A thin, weary woman carrying a small child on her hip emerged from the cabin and blew on a long, hollowed-out horn, summoning her husband and sons in from the fields. It was a lonely, plaintive sound. The woman shaded her eyes and stared, unsmiling, as the wagon drove past.

Shiloh felt sorry for the woman, whose life undoubtedly consisted of scratching out a living on the prairie, facing Indian raids and drought, and being subjugated daily by her husband. Silently Shiloh renewed her commitment to pursue her career, to live independently as she pleased. She only hoped that her blunder with McCord wouldn't prove fatal to her ambition.

From the top of a sharp rise in the road, Houston came into view. It was a sprawling, mud-spattered town clinging to the brown banks of Buffalo Bayou. One of the most populated places in the republic, it boasted numerous grog shops and inns, government buildings, and trading posts. Settlers arrived daily from the East, from Europe, from Mexico, and from the port of Galveston. None of these hurrying strangers found anything remarkable about the tense-looking couple approaching from the west end of town.

Justin pulled the team to a halt and looked at Shiloh, a question in his eyes. She lifted her chin and glanced away, unwilling to speak to him. He shrugged and drew the wagon up to a small whitewashed church. A rainbow of untended wildflowers grew in profusion beside the steps leading to the double doors.

By now, Justin McCord had done the unexpected too many times for her to be surprised. She raised an eyebrow at him. "Come to repent for your sins?"

He reached behind the seat and took out her serape. He placed it around her shoulders and softly answered her question.

"No, Miss Mulvane. I've come to commit one."

Shiloh froze as she felt the thrust of his six-gun against the small of her back. She tensed, ready to spring to the ground.

"I wouldn't," McCord threatened, his voice still soft, almost intimate. "You've backed me into a corner, Shiloh, and I don't much care for it. Let's go."

Heart pounding, Shiloh got down. She glanced about, seeking help. But the narrow lane leading to the church was deserted. Besides, McCord's gun was concealed by her serape. To the unsuspecting eye, they would undoubtedly look like a couple in love, with Justin's hand guiding her solicitously up the steps.

Shiloh hesitated at the door. "What are you going to do? I think I have a right—"

He pushed her, none too gently, into the church. "You gave up any rights you might have had when you went to work for Judge West. Now, keep your mouth shut and you won't get hurt."

The church was empty. Golden shafts of afternoon light slanted in through the high half-wheel windows. Benches were arranged in neat rows facing a raised pulpit. Justin pushed her up the aisle and through a door in the back. This led to a small, dim drawing room. A faint smell of roasting meat hung in the air.

"Hello!" Justin called out.

Shiloh heard the sound of a scraping chair, and then a small, rotund man appeared, wiping food from the corner of his mouth with a napkin.

"Howdy, folks," he said, eyeing Justin with a faint flicker of nervousness. "What can I do for you?"

"We want to be married," Justin stated. "Now.

TWO

Shiloh staggered, her mouth working in shocked silence. Justin held her tightly against him, his gun a constant reminder of his cold ruthlessness.

The preacher seemed flustered. "Now, look, mister, I can't just—"

Justin drew a small cloth bag from his pocket and tossed it on a low table. Yellow-gold coins spilled out. Shiloh guessed there was better than a hundred dollars in double eagles there.

The preacher's moon-shaped face grew suddenly very friendly. He picked up the coins and stashed them in his vest pocket.

"I suppose," he said, "that we could get things going pretty quickly. Now, my wife knows a good hymn or two, and she's just in from cutting flowers in the garden. For a bit more, you could—"

"That won't be necessary," Justin interrupted. "Just do what you have to do to make it legal." He glanced down at Shiloh, whose face had drained of color. As she studied the lattice design on the carpet, Justin felt a small, unfamiliar stab of regret. She looked so vulnerable, so damned childlike. He'd seen more cheerful faces on men doomed to be executed.

Justin let out his breath with a soft hiss. He reached into his pocket and tossed out another coin. "I guess a flower or two wouldn't hurt."

"Of course," the preacher said. "I won't be a moment."

Suddenly, Shiloh seemed to snap out of her stunned silence. "Wait!" she cried.

The preacher turned, eyeing her curiously.

"Sir, you can't do this," she said. "This man is a stranger to me. He's forcing me against my will—" She gasped as she felt the gun press into her back.

"There, now, sweetheart," Justin drawled, sending the preacher a knowing look. "Don't make a fool of yourself in front of the gentleman." He appeared to give her a reassuring squeeze, but thrust the gun even more firmly into her.

Then he faced the preacher. "I guess she can't believe she finally got me to the altar." He grinned. "Trailed me all the way to Washington-on-the-Brazos just to get me hitched, didn't you, sweetheart?"

Shiloh shook with outrage. "I—I—*damn* you . . ."

Justin gave the preacher another coin. "A little case of cold feet, that's all."

The man scurried away to fetch his wife.

When they were alone, Shiloh turned to Justin. "You'll be sorry you did this."

"I've no doubt you'll do your best to make me regret it, Shiloh. But you left me no alternative—"

He broke off abruptly as she twisted in his grip and kicked out viciously. Justin subdued her by squeezing her so tightly that she nearly lost consciousness.

"I'm calling your bluff, McCord," she gasped. "Go ahead and shoot me. I'd rather die than become your wife."

"You don't mean that," he told her. "What would your father think if you got yourself killed on your first job? And didn't you say he was ailing? He may not be able to get along too well without you."

The mention of her father seemed to subdue her. The anger in her eyes melted into quiet defeat. She deflated a little in his arms. Still, the spark of defiance hadn't quite gone out. "You won't get away with this, McCord."

The preacher bustled in again, followed by his wife, whose plumpness and round face matched his. She held out a bunch of wildflowers: lavender foxglove, yellow agarita, tender little wild roses. Shiloh took them, trying to keep her hands steady. His face unreadable, Justin plucked a single rose from the bunch. It was perfect: dewy, on the verge of opening fully, the color of fresh-churned butter. He gently tucked the blossom into Shiloh's hair.

With a grunt of satisfaction he turned back to the preacher. "Let's get on with it."

The preacher cleared his throat and opened a small black book to a page marked by a red ribbon.

"Dearly beloved," he began, "we are gath—"

Justin shifted impatiently. "Can you make this as short as possible?"

The preacher looked up, one eyebrow raised high. He glanced over his shoulder toward the door, obviously thinking of his unfinished supper. Shrugging, he flipped forward a few pages. "I don't suppose you have a ring."

Justin started to shake his head and then hesitated. Working with his thumb, he slipped the curious gold ring from his fourth finger and handed it to Shiloh. Dazed, she placed it on her left hand. It felt warm, comfortably heavy, and the small design of a willow tree glinted in the dim light.

The preacher was already speaking again. ". . . and by the power vested in me by the Republic of Texas, I hereby declare the two of you man and wife."

Silence reigned. The preacher and his wife were looking at them expectantly.

"It's customary to kiss the bride," the preacher prompted.

Shiloh opened her mouth to protest, but Justin's eyes cautioned her. He leaned down, taking his time for once, and captured her lips. His mouth held hers for perhaps a beat, but in that moment his action conveyed volumes. She belonged to him now; that was obvious from the possessive way he kissed her. Shiloh felt weak with relief when it was over.

They signed the preacher's register and a document printed on cheap paper, which the preacher sealed with a stamp.

Numb with disbelief, Shiloh lost her footing as she climbed up onto the wagon. Justin's strong arms were there to catch her. As he held her, amazed at the softness of her body, she felt small and oddly vulnerable to him.

Yet her reaction was terse. "I can manage by myself," she snapped, and brushed him away. Justin shrugged. He didn't blame her. He knew he wouldn't be feeling too kindly toward someone who'd just forced him into marriage without his consent.

As he drove away from the church, Justin studied Shiloh's profile. She held her chin high and looked straight ahead. She had a small, well-shaped nose that was sprayed with tiny freckles, and pretty coral-colored lips. In the past few days, Justin had grown to appreciate Shiloh's looks. She could never be termed a great beauty, not with such an intense face and lean, almost spare body. But there was something about her that he found incredibly appealing. It was more than the pale, perfect vision he'd glimpsed when he'd watched her bathe; it was her spirit, her quick mind, even her sharp tongue that intrigued him. And although Shiloh was fiercely independent, he knew that her bravado masked a wealth of softer feelings. This mixture of gritty self-reliance and childlike vulnerability made Shiloh different from any woman he'd ever known. He wanted nothing more to do with lush, lying beauties like

Isabella Hernandez or the grasping Jessamine West.

It was a pity he'd had to treat Shiloh this way, to involve her in the twisted, murky web of affairs Thaddeus Stripling had burdened him with.

"I'm sorry about what happened back there."

She turned quickly, green eyes smoldering. "You don't need to bother apologizing. It's not going to change the fact that you just forced me to marry you."

Justin shrugged. "The idea of a shotgun wedding didn't seem to bother you much when *I* was the one being forced."

"That was different. I was doing a job."

He leveled his gaze at her. "I, too, have a job that must be done. It would have been disastrous if I'd had to marry Jessamine."

Shiloh sniffed. "You should have thought of that when you seduced her."

Justin scowled. It was true, but he'd had something entirely different in mind as he'd wooed Jessamine.

He guided the wagon down Texas Avenue, wishing that Shiloh weren't so damned silent. Why didn't she rail at him, call him all manner of names, ask a passerby for help?

"Where do you live?" he inquired. "I think the first thing we should do is see your father."

She swung around abruptly, her eyes troubled. "No! I don't want to see him."

"Why not? You've been gone at least a week. Won't he be worried?"

"I told him I was going to visit my aunt Sharon at her farm north of town."

Justin frowned. "You mean you came after me without his knowledge?"

"Of course. I told you, he'd never have allowed it."

Justin let out a low whistle. "Damn. I expect he won't be too happy when he hears we've married."

Shiloh smiled grimly. "On the contrary, he'll be delighted that someone's agreed to take me off his hands. He's been badgering me to 'settle down' since I was sixteen."

"Then why don't you want to see him?"

Shiloh didn't answer right away. As Justin watched intently, she looked down at her small, work-roughened hands. Deep-auburn lashes veiled her eyes. She blinked and swallowed as if fighting back tears. Justin's jaw tightened as he suddenly realized the pain she was in. The pain of having an uncaring father and the pain he'd inflicted on her. Cursing himself, he drew the wagon to the side of the road and halted it beneath a broad live oak.

Gently he touched her arm. "What is it, Shiloh?"

She pulled away and regarded him fiercely. "I don't know why you bother to ask, but if you must know, you've ruined all I've ever dreamed of."

Justin cringed inwardly. "Was there another man, Shiloh? Were you courting—"

"No! I never have. That sort of thing means nothing to me." Her eyes sparkled with the sheen of unshed tears. "All I've ever wanted was to be a detective, like my father. Don't look so dubious, Justin. A few women have done it quite successfully. Doña Estebana of Goliad, for example. But my father was like you. He didn't think a woman could make it. Even when I learned to ride and shoot like a man, he thought it was only a matter of time before I closed my world until it was nothing more than a hearth and home, a husband and children."

"But you had other ideas."

Shiloh nodded, her eyes still moist but oddly cold. She spoke not to him but almost to herself, staring at some distant point beyond the bayou.

"For as long as I can remember, all I wanted to do was be a detective. I knew I was good, from the time I found a Mexican arsenal stored beneath the hall of justice in San Antonio when I was fifteen years old. There was enough ordnance there to bring down half the city, but I saw that it was given over to the proper authorities. After that, my father let me play at spying, posing as a belle at a Spanish *baile* or delivering correspondence here and there. Father would never admit it, but I was getting good. Detective life was ruining him, driving him more and more to his bottle, but I was thriving." She shot Justin a contemptuous look. "I know you proved my ineptness, but this is the first time I made such a large error in judgment."

He could see that she was trembling. She looked small and fierce, like a cornered bobcat. Again he touched her arm.

"This job that Judge West sent you on—it was important to you, wasn't it?"

She nodded. "The judge paid well, and my father had some pressing debts. I had hoped to prove myself to him, so he'd take me seriously at last."

Justin felt an unaccustomed tightening in his gut. Wrapped up in his own affairs, he'd never paused to consider Shiloh. He'd merely used her as a vehicle to avoid being placed under Harmon West's control. Now, too late, he was discovering that she was more than a money-grabbing bounty hunter. She was a many-faceted individual, with hopes and dreams of her own.

Justin frowned as a wave of guilt washed over him. He spoke gently, wanting to soften the hard line of Shiloh's pressed-together lips and the creases in her brow.

"I still think we should see your father. You can't put it off indefinitely."

Shiloh expelled her breath slowly. Without looking at him, she said, "Main Street, the east end."

Eb, the aging freedman who worked for Nate Mulvane, came around to the front of the dusty white frame house to see to the wagon and team. His bright, expert eye quickly evaluated Justin's fine mount, a deep bay.

"Evenin', miss," Eb said. He nodded his grizzled head at Justin, taking the man in with a sweep of his eyes, and led the team away with an obvious lack of curiosity.

Looking after him, Shiloh suppressed a wistful sigh. Only Eb understood her ambition and, in his quiet way encouraged it. How proud he would have been of her if she'd only pulled this off. . . . Feeling Justin's eyes on her, she tossed her head.

"This way. I expect my father will be having his supper." She led the way into the house. There was a large room with a heavy table and benches and a good-sized kitchen hearth. Eb kept the place tidy and swept, and a pot of his good beef stew filled the air with a delicious aroma. An iron safe stood in the corner, its top stacked with numerous papers and account books.

"Eb? Eb!" A gruff voice called from beyond a curtained doorway.

"It's me, Father," Shiloh answered. "I'm with my—with a visitor."

"Well, come on in, girl," Mulvane blustered.

They stepped inside the tiny bedroom. The air was thick with blue-gray smoke. Nate Mulvane sat propped on his bed, his lap strewn with papers and ashes. A plate of stew was on the table beside him, untouched. A bottle of whiskey and a small glass stood beside it, the bottle half empty. Mulvane looked up, his florid face seeming even more ruddy because of his great profusion of red hair. Eyebrows as thick as cattails descended as he viewed his daughter and her guest. He rubbed a hand across his unshaven face.

"How's Sharon?" he inquired.

"She—Father, I didn't go to see Aunt Sharon."

His green eyes, aging mirrors of her own, narrowed slightly. "Oh?"

Shiloh glanced at Justin. He leaned against the door frame, his face impassive. Drawing a deep breath, she framed an explanation.

"Judge West paid me to go to Washington-on-the-Brazos after this man—Justin McCord."

Mulvane's fist came down, scattering the papers in his lap. "Damn it, girl, why didn't you tell me?"

"Because you wouldn't have let me go."

"You're damned right I—" Mulvane looked fiercely at Justin. "What does Harmon want with you?"

Justin sidled into the room. "I suspect he had a number of things in mind, but he had some idea that I should be compelled to marry his daughter."

"Hmph." Mulvane puffed on his cigar, bringing the dwindling ember to life. "I'd heard Jessamine's finally set her sights on one man." His eyes flicked over Justin's uncombed hair and dusty clothes. "Didn't figure it'd be someone like you."

"Don't worry, Mulvane. It won't be."

The bushy eyebrows shot up. "What the devil's wrong with you, boy? Jessamine's damned pretty, and rich to boot."

Justin shrugged. "It doesn't matter. I couldn't marry her. Being Harmon West's son-in-law would be directly at odds with my work."

"Are you a Ranger, boy?"

"No. Why do you ask?"

"You've got that look about you. Cold eyes, fast hands, a go-to-hell attitude . . ."

"I've ridden with Jack Hays and Big-foot Wallace."

Mulvane nodded. "It figures. Well, son, since you're not going to say any more about what you do, why not tell me how it is that you let a hundred-pound girl drag you back to Houston?"

Shiloh gritted her teeth, but Justin grinned broadly. "She did a damned good job. Nailed me when I had my back turned outside a saloon."

Mulvane scowled at his daughter. "I spent most of my life savings sending you to that fancy girls' school in the East. Didn't they teach you not to go near saloons?"

Justin gave a short laugh to dispel the momentary tension. "Her sombrero and serape concealed her identity."

Mulvane relaxed against his bolster. "Well, now, maybe this deal wasn't as foolhardy as I'd thought. How much did Harmon pay you, Shiloh?"

She merely stared, her gut twisting in anticipation of her father's reaction when he learned the truth.

"Well?" he prompted.

"Justin didn't tell you everything," she said, her voice toneless. "He overpowered me, and—"

Mulvane sat forward, his hand going for the barrel of his six-gun, which lay on the floor where he'd been cleaning it.

"And what? Speak up, girl."

"And we were married." The admission was little more than a whisper in the smoky haze of the room.

Mulvane froze in midaction. His green eyes narrowed and his lips thinned. Then, suddenly, he threw back his head and burst into laughter. It was the worst possible reaction in Shiloh's eyes. She could have withstood his anger much more easily.

"Married!" Nate roared. "Sweet tarnation, my daughter's married! Eb! Bring a glass for Mr. Mc-Cord. We've got some celebrating to do. Now, get over here, son, and shake my hand. I'd stand and salute you if it weren't for this dadblamed leg. You're a rare man indeed to stand up to Shiloh's nonsense. I can't tell you how many perfectly decent men she's chased off." Mulvane's broad grin disappeared for a moment. "That isn't to say, Justin, that she won't make you a good wife. In spite of all her malarkey about careers and such, my daughter's a fine woman."

Justin looked from Nate to Shiloh, his face oddly tender. "I know," he said, and took the proffered glass from Eb.

Mulvane looked at her, too. "Go on, now, Shiloh. We've got some serious drinking to do. Go get yourself cleaned up, and for God's sake, put on a dress. It's your wedding day!"

As she lay on her rope-frame loft bed, watching gilded dust motes spin through the air, Shiloh bit hard into her lower lip. She felt as if her life had ended when it should have been just beginning. A dull ache throbbed behind her eyes. She had no idea what would become of her. She didn't know how to be a wife. All she knew was the uncertainty of a detective's life: endless days in the saddle, stealthy observations, the tingle of imminent danger, the sense of supreme satisfaction when a job was done. . . . There would never be any more of that for her.

She squeezed her eyes shut. Conversation, punctuated by her father's deep laughter, drifted up to her ears.

Nate Mulvane chuckled. "Most of these things should be settled before the marriage, but you didn't come to me on bended knee, begging for her hand."

"I had to act quickly, Nate."

"I'm not complaining. But I would like to know where you come from."

"I was born in Virginia. My parents come from old families, and it was always assumed that I'd carry on the family tobacco plantation. But my father and I didn't see eye to eye on a lot of things. Finally, we had a major falling-out and I joined a group that was coming west. That was in 1835. The Texans had already begun their campaign against Santa Anna. Soldiering didn't appeal to me, but I've got a good eye for horse-flesh and can sit a mount decently. Hank Karne, the Ranger, made me a scout. I did a lot of work for him, even after San Jacinto." There was a clink of glass as he refilled his drink. "Recently, I got mixed up in the Mier Expedition, but I managed to escape."

Nate gave a low whistle. "I heard that all the survivors were marched to Mexico City and never heard of again. How'd you get away from those Red Cap devils?"

"I made a friend. A good friend."

Shiloh grimaced. She couldn't imagine anyone as unscrupulous as Justin having a friend.

"I'm surprised I didn't hear about your escape," Nate said. Shiloh recognized the keen probing beneath the casual comment.

"There's a reason for that, Nate. I'd rather not go into it now, but we can talk later."

"You'd be a hero, son—"

"Not interested. There are a lot of things more important than personal recognition."

"Such as . . . ?"

"Annexation. I want to see Texas become part of the United States."

"That's a big dream, McCord. A lot of folks are in favor of it, but not the right folks."

"It's something I've been working for since San Jacinto."

"Working for statehood won't feed my little girl, Justin."

"I have a good piece of land and a house up north of town. It used to belong to Thaddeus Stripling. I'm planning on turning it into a horse ranch. Samuel Colt's Texas-model pistol has made the Rangers a lot more effective, but they could use some better horses. I've seen a lot of good men having to use farm plugs against Comanches."

"Shiloh might like that," Nate mused. "She's always been good with horses."

With a snort of disgust, she sprang from the bed. Justin and her father were cronies by now, drinking and talking without a care in the world. She heard Nate suggest a bath and change of clothes for Justin and decided that she, too, needed to clean up after the dusty, draining trip. She went to the washstand, bending low beneath the roof beams, and poured water into the basin. Sighing gratefully, she peeled off her travel-stained clothes and splashed the sweat and dust from her skin. She used honeysuckle soap liberally, almost defiantly. Both Justin and her father had accused her of being less than feminine, and she meant to prove them both wrong.

She had a few dresses hanging from wall hooks in the corner. None of them were particularly pretty, but the green sprigged cotton frock complimented her coloring, and the full skirt and shirred bodice gave the illusion of fullness to her figure. She brushed savagely at her profusion of carrot-colored curls, not relenting until her hair shone. She swept it back from her face with a pair of tortoiseshell combs, leaving it long in the back. A tiny oval looking glass, cracked years ago when her father was in his cups, showed an image that was barely satisfactory. Days in the sun had darkened her skin and the spray of freckles across her nose. Hastily Shiloh took up a shawl and used it to cover her amber-tinged arms. Taking a deep breath, she descended the ladder.

She hesitated on the bottom rung, looking down with mounting anger at Justin McCord. He was seated at the thick oak trestle table, looking over a sheaf of papers. He was wearing clean clothes: a loose white shirt and thigh-hugging buckskins. His newly washed hair gleamed yellow-gold in the lamplight. His face, clean-shaven now, was drawn into an expression of intense concentration. There was no denying the physical appeal of Justin McCord. Lean and bronzed, with his sculpted features, he was a man of uncompromising masculinity.

Shiloh made a small movement on the ladder.

McCord looked up quickly, his eyes wary, and gathered up his papers, stuffing them back into his saddlebag.

"What are you doing?" Shiloh demanded.

He grinned, taking in the snug bodice of her dress and the turn of her bare ankle with obvious appreciation. "Your father celebrated himself into a long nap. I was just going over a few things." He indicated a large pot on the cookstove. "Coffee?"

Shiloh shook her head. "Where's Eb?"

"He said something about getting one of the horses shod. One of your team threw a shoe."

Shiloh gritted her teeth. Why hadn't she seen that? She'd always been attentive to the animals' needs . . . but she'd been so preoccupied with McCord that she hadn't noticed. She was sure Justin would remember this further example of her incompetence. Without another glance at his handsome, smiling face, she went out to the porch and stood leaning against the railing.

Twilight had given way to another crystalline night. Stars were sprayed across the sky, and the tall, still pines were silhouetted against the light of a waxing moon. The animals in the shed behind the house stamped and snuffed, bedding down for the night.

Familiar sounds, comforting sounds . . . but Shiloh's agitation did not abate. She stiffened when she felt McCord's presence behind her. He was so close that she sensed his warmth, smelled his faint scent of soap and leather.

"For what it's worth, I'm sorry about the way things turned out for you."

She whirled on him, gasping a little as her bosom brushed against his shirtfront. "Spare me your pity, McCord. It has a hollow ring to it."

"Come on, Shiloh. I think you're making too much of this. I promised your father I'd treat you decently, give you a good life—"

Her green eyes blazed in the moonlight. "Have you ever wanted anything, Justin, wanted it so badly you could taste it in the air you breathe and hear it on the wind every night? Wanted it so much you went to sleep thinking about it and woke up with it still fresh in your mind?"

He stared, the lines of his face softening the slightest bit. His eyes took on a veiled, distant look. "Maybe I have, Shiloh."

"Then why can't you understand what this means to me?"

"Because it's wrong, damn it, and you're a fool for dreaming about it. You can't go around masquerading as a man, doing a man's work. Give marriage a chance, girl. You're ripe for it."

Insolently he flicked her shawl away and touched the flesh of her shoulder. Trapped between McCord and the porch railing, Shiloh decided to stand firm and show him that she was not one to succumb to his evocative touch, even though his nearness caused a tingling to begin deep inside her.

"I'm not interested, McCord. That piece of paper we signed today doesn't change that." Still, a curious lassitude was creeping over her, induced by the small, sensual motions of his hand on her bare shoulder.

"So you say," he whispered. "But you're lying." Slowly he bent and tasted her flesh. His teeth grazed the side of her neck, and his hand slid lower to rest against the curve of her breast.

"Don't," she pleaded, but her voice sounded small and distant, so weak a protest that it almost resembled an invitation.

Justin sought her lips, savoring them, devouring their fullness. His arms encircled her, gathering her against him so that she felt the heat of his passion. The lassitude deepened, warming her in places she'd never felt before. His hand played along the narrow length of her back, defying her to make him stop. With a tiny moan of denial, her lips parted. Her arms crept around him, hands roving over the sinews beneath his shirt. He pressed forward until Shiloh arched back over the railing, his strong arm keeping her from falling.

Her heart leaped as his fingers loosened the buttons of her dress. Shiloh was rocked by new sensations, her ears ringing and the world closing down around her, until all that existed was Justin, his bold hands and hungry lips.

Desire knifed through her as she arched against him, beyond thought, beyond reason. Only a moment ago she was hating him for taking away her freedom, yet now she wanted nothing more than to clasp him to her.

"Say you were lying about not wanting me." His hand flicked across her naked breast.

"I—"

"Say it, Shiloh."

The night breeze cooled her bosom and left her longing for him to continue his caresses. Her faint whisper was nearly drowned out by the buzzing of cicadas.

"I lied, Justin. Damn you." She closed her eyes in anticipation of his next searing kiss. When he made no move, she opened them again.

The barest hint of a smile curved his lips. Gently he set her on her feet and pulled the bodice of her dress back in place. While Shiloh stared in confusion, he reached around and did up the buttons. Finally, he drew her shawl back around her, brushed his lips across her brow. His arms dropped to his sides.

"I'll be bedding down out back, with Eb," he said. "Holler if you need me." He ambled down the steps and around back, whistling.

Shiloh gaped, speechless. As he had so many times before, Justin McCord had made a fool of her. Brought her, with his masterful hands and sensual lips, to the brink of surrender, only to leave her stone-cold and seething, despising her own weakness as much as she loathed the man who brought it out in her.

Justin scowled up at the dawn-gray cracks in the top of the shed. Nearby, Eb snored softly, and the horses were just beginning to stir. Justin had passed a nearly sleepless night, haunted by a vision of wide eyes, pale skin, Shiloh's artlessly passionate lips. He couldn't explain what had induced him to begin to make love to her the night before. It was bad enough that he'd made her marry him; he hadn't meant to complicate things further.

But something about Shiloh's contemptuous attitude had challenged him. Perhaps he'd wanted to show her that, contrary to what she believed, marriage to him wasn't the end of the world.

It had taken every ounce of his restraint to leave her, just when she would have given herself to him. But he knew she wasn't ready, although her body had responded to his touch. She would have come to her senses soon enough and despised him all the more for taking advantage of her.

Justin sighed. He was as unready for marriage as Shiloh. There was too much to do, too much uncertainty in the future. He decided that, come morning, he'd explain as much to Shiloh. He'd hold her to their marriage only until the threat of Jessamine West was past, and then he'd give her back her freedom. Surely even Shiloh would agree that that was reasonable.

Although a small voice in the back of his mind protested against letting a woman like her go, Justin thought it a satisfactory solution. Flinging his arm across his eyes, he decided to get a little sleep.

Just as he was drifting off, he felt a circle of cold metal against his neck and froze. Shifting on the bed of straw, he found himself looking into a vengeful pair of moss-green eyes.

THREE

A morning rain had dampened the lush green lawn of the Villa, Judge Harmon West's new house beside Buffalo Bayou. Small, yet cunningly styled after the graceful plantations of Georgia and the Carolinas, the Villa had glass windows and a white-railed verandah wrapping around the flower-decked front porch.

The sparkling lawn bloomed with drooping lavender wisteria and clipped bushes of white-flowering hawthorn. Spanish moss dripped from ancient live oaks. Yellow blossoms of jessamine, for which the judge's only daughter was named, draped a wrought-iron fence. It was a picture of formidable wealth, which Harmon West had come by, some whispered, without total regard for the laws he now upheld.

Justin McCord shifted uncomfortably on the hard cart-bed and was jolted when it came to an abrupt halt on the drive in front of the house. He stared at the stiff, narrow back of his defiant wife and tried to rub his shackled wrists. Glowering, he chastised himself for having goaded Shiloh. He'd been too damned sure of himself, too hasty in dismissing her, thinking she'd given up her crazy notion of delivering him to Judge West.

It was not like him to be so incautious; in his line of work one couldn't afford to make stupid mistakes. But he'd done just that, convinced by Nate Mulvane that the girl had been tamed, letting himself be provoked by Shiloh into taking her into his arms last night.

"You're making a mistake," he muttered.

She swung around, her eyes hard as emeralds. "No, the mistake was yours. You and my father are both dead wrong about me. It's going to take more than that worthless piece of paper—and a few kisses—to turn me into a meek little homebody."

Shiloh's treachery shouldn't surprise him. It wouldn't be the first time a woman had betrayed him.

Justin let a sneer curl his lip. "I'd never accuse you of being meek, my dear, but last night I got the idea that you might be just the slightest bit interested in being a wife to me."

Her hands shook as she held the reins. "You had no right to do that to me, Justin McCord."

"On the contrary, as your husband, I have a right to far more than I took last night. I hadn't planned on taking advantage of it, but this latest stunt of yours may cause me to change my mind."

A servant came out of the great double doors and two mulatto grooms appeared to see to the cart and team.

Shiloh nodded at them and turned to the servant. "Tell Judge West it's Shiloh Mc—Mulvane." She glanced back at Justin. "Making the delivery he requested."

Justin grinned lazily, inclined his head. "Congratulations. You brought this to a successful conclusion, after all." He stretched out his iron-bound ankles, then reached up with both shackled hands and ran them along the silken flesh of her bare arm, flesh that was warm and honey-colored from the sun.

She drew away. "You'd better save your caresses for Jessamine."

"You're a cold woman."

Her green eyes grew hard. "You're nothing to me. Nothing but a hundred dollars in my pocket as soon as Judge West gets out here."

Justin shook his head. That kind of hardness seemed unnatural in one so young. "I'm curious. How do you propose to get around the fact that we're married?"

She scowled at him. "The judge himself will take care of that. No court in Texas would uphold a marriage made by force. Or one that hasn't been consummated," she added.

"It's your word against mine. Your father was mighty pleased with the way things turned out. He's not about to let anything jeopardize our marriage."

"We'll just see about that, Justin." She turned her back and refused to look at him again.

Presently Harmon West arrived, flanked by two

burly black men. He was a man on whom middle
age looked good: tall, silver-haired, still trim
around the middle. He was impeccably clad in a
tailored black frock coat and trousers. His polished hardwood cane was probably an affecta-
tion, for West had the gait of a much younger
man.

He barely nodded at Shiloh but took the keys
she offered and freed McCord's hands and ankles. The two guards stood close by, watching for
trouble. Justin flexed his wrists and jumped
down.

"I appreciate the reception, Harmon," he said.

"Let's go inside, McCord. We have some business to—"

"Justin!" A feminine voice rang out. Jessamine
West ran across the lawn, her ribbon-trimmed
yellow dress drawn back over a lacy petticoat. Her
plump pink cheeks were flushed with exertion,
her blue eyes wide and shining. Yellow ringlets
bobbed about her face.

For perhaps the hundredth time, he rued his
indiscretion with the girl. The liaison hadn't
been anywhere near as fruitful as he'd hoped.
Jessamine had been willing enough to talk, but
her knowledge of her father's involvement with
the British and Mexicans had been scant.

He removed his hat and nodded a greeting.
Jessamine thrust her hand at him. As he bent and
raised it to his lips, he heard Shiloh's soft snort of
disgust.

"I'm ever so glad you're back," Jessamine said. "I was afraid you'd gone for good."

Justin extracted his hand from hers. "You'll have to excuse us, Jessamine. Your father and I were just going in to talk over some business." He turned to follow Harmon into the house.

"Judge West." Shiloh called him back.

The gentleman turned, his jaw twitching in irritation. "Yes? What is it?"

"There's a small matter I must discuss with you."

The judge coughed. "I'll send Mr. North out to pay you."

"Judge, it's not—"

"Now look, miss, we agreed on what the payment would be."

"But I—"

Jessamine frowned, and her small rosebud mouth drew into a pout. "Payment? What payment?"

Feigning innocence, Shiloh raised her eyebrows. "Oh dear, Jessamine, I thought you knew. Your father thought Mr. McCord might need to be persuaded to return to you, since it didn't seem likely he'd come back on his own."

Jessamine's cheeks flamed and her curls bounced wildly, the longer ones striking her ample, heaving bosom. "You're a liar, Shiloh Mulvane! You're just jealous because you'll wind up a skinny old maid, parading around in boys' clothes."

Shiloh tossed her head. "I intend to. Just as

soon as my business with your father is concluded."

Justin suppressed a grin. Jessamine was no match for Shiloh.

Harmon West's office was predictably tidy and handsomely appointed. Books lined the shelves from polished floor to wainscoted ceiling, and the furniture was of finest fruitwood, polished and fragrant with verbena. West was one of the first to bring Eastern style to Houston, which was fast growing from a boggy outpost into a city.

Justin waved away a servant who offered him whiskey, and seated himself on a leather wingback chair.

"What can I do for you, Harmon?" he asked.

The judge selected a fat cigar from the humidor on his desk and clipped the end with a vicious stroke. "I don't much like the way you treated my daughter, McCord."

Justin's lips thinned. "And I don't much like your sending Shiloh after me."

Harmon chuckled. "A blow to your ego, McCord?"

"No, damn it!" Justin's fist pounded the arm of his chair. "What the hell were you thinking of, sending that girl off alone? You know what it's like on the trails—"

"The young lady assured me she had no fear of outlaws, redskins, or Mexican bandits."

"I don't doubt that that's true, Harmon.

Shiloh fears nothing. But you sent her off knowing of the dangers involved. What the hell kind of man are you?"

Unruffled, the judge steepled his hands. "The question is, McCord, what sort of man are *you*? Your concern for the Mulvane girl is touching, but we are here to discuss a more important matter: you and my daughter."

"I have no interest in Jessamine. You wasted Shiloh's time and your money bringing me here."

Harmon West had small eyes of no particular color. They narrowed in a cold, calculating way. "Jessamine needs a husband. Since it was you who stole her innocence, then it will be you who will wed her. You should consider yourself lucky. Men in these parts have been killed for less."

Justin declined to mention that Jessamine's innocence had been long gone by the time he'd taken up with her, knowing that it wouldn't matter to the judge.

West drew a document out of a drawer. "Here is the contract. I've been generous with Jessamine's dowry—"

"Sorry, Harmon. I can't marry your daughter."

"You don't have a choice."

Justin's jaw tightened. "Is she pregnant?"

"No. But that doesn't change a thing."

"I won't sign that contract."

With the quickness of a much younger man, Harmon drew his heavy revolving pistol from the drawer and pointed it with a cold metallic click at Justin's chest. "No one would raise a finger of protest if I killed you now."

Smiling slightly, Justin leaned back in his chair. "I can understand your wanting to marry Jessamine off, Harmon. God knows, the girl spends enough of your money. But my marrying her would make me a bigamist, and that could taint your image pretty badly."

"What the devil are you talking about?"

Justin spread his hands in guileless fashion. "I'm already married." He leaned forward and helped himself to a cigar from Harmon's humidor.

The older man lost his composure for a moment, letting his jaw drop. Recovering, he said, "That's a damned lie. You said you were a bachelor the first night you met Jessamine."

"I was. But then I met Shiloh Mulvane." Justin was a little surprised at the pride he heard in his own voice. He'd never wanted a wife, preferring the nomadic life as an agent of the government. But now that he was compelled to settle down, who better to do it with than the volatile, intriguing Shiloh?

Judge West shook his head in confusion. He lowered the gun but kept his hand close to the handle. "Perhaps you'd better tell me about this."

Justin grinned. "Shiloh and I were married yesterday."

"Either you're lying, McCord, or Shiloh is as

crazy as people say. If she's your wife, then why in tarnation did she deposit you here?"

Justin's grin faded a little. "You know how it is with young folks just starting out. Shiloh has some fool idea about taking up with her father. She accepted your job to prove to Nate that she could do it on her own."

Harmon's hand came down hard on the desktop, causing the lamp and inkwell to jump. "I paid that woman good money to bring you here."

"And she did, Harmon. I don't believe she was charged with insuring my bachelor status. If the money means that much to you, I'll see that you get it back. But it isn't the money at all, is it, Harmon? And it's not Jessamine's happiness you're worried about. The only reason you wanted me to marry her was to get me under your thumb. So I wouldn't stand in the way of your plans to prevent statehood for Texas."

Judge West smiled grimly. "So the cards are all out on the table now, aren't they, McCord? It doesn't matter, though. I admit, things would've been a lot easier if you were one of the family. But I'll manage." His hand moved caressingly, meaningfully, over the butt of his Colt's. "And you'll be one sorry son of a bitch before I'm through with you."

He rode hard over the rolling acres of meadowland, rounding a deep, murky pond and climbing the rise that led to the ranch he'd named Post Oaks. Thaddeus had left some livestock, and a few Mexican workers had stayed on to work for Justin.

He let himself in through the heavy front door. The house smelled musty, of disuse. Most of the furnishings were still draped with sheeting. The small study was the one room Justin had opened. The hand-hewn furniture was unattractive but sturdy, and the desk was well equipped with paper, ink, and wax for his correspondence. With muttered curses, he rifled through his papers. He drew out the documents that he'd intended to pass on to Delgado in Washington-on-the-Brazos and frowned. Shiloh had seized him before he'd been able to meet with his colleague. And now Delgado would miss the opportunity to present damning evidence against the Accord at a hearing in San Antonio.

Harmon West had known that. He'd succeeded in outsmarting Justin on that count. But there was one thing he'd overlooked. Justin's lips thinned into a cold smile. Shrewd as Harmon West was, he had erred badly in sending Shiloh after Justin. She'd provided the perfect dodge.

Perfect? Justin frowned again. He paused to consider the type of woman he'd married. Hoydenish, temperamental, and proud, she was enough to give any man pause. When she was angry, nothing was safe from her wrath. Yet when she smiled—rarely enough—the whole world seemed to light up. And there was an aura of sensuality about her that she didn't even know she possessed. Justin had first glimpsed it when she'd bathed in the river. And last night, when she'd responded to his kisses with surprising intensity. She was naive and untried, but Justin recognized the promise of passion.

It was a promise he was tempted to see fulfilled. Something about Shiloh challenged and defied him.

He returned his papers to the safe and went to find Ina. The maid was in the kitchen, her inky hair braided and her apron smeared with grease.

"There will be two for supper tonight. And put fresh linens on the bed. My wife will be joining me."

Shiloh jumped down from her lathered mount and led it around to the yard behind the house. She'd spent the morning ranging through the wild bayou country as if pursued by demons. Finally, she'd turned her big piebald stallion to the north, where her aunt Sharon lived. Two ferns on pedestals stood inside the door, quivering as Shiloh burst inside.

"Aunt Sharon! It's me, Shiloh."

A small woman came around from the kitchen, wiping her flour-dusted hands on her apron. Nate Mulvane's sister looked enough like Shiloh to be mistaken for her mother, with the same tightly curling red hair, green eyes, and perpetually intense expression. But time and care had mellowed Sharon, made her cautious and prudent where Shiloh was not. Smiling affectionately, she led Shiloh by the hand into her tiny calico-curtained parlor, and they sat down together on a fading brocade settee.

Shiloh swallowed hard. "Aunt Sharon, could I talk to you about something?"

The older woman's eyes softened. A childless widow, she had always lavished her love on Shiloh. "You know you can tell me anything."

Taking a deep breath, Shiloh began at the beginning, when Judge West had sought her out. The words poured out in a torrent, describing her triumph at capturing Justin McCord, and her mortification when he'd turned on her and forced her to marry him.

When it ended, Sharon said, "My dear, you should have considered the consequences of going off like that without your father's knowledge."

"I thought I was prepared for any possibility, Aunt Sharon. But how could I have known that he would make me wed him?"

"I suppose you couldn't have foreseen that. What sort of man is this Justin McCord?"

"Some women might call him handsome: tall and broad, with a great shock of blond hair and white teeth and a dimple. He's from a wealthy Virginia family. I heard him tell my father that he came west after a falling-out with his father, and then he served as a scout in the revolution. Now he's planning on starting up a horse ranch. Father seemed to like him, but I know better. Justin's impossibly arrogant, scheming, and unscrupulous."

"Oh, dear, did he hurt you, Shiloh?"

"No, no, nothing like that. He was quite gentle with me, in fact. I don't know why, but at the wedding he put a flower in my hair and gave me this ring." Shiloh held it out for her aunt to see.

"You could do worse than a man like that."

"But I don't want to be his wife, or anybody's. He won't ever let me work with Father as I'd planned."

"Are you sure of that? Have you asked him?"

She shook her head. "I'm sure he expects me to be a proper farm wife, seeing he's fed and his clothes are laundered." She lowered her voice almost to a whisper. "I just can't live like that." She twisted the ring around her finger.

The older woman stood and moved about the room in her brisk way. "Well, it's done. Now you must decide what you are going to do."

"I'll go to Judge West. He wouldn't listen to me this morning, but now Justin's probably told him everything. Surely he knows a way to invalidate the marriage."

Sharon frowned. "I don't like Harmon West. Never have. When your uncle was with the Rangers he suspected that the judge was supplying the Mexicans with ordnance. Six weeks later, Elihu was dead. Killed in a Comanche raid, or so they said. But I've never been able to get it out of my mind that Harmon had something to do with it."

Suppressing a shiver, Shiloh went and took her aunt's hands. "You never told me that. Why didn't you do something about it?"

"There was no proof. And nine years have passed. Yet I still believe Harmon is not to be trusted."

Shiloh didn't like the judge either, but his money had made her overlook that. Still, she clung to the idea that perhaps he could do something about her predicament. "He's a judge. And it's to his advantage to help me."

"You don't understand, child. If Justin refuses an annulment and your father backs him up, there's no way anything can be done. I'm afraid we women have very little to say about such things."

"I won't go to the judge, then. But neither do I want to be Justin's wife. Can I stay here with you?"

"I was afraid you'd ask that." She gently smoothed a wisp of hair from Shiloh's cheek. "Child, you know I love you like a daughter, but if you stayed here, you'd be running away. You've never been one to do that. You're going to have to face up to this, and the sooner the better."

The sun was lingering low as Shiloh climbed the steps to her father's house. Nothing had changed, but she'd resolved to work something out with Justin. Despite everything, she couldn't deny that there seemed to be a thread of decency in the man. She remembered the yellow rose and the ring on her finger and told herself that maybe he'd understand—

A pair of strong, unyielding hands grasped her from behind, one of them clamping over her mouth to stifle a protest. She recognized Justin instantly from his scent and the low chuckle that rumbled in his throat.

"Evening, Shiloh," he drawled. She struggled ineffectually against his tall, hard frame. "You know," he said, "I don't take kindly to being tricked. You bested me this morning, but it won't happen again. The game is over. Let's go home." He dropped his hand from her mouth when her struggling ceased.

"This is my home," she said through gritted teeth.

"Not anymore."

Nate Mulvane appeared on the porch, leaning heavily on a gnarled cane. Shiloh gave him a pleading look. If ever she'd wanted something from her father, it was this.

Don't make me go, she said in a silent message with her eyes. *Don't make me go.*

A shadow crossed her father's face and he looked away, concealing an odd glint in his eyes. He spoke to Justin.

"Take care of my girl, McCord."

Shiloh couldn't believe her ears. *"Father—"*

"It's for the best. Justin will give you a better life than I ever could."

Stiff with anger, Shiloh preceded him into the house at Post Oaks. At one time it had been quite comfortable—grand, even, by frontier standards—but now the mustiness of neglect hung in the air. By the light of a table lamp in the large main room, Shiloh noted the dusty wainscoting and the cloth-draped parlor furniture. Fading wallpaper peeled from the wall leading upstairs.

"What do you think?" Justin asked.

She whirled on him. "I think you are a boor."

Justin laughed. "I know that. I was talking about the house."

"It's a relic." Shiloh sniffed. "It should have been left to die a natural death."

"Perhaps it just needs a woman's touch."

"I'm not going to spend my days cleaning up your house."

"Of course you won't. We've a maid for that."

Shiloh stared in surprise. "A maid?"

"Ina. You'll meet her later. But now it's time to get ready for supper. This way." He started up the stairs.

Shiloh opened her mouth to object, but she knew by now that Justin was oblivious to normal reasoning. She followed him up to a large room, the master bedroom. This room, at least, had been aired out and the furniture uncovered. There was a pair of matching armoires, the blond pine doors gleaming with polish. A heavy table and chairs were arranged in a corner, and there was a pair of sturdy chairs at the hearth. But the focal point of the room was the huge tester bed. It was draped with colorful quilts and bolsters and looked almost decadently soft.

Justin went to the hearth and stirred the fire to life. He opened a door to reveal a good-sized dressing room. There a copper tub steamed.

"I thought you might like a bath," he said. Returning to the room, he indicated one of the armoires. "I also took the liberty of getting you some clothes. There wasn't much to be had ready-made, so I bought some bolts of cloth as well. Ina is clever with a needle; she'll help you."

"I have my own clothes."

"Dungarees, men's shirts, moccasins, a faded dress or two." Justin laid his hands on her shoulders. "You're not a little girl anymore, Shiloh, playing at being a spy." Abruptly he turned on his heel and left.

Shiloh glared at the closed door. Never had she felt so trapped, so helpless. After talking with Aunt Sharon, she'd had a small hope that she could reach some sort of understanding with Justin. But he'd proved her wrong by unceremoniously snatching her from her father's house and dragging her here.

Sighing, she went to the dressing room. She stood for a moment looking at the tub. She'd never had a real bath, not even at school in the East. It did look inviting, the steam rising in gentle wisps, a fresh cake of soap and a pile of snowy linens nearby. Shiloh wondered whether it would seem as if she were giving in to Justin if she took advantage of the inviting facilities, but convinced herself it would not. She shed her clothes and stepped into the tub, submerging herself up to the neck.

The luxury of basking in the warm, soft spring water engulfed her. For a moment she forgot her troubles and gave herself over to the exquisite sensation of the water lapping up between her breasts, around the tense muscles of her shoulders. She lifted a languid hand and watched the droplets run down her arm. Taking up the cake of soap, she rolled it slowly between her hands.

Honeysuckle. The scent of the lather wafted up, taking her by surprise. Was it possible that Justin had—no, of course not. It was an accident that he'd found her favorite soap.

She noticed a cut-glass decanter and glass on a small stand by the bath. Removing the stopper, she sniffed it. Sherry. Shiloh poured herself a glass and drank it quickly. It tasted so pleasant that she had another. By the time she'd downed her third glass, the warmth pervaded her and augmented the languor of the warm bath.

When she finally, reluctantly emerged from the bath, Shiloh's mood had lightened. She'd never felt so fragrantly clean or so totally relaxed.

Her skin glowed as she patted it dry. Her hair fell in dozens of damp, gleaming ringlets down her back. She stepped into the bedroom, which was dimly lit by the fire. The bed, with its rounded billows of quilts, beckoned irresistibly.

Shiloh went over and sat down. The languor imparted by the bath and the sherry overwhelmed her. She sank back onto the pillows and slid beneath the sheets. She hadn't forgotten that Justin was waiting for her. *Let him wait,* she thought with a slow, catlike smile. *He'll just have to learn that I'll not be at his beck and call. . . .* Stretching luxuriously, Shiloh dropped off to sleep.

The lamp on Justin's desk wavered. He looked up from his work, rubbed his eyes, and folded up the map he'd been studying. Glancing at the clock on the mantel, he saw that more than an hour had passed since he'd left Shiloh. Frowning, he climbed the stairs to see what was keeping her.

He knocked. No response. Swearing, Justin swung the door open. He'd half expected her to flee, but not this soon. Not without being noticed by him or any of the ranch hands, who had been alerted. The room was quiet except for the soughing of the night breeze through the window.

Justin's tenseness left him when he saw Shiloh asleep on the bed. He approached quietly so as not to awaken her. He sucked in his breath at what he saw.

Supper could wait; the heat in Justin's blood couldn't. He bent and nuzzled her cheek. She smelled of sweet honeysuckle and—Justin laughed softly—sherry. Her hand reached toward him, touched the fabric of his shirt. Encouraged, he reclined beside her and tasted her lips, gently at first so she wouldn't be startled. As his tongue traced her soft mouth he felt the beginnings of a response.

Shiloh gasped and her eyes fluttered open. "Justin! What—what are you doing?"

He nipped at her ear. "I just came to see if you've made yourself at home." His hand moved up her thigh. "You seem to be quite comfortable."

"Yes . . . yes, I am." She sounded groggy from sherry and from sleep.

He looked down at her tousled hair, her heavy-lidded, bleary eyes. As suddenly as passion had come upon him, it cooled. He knew that if he took her now, she'd regret it in the morning. It would be just like her to accuse him of taking advantage of her. With a muttered oath, he disentangled himself and stood up.

Shiloh brushed a curl from her cheek. "What's wrong?"

"Supper's waiting." He crossed the room to the armoire and began flinging things onto the bed. A chemise, a wispy pair of pantaloons. "The lady in the dry-goods store told me these were necessary." Last, he took out a yellow cotton dress.

"I don't understand you, Justin McCord. One minute you're—you're making love to me, and the next you're ordering me about." She was so angry that she didn't protest when he held out the chemise and slipped her arms through the sleeves.

"I married an unwilling woman," he said. "I figure the least I can do is wait until you're completely willing to be bedded." He held out the pantaloons, which she snatched away with an oath that would have done a Ranger proud. Keeping the quilts over her, she donned the undergarment. Patiently Justin held out the dress.

Rising from the bed, Shiloh stepped into it. As Justin fastened the buttons in back, she asked caustically, "Are you to be my nursemaid as well?"

He leaned forward and inhaled the scent of her hair. "I could be a lot more to you, if you'd let me."

She spun away, curls flying and eyes flashing. "I want nothing from you,."

Anger pricked at him. He'd gone to no little trouble to get her some decent clothes and prepare the room for her.

As she sullenly picked at the large, flavorful meal Ina and Prairie Flower, the aging Comanche cook, had prepared, Justin began to wonder about the advice Nate Mulvane had given him: *"Romance the girl a little; no need to be heavy-handed. She'll come around."* Justin doubted it seriously.

He watched her eyes flick around the dining room. It had been pleasant in its day, with a beamed ceiling and double doors facing out onto the rolling, oak-studded grasslands. But now the wallpaper and curtains were faded and dusty, and the furniture was dull from neglect.

"You haven't said what you think of the place," Justin said.

"Does it matter?"

"I want you to feel at home here."

Shiloh looked at him suspiciously. "How long have you owned Post Oaks?"

"A few weeks. But I haven't been around much."

"I know nothing of making a home. Back East they taught me how to serve tea and go calling. But I've forgotten that as well."

"Tell me, Mrs. McCord," he drawled. "What *can* you do?"

"I can sit a horse for twenty hours without stopping. Hit a mark at fifty yards. Read sign on almost any terrain. Track a man with the stealth of a Comanche. Oh, yes, I can also read and write and cipher. But I don't suppose those are traits you value in a woman."

He rose and rounded the table to stand behind her. Gently he lifted the curls from her shoulders. "You won't be a caged bird here, Shiloh. I don't expect you to be a housekeeper.

You're free to come and go as you please. But I can't let you do anything dangerous."

She turned and tilted her head back to meet his eyes. "Your concern for me is touching."

He clenched his jaw against an angry retort. "You can have the bedroom all to yourself. If you need me, I'll be in the bunkhouse with the ranch hands."

Shiloh blinked at the ray of sunlight that had slid across her face to awaken her. She sat up in sudden realization of where she was. She ran to the window and looked out. The sun was high over the fields. A pair of hands were driving posts around a corral, their shirts damp with sweat. It was practically the middle of the day. Frowning, Shiloh wondered why no one had awakened her.

Then she remembered. There was no reason for her to be up and about. Justin didn't need her, and she'd refused to run the household.

Sighing, she went to the dressing room and poured water into the basin. She bathed away the puffiness from around her eyes and pulled a brush through her hair, bringing it away from her face with a pair of combs. In the armoire she found another ready-made dress, this one a simple morning gown printed with small lavender flowers. Like the other, it fit her well, hugging her bosom and waist and just brushing the tops of the new black slippers she'd found.

For all his other faults, Justin had done a remarkable job of finding clothes for her. In addition to the two ready-made dresses, there were underthings, stockings, and bed gowns, as well as several bolts of cloth and numerous trimmings. With a twinge of resentment, Shiloh decided that Justin's gesture wasn't made out of thoughtfulness but out of his compulsion to make a proper wife of her.

Studying her much-improved image in the looking glass, Shiloh said, "It will take a lot more than pretty clothes to change what I am."

"Who said anything about changing you?" asked a lazy, deep voice.

She spun about to face him. "It's obvious that you don't care for me the way I am."

He shook his head, giving her a dazzling grin. "I'm not going to get into it with you now, Shiloh. I just came to tell you I'm going into town. I'd be obliged if you'd accompany me."

Shiloh started to refuse immediately, but the afternoon stretched long and tedious before her. Snatching a bonnet from the armoire, she followed him down to the stableyard. A Mexican boy waited beside a handsome cart drawn by a gleaming pair of matched grays.

"I'm Shiloh," she said. "What's your name?"

"I am Tomás." He smiled proudly. "I work for Señor McCord."

"I'm sure you do a wonderful job." Her bright smile faded quickly when she felt Justin's hand at her elbow. She pulled away and climbed into the cart on her own. She saw his jaw clench with annoyance and decided it was wise to court his dislike; with luck, he might lose patience with her and agree to end this farce.

But as they drove toward town, Justin was smiling again. "Tomás was pretty taken with you. You're probably good with children."

"With other people's children, maybe. I don't know the first thing about raising them."

"I'm told it just comes naturally."

"I'm in no hurry to find out." It was ridiculous even to consider having a family with Justin. Fortunately, Shiloh felt safe from that possibility for the moment. He was being unusually reasonable about the intimate aspects of marriage.

Houston was in full swing. The heat-shimmering streets were crowded with people of all shapes, sizes, and color. Laughter and music issued from the numerous grog shops and saloons, and traders worked from hastily constructed storefronts. A sidewheeler that had steamed up from the port of Galveston was swarming with newcomers eager to settle in Texas, where the wild land was practically free for the taking.

Justin rolled the cart to a stop in front of a small log building. "I'll just be a minute," he said, jumping down. "There's a lunch in that basket if you get hungry."

Shiloh watched him amble away, his boot heels clicking on the wooden planks that led to the office. She squinted at a small brass plaque beside the door: *Lamar B. Coulter, Solicitor.*

Taking a biscuit from the basket, she took a bite and chewed thoughtfully. Coulter had come to Nate's house one day, and Nate had been with Captain Charles Elliot, the British chargé d'affaires in Texas. Before Shiloh could show him in, Coulter had mumbled some excuse and fled, as if fearful of meeting the Englishman.

She wondered what business Justin had with the man. She climbed down and stepped into a hot, airless room.

Justin and the solicitor, a tall, rangy man of middle years, were in a small office in the rear, visible through the doorway. They hadn't noticed Shiloh and were conferring in urgent tones.

". . . pretty sure the rumored British offer will turn up in San Antonio," Coulter was saying.

"Christ, no wonder Harmon sent Shiloh after me," Justin said, shaking his head.

"Who the hell is Shiloh?"

Justin laughed harshly. "My wife."

"Your *wife?*"

"It's a long story, Lamar. She intercepted me in Washington-on-the-Brazos before I made contact with Delgado."

"Damn! Then there's nothing we can do."

"I'll go to San Antonio and find Delgado myself."

Lamar shook his head. "Raúl Delgado was murdered yesterday. I had word from a rider this morning."

Justin let his breath out in a thin hiss. "Any word on the letters?"

"Gone. Along with everything else we'd planned to present to the president. I've got these other reports if you want to take a look—" Lamar Coulter stopped short when he reached for a parcel and spied Shiloh.

She crossed the room quickly, as if she'd just come through the door. Smiling guilelessly, she extended her hand to Lamar. "I'm Shiloh Mul—McCord. I'm afraid you've kept my husband a little too long."

Coulter cleared his throat. "I apologize, ma'am. Well, I think our business is concluded, don't you, Justin?"

Justin strode to the door, taking Shiloh by the arm none too gently. "I'll be in touch." As they walked toward the cart, his grip bit into her. "Don't ever do that again," he said, his voice full of quiet rage.

She pulled away, surprised by the intensity of his reaction. The matter he'd been discussing with Lamar Coulter must be very confidential indeed, Shiloh decided with a sly smile.

"You look pretty damned pleased with yourself," he growled as they started up Main Street.

"I didn't appreciate being left to bake in the hot sun while you passed the time of day with Mr. Coulter."

"How much did you hear, Shiloh?"

She gave him a wide-eyed look of innocence. "What do you mean?"

"That was private business between Lamar Coulter and me. You shouldn't have walked in on us."

"I didn't realize husbands kept secrets from their wives."

He turned his hard-eyed stare on her. "You're my wife in name only, Shiloh. I don't trust you with my confidences."

"I see," she said. "Well, you needn't worry. I don't know what you and Mr. Coulter were talking about. But if you're in some kind of trouble, I have a right to know about it."

"I often have business that must be conducted secretly. I have to travel a lot, too. I'm leaving tomorrow, as a matter of fact, for a couple of weeks. I hope you don't get it into that head of yours to go nosing around, Shiloh."

She narrowed her eyes at him. "Don't worry, Justin. I wouldn't dream of tampering with anything that takes you away from me."

They were met at the southern gate of Post Oaks by an agitated Tomás. "Señor McCord, come quickly! It's the big mare. She's foaling right now—this minute!"

Justin extended a hand to the boy and hoisted him up into the wagon. A flick of the reins had the team bolting forward.

When they reached the stable yard, he jumped from the wagon and hurried toward a small outbuilding in the western field.

Sunset was gathering on the grassy knoll where the shed stood. A man about Justin's age motioned them inside.

"What's up, Wylie?" Justin demanded.

The man grinned, revealing a rather poor set of teeth. "The mare's been laboring since this morning. Should be anytime now. Now that you're here, I think I'll go get some supper."

"Thanks, Wylie, for staying with her."

Wylie lifted his hat. "Sure. And I hope you get that filly you've been wanting."

Inside, the smell of dust and sweat hung in the air. A beautiful roan, her sides swollen wide, stood in a hay-covered stall. The mare's eyes, a deep, velvety brown, blinked slowly and rolled back as she grunted with pain.

Justin approached her slowly, hand outstretched. "There now, girl. Easy . . . what's ailing you, Sugar?"

Sugar tossed her head and sidled away. He dodged the softly swishing tail and rolled up his sleeves to examine her.

She sidled again, swinging her head around to regard him in silent reproach. Moved by the mare's obvious pain, Shiloh took hold of her bridle. The mare steadied and held still while Justin continued working.

"Is she all right?" Shiloh asked.

"She's fine, Shiloh. She's about to become a mama."

But the mare was in no hurry. Time seemed to crawl by, the moments punctuated by the animal's grunts and snorts of pain. The sun slid below the horizon, and Justin lit a pair of lanterns and hung them in the stall. An owl screamed somewhere in the distance, and a wolf set up a baleful cry to the rising moon.

The mare let out a high-pitched squeal. "The hooves!" he said. "It's coming—damn!" His hands had slipped.

"Let me try," Shiloh insisted, brushing past him. "You'll hurt her with those big hands of yours." Gritting her teeth, she reached in and grasped the foal. Her eyes lit with triumph as she felt it surge forward. Just as suddenly, it slipped back. Another contraction, and she pulled with all her might. Justin put his arms around her waist and pulled, too.

The foal descended. At long last, a pair of tiny, perfectly formed hooves emerged. Shiloh fell back, awed by the sight. The next happened so fast that she wasn't sure she'd seen it.

With an unearthly squeal, the mare pushed the foal out onto the bed of straw.

Shiloh dropped to her knees beside the limp, still creature. It was tiny, glistening dark and motionless, as quiet as the night air.

"It's stillborn," she said, her voice hollow.

Justin brought the mare around, patting its damp neck. "Here it is, Mother. Looks like a fine filly."

Shiloh stared at him as if he'd lost all reason. "Justin, don't you realize—"

"Hush," he said quietly. "Watch."

The mare nuzzled the still form in the straw, nibbling the slick sac that surrounded it. The tiny filly twitched and gasped, breathing in life for the first time on its own. It let out a thin wail.

Shiloh collapsed against Justin. "Thank God," she whispered. "Thank God."

"I think you and your clever little hands had a little to do with it."

She watched the mare as it cleaned the foal. Unconsciously, she reached for Justin's hand. "Look, it's got a blaze on its face. Oh, Justin, have you ever seen anything so beautiful?"

He turned her in his arms so that they were facing each other. "You," he said. "You're beautiful."

Shiloh searched his face for a hint of the now-familiar mockery. She'd never been more unattractive in her life. Drenched with sweat and soiled by the mare's blood and fluids, she knew she must look and smell abominable. "Justin, this is no time to make fun of me. I'm tired, and—"

"Damn it, Shiloh, I wasn't—never mind. If I told you today was Tuesday you'd say it's Wednesday." He left her side and held the door of the shed open. "Let's go back to the house."

For some reason, Shiloh felt apologetic, although she said nothing. Shaking her head in confusion, she followed him out of the shed. She was amazed to see the first light of dawn rolling down over the fields. They'd been with the mare all night. She stopped in the doorway and breathed in the sweet, moist morning air. She smiled and looked back again at the new little filly. It was already raising its head, feebly but with gathering strength.

"What are you going to name her?" Justin asked.

She frowned up at him. "Name her?"

"The filly. She wouldn't be here if it weren't for you."

"Thank you." A sheen of unbidden tears spread over her eyes as she looked out at the dew-colored fields. "Dawn," she said finally. "I'll name her Dawn, after the most beautiful hour of the day." She looked to Justin to see if he approved, but he was already bolting the door against wolves and coyotes. Then he strode toward the house.

Shiloh had an inexplicable urge to run to him and fling her arms around him, but she resisted it. Justin wasn't an easy man to approach, not even to express simple gratitude.

Weary and filled with a muddle of unfamiliar emotions, Shiloh followed him to the house.

FOUR

Lightning tore through the night sky, bringing Shiloh to her feet. She had been sleeping soundly after spending the day with Sugar, the mare, and the new filly. She'd marveled at the mare's attentiveness to her foal, so meticulous in her cleaning and care, so encouraging as the little creature struggled to its feet to nurse.

Now Shiloh wrapped herself in a robe and ran to the window. The storm had burst upon the fields with ungodly wrath. Leaves were ripped from the trees as rain slashed in through the open window. Lightning struck like brilliant, vertical needles. During one deafening crash, the fields were momentarily lit for Shiloh's eyes. It struck so close to the shed where the new filly lay that she was sure it had been hit. Without stopping to put on shoes, Shiloh rushed downstairs and out to the fields.

She was immediately drenched by a thick curtain of rain, the hem of her bed gown and robe soiled by splattering mud. Driven by a sense of urgency, she ran all the way to the shed.

Her lungs felt close to bursting by the time

she reached it. Wet hands fumbling, she unlatched the door and let herself in. It was dry inside, and the horses were fine. By the bluish glow of another flash, she could see that the mare was standing nervously against the side of the stall. The filly was bedded down in the hay, unperturbed by the storm.

Shiloh stroked Sugar's neck and caught her breath. After spending a few minutes satisfying herself that everything was all right, she went back out into the tempest and secured the door.

"Shiloh!" She heard Justin calling her name, his voice nearly drowned out by the rain and thunder. The sky lit up for a split second and she saw him running toward her, rounding a small oak grove. Waving, she started toward him.

Her foot caught on an unseen root and she slipped. At the same moment, lightning struck. It split a tall, ancient oak tree down the middle.

Shiloh froze, watching in horror as the huge branches descended. She tried to scramble away, but her gown and the mud-slick grass impeded her. But the oak didn't quite reach her, and she was only brushed by small top branches.

A pair of hands gripped her and yanked her to her feet. Weak with relief, Shiloh collapsed against Justin's chest, laying her cheek on him to feel the moist warmth of his sodden shirt.

As he stroked her rain-wet curls, she almost imagined that his hands were shaking. When

he smoothed the hair away from her face, she knew she wasn't imagining it.

With one sweeping movement, he gathered her up into his arms, lifting her from the ground. Shiloh placed her arms around his neck, clinging to his strength.

His mouth crushed down on hers, his lips firm and insistent. The fury of the storm seemed suddenly insignificant compared to the feelings that engulfed Shiloh. She let her lips part to invite the caresses of his tongue. A roar of thunder only heightened the urgency of desire. She answered the questing tongue eagerly, stroking it with her own, amazed at her own wanton boldness. While the wind and rain whipped around them, they brought each other to a fever of passion.

When Justin dragged his mouth away and carried her down to the house, Shiloh was sure their time had come. He thrust the door open with his knee and strode up the stairs, taking them two at a time as easily as if he carried no burden at all. The intensity of the look on his face as he set her down in the bedroom took her breath away.

"Are you all right?" he demanded.

Shiloh wished she had the words to tell him of the longing he'd sparked within her, but she found it so hard to speak that she could only nod.

He gripped her upper arms and bent low. "Christ, you gave me a scare. I thought that tree

had fallen on you. What the hell were you doing up there?"

"I—I was worried about the horses."

"Well, it was a damned fool thing to do, going out on a night like this."

Shiloh began to laugh softly, touched by the brusqueness that masked his concern.

"What's so funny?"

"You," she said, fingering a damp lock of blond hair. "You really do care what happens to me, don't you?"

He took her hand and removed it from his hair, the sculpted angles of his face gone hard. "Obviously, I must," he replied. "I'm sure Jessamine would gladly accept a widower. Besides, I promised your father I'd take care of you."

Shiloh swallowed and looked down to hide a hot blush of humiliation. "I see," she said, fighting a terrible rage. "How thoughtless of me to jeopardize you like that."

"Shiloh, I didn't mean—"

Now her eyes were as cold as his. "I know exactly what you mean. Now, hadn't you better get some sleep before you leave in the morning?"

Justin tightened the straps of his saddlebag and glanced back at the house. The storm had passed by dawn, leaving brilliant green freshness in its wake. He knew better than to expect Shiloh to see him off, especially after last night.

He turned and hooked his hand over the saddle horn, forcing his mind to the journey ahead.

"I don't suppose you'd care to tell me where you're going."

Justin looked back. He hadn't heard Shiloh come out of the house, but there she was, standing stiffly on the porch with one hand on the railing. She was wearing the yellow dress he'd bought, and had pulled her hair severely away from her face. Freckles stood out on the pallor of her face. Her eyes were darkly smudged, as if she hadn't slept well.

"Galveston," he said, mounting the steps. "I'll be back in a week or two. If you need anything, tell Ina or one of the hands." Bending slightly, he brushed his lips across her forehead.

"Take care, Shiloh." Hurrying away from the sweet scent of honeysuckle that clung to her, he mounted and spurred his horse. When he turned to lift his hat to her, he saw that she was watching him, unsmiling, her hand raised in farewell.

Justin spent the ten-hour trip on the side-wheeler *Progress* planning his agenda and avoiding thoughts of Shiloh. By the time he reached the bustling port city, he'd managed to temporarily forget the small, vulnerable girl on the porch.

He went directly to the Tremont Hotel and sent for William Murphy, the U.S. chargé d'af-

faires in Galveston. While he waited in the big
main room, his sharp eyes took in the people
as they came and went.

There were more of them each week, from
all ports of the world, and each was driven by
the conviction that Texas would be their paradise.

And well it could be, Justin thought as he lit
up a cheroot and drew in the pungent, sweetish smoke. Texas had much to offer, but not
in its present state. The government was splintered into warring factions and was hopelessly
bankrupt. The Mexican army threatened from
the south and the Indians from the north and
west. President Houston had been forced to reduce the Texas army by half. When the republic
crumbled, it would be fair game for any nation.

Only statehood would protect it from English,
French, and Mexican interests. Justin hoped
that the news from Washington would be favorable.

William Murphy appeared, a bewhiskered,
well-groomed little man. Justin rose and shook
his hand and they seated themselves on velvet-
covered chairs behind a tall potted plant.

"Good to see you, Justin," Murphy said. "I understand the meeting in San Antonio de Bexar
didn't go through."

Justin nodded ruefully. "I was waylaid in
Washington-on-the-Brazos, and Delgado was
murdered. Much of the evidence we'd gathered
against the Accord has disappeared. It's a seri-

ous setback. Especially since things in Washington aren't progressing."

"What do you mean by that?"

"There are a lot of people who oppose annexation. Mostly Northerners. They're saying they don't want another slave state. But the alternatives are worse. Texas could easily become another English territory within the next few years."

"There's another thing," said Murphy. "The minute Texas signs a treaty with the United States, we'd be at war with Mexico."

"I'm aware of that." No sooner were the words out of his mouth than a flash of brilliant red caught his eye. Through the fronds of the potted plant, he saw a lush form, draped in satin and black lace. Like a dream, a hauntingly beautiful profile was silhouetted against a window across the room.

Forgetting Murphy, Justin rose and covered the distance in a few long strides. Large brown eyes turned to him and widened in unconcealed terror.

"Justin—"

He stepped closer and gripped her elbow, watching the once-familiar swell of her bosom.

"Hello, Isabella."

Shiloh set down the book she'd been reading. In the two days since Justin had gone, the hours had crawled by. There was nothing to do.

Her meals were prepared by Prairie Flower and served by Ina. The ranch hands took care of the livestock and fields. She had never felt so idle in her life.

There was a knock at the door. "It's Ina, Mrs. McCord."

Shiloh let the maid in. "Please, Ina, you must call me Shiloh. I insist."

"Yes ma'am—Shiloh. I was wondering if you'd like to get started on your dresses."

Shiloh smiled apologetically. "I'm afraid I'm not very good with a needle, and I haven't the slightest idea about designing a gown."

Ina looked at her, her olive-tinted face a little shy. "I'm told I can put together a dress quite cunningly. I was taught about it at the mission school in Goliad."

"Very well. If you really don't mind . . ."

Ina hurried to the armoire and opened it wide. She deposited a number of bolts on the bed and took out a drawerful of trimmings. Her middle-aged face was softly handsome. "He has a good eye, your husband. Few men are so well aware of their wives' needs."

Shiloh sniffed. "He presumes too much."

"Do you not find his choices pleasing?"

Shiloh moved her eyes over the pile of fabric, taking in a rich length of gold cotton, an emerald satin, several bright calicos, and some soft pastels. There was no denying that the fabrics were lovely, but she disliked them because of what they represented: Justin's virtual ownership of her, her total lack of freedom to make her own choices. But Ina looked so eager that she smiled.

"I've no doubt that you can turn these into wonderful gowns."

Ina drew several folded pages from her apron pocket and spread them out for Shiloh to see. "These are from London and Paris. Mr. McCord knew I was interested in fashion." She indicated a sketch of a traveling suit. "The cut of this jacket and skirt will look well on you. And this ball gown—think how graceful it will be in the emerald satin. Very simple, but with your coloring it will be stunning."

Shiloh looked at Ina in surprise. The woman must have a vivid imagination to believe she could ever be called stunning. "These are lovely, but why would I ever need such things?"

"Your husband is an important man. He attends many functions. He has been received many times by President Houston and the Allens. You must look your best when you accompany him." Ina's manner became brisk. "Come, let us measure you for your new dresses."

Shiloh submitted to Ina's marked-off ribbon and pins, lifting her arms and turning when instructed.

"You are very small," the woman murmured.

"I'm told my mother was tiny, but I don't remember."

Ina lowered her lashes. "I, too, lost my

mother. My father, too, in the Revolution of eighteen-ten."

"I think you're remarkable," Shiloh said. "I envy you for the way you take care of yourself."

Ina stared at her. "You are lucky to have a man to look after you."

Shiloh snorted. "It was not my choice to marry Justin. I feel he stole my freedom from me. This house, the clothes, everything—I'd give it all up if only I could be on my own again."

Ina laughed. "What a pair we are, each wanting what the other has."

The next day, Shiloh tried her hand at helping Ina, more for the woman's company than from any desire to learn to sew. But she was so inept with scissors and needle that she gave up, with Ina's relieved blessing.

"I'm going riding," she announced after she had cut all the knots out of the seam she'd been sewing.

Ina raised an eyebrow. "Alone?"

"Of course."

"But you cannot! Mr. McCord said—"

Shiloh looked at her sharply. "Said what?"

"Nothing," Ina mumbled, blushing down at her work.

"Did Justin say that I wasn't to leave?"

Ina nodded without looking up. "He is only concerned for your safety."

"The hell he is!" Shiloh said, disregarding the

older woman's cringe at her language. "Justin has no right to keep me here. I won't stand for it!" She flew from the room and went up to don her trousers, shirt, and scuffed boots. Glimpsing herself in the mirror, she smiled grimly. This was the old Shiloh, plain and unadorned, with a devil-may-care, defiant gleam in her eyes.

Her ride took her down along the murky bayou, around thick canebrakes and cypress forests. She galloped wildly until she felt her anger abate to a dull ache. Slowing her mount to a canter, she headed toward town. With renewed determination, she burst into her father's house.

Nate Mulvane showed mild surprise at his daughter's sudden appearance. He was sitting in a chair, his leg propped up on a stool.

"Hello," Shiloh said. "Looks like you're mending."

"Doing better. Could be Eb's infernal liniment is doing some good, after all. What are you doing here, Shiloh?"

She paced up and down the room. "I thought you'd realize that you can't just transfer me to another man like so much horseflesh. You knew I had no desire to be Justin's wife."

"He's a good man, Shiloh. He'll take care of you."

"I don't want to be taken care of. I want to live my own life. Let me work for you. I know money's getting scarce, and you're still in no shape to work. And with new people arriving in Houston each week, you must be inundated with jobs, finding relatives, and—"

Nate shook his head. "Sorry, Shiloh. Things are getting too rough."

They stared at each other with eyes so alike, yet so at odds. Shiloh searched for the slightest softening in his but found none. Without another word, she turned on her heel and left.

Feeling defeated, she returned to Post Oaks. The house on the hill was tinted amber by the lowering sun, and a few horses in the west meadow were silhouetted against a wide, pink sweep of clouds. Shiloh sighed. There was nothing about this place that beckoned her, no welcome in the white-railed porch or the upper dormer windows. To her it was more a prison than a home, in spite of its beautiful setting.

Then she noticed the buckboard in the drive. A driver stood nearby, holding a lantern. A black girl, her face shaded by a wide-brimmed hat, waited on the seat. Shiloh rode up to the house and gave her horse to Tomás. She stopped at the entrance to the parlor, her eyes narrowed to meet the challenge. Planting her feet and placing her hands at her hips, she faced the visitor. "What are you doing here, Jessamine?"

The girl set down her teacup and wiped a crumb of biscuit from her ripe mouth.

"Why, Shiloh, I'd almost given up on you."

"What can I do for you?"

"Isn't it customary for a new bride to receive visitors?"

"I wouldn't know."

"You never were one to practice the social graces." Jessamine gave Shiloh's dusty clothes a meaningful look.

"Since I'm such an oaf, Jessamine, why don't you leave?"

Yellow ringlets bobbed as Jessamine laughed. "I'm curious. I was wondering what you did to make Justin marry you so suddenly."

"Oh, that was easy. All I did was tell him he was going to be forced to marry you."

Jessamine's smiling facade fell away. "You're lying! Justin loves me, not you." She rose and flounced about the room, wrinkling her nose in distaste. "This house is a disgrace. The paint is flaking, the wallpaper and curtains are faded . . . no self-respecting woman would allow her home to look like this."

Shiloh bristled. She didn't care what Jessamine or anyone else thought, but it went against her grain to listen to insults.

"Get out," she said tightly.

Jessamine went to the door, her china-blue eyes gone hard as ice. "It won't take long for Justin to realize the mistake he's made."

"Sorry, Isabella, but I'm not buying it." Justin flicked his cheroot over the saloon balcony. "No one forced you to turn me over to Huerto." Isabella had managed to elude him after that first meeting at the Tremont ten days earlier, but now, on the eve of his departure for Houston, he'd cornered her.

"I had no choice! The *alcalde*'s son, who was once my *novio*, found out that I was hiding you. I would have been punished severely if they'd discovered you."

He leaned easily on the railing, studying her. "Now, suppose you tell me what you're doing in Galveston."

A guarded look came over her. "I am here with my uncle. He owns interest in a small merchantman out of Vera Cruz and has come to do some trading."

Justin shook his head. "You'll have to do better than that, Isabella. I saw you with Captain Elliot last night. What does the Englishman want?"

"Perhaps he is lonesome and in need of company."

"Your lies aren't working, Isabella. Elliot is mighty friendly with the Mexicans and I want to know what he's up to. Now, either you can tell me, or—"

He stopped short, sensing movement behind him. Two thick-set men, dark-skinned and mustachioed, stepped through the curtain onto the balcony. They were as alike as the tooled knife hilts they held in their hands.

Isabella smiled maliciously. "You were saying, Justin?"

He returned her smile as the thugs advanced on him. Then, tipping his hat, he vaulted over the railing and leaped to the street below. He landed on his feet and ambled away, whistling a tune.

At first Justin thought it was relief after a long, fruitless trip that made the house at Post Oaks look brighter, more vivid, than he remembered. As he galloped up the drive, he realized the house had been transformed. Stopping in front, he stared in amazement.

A fresh coat of brilliant white paint adorned it, the trim a handsome grayish blue. The wild tangle of brush had been cleared away from the base of the porch to reveal neatly trimmed hawthorn and azalea bushes. The porch had been swept and a pair of chairs brought out, flanked by potted ivy on wooden stands.

"Señor McCord!" Tomás ran forward to take charge of the horse.

Justin dismounted and tossed him the reins. "What's going on here?"

"Your wife, señor, she has had everybody working for over a week."

Shiloh was full of surprises, Justin thought as he went inside. This, too, was greatly improved. The floors and furniture had been cleaned and polished. The faded wallpaper was gone, the walls painted a pale shade of blue. New curtains graced the windows, and sparkling jars full of wildflowers stood on the parlor mantel and table.

Justin leaned against the door frame, breathing in the scent of lye soap and flowers. He reflected briefly on the home of his boyhood, a plantation called the Willows. The place had dripped with elegance, decorated by his mother to fussy perfection and changed every few years or so. Looking around at his present dwelling, he realized how much he preferred it, with the homey touches of a faded quilt on a stand, a collection of Prairie Flower's baskets at the hearth. After years of living in rough boardinghouses and under the open sky, he found having a home again a welcome change.

He found Shiloh in the kitchen, down on her hands and knees, scrubbing the bricks of the great cooking hearth. Her hair was knotted low on her neck, stray wisps curling about her face. She was humming as she worked.

Justin cleared his throat. "My compliments," he said. "I hardly recognize the place."

Shiloh dropped her brush. As she rose, a ripe-peach blush stained her cheeks. She brushed a stray curl from her brow, smearing it with a thumbprint of gray ashes. But there was not a hint of welcome in her defiant green eyes.

"I see you've been busy," he said mildly.

"I had to do something. If I'm to be forced

to live here, I might as well make my sur-
roundings pleasant."

"Shiloh, no one's forcing you."

"What choice do I have? My father will have
nothing to do with me, my aunt has some fool
idea that I belong here, and I have no money
to live on my own."

"I want you to be happy here."

"Then you're asking the impossible. But I'd
rather be scrubbing floors than mooning idly
about."

Justin ambled over to the sideboard and sampled a crust of Prairie Flower's dark bread. "I
don't suppose you'd accept my thanks for all
you've done."

"It wasn't for you," she said. "And you won't
be so grateful when you find out what I spent
on your credit in town."

Money was one thing he didn't have to worry
about. He had a trust from his grandfather that
would allow him to live comfortably for years.
"I don't mind, Shiloh. I told your father you'd
want for nothing."

She sniffed and wiped her hands on her
apron. "It'll be time for supper soon. I'm going
to get cleaned up."

Prairie Flower came in from the kitchen garden with a basket of greens and onions. The
lines of her nut-brown skin creased around her
small, bright eyes. "Good woman," she said to
Justin. "Hard worker."

"That she is," Justin agreed.

"She is not happy, Mr. McCord."

He nodded his head. "She makes no secret of that."

"She has a fire in her, a spirit. A great desire to prove herself. But she will not do that by simply being your wife." The wizened face challenged him.

As they shared a supper of venison, greens, and field peas, Justin ate in a distracted way. Finally, as the candle on the table burned down to a stub, he spoke. "I have some things to tell you about myself. I'm sure you've realized that I have other responsibilities besides this ranch."

She gave him her coolest stare, resting her chin in her hand. "You're an agent of the United States government, directly responsible to a Mr. Pinckney Henderson in Washington. Your work is supposed to lay ground for an annexation treaty."

He raised an eyebrow at her. "How did you find that out?"

She laughed, enjoying her small triumph. "That outmoded safe in your study isn't much good for keeping secrets."

He set down his glass, tensing in anger. "Damn it, Shiloh, can't you keep your nose out of my things?"

She gave him her sweetest smile. "I'm afraid not, Justin. I guess it's in my blood."

He lit a cheroot and leaned back. "It's not

just a question of negotiating a treaty. There are plenty of influential people around who will go to great lengths to prevent annexation."

"And Judge West is one of them." Shiloh swallowed as a cold feeling gripped her. She knew now how completely Justin had used her to shield himself from Harmon West. The cold feeling turned to bitterness. The marriage had been a wise move for Justin, but what did that make her? Three weeks ago she had been an independent woman. Justin had reduced her to an object of convenience. She knew she must do something to gain back her self-respect. "I want to work with you on this, Justin," she said with quiet determination.

Unhesitating, he shook his head and flicked his cheroot into the grate. "I can't let you do that."

"I'm good at this sort of thing. You said so yourself."

"I don't have the authority to bring you in. It's up to my superiors in Washington."

"That's a lie," Shiloh snapped. "You have a letter from Mr. Henderson giving you license to do whatever you see fit to achieve your goal."

"You really dug deep, didn't you, Shiloh?"

"I wanted to know what you were hiding from me."

He leaned back, folding his arms across his chest. "There is something you can do."

A spark of hope flared within her. "Tell me."

"There's a ball in San Antonio next month,

a big deal put on for the foreign legates in Texas. A lot of important people will be there. I managed to get myself invited. I'd be much less conspicuous if I arrived with my wife."

"In other words," she said coldly, "I'd come along as part of your disguise."

Justin stood up to leave. "Just be sure you have something decent to wear."

Shiloh stared after him, making a silent vow. She'd go to San Antonio de Bexar, but her presence wouldn't make Justin inconspicuous. Far from it.

FIVE

Shiloh lifted a leather flap and looked out the window of the hired coach as it creaked its way along the old San Antonio road. She'd stopped counting the hours of travel long ago, her mind numb with the monotony of the trip.

Ina rode behind in a similar, hooded wagon with—of all people—Nate Mulvane. For some reason, he'd volunteered to drive Ina and Shiloh's ridiculously large load of baggage.

Across from her, on a fading upholstered seat, Justin sat, as absorbed in his thoughts as Shiloh was in hers. She glanced at him and looked out the window at the endless summer sky and green rolls of grassland.

The first four weeks of her marriage had been fraught with tension. Justin refused to discuss his business with her and actually seemed to avoid her. While she continued with her clean-up of the house, he threw himself into developing the ranch. He and the hands repaired the main barn and well-house and built a sturdy corral. A dozen horses were added to the stock. And already there had been plenty of buyers with ready cash.

On the surface, it looked as if the newlyweds were prospering early in their life together. But beneath that thin surface, there existed nothing but discontent and occasionally dangerous moments of passion.

Most of the time, Justin maintained a maddening aloofness. But every once in a while, she would find herself caught in his steel-banded embrace, her mouth plundered by his kisses. She hated the weakness of her own flesh even more than she hated the hollow, empty feeling when he left her raw with desire, as he invariably did.

As she tried to push aside the turmoil of her thoughts, Shiloh sensed a subtle change in the land outside. The long stretches of nothingness became tamer, the small farms more frequent.

"La Villita," Justin said, indicating a row of diminutive houses. "We've arrived, Shiloh. Look up to the north."

She moved to the opposite side of the coach. In the distance, the sand-colored facade of the Alamo rose against the late afternoon sky. She'd grown up hearing tales of the brave, doomed Texans who had fought and died there. Now the building looked ordinary, unremarkable, vendors plodding past with their flatbed carts, and cats sitting upon its walls. Shiloh couldn't imagine those same walls breached by the bloodthirsty host that had slaughtered every

last man within. Yet she knew it had happened, and an almost reverent feeling welled in her heart as they passed the mission.

"Did you know any of them?" she asked Justin.

"Nearly all. I was on a scouting mission down San Pedro Creek. By the time I got back it was too late to join the battle."

She felt her throat constrict at the look of pain etched on his face. She had a sudden urge to reach for his hand, but she didn't dare. That might make him angry, or worse, he might pull her into his arms for another of his punishing embraces.

The coach rolled to a stop beside the clear, quiet river that meandered just east of the city. Justin got out and Shiloh followed, eager to stretch after the long journey. He caught her by the waist and swung her down, his eyes laughing at her surprise.

"We're in San Antonio now, remember? You've got a role to play."

She forced a honeyed smile. "I'll see to it that no one guesses I'm anything but your docile wife."

His look told her he didn't believe her for a minute, but he offered her his arm and they entered San Antonio by way of a footbridge. It was an attractive old town, with tall trees and brick and adobe houses graced with bright summer flowers. They walked through the plaza, which was dominated by a clock tower and a giant cypress in one corner. Justin took her to a small hotel, where they were greeted by a congenial Mexican gentleman who appeared to know Justin.

"For you, Señor McCord, I have a terrace room overlooking the plaza. You will find it most pleasant."

"We're traveling with my wife's maid and her father."

The gentleman knitted his brow. "Every place in town is full, I'm afraid. But I will find something."

Their room wasn't elegant, but it was clean and comfortable and rather spacious. The iron-railed terrace was decked with potted plants, the tall French doors draped by sheer white curtains that billowed in the summer breeze. A dressing area was enclosed by a folding room divider and furnished with a washbasin.

"What do you think?" asked Justin.

She refused to admit to him that she'd never seen the inside of a hotel room before. "There's only one bed," she said dubiously.

He laughed. "What did you expect?"

Blushing, she stared out the window. She tried to avoid thinking about the intimate aspects of their marriage.

"I could try to find another room," he suggested, "but that wouldn't be very convincing."

"There's no need," she answered. "We're both adults. We can be reasonable about this."

She thought she saw a hint of derision in his

eyes. "Of course we can." He went to the door. "I'm going to check on Ina and your father."

Soon after he left, Shiloh's baggage arrived. With great relief, she shed her traveling gown and washed at the basin. Then she donned her lavender cotton frock and went out. She knew that Justin had intended for her to stay where she was, but she didn't think twice about displeasing him.

She walked across the plaza, noting the stone and adobe shops and houses with their shady patios. Before long, she came to the military plaza where she had discovered the cache of munitions five years earlier. Although she barely remembered the cathedral or the elegant dormered mansion of Jose Cassiano, she recalled with searing clarity the thrill of triumph she'd experienced at her own success.

Sitting on a stone bench, Shiloh felt a wave of desolation wash over her. She'd been so busy with the house that there hadn't been time to regret the abandonment of her career. At times she'd even forgotten her ambition. But now it all came back, the impossibility of it taunting her. She sat for a long time, watching the people pass, yet not really seeing them.

And then a shadow blocked her view, and the sweet scent of magnolia assailed her senses. She looked up in surprise to see a black-clad gentleman smiling down at her. The first stars of twilight winked above his head.

"What a pretty sight you make," the man said, holding a cream-colored blossom out to her.

She didn't much care for the man's manner and quickly realized that she would be wise to return to the hotel before dark.

"I have been watching you," the man said, his English enriched by the hint of a Spanish accent. "A more lonely lady I have never seen."

"Sir, I am not looking for company. If you'll excuse me, I must be on my way." She started off and nearly collided with another man, more oily-looking than the first.

"Look, Franco, what I have found," the man was saying. *"La roja . . ."* Behind him stood a third man, compact and handsome in the Latin way.

"A good find, Tonio," that one said. "I was hoping for luck in locating her."

It was not chance that brought these men to accost her. But who were they, what did they want?

Tonio grinned. "Do not be frightened, señora. Come, there is someone we want you to meet, there, in Madame Bustamente's fandango hall just across the way."

"I'm afraid I don't wish to go, gentlemen." She was doing her best to remain calm, but the three of them had closed in on her and there was no way to elude them.

Tonio stroked her bare arm. "Come, now, you will enjoy our company."

Shiloh jerked away, only to find herself

grasped from behind by Franco's arms. He circled her waist and dragged her against him. "Look, Felix," he said to his companion. "I think she likes me."

She struggled with every ounce of her strength, kicking at booted shins, scratching at grasping hands and laughing faces. She cried out, praying someone would happen by.

"Dios!" Franco cried, releasing her to clutch at his leg. *"La diabla—"*

Shiloh seized the moment to run, but she didn't get far. Felix and Tonio caught her and tormented her with rough caresses. They passed her back and forth between them, laughing at her panic.

She felt herself growing fatigued. When a muscled arm wrapped around her neck from behind, she felt herself sinking slowly, almost gratefully, into a deep-velvet void of unconsciousness.

Seconds before she slipped over the brink, Shiloh heard a new voice above the jeering laughter of her assailants. An animal snarl, a growled oath . . . A dark form sprang forward out of the dark-blue twilight. A flash of golden hair, a glint of steel in angry eyes . . .

"Justin!" she said, her voice a harsh whisper because of the pressure on her neck.

She heard a grunt as Franco released her and slithered to the ground. His jaw hung at a crazy angle.

Justin lunged toward the other two, quick and

lean as a cat. One blow split Tonio's lip wide, and another glanced off Felix's cheekbone. Felix cursed, and Tonio spat blood-drenched teeth to the ground.

Giving no quarter, Justin advanced again. But Felix was ready now and kicked him with swift force in the midsection. Shiloh heard his air passages empty out as he sprawled to the dust.

In the second it took him to scramble to his feet, both Felix and Tonio produced knives.

Crouching low, they stepped toward Justin, stabbing out and slicing the air. He twisted away with the grace of a dancer, but still they pressed closer.

Felix jabbed and Justin caught his wrist, squeezing to force the knife from the man's hand. Felix yelped with pain but held fast, pushing the shining blade ever closer to Justin's enraged face.

While those two struggled, Shiloh saw Tonio move toward them. There was no time to think. Her feet left the ground as she leaped at him. His knife dropped several feet away. Shiloh scrambled up, battling the fullness of her skirts, and seized it.

Tonio reached for her and instinctively she brought the knife up, tearing through his sleeve and cutting his arm.

"Puta!" He lunged for her again and she spun away, eluding him. Then, just as she raised the knife in defense, a hand came from behind and grabbed it away.

Justin's voice rumbled low with rage as he addressed Tonio. "You lay a finger on my wife and you're a dead man."

Tonio turned and fled, his boots echoing through a darkened alley. The others limped and scrambled after, cursing the *diablo tejano*.

In the quiet aftermath, music drifted faintly from a dance hall. Shiloh took a deep breath, fighting a fearful trembling. Only now, when it was all over, did the terror of the incident strike her. She took a step toward him, drawn to his strength. The intense look in his eyes made her hesitate. She swallowed, knowing better than to expect sympathy from him. She started to turn away.

"Shiloh." His voice brought her back around. Unsmiling, yet with an unmistakable softening of his eyes, he held out his arms to her.

With a cry of gratitude, she fell into his embrace. His arms curved around her protectively, crushing her to the warmth of his broad chest. As her trembling abated, he stroked her hair and her cheeks, murmuring into her ear. After a moment, he placed his arm across her shoulders and led her back to the hotel.

Justin sat in dimness and watched Shiloh undress. She was unaware that the lamp behind the folding screen silhouetted a shapely leg as she brought it up to roll down her stocking.

Suppressing a groan, Justin forced his gaze

away. He didn't know how long he could go on like this.

She stepped from behind the screen, looking impossibly sweet and girlish in a floor-length white bed gown, which was pleated at the high bodice and gathered demurely at the wrists.

"Are you all right?" he asked.

Shiloh nodded. She was still wide-eyed and pale, but she appeared quite calm.

"Then would you mind telling me what the hell you were doing out alone?"

"I wanted to walk around, stretch my legs, see some of the city."

"Didn't it occur to you that it would be dangerous?"

She shrugged, managing to look both defiant and forlorn. "Not really."

He gave a snort of disgust. Shiloh drew herself up. "Justin, there's something I have to tell you. Those men seemed to know who I was. They said something about taking me somewhere, to see someone."

"The Accord. Probably the same thugs that murdered Delgado."

"I don't understand, Justin."

"Someone doesn't want me at that ball tomorrow night, and they were trying to send me on a wild-goose chase after you." He drove his fist into his hand. "Damn! I knew I shouldn't have brought you along."

Shiloh tossed her head. "You needn't bother chastising me about this. I admit I was wrong to go wandering alone in a strange city. I'm only sorry you had to get involved. But at least you know someone is working against you. Now, I'd like to go to bed."

She slipped beneath the covers and pulled the quilt up around her.

Justin didn't much care for her attitude. The sight of her lying stiffly on the bed in that dismissive pose struck an infuriating chord in him. He crossed to the bed and flung aside the quilts. Shiloh drew her knees up in a gesture of self-protection. "What's the matter?" she asked. "Did I rob you of the opportunity to belittle me?"

He grabbed her by the shoulders and pulled her into a rough embrace. "That's not quite what I had in mind, Mrs. McCord."

His mouth forced its way down onto hers, reminding her of her undeniable attraction to him. His hands plucked at the laces of her bed gown, pulling it down to bare her shoulders to the night breeze.

Shiloh felt her will crumble as Justin's hands moved over her. His caresses were relentless, evocative.

The white heat of passion consumed her. Despite her rage, she found that she was no longer struggling away from him but toward him, toward the searing brand of his touch. Heated longing chased away all resistance, and suddenly, her desire became as fierce as her husband's. She reached for him in feverish want.

An involuntary groan issued from Justin. She knew then that she had a certain sensual power over him, and she meant to exploit it to the fullest.

He raised an eyebrow at her, smiling sardonically. "And all along," he drawled, loosening his trousers, "I thought you were so innocent."

Shiloh didn't think she could cope with the rush of confusing emotions that washed over her. She dreaded what was to come next, yet she thought she would die if she was denied it. She swore and wrapped her arms about Justin's strong neck.

There was a scratching at the door. Justin muttered something vile and tried to ignore it, but the caller persisted. He stood and straightened his clothing.

"I'm not through with you, Mrs. McCord," he promised, going to the door.

But the moment he left her, Shiloh vowed otherwise. She pulled the quilt up and watched Justin with wary eyes. The unseen person at the door had given him a letter. She silently thanked the person who had interrupted them, and turned over to go to sleep.

After scanning the note, Justin removed the lamp's blackened chimney and held the paper to the flame. He glanced over at Shiloh, who was doing a good imitation of sound sleep. He poured himself a glass of whiskey and sat down to think about the letter.

It was from a local Latino agent, confirming

the worst of his suspicions. The government of the nearly bankrupt Republic of Texas was about to be bought. Lord Aberdeen, the British secretary of foreign affairs, had concocted a scheme in which England would pay interest on a loan to Texas. All that was expected in return was a promise to avoid annexation. While not exactly becoming part of the British Empire, Texas would become her puppet, bound by the strings of obligation.

Captain Charles Elliot, the British chargé d'affaires, possessed a letter penned by Aberdeen himself, detailing the offer. Elliot would submit it secretly to a Texas official, whose name Justin hadn't been able to discover.

He had to intercept the letter; it was his sole reason for making the trip to San Antonio de Bexar. His best chance would be at tomorrow night's grand ball at Las Alamedas. Elliot would attend, of course, and he'd have the letter with him. The Englishman would try to pass it on at the party.

Justin vowed that Elliot would never have the chance.

A night shower had freshened the town, cleansed the stone and adobe buildings of dust. Shiloh stepped out onto the terrace and looked down at the plaza. In the brilliant morning sunlight, it was a colorful, rustic scene. But now Shiloh knew that nightfall could transform the plazas and narrow alleyways into a haven for thieves and carousing gangs like the one she'd met last night. Her fear was gone, but the lesson would never be forgotten. Justin wouldn't forget either. He hadn't said anything before he left on some obscure errand, but she'd seen him watching her critically, probably wondering if she'd repeat her blunder.

Waking up to Justin had been a shock. She'd opened her eyes after a sound sleep and found herself staring across the tanned, muscular expanse of his chest. His arms were around her. What stunned her more than anything was that their bodies seemed to fit together perfectly, as if they'd been designed for each other's comfort.

Shiloh went back to the room and tied on a bonnet. Her father had invited her and Ina to a picnic down at the riverside. She decided to wait for them on the patio, where she could sit and ponder her father's strange behavior. She'd never known him to go on a picnic in his life.

She locked the room and went downstairs to wait. The patio of the hotel was a shady, flower-decked refuge from the summer heat. She sat watching bees drift in and out of ligustrum bushes, and mockingbirds flitting through the branches of a fig tree. But her enjoyment was shattered by a shrill greeting.

"Why, Shiloh! I'd heard you were here!" Like a great, billowing confection, Jessamine West swooped down upon her.

Shiloh fixed a smile on her face. "Hello, Jessamine."

The young woman's eyes took in Shiloh's appearance with one sweep. "I must say, you're looking rather well."

"What brings you to San Antonio?" Shiloh inquired.

"The grand ball at Las Alamedas, of course. All the best people will be there, as well as many important European dignitaries. So tell me, Shiloh, what are *you* doing here?"

Shiloh gave her a cool stare. "Although I'm certain to disgrace all Texans, I'm going to Las Alamedas, too."

The blue eyes widened incredulously. *"You?* But of course; I'd nearly forgotten you're married to Justin. After all, his father *is* one of the richest planters in Virginia. I assume Justin has told you how to act in dignified company. But there's so much to remember! You must be consumed by nerves."

"Actually, Jessamine, I haven't given much thought to how I'll act."

Jessamine gave her a dubious look. Then, slowly, a honeyed smile appeared on her porcelain face. "I think we'll find your presence quite amusing tonight."

She sailed proudly away.

At last Nate and Ina arrived and they walked down to the river, where willows swept down to dip their branches into the crystalline water. When Ina asked her if she'd passed a pleasant

night, Shiloh nodded and looked away. There
was no need to speak of the attack, for it
wouldn't happen again.

She quickly turned the subject to other mat-
ters, asking her father what he knew of this
widely anticipated evening.

Nate lay back on one elbow and threw a stone
into the water. "Seems to me Justin would've
told you all you need to know."

Shiloh let her hair fall forward to hide her
blush. She wasn't sure how much her father
knew of her and Justin's relationship—or the
absence of it. She looked hard at a webworm as
it crept along a blade of grass. "Justin always
seems to be busy. Besides, I didn't really give
the party much thought until today. I ran into
Jessamine West."

"Harmon West is never far from big money
and power."

"What is this really about?"

"Like I said, money and power. Mexico will
declare war immediately if a statehood treaty is
signed. And the foreigners like things just the
way they are. You'll see tonight: we're being ro-
manced by the French and British alike. They
couldn't stand to see the United States get any
bigger."

Shiloh and her father talked on, and for a
time it was like it had once been between them.
Her father had never been affectionate with
her. But his appreciation of her mind was something Shiloh valued even more.

During a lull in the conversation, she looked over at Ina, who had been watching both of them curiously.

"You must be tired of hearing about this," Shiloh said.

"Not really. I was just wondering what will happen when Webster leaves his post as secretary of state. There is no doubt he will, since he and President Tyler don't get on at all." She matter-of-factly began unpacking the lunch they'd brought. Nate caught Shiloh's eyes and grinned.

"Still waters run deep, as the saying goes," he said.

They feasted on tortillas and spiced beans and strips of cabrito, idling the afternoon away. Shiloh gathered ripe plums and figs from the trees, and they ate those when the other food was gone.

Then Shiloh lazed by the river, trailing her bare feet in the water. Behind her, Nate and Ina spoke in low voices, like comfortable friends. She couldn't remember her father's ever having a female companion. She looked back and saw Nate hand Ina a tiny figure he'd whittled from a bit of wood. Perhaps Ina would be the one to soften her father's rough edges.

In the hotel room, Justin stood with his back to the door, facing the terrace. Shiloh stopped and caught her breath.

He was clad in a beautifully tailored suit of

evening clothes, a black waisted coat with tails, and fine fawn trousers tucked into tall, highly polished boots. A gleaming top hat rested on the table beside him. His blond hair shone like locks of the sun's rays. He held himself stiffly, accentuating the perfection of his appearance.

Finally, he spoke without looking at her. "I was wondering when you'd decide to come back."

"I'm sorry. I didn't notice the time."

He swung around, and she stopped speaking and gaped at the rest of his garb. His neck was encased by a starched collar and black cravat. A vest with brass buttons hugged his torso, and pleated cuffs peeked out from his sleeves.

Just as she was about to form some compliment, his eyes flashed over her, from her tousled hair to her bare feet. "Is this some sort of joke? Did you hope to make a fool of me by abandoning me tonight? Or is that what you're planning on wearing?"

"No, of course not."

"God knows, I ask little enough of you. All I wanted was to arrive at Las Alamedas with you on my arm."

When Shiloh found her voice, she was equally angry. "I never asked to be married to you. It shouldn't surprise you that I'm at a loss when it comes to behaving like a wife."

"I'm afraid I won't be able to escort you tonight, Shiloh. I promised someone I'd meet him at six-thirty." He gave her another long, hard-eyed stare. "I've had a bath drawn for you.

If you can make yourself presentable, you could come later with your father."

Ina, beautifully groomed and gowned in black, bustled in, followed by a pair of chambermaids.

"What are you doing just sitting there?" Ina demanded. "We must get you ready."

"I'm not going," Shiloh said, still looking out the window at the empty plaza.

"What?"

"Justin left without me. He said I could come later, but I don't think I will."

"Of course you will go. Here in San Antonio they keep later hours. No one is expected to arrive until at least eight o'clock. It is the Spanish way."

Eyes bright with unshed tears, Shiloh whirled about. "I don't *want* to go. If you could have heard the things he said to me, the way he looked at me . . . Justin doesn't want me there, either. He obviously thinks I'll shame him as the plainest, most ill-bred woman there."

A canny gleam appeared in Ina's eyes. "There, you have proven it yourself. You must attend."

"But *why?*"

"To show Justin how wrong he is."

Thirty minutes later, Ina was fussing over her like a mother hen. She brushed Shiloh's hair until it shone. With artful twists and loops, she piled it atop the girl's head and secured it with pins, leaving the shorter tendrils to fall like tiny flames around her face and neck.

Then began the laborious process of clothing her. She slipped on a thin lawn shift and drawers embroidered with white thread. Over that went yards of petticoats to give fullness to the skirt. The gown itself was a masterpiece. It had a wide, low bodice and dozens of tiny pleats leading out to billowing gigot sleeves. Ina had designed a panel of shiny gold beads on the front of the bodice and at the wide hem of the gown. The emerald satin shimmered, catching the lamplight in its myriad folds.

Finally, Ina overrode Shiloh's protests and added faint smudges of rouge to her cheeks and lips.

Shiloh stood before the mirror, feeling as though she were looking at a stranger.

"You see, Shiloh," Ina said with a smile, "there has always been a great lady hiding within you."

Shiloh enjoyed the free-floating motion of her voluminous skirts as she swayed before the mirror. "I only hope that I remember to behave as well as I look."

"Do not worry; I will see that you do."

Shiloh was delighted. "You'll be there?"

A blush rose to the older woman's cheeks. "I will be escorted by your father."

Shiloh stared. *"My father?"*

"Yes. That is, if it doesn't bother you."

"Of course it doesn't bother me. It's just that my father has never entertained a lady—a respectable one—before. I must say, I admire you for putting up with all his gruffness and bad habits."

"He is not so terrible. Beneath all his rough ways, he is a man of good heart. Perhaps he just needs the right person to bring out his finer qualities."

Her father, looking uncharacteristically natty in his best black suit, proved to be an elegant escort. He conversed pleasantly during the short coach ride to Las Alamedas, an elegant Spanish-style villa north of town, which belonged to don Enrique Valdez.

As they drove up between twin rows of graceful poplar trees, Shiloh felt butterfly wings of nervousness beating within her. It was her first formal evening, and she was essentially untrained for such company. As a footman handed her down from the coach, Nate whispered in her ear, "You'll do fine, girl. Just be yourself."

She followed him and Ina into the beautiful tiled foyer. The double doors leading out to the flower-strewn patio were held wide open, revealing a glittering throng that danced in the glow of torches and hanging lanterns. A pair of liveried men stood in the doorway, announcing the arrival of various guests.

Nate extended an arm to each woman. "Shall we, ladies?"

Shiloh held back. "I think I'll go in alone. It will give the gossips something to twitter about."

SIX

A graceful quadrille ended and the dancers applauded politely, migrating toward the tables that flanked the patio to refresh themselves with *aguamiel* or chocolate. Justin stood leaning against a stone pillar, speaking in low tones with his associate, Duff Green.

"I'm glad you came early," said the compactly built, bewhiskered man. "I figured Elliot would have something up his sleeve tonight."

Justin scanned the throng on the huge patio and focused on a handsome man with silvering hair. "I just wish I knew who his contact is. I don't much fancy picking the Englishman's pocket."

"The letter would be a damned good piece of evidence." A servant passed and handed them each a goblet of dark liquid.

Duff tasted his and grimaced. "What the hell is this stuff?"

Justin grinned. "Mustang grape. You have to develop a taste for it."

Duff set his goblet on the sideboard. "I heard you got married," he said, puffing on a thick cigar. "Thought you'd want to show her off tonight."

Justin thought of how he'd left Shiloh in the hotel room. Barefoot, tousled-haired, head flung back in defiance. "I doubt she'll come," he said ruminantly. "Shiloh isn't cut out for this sort of thing. She's . . . different. Plain, even simple, I guess some would call her, and not given to pretty dresses and socializing."

Duff beetled his thick brows. "That's a hell of a thing to say about your wife."

"I don't mean to run her down, but Shiloh would be as awkward as a duck on a lake full of swans. But she's a good woman—"

He broke off as the steward announced a couple he recognized. "Mr. Nathaniel Mulvane. Señora Ina María Ruiz y Garza."

They were an impressive couple: Nate, with his fiery hair and beard, and Ina, darkly elegant beneath her black lace mantilla. But there was just the two of them.

"Mrs. Shiloh McCord," the steward called out.

Duff clamped a hand on Justin's arm. "Jesus," he hissed. "I can't say I blame you for wanting to hide her away."

Justin froze, his gaze riveted on the vision in the arched entranceway. In the cool eyes and red-gold cloud of hair, he recognized the Shiloh he knew. But she had been transformed. As she floated down into the patio on a shimmer of green satin, the gold beads reflecting hundreds of points of light, she smiled and extended her hand to Mayor Seguin and then to his portly wife. Her face exuded a glow so intense that Justin felt a knot in his gut.

Her entrance had not gone unnoticed by the other guests. Vaguely, Justin became aware of a sudden collective intake of breath, followed by low murmurs of pleasure and appreciation.

How had he missed it? Justin wondered, wending his way through the crowd. He just hadn't been able to bring himself to acknowledge her beauty fully, for fear of what it might do to him.

But now there was no denying who Shiloh was—what she was. And Justin knew he could no longer deny his response to her. He approached just as she finished speaking to don Enrique.

With a murmuring laugh, she said, "Here is my husband now. He was in such a hurry to get to Las Alamedas that he found it expedient to leave without me."

Don Enrique shook a finger. "Unforgivable. But then, a bird of paradise needs no escort, does she? Your wife, señor, is enchanting."

The sweet strains of a slow waltz filled the night air. "I couldn't agree with you more, don Enrique." He slid his hand around Shiloh's waist and led her to the dance floor.

Shiloh knew, as they whirled around the lighted fountain, that she and Justin had every eye in the house on them. She felt glorious. Even though Justin had abandoned her, she'd triumphed over his slight. And she could tell by the way he gazed down at her that he knew it.

"I forgot to say good evening," he murmured.

"There's still time."

He flashed a smile, showing his dimple and small fans of creases beside his eyes. "Good evening, Mrs. McCord."

She inclined her head, hiding her reaction to his infectious grin.

"Do I need to tell you how beautiful you are?"

She met his eyes, searching for a hint of the familiar mockery. Seeing none, she said, "Yes, Justin. You do need to tell me."

He pressed closer, squeezed her hand. "You're beautiful, Shiloh. You're so damned beautiful you make my head swim. When I saw you come through that door tonight, I thought I'd died and gone to heaven."

A warm glow spread through her, and with it a tiny throb of longing for him.

As he spun her about, his lips brushed the column of her neck, making her shiver with delight. "Am I forgiven, then?" he asked, his breath warm beside her ear.

"I suppose," she said, "that no respectable married lady has ever been so affronted. But then"— here she grinned wickedly—"most ladies have respectable husbands."

Justin bent low so that only she could hear. "Better stop smiling like that, girl. I might just show you how disrespectful I really can be." His hand began a slow, sensual exploration of the back of her gown, reaching up to her bare shoulder blades with roving fingers.

Just as Shiloh felt her knees begin to weaken,

the waltz ended on a lingering note. Then, it was as if half the gentlemen on the patio converged upon her. Justin laughed at her confusion.

"Now that the formality of the first dance with your husband is over," he said, "it looks like you're fair game for anyone."

Her feet never rested as gentlemen of every age, shape, and size claimed her for quadrilles, gallopades, and contredanses. She even danced the dangerously suggestive fandango with Mayor Seguin himself. Only when she was certain she'd trodden her green kid slippers through to the floor did she gravitate to the tables for a cooling drink.

"You're having a high old time for yourself," Nate Mulvane commented.

Shiloh sat down, her face glowing with exertion and excitement. Her smile disappeared, though, when Jessamine West pushed her way to the table. She looked like a giant flower, in a pink bell-shaped dress cinched in so tightly at the waist that Jessamine's eyes appeared unnaturally wide, as if they might pop out of her head.

"You look quite well tonight, Shiloh," she said, allowing amazement to tinge her remark.

It was a totally new sensation to see envy in another woman's eyes. "Thank you," she said. "And you look lovely, Jessamine."

"Your dress is most unusual, but it seems to suit you. And"—she leaned forward conspiratorially—"you must remember that people will talk if you continue to dance with each and every gentleman present." Jessamine glided off to attach herself to the Viscount Jules de Cramayel, the French chargé d'affaires.

Shiloh turned immediately to Ina. "Never mind her," she said. "I've been asked several times for the name of my seamstress."

"It is not the dress, *mi amiga.*"

Shiloh squeezed her hand and looked up to ask her father how he was enjoying himself. But he wasn't paying attention to her; he was staring intently across the patio.

"What is it?" she asked, following his gaze.

"That's Captain Charles Elliot. I've been watching him all night." He glanced over at Shiloh. "So has your husband."

"Why?"

"I suspect it has something to do with that envelope he's carrying in his coat pocket. I'll bet Justin would love to get his hands on it—before someone else does."

Elliot smiled charmingly and spoke to a passing group, and accepted a drink from a tray. But she noticed the tenseness of his jaw, the watchful looks he cast about.

"Excuse me," she murmured to Nate and Ina, and crossed the patio, politely declining several invitations as she went. "Captain Elliot?"

He looked at her, distracted, and then with growing interest. His stare almost made Shiloh back away. He had the coldest pair of pale eyes she'd ever seen. His smile was suave but did nothing to warm the icy chill of his gaze. "I'm sorry, but you have me at a loss. Have we met, Miss . . . ?"

She smiled at him. "Unfortunately, no. But I'd be delighted if you'd call me Shiloh." She covered her relief. She'd counted on his not knowing she was Justin's wife.

"An unusual name," he commented. His British accent lent a haughtiness to his every word.

"My mother named me after the county where she was born," she explained.

"Enchanting." He extended his arm. "I'm quite ignorant of your Texas dances, but for the sake of a beauty such as yourself I could try to blunder my way through."

"To be honest, Captain, I'd much rather take a stroll out into the water gardens. That is, if you aren't occupied with something else."

For the smallest fraction of a second, Elliot's icy gaze swept the room and then returned to Shiloh. "I'd be delighted," he said, and led her back behind the orchestra, down a few stairs to the garden. As they walked beneath the magnolia trees and down between a cement channel of running spring water, the sounds from the patio grew faint. What Shiloh spoke of she couldn't remember later, but she must have managed to allay any suspicions the Englishman might have had.

When she affected a delicate shiver and asked for his coat to wrap about her shoulders, he readily obliged. Within seconds, she had found the small envelope and slipped it into the bodice of her gown, next to her rapidly beating heart.

When they returned to the patio, she returned his coat with smiling thanks and went back to the dance floor. As two different men approached to claim her for the zopilote, she put her hand to her brow. She let her nervousness work for her, allowing her face to drain of color.

"Mrs. McCord, what is it?" someone asked.

"I—I feel dizzy." Letting her voice dissipate into the flower-scented air, she sank with dramatic slowness to the tiles.

"Stand back," someone ordered. "Give her air!"

"Smelling salts!" said another. "Bring smelling salts, and some water!"

Shiloh felt a pair of strong arms lifting her. She recognized Justin from his unique scent and the hard musculature of his frame. She allowed her eyes to flutter open. "Justin, I'm ill. Oh, please, take me back to the hotel." She took a deep breath and feigned another swoon.

She was the only one who heard his vile whispered oath. Aloud, he spoke to her father. "Nate. Could you—"

"Sorry, lad. I was just about to dance with this lady on my arm. Go ahead, take the coach. We'll get back another way, and I'll take your horse to the livery."

Shiloh felt Justin tense. Then he strode away so quickly that she could feel the wind in her hair. He paused twice on the way out. Once to

promise a future meeting with someone called Duff, and again to decline don Enrique's offer of a room in the villa.

Shiloh had planned on showing Justin her prize once they were in the coach, but as it bounced and clattered down the tree-lined lane, she thought better of it. If Captain Elliot overtook them, he was unlikely to commit the offense of searching her, but he wouldn't show that much restraint with Justin.

Besides, it was undeniably pleasant lying in Justin's lap with his arms about her, hearing his heartbeat and breathing in his clean smell.

Only when he had dashed with her up to the room and laid her on the bed did she allow her eyes to open again.

By the light of a low-burning lamp, she saw Justin's face and the golden gleam of his hair. All anger was gone from him as his brows knitted in concern.

He spoke her name and she smiled a little. "Shall I send for a doctor?" Before she could answer, he was going toward the door.

Bringing her charade to an abrupt end, she sat up on the bed. "That won't be necessary. I'm perfectly all right."

He whirled around to face her. "Are you sure?"

She brushed a stray tendril from her neck. "Quite sure."

He returned to the bed and sat on the edge, holding her by her upper arms. "I thought something was seriously wrong."

She smiled in anticipation of revealing her triumph. "I've never swooned in my life. But apparently, I was pretty convincing."

His grip on her arms tightened. "But—*why?*"

"I thought it best to leave right away. I'll admit fainting was an amateurish ploy, but it was the best I could do under the circumstances. And it did work. Here we are."

Now the hands were biting into her soft flesh. "Of all the foolish, idiotic—"

"Justin, please! You're hurting me!"

His face was very close to hers, darkly flushed with anger. "Not half as much as you deserve to be hurt," he raged. "Damn it, Shiloh, do you know what you just did? That party wasn't just a social engagement for me. I had a job to do, and you stood in my way. I've spent weeks trying to pin down some evidence against the Accord, and now it's all lost. I'll never have a chance like this again. Damn! I was so close . . ." His tirade went on, punctuated by curses that even Shiloh found impressive.

She forced herself to listen calmly and resisted wincing in the steel trap of his hold on her. When he finally paused to glower at her, she removed his fingers one by one until her arms were free. "Are you finished?"

"In more ways than one."

Slipping a thumb and forefinger into the bodice of her gown, she extracted the envelope she'd stolen from Charles Elliot and held it out to Justin. "Is this what you were so all-fired eager to get your hands on?"

He snatched it away and broke the seal. His eyes scanned the tiny writing on the page. He looked up in amazement. "My God. Shiloh, how the hell did you wind up with this?"

She permitted herself a touch of smugness. "I went for a stroll with Captain Elliot. He very kindly offered me his coat when the air got chilly."

"Why, Shiloh? Why did you do it?"

"I knew you were after it. My way was a lot more discreet than your trying to pick his pocket."

An intriguing succession of emotions crossed Justin's face as he stared at her. Anger, suspicion, disbelief, and finally elation lit his eyes. Then, like the sun bursting from a thundercloud, he grinned his marvelous grin and let out a great whoop.

Shiloh's breath left her as she was swept into his embrace. His joy was infectious, and she brought her arms around him in response.

"Shiloh, my girl," he said with a rich laugh, "you've just outsmarted the wiliest fox that ever left England's shores."

She fell laughing against his chest, in the full flush of her victory. Then she looked up into his smiling eyes, still laughing. Almost by accident, their lips met, bumping together as they smiled at each other.

Shiloh's smile faded as quickly as Justin's, and

they regarded each other from the distance of a single breath, a heartbeat.

Now Justin's every movement became deliberate. With tantalizing slowness, he lowered his mouth to hers, drawing her soft gasp of surprise into his lungs. For a moment there was light pressure as his lips explored hers. Then he began a slow, sensual movement, deepening the pressure and wrapping his arms more securely around her.

Heat pervaded her most secret places. Her lips parted, hungry for a taste of him. Justin's tongue traced the lines of her mouth and slid with unmistakable suggestion into hers.

Finally, when Shiloh lay weak and flushed in his arms, Justin lifted his mouth from hers. His eyes burned with an intensity she'd never seen before.

"Justin?" Her voice was breathless. "What— what is happening? You've never kissed me like that before."

"That's because I never meant business before, Mrs. McCord."

She frowned, trying to still the quaking within her. "What's that supposed to mean?"

He traced his finger along the outline of her lips. "All these weeks I've watched you, Shiloh. But I swore I'd never force myself on you. I said I'd wait until you were willing. . . ." His fingers left her lips and trailed down the column of her neck to the top of her bosom. "But now," he continued, "now I can't wait any longer. You'd best tell me to go away now, Shiloh, or I won't be responsible for what happens."

She was mesmerized by the deep timbre of his voice, the fire in his eyes, the sensual circling of his hands. She didn't think before she spoke; the words seemed to form of their own accord.

"Don't go, Justin. Stay with me. Stay and show me. . . ."

"What? Tell me, Shiloh." He urged the admission from her.

"Show me what you want from me. What—what I want from you."

Her words seemed to cause the fire in his eyes to blaze wildly. "Stand up, Shiloh."

"What?"

He stood and pulled her to her feet. His heated gaze swept over her, and a smile of soul-searing intimacy crossed his face.

"That dress showed me how beautiful you are, Shiloh. But the creature beneath is something much, much more special." He punctuated his speech by drawing, one by one, the pins from her hair. Curls spilled over her shoulders and down the hollow of her back. Then his hands reached behind, freeing the gold buttons from their loops. He pulled at the fullness of her sleeves, bending to nuzzle her neck as the bodice of her gown fell to her waist.

With agonizing slowness, he pulled at the drawstring of her chemise, standing back to watch as it, too, fell away. He brought his mouth first to one breast, then the other, teasing the nipples with teeth and tongue until Shiloh gasped aloud.

He looked up, smiling. "Do you like that?"

"I— It's—"

"Do you, Shiloh?"

"Yes."

He slid the gown over her narrow hips, pulling her toward him so she could step out of it. His hand untied the strings of her pantalets and he slid them, along with her silk stockings, downward.

Shiloh's trembling increased as he knelt, revealing a triangle of red-gold hair and the curve of her buttocks. Sensation rocked her as he kissed every inch that was bared to him: the side of her hip, the whiteness of her thigh, the back of her knee. Then he stood back and regarded her, like an artist admiring his own creation.

"Justin." Her whisper sounded distant, rough with both fear and longing.

"Undress me, love," he said.

She looked up at him, shocked.

"Come. I'll help you." He took her trembling hands and placed them at his lapels. She watched his jacket drop away. Then she cast aside his cravat and unbuttoned his vest and broadcloth shirt, her fingers clumsy and shaking.

Tentatively, then with growing confidence, she stroked his shoulders and strong arms and laid her cheek upon his chest. She heard the thundering of his heart and marveled that it was she who caused his pulse to race.

Justin kicked off his boots and cast aside his belt. He bent to kiss her, his mouth holding hers even as he laid her on the bed. The frame creaked as he settled himself beside her. Propping himself up on one elbow, he lifted his lips to gaze down at her.

His other hand was everywhere, stroking her with long, sensuous caresses. "You're a wonder, Shiloh," he said. "A woman in every way, but still a child, too. Do you know anything about this?"

"I—" Shiloh reddened. "No."

"I only hope, Shiloh, that I can do justice to your beauty—your innocence."

Then he began kissing her in earnest, relentlessly, while his hands played her as if her body were a tightly strung instrument. Shiloh gasped at the shock his touch produced.

"Easy, love," Justin muttered, nuzzling the leaping pulse at her throat. "Easy . . ."

She forgot to breathe as his fingers began a slow, tantalizing caress. Shiloh cried out but again was quieted by Justin's soothing whisper. His tongue thrust into her mouth, and the motion was imitated below. And all the while, his thumb stroked relentlessly.

Shiloh felt her hips begin to rise. Her head pounded with the waves of sensation that flooded her. She teetered on the brink of a precipice and waited, breathless, to drop over the edge.

Her eyes flew open as she was catapulted into a dark world of sensation so intense that it caused her to cry out.

He kissed her until she finally relaxed. Then, as she lay bathed in the glow of passion, he slipped off his trousers.

She shuddered as he lay down beside her. "What shall I do, Justin?" she asked.

He caressed her cheek. "Whatever you want."

"But what about you?" She realized that their lovemaking had been one-sided.

"You're everything I want," he said roughly. And then his hands rekindled the fires that had never quite gone out. Before long, Shiloh was quaking in his arms, straining for completion.

But Justin was different now. Besides simply giving her the exquisite pleasure her body craved, he began to reveal, gently, demands of his own.

Shiloh touched him. She didn't know where she got the nerve to do it, but she bestowed on him a caress so evocative that he groaned aloud.

He knelt between her legs and looked at her, his face hard with restrained desire. "I'll try not to hurt you, love."

Hurt her? Shiloh had no inkling of what he was talking about. She closed her eyes and gave herself up to him.

A moment later, she clawed at the rigid back, moving her head from side to side in protest.

Justin's lips whispered into her ear, crooning to her, "Just relax, sweetheart. It'll pass, you'll see. . . ."

He began to move. Slowly, the pain gave way to sheer pleasure. The rhythm Justin had taught her was so exquisite that tears sprang to her eyes. She felt the moment build and again experienced an ecstasy even sweeter than the last.

Justin shuddered and thrust deeper, and then relaxed, covering Shiloh's sated body with his.

They lay still, neither daring to move. Finally, when their heartbeats had slowed to normal, Justin kissed her and moved to one side. "Regrets, Shiloh?"

She hesitated, wondering. He had stolen her freedom, but she'd never felt like his possession. Yet now, bathed in all the new feelings he'd awakened in her, she knew that he had truly made her his own. She belonged to him as much as the stars belonged to the wide Texas sky. And he was asking her if she regretted that.

Shiloh was awakened by an odd, tingling sensation. It was as if a feather were being drawn up and down the length of her side, from her ear to the back of her knee. It was so pleasant that she thought she might be dreaming, but when her eyes fluttered open, she knew she was not.

It was beyond the capacity of her imagination to conjure an image more exquisite than the one she saw. Justin reclined beside her, looking like a young god.

He had plucked a wildflower from the jar on the bedside stand and was trailing it lightly over her naked body. "Did I startle you?" he asked.

Shiloh couldn't help smiling. "I've never been awakened quite like this before."

He grew bolder with the flower, dipping it down between her breasts and over her belly to tease the responsive flesh of her thighs. Shiloh allowed the sweet torture to continue until she could stand it no more. Then she snatched the sprig away and cast it to the floor.

Laughing at her impatience, Justin gathered her to him, and Shiloh realized that nothing would ever be quite the same again.

SEVEN

A cloaked horseman plunged into the twilight shadows of a canebrake along Buffalo Bayou, looking this way and that to assure himself he hadn't been seen. An owl screeched, and an armadillo scuttled into the underbrush, but otherwise the murky locale was silent. The horseman slid to the marshy ground, tethered his horse, and went to a spreading live oak. There, another dark figure awaited him.

"Well?" asked Harmon West, peering at the approaching man.

"A disaster." Charles Elliot's clipped accent cut through the heavy night air. "Lord Aberdeen's letter was stolen from me at Las Alamedas. By the charming wife of Justin Mc-Cord, I later learned."

"Damn! You should have been more careful."

"This whole thing could have been avoided if you'd been there, Harmon."

"I was laid up with the damned gout. Couldn't move a muscle."

"What are we going to do about the letter?"

"No point in trying to get it back. Justin Mc-

Cord wouldn't let it slip through his fingers. No doubt he's waiting for Sam Houston to return to town, so he can present it to him."

"I'm not worried about President Houston. Lord Aberdeen will, of course, deny any knowledge of the letter, and that will be that. But the real tragedy is that an ingenious plan can never come into being. The Americans would cry foul the minute they heard of it."

"You're right about that. But we don't need to get alarmed just yet. Houston isn't leaning too hard toward annexation, and the Texas legislature won't be meeting for a couple of months, at least. We've got plenty of time to think of a plan of action."

Elliot sighed wearily. "Whatever we do, let's try to keep McCord and his wife in the dark about it. I've a feeling those two don't miss much."

Harmon West snapped his fingers. "That's it, Charles. The *two* of them. We were on the right track when we tried to have the woman abducted in San Antone. If we can somehow get them working against each other instead of together, they'd be a lot less effective."

"They're husband and wife."

"Their marriage was no love match. Maybe we could get the girl to sympathize with us. We could use the slavery argument. Her father's a known abolitionist."

"What do you propose we do?"

"Justin has a reputation as a real ladies' man,

and I doubt Shiloh would sit still for his fooling around. I'll get Isabella Hernandez to come in from Galveston. She managed to turn his head once, down at the border. And meanwhile, Charles, you can talk to Shiloh."

"Good God, Harmon, I'm twice her age."

"I'm not suggesting you sweep her off her feet. But you've got a way with words. Let her think your sole purpose is to prevent the United States from winning another slave state."

"Very well," said Elliot. "Now, what are we going to do next?"

Harmon grinned into the thick darkness. "I think it's time we brought our Mexican friends into play. We've had them waiting down at the border for a long time. Now would be a good time to demonstrate to people just what would happen if a treaty were made with the United States."

A dark shape slithered down the bank and dropped into the bayou with a small splash. Elliot recoiled. "What was that?"

"A moccasin, probably. Poisonous as they come."

"I don't believe you, Justin!" Shiloh snapped, whirling on him so quickly that her robe gaped open in the front.

He looked at her with unconcealed lust, eyes alighting on her breasts and the tiny red bite marks he'd bestowed on her the night before as they'd celebrated coming home to Post Oaks.

"It's business, love." He crossed the sun-flooded room, catching her against him, his arm slipping inside her robe. Immediately, he felt her soften. Desire flooded through him and he bent his head to inhale the honeysuckle scent of her silken skin. Her innocence and vulnerability were coupled with pride and strong will, and a passion that left him fighting for air like a drowning man. Justin refused to question his passion for his young wife. He didn't want to know why he was so drawn to her; he only wanted to feel and taste and smell her, and hear her unabashed cries of ecstasy ringing in his ears.

"Justin."

"Mmm?" He kissed her cheek, the edge of her jaw.

She placed her hands on his chest, pushing away so that she could look at him. "Tell me what was in the letter."

He groaned aloud. "We've already been through this." He bent to kiss away her mounting anger, but she turned her head aside.

"I have a right to know. After all, it was I who got the envelope for you."

"I never asked you to do that."

"Nevertheless—"

"It's too dangerous for you to get involved in all this."

She wrenched herself out of his embrace. "Then we have nothing more to discuss."

"It didn't take you long to learn to use yourself as a weapon," he observed. "You almost had me fooled, Shiloh. But you're no different from any other woman. The minute you don't get exactly what you want, you declare yourself off limits."

"That's not true."

He raised an eyebrow. "If I'd shown you the letter, you'd be flat on your back, begging for me."

She walked stiffly to the window, hiding her face from him. Suddenly, she turned again. "What about you, Justin? You wouldn't have been a husband to me if I hadn't shown up at Las Alamedas, dressed like a perfect lady. You didn't even want me until it became obvious that other men found me desirable."

"I only did you the courtesy of waiting until you were ready."

"You were waiting to see if you could mold me into a proper wife. Well, you can't. I'm the same person you found so disagreeable at first. I still have the same dreams, the same goals. If you refuse to share your secrets with me, I swear I'll find out on my own."

"Shiloh," he said, "when I was in San Antonio I had a report about Raúl Delgado, my associate who was killed. It wasn't a simple case of murder. The man had been tortured. And then, after he told all he knew, they did him the favor of putting him to death. Don't go snooping around, Shiloh. It's too dangerous."

"Is it too dangerous for me? Or for your overblown male pride? You're jealous because I was able to get the letter."

"Of all the . . ." He stopped speaking. There was simply no reasoning with the woman. Cursing under his breath, he pulled on his clothes and boots and took his hat from a peg by the door. "I don't have time to argue with you, Shiloh. A couple of dozen wild horses are being driven in from Goliad, and there's going to be a lot of work to do around here in the next few weeks. But think about what I said. It's not a game, Shiloh."

"You did not touch your dinner," Ina observed, removing Shiloh's plate from the table.

"I don't have much of an appetite these days, Ina." Shiloh was surprised to see the maid's handsome face smiling broadly at her. "What's funny?" she demanded, getting to her feet.

"It has been seven weeks since we returned from San Antonio. Often that is soon enough to tell."

"Tell what?"

"Ah, I keep forgetting you did not grow up with a mother. There has been no one to tell you about the first signs of motherhood."

Shiloh stumbled back, stricken. The possibility of having a child filled her with cold dread. She wasn't ready for a baby; she never would be. "Tell me more about these signs."

"The symptoms are quite mild. I have never experienced them myself, but I am the oldest of eight children and I remember my mother well. A woman will feel nausea and headache. And, of course, the monthly bleeding stops."

Shiloh brightened. "It does?"

Ina stared at her, first with disbelief and then with great sympathy. "Poor little one," she crooned. "You are truly a child in many ways. Now. Do you think you are carrying a baby?"

"It's not possible. I had my courses after—after—" She swallowed, stifling a sob of misery.

Patting her hand, Ina said, "After Señor McCord moved back to the bunkhouse."

Shiloh nodded glumly. "I was so stupid. I thought everything was going to be all right, and then we had that terrible row. In the past month, Justin has either been away on business or busy with the ranch hands."

"There is a new herd to be broken. More space must be built for them. Do not worry, Shiloh. He will realize soon that he has been neglecting you."

"I *want* him to leave me alone. I want nothing to do with him."

Ina regarded her sagely. "Then why do you miss him so terribly?"

"I don't, Ina. I swear it! I've just been melancholy because there is so little for me to do. If

I were on my own I could be making a living the way I choose."

"You have been working very hard, Shiloh. You have been doing as much with the horses as any ranch hand."

"That's because there's nothing else to do. But I have half a mind to quit that, too. Justin doesn't seem to care one way or another."

"He cares, Shiloh. I have been watching him. You must understand a man like Señor McCord. He is proud and has never failed at anything he has tried to do. He is afraid to find out whether or not he has won your love. And you are much the same. Stubborn." Ina gathered the dishes from the table and left Shiloh to her thoughts.

She stood for a long time, looking out across the wide, shimmering fields of autumn. The sorrels and palominos grazed within the confines of a newly built fence. The hands worked tirelessly, transforming Post Oaks into a prospering ranch.

Shiloh ran down to the stable yard. She could no longer tolerate this silent limbo. She squared her shoulders and stepped into the dimness of the stables.

"Where's Mr. McCord?" she asked Tomás.

"He has just left for town. He said he had to meet with someone."

The afternoon stretched long and restless ahead of her, and she didn't relish the idea of waiting for Justin to come home. "Saddle my horse," she said. "I'll go get my boots on."

* * *

Justin sat at a battered table, clenching his jaw against an angry outburst. He, Lamar Coulter, and Duff Green had gone to hear Sam Houston's reaction to Elliot's letter.

"You have it right there in front of you, sir," he said. "I don't know what more you need."

The president shrugged his massive shoulders and puffed on his cigar. He was the man who had chased Santa Anna back to Mexico, tamed the Indians of the frontier. And he looked exactly like the hero that he was. But perhaps that was the problem, after all. How could a man as proud and powerful as Sam Houston allow the republic he'd built to disappear, joining the Union as a state?

Houston cleared his throat. "You've done the republic a great service in bringing this matter to my attention, Mr. McCord. Please extend my thanks to your associates." He shook his head in disgust. "The government's broke; that's no secret. There are a lot of people who would think this a reasonable solution."

"May I ask, Mr. President, what you intend to do about it?" Lamar asked.

Houston slapped his hands down on the table and rose to his full height, well over six feet. "Nothing, gentlemen."

Duff Green moved agitatedly about the tiny office. "Just a minute, sir. I know we can't touch

Elliot—he's a foreigner. But what about Harmon West?"

"He'll deny everything, as will the English."

"But he's got to be stopped! West is known to have illegal dealings in Caribbean sugar and rum."

"That's never been proven." Houston went to the door and turned back, his roughly handsome features set in an apologetic expression. "Sorry, gentlemen. Texans are always being accused of meting out justice rashly. We'll just have to let this one blow over." Taking down his hat, he left Coulter's office.

Shiloh caught sight of Justin's deep-chested bay tethered at a hitching post outside a grog shop. It was the noisiest one in town, alive with piano music, loud yells and laughter, and the endless clink of glasses.

Justin wasn't a drinking man and didn't seem to have a penchant for card-playing. She wondered what he was doing in such a place.

She brushed the wrinkles from her skirts and took a deep breath. Ladies, of course, didn't ever show their faces in Houston's grog shops, but Shiloh knew her presence wouldn't shock many people. Her father had often brought her along on his drinking bouts, and occasionally she'd had to fetch him after he'd imbibed too much.

She stepped inside and let her eyes adjust

to the dimness. The air was thick with smoke, the taproom crowded with bodies. It was easy to spot Justin. Standing at the far end of the bar, he towered over all the others. He was grinning and speaking to someone.

As always, Shiloh's heart lurched at the sight of him. Even in the murky environment of the saloon, his hat dusty and his shirt damp with sweat, she noticed something unfamiliar in his eyes. They seemed to lack their usual sharp intensity. As he lifted a glass to his lips and tossed back the amber liquid, Shiloh realized what it was.

Justin was drunk. Not in a loud-mouthed, staggering way, but quietly in his cups. Justin wasn't the stoic she'd thought him. Perhaps he was more affected by the rift between them than she'd thought.

She jostled her way down the bar, ignoring a few leering glances, a sly suggestion or two. Justin hadn't noticed her yet. He was still talking, laughing a little at some joke. When she was only feet away, Shiloh froze. One of the men in front of her had moved aside to reveal Justin's companion.

She was a Mexican woman, her profile stunningly beautiful. Her hair gleamed ebony, her full lips a vivid red. A shining gown showed off lush curves, which she pressed intimately against Justin. He bent and wrapped his arm about her, his face intense, unsmiling. Shiloh knew the look of passionate hunger. She couldn't stifle a gasp of outrage when he bent low to the ripe ruby lips.

The woman stepped back abruptly. It was then that Justin spied Shiloh. Their eyes locked for a burning moment; she saw her name form on his lips. Her heart pounding wildly, she fled.

Justin burst from the saloon and called to her, but she ignored him and leaped into the saddle. She slapped her horse, urging it to a gallop, and rode as if the devil himself were at her heels. Her piebald wove between carts and pedestrians as it bore her away from town.

She wished a great wind would come up and carry her far away, never to return. Yet she knew there was no escaping the demons that pursued her. How many times had Justin gone to the arms of the Spanish beauty?

Shiloh hated him. He had robbed her of her freedom by marrying her, then awakened her passion only to discard her for a sophisticated beauty with worldly ways. The loss of her dignity was more than she could stand. Probably half of Houston knew about Justin's wandering.

The landscape blurred before her, an expanse of painted flowers and grass as she thundered across a field to the north. She ducked low under the branches of a moss-hung tree and then gave the horse its head.

Minutes later she sat in her aunt's snug house, sipping lemonade and glowering at the cold hearth.

"Can I get you something to eat?" Sharon asked.

"I'm not hungry."

"Let me know when you're ready to talk about it."

Shiloh held fast to rage, knowing she could dissolve into tears at any moment. Finally, she began speaking in a flat monotone, telling her aunt about the trip to San Antonio, the terrible row they'd had their first day back at Post Oaks, and finally, the scene she'd just witnessed in town.

Sharon tucked a wisp of gray-streaked red hair into her dustcap and looked hard at Shiloh, as if trying to see the true feelings that lay beneath the hurt and anger. "What will you do?"

"I can't go back to Post Oaks."

"I don't know much about your husband, Shiloh, but I did talk to Nathaniel about him. That business in the saloon doesn't sound like something Justin would do. You need to give him a chance to explain."

Shiloh folded her arms across her chest. "Even if he bothers to explain, it'll all be lies."

They sat together in lengthening silence. A mockingbird trilled outside the parlor window, scolding one of Sharon's cats, which sat on the sill. Finally, Sharon stood up. "I just brought in a basket of field peas. I could use some help hulling them."

Shiloh ate little of her supper and hastened to clear up afterwards. Her stomach was a tight ball of nerves. She couldn't rid herself of the image branded on her mind: Justin, bending down to the dark-haired beauty. The vision tormented her, tore at her until her hands shook and her breath came in short gasps.

She could no longer deny what she felt. Several times she started toward the door, but stopped herself. She was the one who had been wronged. Let him come to her—if he could manage to tear himself away from the Mexican woman.

As evening descended, a knock sounded at the door. Shiloh flew to answer it. She jerked the door open, aware that her face would reveal all that she felt, yet powerless to conceal it.

She found herself staring, confused, at a composed face and icy pale eyes. "Captain Elliot!"

"I'm pleased you remember me, Mrs. McCord." He used her name pointedly, reminding her that she hadn't revealed her identity to him in San Antonio. "May I?"

Shiloh stepped aside. "Of course. Captain Elliot, this is my aunt, Sharon Bledsoe."

The two of them shook hands. "I apologize for the intrusion, Mrs. Bledsoe," said Elliot. "I have been wanting to speak to Mrs. McCord."

"How did you find out where I was?"

"Someone at your ranch mentioned Mrs. Bledsoe's place."

Shiloh stepped away from him, watching distrustfully. "What do you want from me?"

He indicated the settee in the parlor. "Shall we sit down?"

"I'll fetch something to drink," said Sharon, and she hurried off to the kitchen.

"Imagine my surprise," Elliot began, seating himself, "when I discovered that a certain young woman had relieved me of a rather personal document."

Shiloh raised an eyebrow. "Was it so personal, Captain?"

"I'm sure you know exactly what that letter said. My superiors in London were very specific."

"They were, indeed," Shiloh bluffed.

A tic of agitation began to jump beside his right eye. "In betraying official confidences, you have condemned the Republic of Texas to total bankruptcy."

Shiloh drew herself up. "Texas will not be manipulated by foreign powers."

"You're a proud woman, Mrs. McCord. And Texas is a proud nation. It surprises me that you wish your country to be swallowed up by the United States."

"The people—myself included—want annexation."

"Texas is a sovereign nation, independent of all others. If the United States takes over, you'll be subject to the whim of legislators thousands of miles away."

"If we don't sign a treaty, sir, we'll soon be so

impoverished that the republic will simply dissolve."

The Englishman gave her a measuring glance. "Are you in favor of slavery, Mrs. McCord?"

"Certainly not." She accepted a glass of lemonade from her aunt.

"Slavery would be prohibited as a condition for the loan."

"I have a feeling, Captain Elliot, that abolition is not the only condition of the agreement. England is a great nation, but I doubt it can afford to be philanthropic. It's no coincidence that your interest happens to be in a fledgling republic that lies at the western edge of your greatest rival in trade."

"I hope your husband hasn't convinced you that his way is the only way."

"My husband has convinced me of nothing," Shiloh stated. "My views are my own. Your cause doesn't have my sympathy, Captain, but I won't be too hasty to condemn it."

The Englishman stood, his mouth smiling charmingly but his eyes bitterly cold. "On that encouraging note, I must be going," he said. He thanked Sharon for her hospitality and rode off.

"What was that all about?" Sharon demanded.

"I think Captain Elliot might want to make friends with me. Perhaps he'd like me to ally myself with him against Justin."

Sharon shivered. "Dreadful man."

Shiloh's face hardened. "I won't need any persuasion to disagree with Justin."

A horseman came to the top of a rise and drew up, shading his eyes to watch Captain Elliot as he disappeared in the opposite direction. Then he wheeled his horse and galloped toward the house.

"It's him," Shiloh said.

"He's magnificent," Sharon commented. They stood on the small porch, watching as Justin dismounted and ambled toward them. An evening breeze lifted his golden hair as he removed his hat.

"Evening, Shiloh." He cracked a smile at Sharon. "Ma'am."

"I'm Sharon Bledsoe. Welcome, Mr. McCord."

"I'd be obliged if you'd call me Justin, ma'am."

"Of course, Justin." Sharon wiped her hands on her apron. "Please excuse me. I've got some washing up to do." She disappeared, closing the door firmly.

"You favor your aunt," Justin said, unsmiling.

Shiloh tossed her head. "So I've been told."

He took a step toward her. Shiloh was sure he could hear the wild hammering of her heart.

"What were you doing in town today?" he asked.

"I don't have to tell you that."

"You were looking for me, weren't you?"

"So what if I was?"

"What did you want to say to me?"

"I was going to ask if things would ever change with us; I was tired of going on like we were at Post Oaks. But I got my answer, didn't I?"

"That wasn't what it seemed, in the saloon," he said, the lines about his eyes deepening with intensity.

"It's too late for lies, Justin. I saw you kiss that woman—"

"No, you didn't."

Shiloh tried to walk away, but she found herself in his iron grip.

"The woman's name is Isabella Hernandez. She's an old acquaintance. I was shot at the border last March, and she helped me. But I didn't read her right back then. She's in with the Accord. She gave me over to the executioners of the Mier expedition."

"No wonder you find her so fascinating."

"Just listen to me, will you? Isabella found me in the grog shop and began acting very friendly. I humored her for a while, thinking maybe she'd let something useful slip."

"In other words, you kissed her in the line of duty."

"I didn't kiss her at all. I merely bent down to take something from her. From where you were standing, it probably looked like something else." Abruptly, he released her. Like a striking snake, he drew a tiny, evil-looking blade from his belt and pointed it at her. Shiloh gasped, thinking he'd lost his reason.

But he retracted the blade back into its elegant, almost feminine-looking handle of mother-of-pearl. "A parting gift from Isabella."

Shiloh didn't want to believe his story, yet it made perfect sense. "What were you doing getting drunk in a grog shop in the first place?"

"I'd just come from a meeting with Sam Houston. I wasn't happy with what he'd had to say, so I had a few drinks to cheer me up. That was when Isabella found me."

She thought of her father. "I know all about men who turn to the bottle when things don't go their way."

His lips grew stiff with anger. "Most men have a home to go to, a wife's soothing arms. I've had nothing but cold stares and snide remarks for weeks."

"Forgive me if I'm not the woman of your dreams, Justin. I never pretended to be."

He let out a long, weary sigh. "I made a mistake, Shiloh. And I'm sorry; I know things haven't been easy for you, either. Let's say goodbye to your aunt and go home."

Shiloh planted her feet. "I'm staying right here."

Sharon stepped out onto the porch. "No, you're not, dear. Running away from each other isn't going to fix things. You go on home and try to treat each other right." She grew severe and spoke to Justin. "I love my niece like a daughter, Justin. I'd like nothing better than to keep her at my side if I thought that would be best for her. I'm trusting you, young man, to put the smile back into her eyes."

Justin placed his hat back on his head. "I'll do my best, ma'am."

Shiloh couldn't sleep. She'd bathed, hoping the warm water would relax her, but she only became more restless as she moved about the bedroom. Crossing to the window, she noticed that the night sky was as unsettled as she. Heavily bunched clouds scudded in from the Gulf across the moon, and heat lightning flickered in the distance. A hot, heavy wind blew the curtains inward, plastering Shiloh's robe against her body. The storm, when it rolled in off the Gulf, promised to be severe. Shiloh wrapped her arms across her chest and shivered.

"God, you're a sight," said a husky voice behind her.

She spun around, taken by surprise. Justin stepped close, his hands resting on her shoulders. He, too, had cleaned up. His hair glistened damply, and his clean-shaven cheeks smelled faintly of bay rum.

"I couldn't forget you," he said. "All those nights in the bunkhouse, all I could think of was your face, your body, your voice calling out to me. . . ." His lips descended, seeking hers.

It took all of Shiloh's willpower to turn her head aside. Despite the throbbing ache deep within her, she couldn't give in to her weakness.

She had too many unresolved feelings to sort through.

Justin caught her chin with his thumb and forefinger and lifted her face to his. "Don't do this, Shiloh. Let's forget all the arguments."

She shook her head, feeling the burn of tears in her eyes. She prayed he wouldn't notice. "I can't, Justin. I can't forget that you wouldn't trust me enough to tell me about the letter. I had to find out from Captain Elliot."

"Elliot?" His eyes grew hard. "I thought I recognized him as he rode away from your aunt's. What the hell did he want?"

"I think he wanted me to know he's not the scheming villain you made him out to be."

"And were you convinced?"

She tossed her head back, curls flying. "Sometimes I feel I have less reason to trust you than him."

"I didn't realize you were so frightened of me."

"I'm not frightened! I—"

Suddenly his hands were on her, igniting her flesh with knowing, masterful strokes. He laughed softly at her surprised gasp. "Could it be, Mrs. McCord, that you're afraid of yourself? Afraid of all the things you feel when I touch you . . . like this . . . and this . . . ?"

He brushed her robe aside and continued his relentless assault on her, finding all the places that were most sensitive. His hands cupped her breasts, branding her flesh with a heated caress.

Then he circled her waist and pulled her roughly against him.

"Leave me alone," she said, battling the storm of passion that raged within her.

"You don't really want me to stop," he countered, stroking her intimately. His mouth descended on hers. At first Shiloh resisted, pressing her lips together and stiffening in his embrace. But as his hands blazed a path down her torso, she felt herself weaken. Even as she cursed her own failing, she felt her lips soften and part to admit his seeking tongue. Her captive body began to relax against his, leaning toward him, demanding completion.

Even so, she struggled for control, trying to retain something of herself. Yet Justin's determined assault continued. His hand traveled down to her thighs, toying insolently with the sensitive flesh until Shiloh's legs began to buckle.

In her head there were a hundred reasons why they shouldn't play this dangerous, erotic game. But the reasons seemed small in the face of the overwhelming power of their intimacy. Her hands, obeying her heart instead of her mind, sought the rigid lines of his body, moving slowly over his muscled flesh.

She raised her eyes, smiling. "Your heart is racing, Mr. McCord."

"Does that surprise you?"

Shiloh pressed closer. "I guess it does."

He shook his head, half annoyed, half

amused. "Shiloh, why can't you just accept the fact that you're a beautiful, desirable woman? You make me crazy for you." His mouth claimed hers again, tearing a moan of aching want from her. The final shreds of resistance fell away as Shiloh found herself engulfed by her husband—his hard, lean body, his male scent, the exquisite taste of him. His kisses, his searching hands, his intimate murmurs filled her with longing.

Sensing her capitulation, Justin slid her bed gown from her, discarding it in a heap at her feet. His eyes drank in the sight of her until Shiloh began to blush. She held herself still as he disrobed. There was no resisting his magnificent body. Shiloh propelled herself toward him, and in one motion they fell to the bed, mouths locked and limbs tangled together.

They came together with a hunger that had been building for weeks. One raging explosion led to another, and by the time they were finished, the storm rolled in with the dawn. As the tempest raged outside, so did the one in her heart. She knew she was becoming a slave to Justin's touch, but she was powerless to stop it. Drunk with his lovemaking, she finally fell into a deep, contented sleep in his arms.

He was gone when she awoke. The spot where he'd lain was a cold hollow, yet still his scent clung to the sheets and pillows. Shiloh felt a wave of fresh longing, an emptiness that only Justin could fill. Her cheeks flamed as she re-

called the abandonment with which she'd behaved. He controlled her will with a single
touch.

It was preposterous to allow him such power
over her. Flinging the covers off, Shiloh leaped
from the bed, full of renewed resolution. As she
washed away the unsettling traces of their lovemaking, she vowed to be stronger, to protect
herself from Justin. She couldn't let him turn
her again into the weak, panting creature she'd
been last night, or her whole identity would be
lost.

Dressing hurriedly, she went down to see what
the storm had wrought.

EIGHT

It was even worse than it had sounded. Rain lashed against the windows, and thunder roared. The fields had been transformed into a network of streaming, wind-whipped rivers, the corrals deep with mud. A branch had crashed through the top of the stables. Wiping the condensation away from a window, Shiloh saw the hands running here and there, trying to bring the horses to the barn, which sat on higher ground, safe from flooding.

There were too many horses and not enough men. Even young Tomás wrestled with a balking mare. Shiloh ran from the house to help.

The downpour soaked her to the skin, plastering her hair to her cheeks. Her feet sank into the reddish-brown mud as she ran across the stable yard to the corrals. She took the frightened mare from Tomás, slapping it on the haunches, and led it to the barn. It was a slow, slippery uphill climb, made more treacherous by holes that had been hollowed out by the streaming water. Shiloh took care that the horse didn't stumble.

She found Wylie Stokes in the barn, clearing space for the livestock.

"Where's Justin?" she shouted over the din of the rain.

Wylie jerked his head. "Down by the bayou. He's rounding up the sorrel mare and her foal." He scratched his grizzled cheek. "Should've been back by now."

Shiloh's nerves twisted. She ran from the barn and headed down to the bayou. The sheets of rain were so dense that she was unable to see how swollen the bayou was until she nearly slipped into the water. Whole trees were underwater, only their windblown tops showing.

She heard the terrified squeal of a horse and went toward it. The mare called Sugar stood on high ground, bucking and pawing the air, eyes rolling white in her skull.

Deep in the eddying brown waters, Justin struggled to bring the filly to safety. The frightened young horse struggled wildly, hooves lashing out.

Justin sank below the surface and then came up to gasp for air. He was holding fast to the horse's mane, trying to guide it to the edge. But the panicked animal twisted and bit, impeding his efforts.

Shiloh paused to discard her gown and petticoat, which would drag her under. Clad only in her soaking shift, she waded in. She was a fairly good swimmer, but the current dragged at her legs. Reaching out, she could almost touch the flailing horse.

Justin was so intent on his battle that he didn't notice her until she called to him. His face contorted with anger. "Shiloh! Damn it, woman, you can't—"

"I'm here to help you," she shouted.

He shook his head, beads of water flying. But there was no time for arguing. The current was growing stronger by the minute and the filly's panic was rising. Shiloh planted her feet and took hold of the sodden mane.

The horse tossed its head back, dragging her into the water. As she plunged beneath the surface, Shiloh's mouth and nose filled. She was frightened, yet her fear gave her strength. With a great kick, she came up and gulped for air. Setting her jaw, she hauled back on the mane. With Justin pushing from behind, the filly came forward, closer to the edge.

"Good girl!" Justin shouted. "One more time, sweetheart—pull!"

The filly advanced again, and its forelegs touched bottom. With the feel of solid ground under its feet, it surged toward its mother.

"She's out!" Shiloh yelled.

Justin's whoop of jubilation was cut off. The filly kicked out with its hind leg in a final effort to scramble ashore. The hoof caught Justin on the temple, opening a deep crescent in his scalp. As Shiloh watched in horror, he lost consciousness with a hiss and sank down. The current whirled around him, and a cloud of bright red puffed out into the murky water.

With a strangled cry of abject terror, Shiloh plunged in. The rushing water pulled him downstream. She lunged after him. She dragged him toward the shore. His inert, waterlogged body was abominably heavy, but Shiloh barely noticed the weight. In seconds, she had him lying on the grass.

The sight of him filled her with a dread that felt like a physical pain. His face was colorless except for the gaping, curved gash at his temple. Blood pulsed from the wound. With a sob of fear, Shiloh staunched the flow with her wet gown. His flesh beneath her trembling hands felt cold.

Just as she began to wonder how she would get him back to the house, four of the ranch hands, led by Wylie Stokes, came running across the sodden grass. They gathered Justin up, forming a human litter by locking their hands and wrists together. As Tomás drove the mare and filly up to the barn, the others bore Justin to the house.

By evening, the rain had abated to a thin, steady mist, and the ranch hands were already at work removing the branches and debris from the stable area.

In the big bed upstairs, Justin lay motionless. Prairie Flower, assisted by Shiloh, had painstakingly closed the wound with a needle and a length of thread. It stood out like a black seam upon cool, grayish flesh.

Shiloh sat and looked upon her husband, hardly less terrified than when they had brought him in. He hadn't stirred, even when Prairie Flower had stabbed him with her needle. With a soft sob, Shiloh took his limp hand and brought it to her cheek, wetting it with frightened tears.

Prairie Flower came in with a tray of damp compresses and an array of herbs and special salves. She padded on bare feet to the bedside, her bright eyes assessing Justin and the trembling girl at his side.

"You love him well," said Prairie Flower.

Shiloh looked up, shocked to hear the words. She shook her head in mute denial. How could she love him when she didn't even know what the feeling was? "I'm worried about him. And— and I feel responsible. I was trying to help him."

Prairie Flower gave a little grunt and bent over the tray, making a strong-smelling poultice.

Shiloh leaned forward to see. "What is that?"

"Beth root, wormwood, indigo . . . it will help in the healing." She placed a compress on the wound and expertly wrapped it to hold it in place. She looked up, patted Shiloh on the hand. "You rest. He will need your strength." She left quietly.

Shiloh sat on until the candle guttered and

she had to light another. She stared hard at
Justin, watching his shallow breathing and
stroking his hand, willing him to open his eyes.
Prairie Flower's observation niggled at her
brain, insinuating itself into her thoughts.

Love . . . could that be what she felt for Justin?
Was that why the sight of him lying so still and
pale tore a hole through her and left a great
gulf of emptiness? She ran her hand through
her tangled curls, wondering if she could make
such an admission. Thinking back on her
strange, lonely childhood, she knew she could
not. She hadn't learned enough about love to
recognize it when it touched her heart.

All she knew as she stared down at Justin was
that she wanted him to be well, wanted it more
than anything else. But he ignored her silent
appeal and remained still throughout the night.

She was awakened from a nap in her chair by
her father.

"I came to see how you'd weathered the
storm," Nate said gruffly. He gestured at Justin.
"How's he doing?"

Shiloh blinked the sleep from her eyes and
stretched her stiff legs. "He hasn't moved."

Nate handed her a glass of water. "He'll buck
up, girl. Just needs time to sleep it off."

"You don't know that."

"There, now, you've never been one to give
up hope." Nate gave her a canny look. "Or could

it be that you've found a way out of being a wife?"

"How dare you?" Shiloh demanded. "How can you even think such a thing? I may not have wanted to be married to Justin, but that doesn't mean I wish him ill."

"There, there, of course you don't. It appears to me you care for the man. Leastways enough to sit up with him all night." Nate reached out as if to touch her but then hesitated and stuck his hand into the pocket of his breeches. "Let me know if there's anything I can do. I hope he gets better, Shiloh. For both of your sakes."

She squeezed her eyes shut and pressed her fists into them when she heard the door shut. She took Justin's hand and fell asleep again.

A light pressure on her hand awakened her. Her eyes flew open, blinking at the afternoon light that flooded in through the curtains. At first Shiloh thought she was imagining what she felt. But Justin's long fingers closed around hers again, more firmly this time. Her heart thumped wildly in her chest. "Justin?"

His eyes fluttered open, squinting against the sunlight. "Hello, Shiloh." His voice was gravelly with disuse.

"How do you feel?"

He groaned. "Like a herd of buffalo stampeded over my head. What happened?"

"You were kicked by the filly. She got out of the bayou, though."

Justin felt the bandage around his head. "Wasn't that your little foal?"

Shiloh nodded. "I should disown her after that."

"That was some storm."

"It's over. The men have almost finished clearing up. Are you hungry? I could bring you some soup, or—"

He waved his hand in refusal. "I'd rather just keep you right here, Mrs. McCord. I kind of like having you nurse me. Do you realize we've just had an entire conversation without ending up at each other's throats?"

Shiloh stiffened. "So what?"

"So maybe, my dear, there's hope for us yet."

Shiloh turned her head aside, wondering if it could be true. She could not deny her relief at his recovery. But it was more than that. Perhaps Justin's brush with death would change the way they acted toward each other. She took his outstretched hand in both of hers. "Time will tell, Justin," she said.

Justin's youth and strength served him well. Within a week, he was up and about and Prairie Flower had snipped the stitches from the gash. Shiloh cringed when he scaled up to the top of the stables to repair the broken beams or when he worked with the wild horses, but she said nothing. She knew he wouldn't slow down, no matter what she said.

The only time he appeared to relax was at night. Although nothing was actually said, there was no question about his staying on in the master bedroom. For several nights they slept together, holding each other gently, making no demands. But inevitably, the low-burning flames of desire flared up and there was no holding back.

By day, Shiloh blushed when she recalled their nightly passionate adventures, but all hesitation fell away when Justin gave her the hard look of desire and ignited her flesh with his masterful touch. She knew that his lovemaking left her weak and gasping, as pliant as clay in his hands, but she had no defense against him.

Some days, she caught herself smiling lazily as contentment crept over her. Still, there were other times when the old restlessness took over, after the work of the ranch was done or the endless jobs grew tedious.

On one such day, she went to her father's house.

When he recognized the glint of determination in her bright eyes, Nate Mulvane shook his head.

"Not again, Shiloh. I'm not about to put you to work."

"Come on, Father. You need help. I heard about the cattle-stealing case."

"My answer is still no. This is a slippery one, dangerous to boot. They'll knife you in the dark and ask questions later."

"I can handle that."

"You've got to stop trying to fill your life with my affairs. You have your own life now. Take care of your home, your husband, maybe have a couple of kids."

Her face reddened. "That's not what I want."

"Then talk it over with Justin. I imagine he has his hands full, what with all those new appointments in Washington."

She leaned forward. "What are you talking about?"

Nate pushed a newspaper across the table to her. "It's all there in the *Morning Star.* Apparently, Black Dan Webster had his final falling-out with President Tyler. There's a new secretary of state, name of Abel P. Upshur. He's a real pro-Texas man. Justin'll have to watch Harmon West like a hawk now. The old judge is sure to have something up his sleeve—"

Shiloh left before he had a chance to finish.

She was panting and sweaty when she burst into Justin's study, where he was puffing reflectively on a cheroot.

"Why didn't you tell me about Upshur?" she demanded.

He looked at her levelly. "I didn't think you'd be interested."

"Liar! Just because we've been getting along decently for a change doesn't mean I've become a meek little housewife."

He studied the play of her fiery hair about her shoulders, the snapping green eyes, the incredible trimness of her figure in a crisp split riding skirt and jacket. Unable to resist a smile of pure pleasure at her appearance, Justin said, "I'd never make that mistake about you."

"Then why haven't you talked to me about this? It's as if half of you is a secret from me, while every night I give my whole self to you."

Justin's eyes narrowed. "I didn't know there was a trade-off involved. Is that why you let me into your bed, Mrs. McCord? To swap your favors for my confidences?"

Her eyes widened in outrage. "How dare you—"

"I don't buy it, Shiloh. You're a man's dream at night, but I won't let you use your charms to milk me for information."

"If that's what you think, then I have nothing more to say to you." She stormed from the room, crashing the door shut with a mighty heave.

Justin rubbed his hand through his hair. "No, Shiloh," he said, "that's not what I think." He hated what he'd just said to her, but he had to do it. Had to sever the lines of communication for her own good. Shiloh was too damned smart to deceive; it wouldn't have taken her long to guess that he was about to investigate a dangerous matter. And she wouldn't sit still once she learned what was going on.

He should have known that the blissful time wouldn't last. But God, how he wished it could.

The comfort of her arms around him after a long day, and her company during meals and quiet times was more pleasant than he'd ever imagined it could be. If only Shiloh would forget her crazy notions and settle down . . . but of course, then she wouldn't be Shiloh.

He dialed the combination on his safe and withdrew a letter. It had arrived only that morning from Francisco Reyes, a trusted contact in the border town of Matamoros.

As Justin had feared, the members of the Accord were wasting no time in reacting to Upshur's appointment. The new secretary of state was sure to press the issue of annexation, and Harmon West needed to act quickly to turn the tide of public sentiment against it.

The judge's plan was coldly simple. Reyes wrote that the Mexican forces in Matamoros were expecting a large shipment of arms from "an unnamed Houston gentlemen." Once equipped, a small but well-trained army would march up the Texas coast to Corpus Christi in a brash show of force. The impoverished Texas army would be powerless to stop them. And Texans everywhere would have a taste of what Mexico thought of annexation.

Justin hoped to accomplish two things: to foil the planned march and to catch Harmon West in the treasonous act of providing arms to the Mexicans. Drumming his fingers on the table, he searched for answers. West had known about Upshur's appointment in advance. That would have given him time to get a shipment of British-made arms and ordnance from forts in the Caribbean. The question was, where would such a large shipment be hidden?

Down the bayou from Houston, West had a derelict cotton warehouse with docks providing access to the water. It sat on isolated marshland; no one would go near it.

Reyes had found out that a Mexican boat would collect the arms on October first. Tomorrow. Justin took up a stub of a pencil and scribbled the date and place on a piece of paper. He sealed it securely and went to give it to Leonicio, one of the ranch hands who couldn't read. Leonicio rode off to Houston, bearing the message to Lamar Coulter.

Justin stood on the porch, stretching and flexing his legs after hours of sitting. The night birds had arrived with the dark, mingling their voices with the ceaseless buzzing of cicadas. In the distance, he heard Prairie Flower crooning to her chickens in her guttural native tongue as she closed their roosting house against marauding predators for the night. Faintly he smelled her good venison stew in the air and realized he'd missed supper.

In spite of the angry words, his body craved Shiloh's closeness. There was little hope of a reconciliation tonight, but Justin was through with sleeping in the bunkhouse.

He let himself into the dark room and shed his clothing. As he splashed water over himself at the washstand, he smiled ruefully. A few months ago, it never would have occurred to him to clean himself up for bed, not if bed was a dusty roll under the stars, or a bug-infested boardinghouse mattress. Having a home and a wife had civilized him, without a doubt.

He slid beneath the covers, his arm wrapping around Shiloh's middle. She stirred in her sleep and settled against him with a sigh. He willed away the desire that filled him and fell asleep.

Shiloh held herself still with a great effort. She waited patiently, steeling herself against the warmth of his breath on her neck, until his breathing became deep and regular. Then, with painstaking slowness, she extracted herself from his loose embrace and slipped from the room.

In his study, her match flared and caught, and she lit the guttered stub of a candle. She went directly to the safe and whirled the tumblers around. It wasn't the first time she'd gone into the safe, and she knew the combination by heart.

The door swung open. Shiloh moved aside an astoundingly large supply of banknotes and U.S. currency and took out a handful of papers. Setting the candle down, she thumbed through the pages.

A few finely printed documents, a number of letters signed by W. S. Murphy and Pinckney Henderson, all dated months ago. Their marriage certificate. Shiloh stared at Justin's firm signature, her own shaky one. She thought it strange that he considered the document important enough to lock away. But of course he would, she thought again. It was his safeguard against having to marry Jessamine.

Then she found what she was looking for: a recently dated letter. It was written in poor English, signed by F. Reyes, Matamoros. As she read the letter, cold shock gripped her. If this Reyes was correct—and Justin obviously believed that he was—there would be a Mexican invasion. That meant outlandish atrocities, not just against the men, but against women and children as well. The Mexicans despised the Texans, whose ragtag army had driven them home years before. They took their revenge whenever they could.

It would all begin tomorrow, Shiloh noted. But how? Where? She leafed through the rest of the papers. Finding nothing, she replaced everything as she'd found it and closed the safe. Then she went to the desk and looked there. She saw only a stack of blank paper, a bit of graphite, an empty inkwell.

As she sat thinking, the candle flickered across the blank paper. A tiny impression, the shape of a letter, caught her eye. Justin had written something, and the top sheet bore the imprint of it. Holding the candle so that it cast a long shadow, Shiloh decoded the message.

Justin had a firm hand, making the impression quite visible.

Tomorrow's date, and then a meeting place. The warehouse at LeBoyer's Crossing. Closing her eyes, she tried to think where she'd heard the name before. Nothing came to her. She decided to go back to bed and mull over the puzzle until she remembered.

The flame of the candle angled toward her. Justin's tall form filled the doorway. "What are you doing?" he demanded, striding into the room.

"I couldn't help it. I knew something was up by the way you talked to me this afternoon. I read Reyes's letter. And I know the Mexicans are going to LeBoyer's Crossing."

Justin cursed bitterly. "You have no business—"

"We don't have time to argue about it. If the Mexicans get hold of that shipment, people will die!"

"Don't you think I know that?"

"Then what are you waiting for? All we have to do is get to the warehouse, make sure the arms are there, and dump everything into the bayou."

"*We* are not going to do anything. I'll handle it on my own."

"There isn't much time. Why bother waiting?"

He heaved a tired sigh. "I have to catch West in an act of treason. To do that, I'll need to wait until he is actually making the transaction."

Shiloh shook her head. "Too risky. It's more

important to prevent the march on Corpus Christi."

He crossed the room and gripped her by the shoulders. "I've got a job to do, and I'll do it the best way I know how. Now, go back to bed."

Shiloh's hands clenched around the porch railing. It was a glorious autumn day, alive with singing birds and colored by ripening fruits and vegetables in Prairie Flower's kitchen garden. Yet Shiloh remained pale with worry and lack of sleep. She was watching Justin as he prepared to leave. With growing alarm, she saw that he carried both of his revolving pistols and his bowie knife and had lashed a long rifle to his saddle. He packed away enough powder and balls for a small battle.

As she watched him mount up in the stable yard, she was struck by the idea that this could be the last she ever saw of him. If he was caught, he was a dead man. Harmon West would never allow him to carry tales of treason to the authorities.

She started toward him, not knowing what she would say. Then she hesitated. The words he'd said to her last night had laid open wounds that were still raw by light of day. She wasn't ready to forgive him, and it was obvious he wasn't of a mind to apologize. And so she stood quietly, hands clasped in front of her.

He looked over at her and their gazes locked.

Neither betrayed the slightest emotion. Autumn bees hummed through the flowers and there was a smell of ripe apricots in the air. After a tense moment, Justin raised his hat to her, wheeled his horse, and spurred it off down the road.

Shiloh watched until he was out of sight, and then she ran back into the house to prepare for her own journey.

Four hours later she was traversing brambles so thick that her horse had slowed to a clumsy walk. The bayou, which she'd kept in sight, crept sluggishly toward the bay, obscured from time to time by dense brakes of cypress and cane. Strange birds—egrets and long-legged cranes—picked their way in and out of the marshes, poking their heads on thin necks into the silty ground. The mosquitoes were thick and merciless. Even with a coating of Prairie Flower's pennyroyal solution, Shiloh was plagued by the insects.

But not for one minute would she consider turning back. Her father had given her directions to LeBoyer's Crossing, and she meant to reach it as fast as was humanly possible. Maybe Justin wouldn't need her; maybe it was all a waste of time, but she had to be sure she was there in case something went wrong. If the Mexicans got hold of the arms . . . she tried not to think about it.

Voices drifted across the bayou, and she drew up her horse. Slipping to the ground, she went to investigate.

It was Judge West, standing upon a stout raft as if he were captain of a lofty vessel. He was dressed in his usual impeccable black and held a cigar in one hand while he gestured with the other. His burly slaves poled the raft down the bayou and listened indolently as the judge spoke.

Shiloh couldn't hear the words, but she could see that West was prepared for trouble. He himself was armed, as were the pair of buckskin-clad men with him. One of them was small and compact, with dark Latino features and a ruthless, hard look about him. The other was Anglo, tall and lanky, with eyes that lacked depth. *Lackeys,* Shiloh thought contemptuously as she returned to her horse. No doubt Judge West had selected them because they would follow his orders without question.

Although the raft was moving sluggishly, Shiloh felt a sense of urgency. She spurred her horse and whispered encouragement over the piebald's neck as it stepped through the tall reeds and marsh grasses.

She almost missed seeing the warehouse. Abandoned years earlier, when it had become known that the Allen brothers were taking their city farther north, it was overgrown by vines and grass and roof-high cattails. Had she not been looking for it, Shiloh might not have noticed the gray, weathered structure. She tethered her horse on dry ground and made her way toward it, carrying a heavy cloth sack over her shoulder.

She saw no one. The only sounds were made by birds and the quiet lapping of the water around the rotting dock. When she crept around to the front of the warehouse, she spied a man, a guard.

She recognized him from town. He was one of the scores of eager-eyed, hollow-cheeked newcomers, who'd probably spent his last cent getting to Texas and was now desperate for work. Shiloh doubted the man knew what he was doing. He'd shed his shirt and drawn his hat down over his face, evidently for a late-afternoon nap. One hand rested on a rusting shotgun; the other loosely held a rope attached to a small rowboat.

Shiloh took a deep breath and pulled her hat down more securely, checking to see that no stray red curl escaped to betray her sex. She drew out her gun and stepped soundlessly toward the dozing man.

With one kick of her boot, she sent his shotgun into the bayou. At the sound of the splashing water, the man started.

"What the—?"

Shiloh aimed her gun at his face. "Don't ask questions, mister," she said hoarsely, almost whispering. "Just get in that boat and start rowing downstream."

He tensed but didn't move. His hungry eyes watched her, and his ribs poked through his gaunt frame. Knowing Judge West, the man wouldn't be paid until his job was done. Silently she begged him to go. Aloud she said, "Don't make me use this."

She must have sounded convincing. The man scrambled down to the boat and began rowing with long, frantic strokes.

Replacing her gun, Shiloh stepped into the warehouse. She gasped, tasting dust and the tang of powder in her mouth. The building was packed to the walls with unmarked wooden crates. There were enough arms to outfit a small army. She climbed the crates until she reached the highest rafters, and then carefully put her head up through a jagged hole in the roof. She wanted to make sure the guard was well on his way before she proceeded.

He was on his way, all right. Although he'd headed downstream at first, he had circled back and was sculling toward Judge West's raft, perhaps a quarter-mile off. Shiloh had no doubt the man would alert the judge. And downstream was a sight that chilled her blood.

A shallow-draft shallop crept up from several hundred yards off. Although it was unmarked, even unremarkable, she knew it must be the Mexicans.

Turning, Shiloh saw movement in the tall grasses a good distance behind the warehouse. The horsemen appeared for an instant, then receded again into the foliage. In that moment, Shiloh recognized Justin's worn black hat and bay horse and the slouching posture of Lamar Coulter.

They wouldn't know how close they were to danger. Not one but two separate enemies were about to converge on them, with the judge now warned by his confused guard. Shiloh knew she couldn't wait to see what happened. She had to act. Although she agreed with Justin that it would be best to catch Harmon West, it was more important to avert the coming disaster. And there was only one way to do that.

Once she'd made her decision, Shiloh's trembling ceased. She leaped to the packed-earth floor and drew a large jar of lamp oil from her sack. Working methodically, she sloshed it over the crates and the walls of the building. Outside, she emptied the jar in a circle around the entire structure.

Her hands began to shake again as she struck match after match, throwing the small flares around the building. None of them appeared to catch fire or stay lit long enough to ignite the warehouse. Almost crying with frustration, Shiloh tore down a long, brown-tipped cattail and loosened the pod until it resembled a ball of cotton wool. She doused this with the remaining drops of oil from the jar.

The makeshift torch caught fire, as did the grass and the outside wall of the warehouse when Shiloh touched it. She ran the entire perimeter until a steady blaze crackled and the flames licked toward the roof. Then, flinging down the cattail, Shiloh ran to her horse.

By the time she'd mounted and spurred, the fire roared. Shiloh looked back to see heat shimmering wildly above the bayou. Then, with an earthshaking explosion, the building detonated, sending plumes of fire high into the air and flinging debris in all directions. Several more explosions followed. Finally, the fire engulfed a black hole where the warehouse had once stood.

Shiloh smiled grimly. "So much for your invasion, Judge West," she murmured, and started on the long ride home.

Hours later, she was startled from a deep sleep by the bang of the bedroom door being flung open. Justin advanced on her, dark fires burning in his eyes. His voice was a growl in his throat.

"You've gone too far this time, Shiloh."

NINE

Shiloh sat up and rubbed her eyes. Justin set a candle down on the bedside stand. His rage hung in the air between them like a thick fog.

"Don't try to deny it," he snapped even before she had a chance to speak. He flung a heap of clothes onto the bed. Her trousers and the cotton shirt she'd worn on her journey down the bayou reeked of smoke and powder.

"I don't deny anything, Justin. I set that fire today."

His fist slammed against the wall. "Why, damn it?"

"Because I didn't want the Mexicans to get at the arms and munitions. I didn't want them to go anywhere near Corpus Christi."

Justin shook his head. "We were so damned close. Another few minutes and we would've had West, maybe even gotten a censure against Mexico."

"You're wrong," Shiloh said. "I saw what happened. Judge West was armed to the teeth. There was a guard at the warehouse. I sent him rowing downstream, but he doubled back to warn the judge."

"Well done."

She ignored that. "The Mexicans coming up the river were probably armed, too. You and Mr. Coulter didn't stand a chance."

"I see. I suppose you think I should thank you for saving my life."

"I'm not asking for gratitude. But I wish you'd understand that there wasn't anything you could have done. Everything is fine now, Justin. No one was hurt. And no one will get hurt—"

"Until Harmon West tries something else. Thanks to you, he's free now."

Shiloh bit her lower lip. "I'm sorry he got away. But at least he has nothing to give the Mexicans now."

Justin hissed out a sigh and tossed his hat onto a hook. "I guess what's done is done."

"Why are you so late?" she asked.

His steel-hard eyes bored into her. "Because, Mrs. McCord, I was looking for you. That explosion was big enough to take you with it."

"I'm not stupid," she said. "I got well out of the way. Now, if you don't mind, I'd like to go back to sleep."

"Fine," he said, sitting on the edge of the bed and pulling off his boots.

"What are you doing?"

He ran his fingers through his hair. "I'm going to get cleaned up and then come to bed."

"Oh . . ."

He gave her a sardonic smile. "Don't worry, Mrs. McCord. I won't bother you tonight. It's kind of hard to make love to a woman who makes a practice of lying and interfering in a man's work."

A week later, Shiloh was in the stables rubbing down one of the mares that had been brought from the wild to Post Oaks. The palomino flanks gleamed from the dedicated application of Shiloh's metal currycomb. The lean, rangy look of this mare and the others was gone since they'd been fattened on corn and good mash. Every one of them had been broken to the saddle. They were ready for the auction house.

Shiloh finished with the mare and moved on to a three-year-old, another palomino. She had taken to caring for the horses daily. It was something she enjoyed, and it was a way to avoid Justin.

He seemed to be satisfied with their lack of communication. Each morning he was gone by the time she awoke, working tirelessly on the ranch. At night he'd tumble exhausted into bed after Shiloh was asleep. If they chanced to meet during the day, conversation was strained, and Justin seemed to study her with suspicious eyes as if wondering how she would betray him next.

"It's not as if I'd committed some great crime," Shiloh fumed, attacking the horse's flanks with her stiff-bristled brush. "I only did what I had to do." She went over and over it in her mind, trying to figure out if there could have been a way for Justin to seize Judge West and the shipment as well. But it was no use. If she'd stood aside and let him do it his way, he'd surely be dead by now and the Mexican army equipped. Yet Justin would never accept the truth of that. And now he was doubly angry because Harmon West and his daughter had left town for a while, to lie low after the fiasco at LeBoyer's Crossing.

Sighing, Shiloh finished up in the stable. The mares they were taking to auction had never looked better. Their coats gleamed, manes and tails combed free of tangles and debris. Even their hooves shone with the polishing Shiloh had given them.

Looking down at her dusty trousers and sweat-stained shirt, Shiloh shook her head ruefully. She'd let her appearance go this week. The work clothes were functional, as was the thick tail of hair she tied at her neck. But she decided to make some changes for the trip to Houston. Buyers might take more notice if she looked decent.

Tomás brought water for her bath, and Ina laid out her new riding habit. The sky-blue skirt hugged Shiloh's hips and fell in a long, pleated line. The matching jacket covered a blouse trimmed with a bit of cream lace, tatted by Ina's own fingers. Ina piled her hair cunningly and pinned on a small hat. Then she handed Shiloh a small velvet purse.

"From your husband," she said.

Frowning, Shiloh loosened the laces and drew out a wide blue ribbon to which was attached an oval-shaped piece of porcelain, exquisitely painted. A brush no bigger than an eyelash had depicted a stalk of wild bluebonnet.

"It's beautiful," Shiloh whispered.

Ina took the ribbon from her and fastened it around her neck.

Shiloh felt oddly nervous as she went downstairs. Her heart fluttered a little, reminding her that her feelings for Justin—such as they were—could not be denied. He was waiting for her at the foot of the steps, neatly dressed, his tall boots gleaming.

"Very nice," he murmured, unsmiling.

Shiloh nodded. "Ina is a genius with the needle." She reached up and fingered the brooch. "Thank you for this, Justin."

He shrugged and held the door open for her. "There's a German immigrant in town, name of Bruckner, who does that sort of thing."

As Shiloh passed in front of him, she caught his scent, and warmth flooded through her. She had to resist the urge to touch him. Her voice faltered a little when she said, "It—it's very thoughtful of you."

He tossed her the reins of her horse and took his own from Tomás. "You earned it," he said matter-of-factly. "You've gotten these nags looking like champions for the auction. I expect they'll get us a hundred dollars apiece."

Shiloh sat stiffly in the saddle as they headed up the string of horses. She was angry at herself for having gone all soft over Justin's gift. She should have seen it for what it was: payment for services rendered.

"Maybe," Justin said, "it's a peace offering, too." The corners of his mouth lifted slightly, and a smile deepened the lines about his eyes.

"What are you saying, Justin?"

"That what's done is done. I'm willing to forget what happened last week if you are. We both want the ranch to succeed; we've worked our tails off for it. There's no reason for us not to be friends."

"Friends . . ." she repeated quietly. She'd never thought of being friends with Justin. He always seemed so unapproachable. She smiled at him, feeling a little shy, and he raised his hat with mock cordiality. It was a tenuous truce at best, but immediately, Shiloh felt some of the tension flow out of her. By the time they reached Houston and led the mares into the auction corral in Commerce Square, she was excited.

It was the first time they had appeared together at a large gathering in Houston. Shiloh couldn't have anticipated the reception they received.

Mrs. Charlotte Allen, the wife of one of Houston's founding brothers, descended on her like a large, colorful butterfly. Her big, jowled face smiled, and her voice rang with deep, cultured tones. "Shiloh Mulvane—or McCord, I should say. Who would have thought you'd end up like this?" She embraced the girl, giving her a generous whiff of mimosa toilet water.

The society matron had never said so much as "good day" to her before. Indeed, she'd been quite vocal about her disapproval of "that Mulvane girl," shaking her head as Shiloh passed through town at her unkempt father's heels.

But now, apparently, things had changed. As the ladies of the town gathered around to greet her, she longed to inform them that decent clothes and a socially acceptable husband hadn't changed her.

"I always knew you'd come around, dear," said Vera Hanks, squeezing her hand. "It just took someone like Captain McCord to get you to settle down."

Shiloh looked quickly at Justin. *"Captain* McCord?"

"Of course," said Mrs. Hanks, clasping her hands. "And who would have thought you'd become such a beauty? Oh, the two of you make such a *handsome* couple. . . ." The woman gushed on as the others murmured agreement.

Justin extracted Shiloh from the circle of women and led her to a seat overlooking the corral. "Sorry about that," he said. "I should've realized you'd cause a stir."

"It's as if I'd been legitimized overnight," Shiloh remarked. She gave him a sideways glance. "I guess I have you to thank for that, *Captain* McCord."

He grinned. "Somehow, I don't think your goal in life is to join the ranks of 'proper' ladies."

She had to smile. "I doubt you'll find me joining quilting bees or church clubs. Justin, why didn't you tell you were a captain in the Texas army?"

"Would it have made you like me better if you'd known?"

"No."

He laughed deeply. "There you have it."

They shared a smile, and Shiloh found herself relaxing even more. It was so much better this way, being friends.

Their horses were a great success, adding to her enjoyment of the day. They walked away from the auction that evening in high spirits, some eight hundred dollars richer.

Justin took her to Houston House, a hotel that had a reputation for good food and elegance. His mood was understandably expansive. He ordered wine and a lavish meal of steak and potatoes, spiced squash, and English peas. As they lingered over a dessert of Mexican flan and a delicious amber liqueur, Shiloh looked around the draped dining room, where the crowd had begun to thin. "Shouldn't we be getting back to Post Oaks?"

"No need," Justin said, placing his napkin on the table. "We're staying here tonight, Mrs. McCord. I thought you'd like a change of pace, and there's a new string of wild mustangs in from Goliad. I'd like to buy a dozen or so in the morning."

"But I haven't brought anything to sleep in."

He reached across the table and grasped her hands. "The way I feel tonight, Mrs. McCord, you won't need anything."

Shiloh gasped at the look on his face and at the sensation that flooded her. Mesmerized by his intimate caress, his intent stare, she rose from the table and followed him to the foyer.

The man at the desk handed Justin a key. "Everything has been arranged as you requested, sir," he said.

Discreetly Justin pressed a coin into the man's hand.

Shiloh looked with wonder around the hotel's best room. The canopied bed was enormous, billowing with quilts and shrouded by a gossamer mosquito net. There was a painted screen near the hearth that only partially concealed an enormous zinc bathtub. Steam curled from its surface.

"A bit of luxury for the lady," he said with an exaggerated bow. "I need to go down to the livery and check on the horses."

She knew their horses were fine; Justin seemed to sense her modesty. He dropped a kiss on her forehead and left. Shiloh disrobed and sank down into the bath with a contented smile. It was the first time she'd ever bathed twice in one day, and she found she didn't object to it in the least. The water was the perfect temperature and felt as soft as rain as it lapped up around her shoulders and neck. She luxuriated for some minutes, closing her eyes and giving herself up to pleasant sensations. She heard the door open and close, the latch slide into place.

"It's me," said Justin. "Can I get you anything?"

"I couldn't find any soap."

He stepped around the screen, holding a glass of brandy in one hand and a new, embossed cake of soap in the other.

Shiloh instinctively hugged her arms across her chest and drew up her knees.

"Modest, Mrs. McCord?"

Her heart thumped at the look on his face. "Just set it there, by the towels, thank you."

But Justin only shook his head. He held the soap just out of her reach. If she wanted it, she'd have to unfurl her arms.

"Justin, don't tease."

His grin broadened, deepening the dimple on his cheek. He leaned forward, but he still wasn't close enough.

"You're impossible." Covering herself with one arm, she reached out. Abruptly, he released the soap and it dropped into the water.

"Sorry," he said as Shiloh began running her hands along the bottom of the tub. "Here, I'll help." In seconds, he had shed his coat and shirt. Shiloh gasped as he knelt and plunged his hands into the water. Slowly, holding her eyes with his, he dragged the bottom. Shiloh tried to shrink away from him, but his hands fluttered against her, stroking her silken flesh.

"Justin, please—"

He stopped her protest with a deep, hungry kiss. His mouth mastered hers as his hand, now holding the soap, began to lather her shoulders with slow, circular movements. The scent of honeysuckle wafted upward.

With a moan of agony, she lifted her arms and wound them about his neck, drawing him nearer.

Justin rained kisses on her face, her neck, circling her ear with the tip of his tongue. "I've missed you, my beauty," he whispered. His teeth nipped at her earlobe and then he kissed her again, giving her a taste of brandy from his own mouth. Placing one hand beneath her buttocks and the other around her shoulders, he lifted her from the tub, heedless that she soaked him from neck to boots.

"I—I need a towel," Shiloh said helplessly.

But he only shook his head and carried her to the bed, parting the netting to lay her upon the quilts. Instinctively Shiloh moved to gather the covers over her, but he held her hands still. A glow from the lamplight flickered across the sculpted lines of his face.

"I want to see you. All of you." He handed her a glass of brandy from the table. "Have a sip of this."

Thinking it would still her hammering heart, Shiloh took the glass and drank. But the brandy and the sight of Justin's lean body as he peeled away the remainder of his clothes only added fuel to the fire he had lit within her. She closed her eyes and trembled as he sat down on the bed. His hands found hers and then trailed up her arms, to her torso, her breasts.

"Don't ever hide yourself from me, Shiloh," he said in his low, husky voice. "You're more beautiful than words can say." His hand tilted her chin up. "Here," he said, indicating her upturned face. "And here . . ." Finally he parted her thighs with a swift movement. "And here . . . ," he said, touching her.

Shiloh was so shaken by his sensual assault that she jumped. Brandy sloshed from the glass, spilling down over her breasts and pooling in her navel.

Justin set the glass aside and pushed her back against the quilts. "Allow me," he murmured. And he proceeded to kiss and lick the droplets of brandy from her flesh.

Just as Shiloh thought she could take no more of the exploding sensations, his mouth roved down to the tense muscles of her middle, his tongue lapping the liquid from her navel. She thought Justin had lost his reason when his lips went lower still.

Shiloh thought she would die. She was powerless to stop the assault of his mouth and flicking tongue. She felt she was being torn to shreds by a passion so deep that bright light shimmered before her eyes.

A cry was dragged from her lips as she found the strength to draw Justin atop her.

He slid effortlessly inside her, filling the void that cried out for him. His rhythmic movements finished what his mouth and tongue had begun. Shiloh's senses soared and exploded.

Soon after, she felt Justin stiffen and convulse, and then he collapsed upon her. The moments throbbed by as, in silence, their bodies reveled in the relief they'd given each other. Finally, Justin moved aside and curled her against him.

"How do you feel, Mrs. McCord?"

She shivered. "I don't know what to say, Justin. I feel so naive with you."

He stroked her gently, kissed her temple. "All you have to understand, sweetheart, is that you were made for love. There's no shame in anything we do together, so long as it pleases us both."

"Is it always like this between a man and a woman?"

He gave her a thoroughly disarming smile.

"I didn't ask it to amuse you!"

"Sometimes I forget what an innocent you are. And to answer your question, no. Some women never allow themselves to feel pleasure. And a man can't always—that is, he's got to have some feelings for a woman in order to please her." He stumbled over the words, uncharacteristically awkward.

"You mean they have to be friends."

"To say the least." He turned on his side and

looked down at her, growing serious. "Shiloh, when I touch you, when we're close like this, I feel something deeper than friendship."

She waited, breathless, for him to continue. "Yes?"

"I feel . . ." He searched her face, as if looking for answers there. "You do something to me, Shiloh, that I . . ." Giving up, he leaned down and kissed her deeply, letting his mouth and hands say what he could not voice.

In the morning he left her with a soft kiss before she had fully awakened. She gave him a sleepy smile and promised to be ready to leave when he returned. There was an almost sinful delight in lying naked between the sheets, hugging the pillow that still held Justin's scent.

Maybe things would work out. If she could just find ways to soothe the restlessness in her, the unsettled longing for adventure . . .

There was a knock at the door. Shiloh sat up, clutching the sheets to her bosom.

"Yes?"

"A man by the name of Eb to see you, missus," said a female voice.

"Just a minute." She scrambled into her clothes and yanked a brush through her disarranged curls. Before she opened the door, she carefully pulled the netting around the bed, flushing when she thought of what had occurred there in the dark of night.

Then she let Eb in. The aging freedman moved slowly, with fatigue in his joints.

"Eb," she said, embracing his thin frame. "How did you know where to find me?"

"The name McCord is all over town. Your husband had a good day at the auction."

She saw the troubled shadows in his eyes. "What's wrong, Eb?"

"Your papa's in jail, Miss Shiloh. Drunken brawling. I couldn't find the cash to get him out."

Shiloh grabbed her reticule and spilled the contents into her hand. There were three double eagles and some silver.

"I've got enough," she said. "Let's go."

Nate Mulvane was sleeping soundly on the packed-earth floor of a small cell. Shiloh paid off the deputy, and together she and Eb managed to get her still-drunk father home.

Eb made coffee and Shiloh poured two cups down her father's throat, despite his angry protests and sputtering.

"You're out of money," she accused. "Flat broke. Why didn't you come to me?"

"I'm not going begging to my little girl," Nate blustered. "Besides, it's only a temporary situation. I'm about to clean up on that cattle-rustling deal. Tonight, as a matter of fact."

Mr. Clay Joseph, one of the biggest ranchers in the area, had lost hundreds of head of cattle to thieves. When the lawmen couldn't make any headway, Joseph had hired Nate to break up what appeared to be an extensive, well-organized ring of crime. But one man couldn't be everywhere at once. Joseph's ranch encompassed thousands of acres, and the thieves struck at night.

"But I've got 'em now," Nate said. "Figured out why they never left any sign to speak of. They've been coming by raft. Take the herd right on down to Galveston and on to New Orleans."

"How do you know about tonight?"

Nate took another swallow. "Spotted their raft on the bayou."

"It sounds too simple," Shiloh said.

"There could be a hitch or two. Joseph has a couple dozen *vaqueros,* and I suspect several are in on this."

She said nothing to Nate of her disappointment in him at landing himself in jail, or of her humiliation at having to bring him home. That had all been said before, and it had had no effect.

Eb insisted on seeing her back to the hotel. He spent a moment talking to Justin, and Shiloh caught him looking keenly at her. But she only smiled and started up the busy street.

Justin watched Shiloh carefully through supper that night. By now, he recognized the restlessness that drove her. She picked up one of Prairie Flower's specialties, a squash blossom stuffed with herbs, battered and fried. She sampled it distractedly and set it down on her plate.

"Not hungry?" Justin queried.

"I suppose you know that's not the first time he's spent the night in jail." She turned her water glass around in her hands. "When I was young, Eb used to try to hide it from me, but I always knew. People talked . . . When we lived up in Nacogdoches, ladies would come by with charity baskets from the church. They always made sure I knew exactly why they were there."

Justin saw in her eyes the lonely, frightened little girl she had been. In the determined set of her chin he could see the stiff bravado that had seen her through such times.

A wave of tenderness unlike anything he'd ever felt before washed over him and brought an unaccustomed hardness to his throat. He wanted to gather Shiloh to him, to shield her from hurtful things.

He reached across the table and took her hands. "Shiloh—"

Wylie Stokes burst into the dining room. "Justin!" He snatched his hat from his head. "Excuse me, ma'am. Justin, there's trouble with the new horses. They broke through one of the barriers and they're getting into it with the other horses."

Justin jumped up to follow him. He hesitated at the door and turned back to Shiloh.

"I'll see you later," he told her, and looked at

her so that she could not mistake his meaning. She cast her eyes downward and nodded.

For the better part of an hour, Justin and the ranch hands labored to separate and contain the horses. Dodging flying hooves and viciously snapping jaws, the men managed to get in among the new horses and hood them with cloth sacks.

All the while, Justin cursed his bad luck. He'd meant to stay with Shiloh all evening, just in case she had any ideas about going out to the Joseph ranch. Swearing under his breath, he hauled on the bridle of the last horse and brought it back into the corral.

Then, leaving the others to finish up, he burst into the kitchen to ask Ina and Prairie Flower if they knew where Shiloh was.

"Upstairs," Ina said. "She wanted to retire early."

Justin recognized the ruse. He ran across to the stables. Shiloh's piebald was gone. He prepared to go after her, taking both revolving pistols and his bowie knife.

Fool woman, he thought as he spurred his horse along the bayou path. Didn't she realize what could happen if she rode down among cattle rustlers? Lying low over his horse's neck, he sped beneath moss-hung branches toward the Joseph ranch. He found the rounded-up cattle by the noise they made, lowing and grunting as they were jostled together between four shadowy, hard-riding forms.

Justin brought his horse to the edge of a clearing that was fringed by woods in a semicircle in front of the bayou landing.

"Aqui. Aqui, hombre." The clipped orders carried across the water. The men were trying to haul a log barge up to a muddy bank.

"Are you sure somebody's over there, Jaime?" asked one of the riders.

"I heard voices," the man called Jaime said. "One of 'em's a female."

"Don't worry, we'll just rough her up a bit. Maybe even have a little fun with her later. Let's go."

As they dismounted, Justin spurred his horse. Bunching the muscles of its haunches, the bay leaped from the shadows. Justin raised one of his pistols and brought it down in an arc on the head of one of the men. As that one sank with a groan, the other let out a yelp of warning and started to run. Justin rode down the second man and pistol-whipped him to the ground.

Justin heard the crack of a rifle and the whiz of a ball behind him. As others opened fire, the *vaqueros* left their posts and the panicked herd stampeded. Justin's leg was crushed against the horse's flank as cattle rushed by. He ducked low to avoid the gunfire and urged his mount to fight its way out of the pack. By the time he plunged into a dense thicket, he was bruised and scratched, his horse lamed by a heavy bovine hoof.

But he was safe. The shouts of the *vaqueros* and

boatmen receded as they gave up on the herd and escaped down the bayou.

At Post Oaks, Shiloh met him at the door, still clad in her snug trousers and boots. "I hope you're pleased with yourself, Justin. Every one of those rustlers escaped tonight."

"That's a sight better than letting them get away with a herd."

"Why did you have to interfere? We had it all set up so the law would catch them after they'd stolen the animals."

"There was one thing you overlooked, my dear. A couple of the ranch hands heard you. They were on their way to shut you up for good when I rode them down."

"I don't believe you. You know what I think, Justin? I think you can't stand to see me succeed at a man's job."

"You're the one who can't be satisfied with your own life."

"I never asked for anything from you, except to have a career of my own."

"It doesn't matter what I say, does it, Shiloh?" Justin's shoulders slumped with fatigue. "I just walked six miles with a lame horse. I'm going to turn in."

"Wait a minute, Justin." She stepped toward him, fingers twisting together. "I hadn't planned on attacking you the minute you got home. But I was so damned mad about the rustlers and my father losing his payment that I forgot what I stayed up all night to tell you."

He was impressed by the way she suddenly gathered herself together, becoming coolly reasonable. "Go on," he prompted.

"I've been doing a lot of thinking about the two of us. This marriage started out as something neither of us wanted, and nothing has been right since. If we don't do something soon, we'll tear each other apart."

"What are you getting at, Shiloh?"

"I think we should get out of each other's way instead of being at each other's throats. I'll stay married to you for a while, I guess until Jessamine finds herself a husband. But we can't go on living like this. I'm going to stay with my aunt."

Justin thought he heard a note of wistfulness—sadness, even—in her voice. Part of him wanted to reach out to her, to ask her to try to work things out. Yet he couldn't argue with her cool logic. He stroked her flushed cheek.

"You're a fool woman," he said. "But I'll miss you."

Ina loaded her trunk with tight-lipped disapproval. "Women do not simply leave their husbands just because things get a little hard."

"It's no use. Justin and I will never get along. There's too much distrust between us."

Ina arched a dark brow. "Distrust? I think not.

I think that, even though you will not admit it, you would trust Señor McCord with your very life. I am sorry, Shiloh, but it makes me angry that you would leave a good man when I, who for years have wanted to be a wife to someone, have nobody."

Shiloh took her hands. "Oh, Ina . . ." The woman was taking this as a personal defeat. Then Shiloh had an inspiration.

"Ina, my father needs help." She grimaced, thinking how close Nate had come to earning his pay from Clay Joseph. "He'd never take money from me, but maybe you could take him some things from the garden, a slab of bacon from the springhouse. Perhaps even fix him a meal or two and mend his clothes. That is, if you've no objection."

"No, none at all," Ina said.

Shiloh checked her dove-gray traveling suit in the mirror. "I'm going to send Wylie up for the trunk," she said, leaving the room.

As she descended to the foyer, she saw an unfamiliar hat on the rack beside the door. Wrinkling her brow, she went to the door of Justin's study to knock. She hesitated at the sound of low, urgent voices.

No, she told herself, *I'm through with meddling in Justin's affairs.* But she couldn't help it.

". . . could be in England by the end of November," said the stranger.

"I don't know, Will," Justin said. "That's a damned long time to be away."

"I know it's a great inconvenience, Justin. Especially with you being newly married."

"That's one thing I'm not worried about at all," Justin replied. The coldness in his voice caused Shiloh's throat to tighten painfully.

"I guess there's no reason you can't bring the little woman along," said the stranger.

"I'm sure my wife would have no interest in going to England with me. In fact, I don't even want her to know where I'm going."

"Then I can count on you? We need you, Justin."

He hesitated only a second. "Of course."

"Good. There's a merchantman called the *Falcon* in Galveston. It's going to call at a port in the Caribbean and then proceed to England."

"The *Falcon?*" Justin asked. "Has that smuggler gone legitimate all of a sudden?"

"It appears so, but don't count on it."

Shiloh heard the clink of coins, the rustle of paper. "Here's everything you need. Letters of introduction from Pinckney Henderson and myself, papers of identification. Be careful. The British are really hot on this issue. They'll go to great lengths to protect their interests."

The speakers stepped toward the door. Shiloh jumped back quickly and knocked.

Justin opened the door. "Shiloh," he said, unsmiling. "This is Mr. William Murphy. Will, my wife."

A well-dressed man bent low over her extended hand. "Mrs. McCord, I'm enchanted," he

said. He had the slightly nasal twang of an East-
erner. "I must be going," he added. He gave
Justin a nod and let himself out.

"Who is he?" Shiloh asked.

"An acquaintance. It's not important."

She wasn't surprised by his evasiveness, and
she knew better than to press for details. "I'm
ready," she said.

His eyes, hard as gunmetal, swept her up and
down. "So I see." He went to the safe, whirled the
knob, and took out a leather purse, dropping it
almost disdainfully into her hand.

She weighed its heaviness. "I can't accept this."

"You can," he said. "You will. You've earned it
and then some."

"Earned it, have I?" Rage welled up inside her.
"Is that what I did—warmed your bed for a few
coins?"

TEN

"I'd like you to leave me in Houston," Shiloh said to Wylie Stokes, who was driving the cart.

"Ma'am?"

"I want to stop in town before going on to my aunt's. I've got some shopping to do."

"Whatever you say, ma'am. I don't mind waiting for you."

"I couldn't ask you to do that, Wylie. I'm sure to take all day. You can just leave me at Mr. Burdett's dry goods store. I'll hire someone to bring me out to Aunt Sharon's later."

It was no accident that Burdett's establishment was in Commerce Street, directly across from the busy bayou wharves. Shiloh waited beside her huge trunk until the cart lumbered out of sight. Within half an hour, she'd boarded a big sidewheeler and settled down amid a noisy crowd of traders, families, and slaves for the eight-hour trip to the port of Galveston.

She still was incredulous about her impetuous decision. She knew she had no business following Justin to England, but she had to go. Everything fell so perfectly into place. She had her trunk containing all of her belongings, the money from Justin. Aunt Sharon wasn't expecting her, so she wouldn't be missed.

And adventure beckoned tantalizingly. It was irresistible when Shiloh thought of the endless autumn and winter months ahead at her aunt's farm, the intolerable sameness of it all. She would have died of boredom.

Eventually, the fatigue of her sleepless night took over and she dozed. She didn't awaken until the steamer blew its piercing whistle, signaling the end of the voyage.

Galveston was a strange place to Shiloh; she knew the town only from brief visits when she'd gone off to school. The most populous city in Texas, it was a teeming port. The wharves were crowded with travelers, stacks of crates and puncheons, rolling hogsheads, and enormous, tightly bound bales of cotton.

While a porter brought down Shiloh's trunk, she looked in confusion at a dozen high-masted ships. Finally, she asked a passerby, a barefoot man with rolled-up trousers and a rolling gait, if he could point out the *Falcon*.

The swarthy, muscular man babbled something in a language she didn't recognize and held out his hands.

"You are looking for the *Falcon*?"

She turned, startled by the rich, creole accent of the speaker. She nodded quickly at a lovely, statuesque black woman.

"Yes, I am," she replied.

"Over there, in the farthest slip, missy. But are you sure it is what you are looking for?"

"Of course." But something about the dark-eyed woman's dubious glance unsettled her.

"It is not the place for you. There is danger on the winds that carry that ship."

Shiloh smiled. "It doesn't worry me."

The woman pointed to a ramshackle building at the end of a row of warehouses. "I am living there. If you need anything, ask for Sylvie."

"Thank you. But I'm sure I'll be fine."

Sylvie looked grim. "I, too, thought the same when I boarded the *Falcon*." She swung her head, long earrings jangling against her slim neck. Her disapproval as she studied the thrown-together buildings, the dusty road, and the sere sea grasses that waved in the autumn wind, was apparent.

Shiloh gave the mysterious woman no further thought. She hired a porter to bring her trunk on a handcart to the *Falcon*. It was a tall, graceful vessel with sleek lines and clean, scrubbed-looking decks. There was nothing at all forbidding about it. Mounting a plank to the upper deck, Shiloh hailed one of the sailors, who was sitting with a lapful of rigging, mending it. "Whom do I see to inquire about passage to England?" she asked.

The man jerked his head toward the raised stern. "See the captain, St. James," he said, his accent markedly British.

Shiloh stepped around crates and coils of rope as she made her way to the captain's quarters.

The door was slightly ajar, and she took a moment to study the interior. It was more like a small, elegant drawing room than a ship's cabin. Evening light slanted in through windows on three sides, illuminating glowing walnut panels and bolted-down furniture, a rich Turkey carpet, and a beautiful silver service on a sideboard.

A tall man stood looking over a spread of charts and strange-looking instruments on a broad-topped table. He was young, perhaps of an age with Justin. His full head of curly black hair framed a handsome profile. Hearing her tentative knock, he turned on her a face so beautiful that it was almost intimidating. "Yes?"

Shiloh took a deep breath. "I'd like to sail to England, Captain St. James. I understand your ship sails tomorrow."

His eyes, dark brown with a vaguely Latin cast and a certain sleepiness, assessed her quickly. Apparently, she pleased him, for he gave her a dazzling smile. "Is that so, Miss . . . ?"

"Mulvane," she said. "Shiloh Mulvane."

He extended a slim, long-fingered hand. "Christopher St. James. Welcome aboard."

She hadn't expected it to be so easy. "You mean you'll take me . . . there's room?"

"There is always room on my ship for a lovely lady," he said. "Provided, of course, she can pay."

"I'd like the best accommodations available, please." She placed a stack of double eagles on the captain's table.

"I'll show you there myself."

A ship's boy was polishing a brass bell on the stern. He ducked his head as the captain passed. The strong scent of musk cologne preceded Shiloh as St. James led the way down a steep ladder and along a narrow passageway. He opened the door to a tiny but immaculate cabin. There was a berth along one wall, a wooden stand with a brass lavatory on it, and a small secretary bolted to the opposite wall.

"If you'll send someone for your baggage, I'll have my steward set another place in my quarters for supper." He hesitated, lazy eyes holding hers. "You will join me, won't you?"

"Yes, thank you. Will there be other passengers?"

"Of course. Let's see . . . an older couple, the Westons, a young French family by the name of Jemeaux, an American called Duff Green, and his companion, whom I've not yet met. And then, when we call at Antigua, we'll be taking on more. You'll have plenty of company." St. James wet his sensual lips.

"It is my good fortune that you are the first to come aboard. We'll have the chance for some uninterrupted conversation this evening." He clapped his booted heels together smartly and left.

She chose her lavender dress with its modest high collar for supper that night. St. James's steward came to fetch her. He gave her an odd, assessing look.

"Is something wrong?" Shiloh asked. Her hand went to her tight red curls.

"No," the man said. But he directed another strange look at her before leading her to the captain's cabin.

Christopher St. James had dressed in black velvet with tails and tall, highly polished boots. He swept Shiloh's hand to his lips, tickling her palm.

"Come, shall we eat?"

It was a meal such as Shiloh had never seen before. Delicate boiled shrimp was served cold on bone china plates, garnished with tiny fresh limes. Then there were generous portions of gulf trout bathed in a rich sauce of butter and wine, with green peas on the side. Finally, a tray of mille-feuille pastry, fruit, and cheese. St. James insisted that she sample at least three different wines.

"You live quite well, Captain," Shiloh commented, plucking a grape from the bowl on the table.

"No doubt you've heard stories of rough life at sea, men dying of thirst and starvation . . . well, that doesn't happen on my ship."

She hid a small yawn behind her hand. "Excuse me," she said. "I'd like to retire now."

St. James placed his lips around a ripe plum and bit down, his flicking tongue catching a droplet of juice before it coursed down his chin.

All the while, his indolent eyes held hers. "So soon?"

"I'm very tired."

"I wouldn't dream of keeping you from your much-needed rest. But I have one question, Miss Mulvane. That ring. Is there something you're not telling me?"

Shiloh blushed and cast her eyes downward. "I'm afraid I may have misled you, Captain. I'm married."

"Oh?"

"But my husband and I are—we've decided to live apart for a time."

"I see," he replied with great interest. "In that case, it will be my pleasure to take care of you."

Through the small, misted portal of her cabin, Shiloh watched the roll and tilt of the white-capped open water. The ship listed to one side and she clutched the edge of her berth, leaning over the chamber pot.

In the first eight days at sea, Shiloh had suffered untold miseries. Nothing could have prepared her for the unrelenting sickness. After the first day, she hadn't bothered to get dressed or so much as poke her head out the door. A steward came several times a day to bring her fresh water and food and to empty her chamber pot. Shiloh looked and felt too wretched to respond to Christopher St. James's frequent invitations. She was so ill that she didn't care to see if Justin was aboard.

Then, on the ninth day, the sun pushed away the billowing storm clouds. With them went Shiloh's sickness, leaving her weak but full of elation, as if she'd been reborn. At first she couldn't believe the churning nausea was gone, but her breakfast tasted wonderful. When the steward came, offering St. James's supper invitation, she accepted. She wore one of her favorite dresses, a gown of cotton shot through with green thread, and smiled broadly across the elegant table at Christopher St. James.

"Never, my dear, have I seen a person emerge from the *mal de mer* so triumphantly."

After dessert, he plied her with wine, keeping her from protesting with a steady stream of conversation. "I was born to the sea," he said, his lazy eyes reflective, hands caressing his glass. "It is the one place where a man is not bound by society's rules. That is important to me."

"Why?" Shiloh asked, intrigued.

"Because of my parentage. I carry the name of St. James, but it was given me only as a courtesy. You see, my father, an Englishman, was not married to my mother." His eyes darkened. "I was given a fine education, but I was never allowed to forget that my mother was a Mexican courtesan in Vera Cruz."

Her own childhood had been painful at times, and she understood.

"But here," St. James said grandly, "I do as I please, and no one disapproves."

They talked on, and when the hour of eleven was called out, Shiloh didn't know where the time had gone.

"I'd like to share something with you," said St. James. "Something very special." He took a pipe from a drawer, along with a small, tarlike substance. Loading the pipe with it, he lit it and inhaled deeply.

"Opium," he said. "Here, I think you'll find it most agreeable."

Shiloh had heard of opium's being used for medicinal purposes, but never like this. "Captain, I don't think—"

"You must call me Christopher. Take it. I think you'll enjoy the pleasurable effects." He held it to her lips, putting a match to the pipe. The slightly sweetish smoke blended with Christopher's musk scent, filling her head with decadent sensations.

Shiloh's limbs went loose; her eyelids could barely hold themselves open. Although Christopher had promised her ecstasy, she was aware only of a creeping lassitude. When he led her to his bed and pressed her down upon it, she could offer only the weakest of protests.

He began stroking her back, his hands traveling the length of her with great intimacy.

"And now," he said, working open her buttons, "I've another surprise." He reached up and pulled a small, tinkling bell, keeping her in his hypnotic gaze. Almost immediately, a slender youth appeared, clad only in trousers. He was as beautiful as St. James, tall and lithe, his chest and shoulders glistening.

"This is Antoine," said Christopher. "He is well versed in the arts of pleasure. I think the three of us are about to embark on a rare journey together."

At that, Shiloh's eyes flew open. Antoine's appearance had the effect of a bucket of cold water being thrown in her face.

"No!" she cried, pushing Christopher away and lunging for the door. He blocked her escape.

"Come now," he said, "don't disappoint us, Shiloh."

She landed a sharp, bone-crunching kick on his booted shin, pulled the door open, and ran out onto the deck. The canopy of stars lit her way, but she was unfamiliar with the upper decks and promptly tripped over a coil of rope. Behind her, footfalls grew louder. Shiloh righted herself and fled to the middle of the ship. But her flight was hindered by her billowing skirts and a network of railings and grates. A pair of strong arms grasped her from behind, and she felt herself crushed against Antoine's bare chest.

In front of her loomed Christopher St. James. "There is something to be said for the thrill of the chase, Shiloh, but this has gone far enough." He leaned down and grasped her face, holding it still to deliver a punishing kiss. Shiloh bit at his lips and screamed when he pulled away.

"I'd always heard pioneer women liked it

rough," he laughed, daubing at the blood with a musk-scented handkerchief. "Very well . . ."

Without warning, he cracked his open palm against her cheek, causing her head to snap to the side. Shiloh's vision swam. As the rough assault continued, the stars spun and swirled overhead.

Things were beyond her control. She wished with every fiber of her being that this were some awful nightmare. Just as she dared open her eyes, she became aware of a shadowy form approaching. Like a great cat, the figure dropped onto the deck. There was a sickening sound of flesh against flesh. The force of the blow lifted St. James from his feet and sent him sprawling to the deck. Antoine's hold loosened.

"Get lost, pretty boy," growled a voice, and the scantily clad youth scuttled off into the night.

"Justin!" Shiloh spoke his name with an exploding gasp of relief and hurled herself into his arms.

"My God, Shiloh," he murmured, stroking her hair.

There was a quiet snarl from behind. Justin set Shiloh aside and spun about to face St. James. The flash of a knife blade glinted in the starlight.

The two men were nearly the same size, Justin having the advantage of a few inches and pounds. But while St. James's face was set in an ugly sneer, Justin's was transformed into a visage of magnificent wrath. He was brilliant light, whereas the captain was a dark threat.

St. James stabbed out and Justin jumped back. Then the Englishman grew bolder with his blade and gave a mighty thrust. Shiloh's scream died in her throat. Lightning quick, Justin's booted foot swept upward and sent the knife clattering down to the deck. The two came together in a vicious melee of tangling limbs and curses.

Shiloh allowed herself to relax against the wooden rail. Now that St. James had been disarmed, he didn't have a chance against her husband's towering strength. In seconds, Justin had slammed the captain down to the planks.

St. James began thrashing and whimpering like a whipped dog. "Mercy!" he cried in his high-pitched voice.

Justin looked at him in disgust. "Don't worry, St. James, I'm going to let you sail this bucket to England." He leaned down, his voice a deadly whisper that Shiloh could barely hear above the swish of the shifting seas. "But if you ever come near my wife again, if you so much as look at her, I'll make you wish you'd never been born."

"I—I promise."

The Englishman ran wildly to his cabin. Shiloh faced her husband, words of gratitude on her lips. But he never gave her a chance to speak. Grabbing her by the arm, he took her below.

A lamp swinging gently from a rafter illuminated his cabin. He sat her roughly on the berth and thrust a mug of lukewarm coffee into her hands. "Drink," he commanded. When she'd had a few swallows, he spoke again. "When will it end, Shiloh? The lies, the deceit—"

"I couldn't help it, Justin. I couldn't stand to live with my aunt, stuck out there with nothing to do. Besides, I'm your wife."

"I believe you decided we shouldn't be together."

"But that was before I learned you were going to England."

His jaw clenched. "It's all been a game to you, hasn't it? A way to alleviate your boredom. Damn it, this time you've gone too far. I've tried so many times to protect you, yet you persist in getting yourself into one scrape after another. What would've happened tonight if I hadn't heard your screams?"

Shiloh swallowed hard as a shudder rippled through her. "I had no idea St. James would try something like that."

"That's because you're so damned ignorant. If you'd known the first thing about the *Falcon*, you'd never have dared to set foot on this ship. Slaves, contraband, stolen goods . . . St. James is notorious. His reputation is known—and feared—in a hundred ports. Good God, even the wharf urchins could have told you about his bizarre appetite for young boys and opium. Of course, few women have lived to tell the rest of the story. St. James keeps them or discards them according to his whim. It's said he keeps a pirate's retreat off Mexico somewhere."

Shiloh began trembling in earnest now as she recalled the warning of the woman called Sylvie. Justin reached out and thrust her head back, using his thumb to raise one of her eyelids. "He drugged you."

Shiloh winced. "I didn't know what he was offering me."

Justin gave a dry laugh. "This from a woman who fancies herself a spy. I wonder what your father will say when he hears what happened this time."

That was too much for Shiloh. She flung herself onto the bunk, quaking with bitterness. She cried because the truth of what Justin said knifed through her like a blade. She *was* a failure. She was incapable of becoming what she wanted so badly to be. Although she'd harbored dreams of glory, the miserable reality was that she'd proven herself to be a bungler. Perhaps her father had known that all along. Perhaps that was why he— and Justin—couldn't love her.

She wept on, heedless of Justin's stolid, silent presence. Finally, the sobs abated to hiccoughs of misery and she went limp upon the berth.

"Do you want to stay here tonight?" His voice was unbearably cold.

Shiloh forced herself to face him. "No, thank you," she said. She couldn't stand to spend another minute in the presence of his disapproving scrutiny.

He escorted her to her cabin. "I guess you'll be safe enough. St. James is a cowardly son of a bitch. But latch the door anyway."

Justin flicked his cheroot over the rail into the clear, aqua-colored water. As the *Falcon* maneuvered its way into Falmouth Harbor at Antigua, he thought again of Shiloh.

She'd spent the remainder of the voyage sequestered like a nun in her cabin. He couldn't be sure who she was avoiding—St. James or him. Grimacing, he recalled how hard he'd been on her the night she was attacked. But, damn it, she deserved every word. She had no business sneaking to England, walking with unbelievable innocence into the hands of Christopher St. James. She had to hear those things before she let something else happen. If she hated him for what he'd said, at least he had the consolation of knowing she wouldn't be so damned blind about people in the future.

He might have gone too far, though. He'd glimpsed Shiloh once when she'd opened her door to a steward. Her face was pale, frightened, and her eyes had the dull look of defeat in them.

Justin caught himself wishing she would come above, just for these last few minutes. He knew her eyes would grow bright with pleasure at the exotic island scenery. Antigua was a matchless jewel in the necklace of the leeward islands.

Towering Boggy Peak stood above lush tropical forests and cane fields of impossible greenness. Justin wanted Shiloh to smell the flowers and feast her eyes on the curling silk-cotton trees, to hear the wild calls of the colored birds.

He was joined instead by Duff Green, who came to stand among the passengers at the rail.

"I figure we'll be here two days at the most," said Green. "Looks like all that cargo over there is meant for us."

Justin looked over at the enormous bundles of cane and crates of rum. "I'm glad there won't be much of a delay," he said. "I'm eager to find out exactly what Lord Aberdeen's up to now."

"Nothing good," Green said. "But I doubt you'll find much to pin on him."

They stood and talked while the ship's crew furled some of its sails and it crept carefully amid the rocky shoals, finally fitting snugly into harbor and dropping anchor.

Lighting a cigar, Green made his way to one of several gangplanks that had been laid. "What do you say, Justin? Shall we hit the grog shops, maybe try to find a little entertainment."

"No, thanks."

Duff looked apologetic. "Sorry. I forgot about Shiloh. What's ailing the two of you, anyway?"

"I said some pretty harsh things to her."

Duff looked concerned. "Maybe this island will coax her out. Closest thing to paradise I ever saw. If you don't mind my saying so, Justin, she's sure as hell worth a try."

* * *

Beyond the white roads of the small settlement, fat goats grazed on a hill. Ancient stone sugar mills stood about. To one side were banana trees, called figs by the inhabitants, and orchards of strange, exotic fruit. And all around were the flowers, growing wild or cultivated near the snug cottages, to be tucked into the hair of dark-skinned island girls.

It was time, Justin decided, to coax Shiloh out of her self-imposed isolation. Tucking his white broadcloth shirt into his trousers, he descended to her cabin. "Shiloh, open up. It's me."

She let him in, keeping her eyes downcast. Never had she looked so small, so vulnerable.

"We ought to go ashore."

"No, thank you," she said. "But you go ahead. I'll just stay here."

He was talking to a stranger. Where was the fire, the ambition, the hunger for adventure? "Damn it, Shiloh," he said, taking her by the shoulders and forcing her to face him. "You may as well wait in Falmouth Harbor for the first boat back to New Orleans or Galveston. You could be back with your aunt in a few weeks."

"No!" she cried, defiance returning to her eyes. "I—you're right. I'll get my things."

The evening light bathed the port city in a shimmer of pink-gold. Trading was still in full swing. Women with brightly painted handcarts hawked trinkets and fruit, and malodorous fish stalls were laden with odd-looking creatures, freshly caught. Justin bought Shiloh a large yellow mango and sliced it with his knife. He watched with pleasure as she devoured her portion. Already he could tell, her zest for life was returning.

They stopped at an open-air cantina and dined on fried blue-marlin steaks, yams seasoned with molasses, and more fruit, and something called goat water washed down with swigs of raw rum. Overhead, a balmy breeze rustled through the palm-thatched canopy of their table. Justin overpaid the smiling, dark-skinned boy who served them.

"Where's the best place for my wife and me to take a walk on the beach?" he asked.

"I know a very good place, sir: Pigeon's Point. Sand white and still warm from the sun. Very private, very quiet. Walk to the end of the road and circle round that large rock. You will pass a glade on your right with a cold spring and then there will be a wide beach."

They strolled at a leisurely pace, inhaling the heavy perfume of flowers and watching the graceful swaying of tall palms. The beach was everything the boy had promised: waves lapped up on a wide, pristine stretch of sand, and a cooling salt-scented breeze blew in.

She bent and removed her shoes and stockings and ran down to the water's edge. Drawing her skirts up above her knees, she waded in. As she felt the fineness of the sand under her feet, she realized that her old vigor was returning.

Justin joined her in the clear water. The rising moon and a spray of stars illuminated the breaking waves, making them glow as they rolled in.

"It's breathtaking." She was talking about the scenery, but her eyes were fastened on Justin's handsome face, on his fine golden hair as the breeze blew through it. "Thank you," she said.

"For what?"

"For making me get off that ship. I hid there too long."

"I was surprised at you, Shiloh. You've never been one to give up."

"But you made everything clear to me. The things you said—"

"Should never have been said. I had no business judging you."

A wave rolled up and propelled her forward. With a small cry, she fell against Justin's chest and grasped his arms for support.

He reached behind her and began unbuttoning her dress.

Her heart leaped. "What are you doing?"

"It seems a shame," he said, continuing to work at the buttons, "not to take advantage of this private beach. Surely you must be wanting to swim."

It seemed as though she'd been thinking it all along. Laughing, she went back to the dry sand and began removing her clothes. When she was clad only in her shift, she started back toward the water.

"What's this?" He plucked at the ribbons of her shift. Without further ado, he swept it off and raked his eyes over her slim body.

Shiloh ran down to the water, modestly burying herself in the moon-glowing waves. She would never get used to Justin's behavior. As she swam through waist-deep water, she felt him grasp her about the middle. He laughed at her cry of alarm and turned her easily.

His kiss was deep. As the water swirled up between them, Shiloh thought she would burst with the longing that flowed through her. She wrapped her arms around Justin, never thinking to deny him now.

Soft moonlight played over his features and flooded his eyes with a silvery gleam. He took one of Shiloh's hands and brought it to his lips, kissing the fingers one by one. "I'm almost glad you decided to follow me on this trip." He sipped the sweetness from her mouth as his fingers, moving secretly, found the small bud of sensation between her legs.

The stars above spun, turning from bright points of light into long, livid streaks. The unending rhythm of the sea thundered in her ears, relentless, compelling, urging her toward Justin.

"Please . . . ," she begged, her voice ragged with emotion.

Justin ceased his sensuous caresses and took her by the shoulders, cursing himself for not being more sensitive to her. The last man who had tried to touch her had scared the daylights out of her. "I should have known you weren't ready so soon after that scare with St. James."

She shook her head, spraying droplets of water. "I wasn't asking you to stop. I want you, Justin. What St. James tried to do to me was evil, and only you can erase that memory for me."

Now there was no hesitation, no teasing. Shiloh gloried in the pure ecstasy of his touch, and she reached out to him. Shifting water eddied between them like a small, warm gulf.

She brought her legs up and wrapped them around his torso, amazed at how much the unfamiliar position aroused her. The lapping of the water, the undulating of their hips, Justin's breath in her ear, all combined in an erotic symphony that rose to a breathless crescendo and then crashed down. She felt as if she were drowning in a pool of exquisite sensations.

She dragged her lips along his shoulder and up his neck. "I must be possessed by voodoo magic."

He traced the curves of her torso. "Is that right?"

A troubled shadow crossed her face. "Justin, I wasn't brought up to be a religious person, but sometimes the things we do . . ." Her voice trailed off as her face grew warm. She looked up at him, her eyes wide and bathed in moonglow. "Justin, what we do—could it be wrong?"

He pulled her through the water against him. "Just because we didn't make love in a proper bed doesn't mean we've committed any crime."

As he spoke, his hands moved discreetly under her and he brought them together again. At her soft sigh of pleasure, he whispered, "How can this be wrong, Shiloh?"

They enjoyed the interlude at Antigua for another day, and then it was time to set sail again. Justin and Shiloh stood together on deck, along with Duff Green.

"Ah, a man could get used to this life," Duff declared, patting his generous middle and puffing on his cigar. "All it takes is a little money, and you get the royal treatment. Perhaps I was hasty in throwing in my entire lot for Texas."

"It seems you're not the only one who thinks that way," Justin remarked. He gestured at an overloaded coach that had stopped on the wharf. A liveried footman handed down an elaborately gowned and bonneted woman. Shiloh raised her head and found herself staring into the china-blue eyes of Jessamine West.

ELEVEN

"What are they doing here?" Shiloh asked that night. By unspoken agreement, Justin had moved into her cabin, and they lay crowded together in the small bunk.

"Harmon West is overseeing his sugar plantation, no doubt. And it appears that Captain Elliot has some interest in it, as well. From what the *Falcon* took on, they should make a tidy profit."

"Is that why Judge West is so dead-set against annexation?"

"That's one of the reasons."

"What are you going to do about it, Justin?"

"I'll hardly need to lift a finger. When President Houston learns how thick West and Elliot are, the judge will be stripped of his appointment. Duff's going to take care of Elliot. This might finish him as a diplomat. The English can't have their representatives getting rich off their policies."

"It could just be a coincidence."

"It doesn't matter. They wouldn't survive the rumors. And don't forget whose ship we're on."

"The opium?" Shiloh shivered, recalling the

mind-numbing effects of the drug the captain had given her.

"I'd be willing to bet that there's a connection there. Elliot was in China during the opium wars. And Harmon West has never been one to turn his back on a big-money deal like that. We've got him up against the wall now."

Shiloh yawned and snuggled against him, savoring the feel of his warm chest beneath her cheek. "I'm glad," she murmured. "I hope we've seen the last of the Wests."

"McCord needs to be silenced." Harmon West crossed the deck where he, Jessamine, and Elliot were standing.

"Any ideas?" Elliot asked.

"I'd like to feed the meddling son of a bitch to the sharks. Sorry, Jessamine," he added.

"I'm a big girl now; I've done a lot of growing up since I found out why you wanted Justin to marry me. By now you should know it's best to include me in your plans." She finished the pastry she was eating and licked the crumbs from her fingers. "Now," she continued, "I think you two gentlemen should use a little imagination. All you have to do is blackmail him, just as you're doing to Mr. Green about his Del Norte land company."

"Unfortunately, our Mr. McCord is utterly devoid of any taint, unlike his friend Duff Green.

What could we possibly reveal about him that would prevent him from revealing us in turn?"

Jessamine grimaced. "It wouldn't have been if he'd married me instead of that appalling bit of riffraff—" She stopped as a smile spread slowly across her face. "Now, there's something."

"Tell us," Elliot and the judge said at once.

"What if he was caught in a clandestine affair with the daughter of the very man he's supposedly investigating? Not only would people think that Justin had sold out; they'd also condemn him for cheating on his poor little wife. Now, all we've got to do is arrange for someone—Mr. Green would do nicely; he is published in many newspapers, isn't he?—to find us together, and then we could offer Justin a choice. Either he keeps quiet about our business, or we allow Mr. Green to carry his tale to Justin's superiors."

Harmon West smiled at his daughter. "If your mother had lived to hear how deviously your mind works, my dear, she'd send you to a nunnery."

Justin was penning a letter in his cabin, where he no longer slept but kept his baggage and papers. Reaching into his pocket, he checked his watch. It was nearly midnight. Shiloh would be asleep by now.

A smile curved his lips. His wife wasn't ever averse to being awakened, not if he did it gently.

The sound of a knock startled him out of his

reverie. Opening the door, he was amazed to see Jessamine West.

She was clad in an impossibly thin dressing gown and nothing else. Her generous curves had once been familiar, but now he saw a stranger who meant nothing to him.

"Justin, I must speak to you." She stepped inside the cabin and closed the door behind her. "I've been waiting to find you alone." She pressed close, her heavy gardenia perfume filling the room.

"What is it, Jessamine?"

"I know you think the worst of Father's being in Antigua, and now bound for England. But I must ask you to say nothing of having seen us. There are many people who wouldn't understand."

"I think it's the other way around, Jessamine. Most people will understand perfectly that your father sympathizes with the English against annexation."

She glowered at him. "So you will slander my father, a public figure—"

"His actions will speak for themselves."

He saw her anger flare, and then she mastered it. She looked up at him through heavy-lidded eyes and moistened her lips. "Really, Justin," she said in a husky whisper, "you're not being fair to us. But we're prepared to be more than fair to you. There's a nice reward waiting for you if you agree to forget about this."

"You know better than that, Jessamine."

"And then," she went on as if she hadn't heard him, "there is me." Boldly grasping him about the waist, she hugged him to her soft body. "Remember how it was with us, Justin, in the spring."

Even as he was extracting himself from her embrace, she shrugged her gown off one shoulder and leaned up to kiss him.

Shiloh was awakened by the ship's bell ringing midnight. She blinked into the darkness of the cabin, immediately sensing Justin's absence. She pulled on her robe and went to look for him. A sliver of lamplight glowed under the door to his cabin down the passageway. Shaking her head, she made her way toward it. She knew of no man who worked harder and slept less than Justin.

She nearly collided with Duff Green, who approached from the opposite direction.

"Good evening, Mrs. McCord," Duff said. "You'll pardon my bed gown and cap; I was sound asleep when a steward summoned me to your husband's cabin."

"*Summoned* you, Mr. Green."

"Yes, ma'am. What could he want at this hour?" He knocked at the door. There was no answer— only a strange bumping sound and muffled voices, one of them unmistakably female.

Duff gave Shiloh a dubious look. "Perhaps we'd better leave."

A chill gripped her heart and squeezed tight. "Open it," she said.

When he hesitated, she pushed the door open. Jessamine West, naked to the waist, was in Justin's arms. The girl's mouth formed a surprised O, and then gave Shiloh a knowing smile.

Shiloh fled, unwilling to subject herself to the humiliating scene. She latched her cabin securely before flinging herself onto the bunk, pounding her rage into the pillows.

Duff Green was not so hasty. Carefully averting his gaze, he stood just outside the room.

"Miss West was just leaving," Justin said. Roughly he pulled her gown back into place and propelled her out of the cabin.

"Good night, Justin," she called sweetly, trilling her voice loudly enough for anyone to hear.

"That wasn't what it looked like," Duff said. "Obviously she wanted something to hold over you, so you'd keep quiet about her father."

"She did just the opposite," Justin said. "She just sealed Harmon's fate."

For the remainder of the voyage, Shiloh kept to her cabin, refusing to let Justin enter. She ventured out on deck only in the company of the Jemeaux, the French family on board. Upon arrival in Bristol and on the subsequent journey to London, she kept herself coldly distant from him.

Only when they reached the huge, smoky city and registered at a hotel in Portman Square was she forced to confront Justin in private. Although she tried to secure a room for herself, the proprietor told her there were no more vacancies. She suspected Justin had lined the man's pockets to compel him to say that, but she didn't want to cause a scene.

And so, stiff-backed and still smarting from his behavior, she allowed herself to be installed in a high-windowed suite overlooking the fashionable square.

"I hope this is to your liking," Justin said.

Her eyes swept the delightful green-and-yellow decor, the slim, elegant lines of the furniture, the ornate plaster molding around the hearth and ceiling.

"The room is fine," she said, deliberately understating her admiration. In reality, she'd only ever dreamed of such luxury.

Justin paid the porters who brought their trunks and ordered up a bath. "Wear something pretty tonight," he instructed. "We're invited to a reception at the home of Lord and Lady Henry Parsons. Expect a lot of flattery. Texans are mighty popular in England these days." He turned on his heel and left.

Shiloh breathed a sigh of relief. Just being near him was painful. His very presence made a mockery of all she'd given him, all she'd foolishly felt for him. The bath arrived and she scrubbed herself with a vengeance, as if trying to cleanse herself of the voyage she wanted so badly to forget.

A young maid helped her dress, speaking rapidly with a pronounced accent. "So it's to the Parsons's, is it? Terribly grand, I'm told. But of course you'll be treated to such things every day. Right friendly we are to Texans, ma'am. 'Tis Lord Aberdeen himself started the whole bit. What's it like, ma'am?"

"Texas?" Shiloh couldn't help smiling. "If you were to go there, you'd probably think you'd landed on the moon. It's nothing like London."

"Oh, do tell," said the maid.

"It's hot and dusty, mostly, but almost like a jungle in other places. The towns are few and small, with simple frame houses or log cabins. You can go for miles in certain areas and never meet a soul."

"And the savages, ma'am, have you seen them?"

Shiloh nodded. "Many times. They trade with the settlers for flannel and trinkets. The peaceful ones, that is."

"And the others, ma'am?"

"There's a whole area beyond the settled regions called the Comanchería. The tribes of the Comanche hunt buffalo and make war on the settlers. I've never been in an attack, thank God, but I've heard stories that would make your blood run cold."

"Are you ready, Shiloh?" Justin stood outside the dressing room, clad for the evening in an elegant gray frock coat and white trousers tucked into his gleaming boots.

"Oh, sir," the maid said, "how handsome you look."

Justin looked slightly uncomfortable. "Yes,

well, finish up, will you?" He went back to the sitting room of the suite to wait.

Because of the chilly London weather, Shiloh had the opportunity to wear her newest gown. It was of lavender velvet, with sleeves and bodice banded by wide black ribbons. The generous hem was drawn up at intervals and fastened with black bows, and the exquisite lace of a dressy petticoat peeped out.

"Lord, now, ma'am," the maid said as Shiloh pivoted before a free-standing mirror. "You didn't say you'd been to Paris. Surely that is one of Mr. Dumalier's designs."

"Actually, it was made by a Mexican woman who works on our ranch."

"No," breathed the maid. "Then a genius, she is."

"I'll be glad to tell her that." She was determined not to let Justin spoil the evening. She meant to show the Londoners that Texas women were not backwoods pioneers. And above all, she would not allow herself to be outshone by Jessamine West.

Justin's reaction satisfied her. He couldn't seem to keep from staring at the wide, plunging neckline of her gown or the beautifully worked bodice. Shiloh only wished that she were not so affected by her husband's looks. Handsome as a prince and smelling faintly of soap and tobacco, he was undeniably appealing.

And he was determined to clear the air with her. As a hired coach bore them to the tall, ornately facaded house of Lord Henry Parsons, he brought up the subject of Jessamine.

"It's taken me a damned long time to get you alone to talk, Shiloh, but I know we've both been thinking about it. It wasn't what you've obviously conjured up in your mind."

"I know what I saw. Don't insult me by trying to deny it."

He ground his fist into his hand. "How the hell can you think I'd have anything to do with Jessamine? Hell, I married you just to avoid the woman."

Hurt knifed through her. "It's comforting to know I am the lesser of two evils."

She erected a silent wall to protect herself from the hurtful things he said. Perhaps Jessamine had thrown herself at him, as had the Mexican woman back in Houston, but it was too much. Justin was a grown man, after all. He had no right to be angry at her, but he was. She could tell by the way he sat, stiffly, not looking at her.

When they arrived, they were presented to a circle of smiling, titled people who extended solicitous hands of welcome. Rather than being nervous, Shiloh was relieved to be away from Justin. Despite the formality of the occasion, she found herself responding easily even to the most daunting aristocrats.

She caught sight of Jessamine in a yellow, multitiered gown. The girl had been cornered by a middle-aged gentleman who leaned toward her, studying her through a quizzing glass as though she were some rare specimen. No one, it seemed, was going to rescue Jessamine from him. Shiloh turned her attention to a dashing young man who'd been introduced as the Viscount St. Amberly.

"The belle of the Texas Republic," he proclaimed grandly. "May we ever be grateful that she has graced our shores."

When the dancing began, Shiloh waltzed with the eager young viscount.

"Thank you for the toast." Shiloh cocked her head in puzzlement. "Is it 'Your Lordship'? I'm afraid I'm quite ignorant of titles."

"Then call me Andrew. It's much simpler."

Shiloh didn't leave the dance floor for hours. Gentlemen of all ages claimed her, and she was exhilarated rather than fatigued. She enjoyed most of her partners, with the glaring exception of Krieger Wilkes, who was some sort of aide to Lord Aberdeen. The odious little man leered unabashedly and even invited Shiloh to his flat later.

"Out of the question, Mr. Wilkes," she said firmly. "Excuse me."

His hand gripped her arm. "It would behoove you to treat me well."

"I think not." She disengaged herself and walked away.

Inevitably, she found herself in Justin's arms.

"A last dance with your husband?" he inquired.

She followed him woodenly through the steps.

"You handled Wilkes quite well," he commented. "The man is a notorious lecher, but he's tolerated because of his connection to Aberdeen. Aside from him, you've captivated the peerage of England."

The following two months were a whirlwind of activity. There were many more balls and dinner parties, picnics in Hyde Park when the winter mist let up, shooting contests, and horse races. Often, Justin was absent from such events. He attended meetings with British officials, who were cautious with him. Charles Elliot had obviously warned them that Justin was a proponent of annexation.

At one such meeting, George Hamilton Gordon, the fourth earl of Aberdeen, was expounding on the various evils of slavery.

"It is the scourge of the American South, and we fervently wish that it not be extended to Texas," he said, thick eyebrows lowering accusingly at his listeners.

"That's commendable, Your Lordship," Justin said. "But what about your own colonies in the Caribbean, which thrive by virtue of slave labor?"

"I'll ignore that comment," Aberdeen replied imperiously. "What we really want, gentlemen, is for your fledgling republic to make peace with Mexico, settle its frontier disputes, and achieve success independently. And England is prepared to help in any way."

Justin ingratiated himself to no one during the many discussions. He probed and questioned relentlessly, trying to force an admission from Aberdeen that England's real motive was to protect its interests in the Gulf of Mexico.

"You're treading on shaky ground," Duff Green commented one day shortly after the new year.

"I just want something concrete to prove to the United States that they'd damn well better get moving on annexation."

"What are you going to do."

"I intend to find out what Aberdeen is planning. I'm going to start by searching his ministerial chambers."

Duff gave a low whistle. "Aberdeen'll have your tail if you're caught."

"There's no other way. And I'm running out of time. I think tonight's as good a time as any to pay a visit to His Lordship's chambers."

They stopped at an alehouse and went over the details of his plan. "I believe I'll make a good thief," Justin said. "I just hope I can make it out of the country before Aberdeen realizes what hit him."

Alone in Aberdeen's chambers, Justin managed to locate a packet of papers in a locked drawer. The papers were written in cipher, but it wasn't a very good one. Scratching with the stub of a pencil, Justin uncovered a plot to move British warships into the Gulf of Mexico, ostensibly to force Mexico to recognize the sovereignty of Texas. But of course, the fleet would have an obvious secondary effect. Not only Mexico but the United States would be intimidated. And Texas, too impoverished to defend itself adequately, would become an outpost of English imperialism.

"Not if I can help it," Justin muttered, replacing the papers. He blew out the stub of his candle and prepared to leave.

The quiet dark of the office was shattered. Justin heard the thud of boots and lunged toward the second-story window through which he'd entered. The steeply slanting tiled roof was slick with nighttime mist, and he nearly lost his hold. His pursuers climbed out after him, but they balked at the sheer drop to the cobbled courtyard below.

Clinging desperately to the rough edge of the roof, he traversed hand over hand to a drain pipe at the corner of the building. This, too, was slick with moisture, and his every limb shook as he made his descent. At last he dropped to the cobbles.

And was promptly seized from behind by two burly men. Although he bucked and struggled in their grasp, they held fast and dragged him, cursing, to a public wagon.

Shiloh dined alone in her suite at the hotel in Portman Square after a hectic day of shopping and sightseeing with some of her self-appointed hostesses. She seemed to be in great demand in London society. Her outspokenness was admired, as were her tales of life in Texas. She, in turn, found the Londoners well educated and interesting. Only the rift between her and Justin marred the visit.

His absence tonight wasn't unusual; he'd been so busy that she'd seen almost nothing of him. Sighing discontentedly, she pushed aside her plate of stewed chicken. She told herself that being with Justin would only compound the hurt. But the hours alone were tedious.

When a knock sounded, she jumped to answer it. Her eyes opened wide at the sight of Duff Green and a very unhappy Jessamine West.

"Forgive the intrusion, Mrs. McCord. I should have done this long ago," said Duff. "Miss West has something to say to you."

"Yes."

Shiloh had never seen Jessamine so agitated. "I'm listening," she said with growing interest.

"What you saw between Justin and me onboard the *Falcon* was only playacting. I—I forced myself on him and arranged for us to be discovered."

Shiloh's head began to pound. "But—*why?*"

"Because your meddling husband won't stop hounding my father. He won't stop until he ruins us."

"And so you decided to have your revenge on him."

She tossed her yellow ringlets. "You're in no

position to judge me, Shiloh. Before you got your claws into Justin, you were nothing but a no-account drunkard's daughter."

Shiloh leaped at her, scratching at the sneering, haughty face. Falling to the floor, they became a tangle of billowing skirts and petticoats.

"Get this madwoman off me!" Jessamine screeched.

Duff took his time lifting Shiloh from her. "You can leave now, Jessamine," she said hotly. "But if I ever hear you insult my father again, if you dare go near my husband again, I'll make sure there's no gentleman around to protect you from me."

Jessamine righted herself with an effort, arranging her skirts around her.

"I was foolish to think you'd accept my explanation gracefully," she said, sweeping with great relief from the room.

Shiloh faced Duff Green. "Would you mind telling me what that was all about?"

"I apologize for meddling, but I felt you deserved an explanation."

"How did you get Jessamine to admit the truth to me?"

He smiled. "There are few people in Texas who know more about the illustrious Miss West than I. There are a number of things I was able to forget in exchange for her confession."

"Thank you, Mr. Green." She closed the door with a quiet click and turned back to the room. It wouldn't be easy to face Justin now that she knew the truth, but she owed him an apology.

How many times had he tried to explain, and she'd refused to listen? How could she ever find the words to tell him that she should have trusted him?

She sat before the lowering fire in the hearth, pondering long into the night. Finally, she dozed off into a fitful sleep, and didn't awaken until the light of late morning slanted across her face.

She squinted and slowly stretched. Pouring herself a glass of water, she went to the bedroom door. Perhaps Justin had slept there, not wishing to disturb her. But the bed was perfectly made, the counterpane drawn tightly, as it had been the previous day.

A cold prickle touched the base of Shiloh's neck. She gulped her water and put on a fresh gown.

Justin's enemies, and there were many lurking behind congenial aristocratic masks, may have finally gotten the better of him. Heart pounding, she hurried down to Duff Green's room one floor below. "Where is Justin?" she demanded.

He wiped a bit of coddled egg from his mouth. "He didn't return last night?" Duff leaned against the door frame as if in sudden need of support.

"He's in some sort of trouble, isn't he?" Shiloh said quietly. When Duff nodded, a strange, unexpected calm crept over her. It was no use going into hysterics. Whatever had happened, she'd need a clear head to face it. She stepped inside the room and pulled the door shut. "Perhaps you'd better tell me what you know."

"Justin and I both suspected that Lord Aberdeen has some unscrupulous plans in the making for Texas. Last night Justin went to the minister's office to try to find out about it. I'm afraid he must have been discovered."

"But where could he be?"

Duff shrugged. "At best, he'll receive a dressing-down from Ashbel Smith at the Texas consulate and be deported."

"And at the worst?"

"Prison. Since he's not an official diplomat, he could be treated like a common thief."

TWELVE

Shiloh kept her hands folded in her lap, carefully hiding her nervousness. After an interminable wait, Lord Aberdeen had deigned to see her.

"My husband is missing," she said, not wasting time on niceties.

Aberdeen raised his quizzing glass. "I'm sorry to hear that, Mrs. McCord. But why do you come to me?"

"I think you know where he is, Your Lordship."

"My dear girl, London is a big place. Your husband could be anywhere. Now, if you'll excuse me, I've work to do."

"My husband is a citizen of Texas," she persisted. "And a guest in this country. Lord Aberdeen, I know you do not wish to have this incident become an international affair."

The man's face reddened beneath his powdered wig. "Young lady, if you make unsubstantiated accusations, it will reflect quite poorly on the country you represent."

She rose to leave. "I can see I'll have to go elsewhere for help, Lord Aberdeen. But you haven't heard the last of me, sir."

Outside his office she slumped, trembling with frustration, against the wall. She squeezed her eyes shut to prevent the flow of hot tears that threatened to erupt.

"Miss . . . ?" Shiloh opened her eyes and saw a clerk staring at her, his pale eyes concerned. "Are you all right?"

"Yes, thank you." Shiloh clutched her reticule and prepared to leave.

"I'll see you out," the clerk offered.

"I can find my own way, thank you."

But the clerk followed her anyway, opening the door to a long corridor. "Never know what you might run up against." He gave her a meaningful look. "Only last night it was, a thief was discovered right there in His Lordship's offices."

Shiloh froze. "What are you telling me, sir?"

He glanced left and right, lowering his voice. "Took him off to Newgate, they did."

She fairly flew down the stairs and out into the street, where her hired cab was waiting. "To Newgate Prison," she told the driver, ignoring his look of astonishment. The ride seemed interminable as they wound through narrow streets among carts and coaches, beneath the overhanging roofs of top-heavy buildings.

Finally, they reached the forbidding gates of the prison. Shiloh practically had to force her way into the day warden's office, pushing past clerks and guards.

The warden was a small, whey-faced individual, dressed in soiled finery, looking like a caricature of a gentleman. His watery eyes appraised her and showed approval.

"I am Shiloh McCord, from the Republic of Texas. I believe my husband was brought here last night."

"Is that so?" the warden asked. He shuffled through a stack of papers and located a blotted list. Scanning it with a dirty finger, he nodded.

"Aye, here's a McCord."

"Please send for him immediately. What is the amount of the fine?"

But the warden only shook his head. "There'll be no release for the prisoner, ma'am. I've a special order here."

Shiloh's heart sank, but she kept her head high. "Suppose, sir," she said, touching the strings of her reticule, "that you decided it would be more profitable to ignore that piece of paper. . . ." She let her voice trail off and allowed him to hear the coins falling to and fro.

The warden licked his lips, and his hands worked nervously at his sides. But he shook his head regretfully. "This order is signed by the secretary of a very highly placed official."

She had no doubt about the identity of the official. "May I see my husband?"

"Alas, no. There's nothing more I can do. Good day, madam."

* * *

"You know I wouldn't be here if I weren't desperate." Shiloh gripped the sides of the wingback chair she was sitting in.

Harmon West looked across his suite, fairly gloating as she finished her tale. Jessamine sat nearby, looking smug.

"You have a great deal of influence," Shiloh continued, hating herself. "More, probably, than Mr. Ashbel Smith. Lord Aberdeen will listen to you."

"Tell me, Mrs. McCord, why should I lift a finger to help your husband?"

"Justin is your countryman."

"He's also my enemy."

Shiloh drew a deep breath. "I can't speak for Justin, but if you get him released I'll do everything I can to see that he doesn't mention what he knows to President Houston."

"You have that much influence over your husband?"

"I don't know, Judge West," Shiloh said honestly. Indeed, when had Justin ever trusted anything she'd said? "But surely, once he's released, he'll feel beholden to you."

Harmon West went to a small wooden secretary. Dipping a quill into the ink, he scratched out a brief message, signed it, and sealed it with a bit of wax.

"Take this to Lord Aberdeen's secretary, Krieger Wilkes," he said. "And Mrs. McCord, don't make me regret this."

* * *

She remembered Krieger Wilkes all too well from several receptions she'd been to. The tiny eyes sharp as needles, the thick, perpetually wet lips, the mottled, pock-marked face. But it was not his physical appearance that repulsed her so much as the transparent lust she saw when he looked at her, and his moist, chubby hands that seized every opportunity to come in contact with her.

Shiloh almost wished she hadn't rushed to his residence, a tawdry little apartment in Philpen Row, so cramped that he slept on a daybed in the sitting room. The smell of cigar smoke and stewed cabbage hung in the air and in the dark, water-marked drapes that covered the single window.

"Mrs. McCord," Wilkes said in his nasal voice. "What a pleasant surprise. Do sit down." He gestured grandly at a stained, musty-smelling chair.

Shiloh handed him Judge West's letter. He broke the seal and squinted at it. "Light's bad," he muttered. "I'll fetch my spectacles." He rifled through a drawer by the daybed. Shiloh's eyes widened at the sight of a small pistol, but she said nothing. Wilkes located his spectacles and read the letter. He laid it down on a table and approached Shiloh, circling her chair like a shark coming in for the kill.

Finally she spoke. "Can you help me, Mr. Wilkes?"

"A release order from me would give your husband immediate freedom. But I'll have to do no little amount of explaining to Lord Aberdeen if I decide to do this. Surely I'm entitled to some sort of payment."

"Certainly," she said, reaching into her reticule. "Name your price."

"I wouldn't think of taking your money." His finger circled her shoulder, causing her to recoil against the back of the chair. "What I have in mind, dear lady, will cost you nothing."

"I'm a married woman," she said, absurdly thinking that Wilkes might have some hidden shred of decency.

"And I am a lonely man. A few hours of your company is all I ask. Surely that is not too high a price for your husband's liberty."

Shiloh's mouth was dry as cotton. "I—I can't—"

Wilkes shook his head regretfully. "Then I'm afraid I can't help you, Mrs. McCord."

She stared at the scuffed planks on the bare floor. "I'll stay," she whispered at last.

"I didn't hear you, Mrs. McCord."

She flung her head back, eyes seething with loathing. "I'll stay," she repeated.

His tongue flicked over his thick lips as they parted into a leering grin. He extended a hand. "Come and sit on the bed. We'll be more comfortable there."

Shiloh obeyed, her every limb stiff with repugnance. As she seated herself, she noticed a stain on the pillow from the macassar oil Wilkes smeared on his hair.

"I'd like something to drink," she told him.

He seemed pleased at her compliance. "Of course. I've nothing for a delicate palate, but if you'd like some gin—"

"Gin is fine." The moment he turned his back, her hand snaked out, fingers closing around the drawer pull. It began to creak as she eased it open. Gritting her teeth, she forced herself to go more slowly. At last, she slipped her hand inside and took out Wilkes's pistol.

When he turned around from his pouring, she had it pointed squarely at his chest.

"Write the release order, Mr. Wilkes."

His face fell. "Come, now, Mrs. McCord, surely you wouldn't do murder just to avoid my company."

"It has been a very long, very frustrating day." Shiloh's finger caressed the trigger. "I'm just about at my wits' end. Now, you can risk crossing me and see what happens, or you can do what I say."

Grumbling about uncivilized outlaws from Texas, he snatched up paper and quill and wrote out the order. Shiloh didn't lower the gun until he'd placed an official stamp on it. Then she directed a nervous Wilkes to the chair and snatched the paper. She extracted a key from the inside lock and locked Wilkes securely in his tawdry lair. As she fled down a flight of narrow, uneven stairs, she could hear the man's enraged shouts.

* * *

Justin moved away from the dank wall of his cell to avoid the droplets of moisture that formed on the stones. The floor was strewn with moldering straw that provided a haven for lice and other vermin.

His cell mates were a rough assortment of petty gamblers and cutpurses. None of them was willing to challenge the tall, grim-faced Texan, although ordinarily there was a crude initiation to establish a pecking order.

The indolent, unwashed men accepted him with surprising tolerance, giving him his pick of the worm-infested biscuits and brackish water that was brought at intervals during the day. Then they pressed him for stories of Texas, tales of Indian wars and the struggle against the Mexican army.

At nightfall the talk subsided, and Justin's thoughts returned to his predicament. Someone had betrayed his plan to Lord Aberdeen; that was the only explanation for his seizure.

It didn't matter now. What was important was getting the details of Aberdeen's plan to his superiors. Justin's request to send a message to Duff had been flatly, laughingly denied. The only hope was escape.

One by one, Justin's cell mates dropped off to sleep, curling against the damp chill beneath ragged blankets. Justin went to the heavy locked door. A brief examination told him he wouldn't be able to budge it. Then he went to the drainage grate in the middle of the cell. An unholy stench of sewage and rot arose from it, stinging his eyes. Grasping the iron grate, Justin pulled until his muscles quivered. At last, the rusting metal gave. But the hole, too dark to see into by the glimmer of light from the corridor outside, offered no promise. It was too narrow for even a child to fit through, and there was no telling where the drain led.

But the grate itself would be useful.

After what seemed an eternity, he heard the jingle of a key in the lock. He stood, flattening himself against the wall, and raised the heavy grate high.

The door creaked open and a figure stepped into the cell. Too late, Justin saw the lace of a petticoat and the fringe of a shawl. Unable to stop the downward momentum of the descending grate, he could only throw it aside.

But it wasn't far enough. The grate struck a glancing blow, and the woman crumpled to the floor.

Justin dropped to his knees. "Shiloh," he said, "Oh my God—"

"A fine way to thank the lady," grumbled the night warden, who had followed Shiloh to the cell. "She went to no little trouble to get you released."

The hastily summoned doctor rose from the bedside. "Your wife should come around shortly.

And you look as though you could use a rest. Get some sleep; she's resting quietly."

Justin stayed beside Shiloh until dawn peeped through the curtains. Finally, catching sight of his grimy, haggard face in the dressing table mirror, he went to clean up.

A few minutes later, a knock sounded at the door. Justin answered it, clad only in his trousers, thinking it was Duff. But Jessamine West sailed in instead. "So it's true," she said. "Shiloh really did manage to get you out of Newgate."

"I—she's been injured, Jessamine, and I'm tired as hell. Now, would you—"

"Injured! Don't tell me that awful Wilkes hurt her!"

"What does Wilkes have to do with this?"

Her lips drew together in a pout. "Oh dear, perhaps I've said too much."

"What's that supposed to mean?" Justin asked.

"Well, you know what Wilkes is like. But I'll leave it to Shiloh to tell you the details—if she's not too ashamed."

Justin felt himself growing taut with anger. "Jessamine, did you come here just to gloat, or do you have something else to say?"

"I only wanted to remind Shiloh about the promise she made my father. But I'll let her tell you about that, too."

As she swept out, Duff Green entered, garnering a stare of pure loathing from her.

"Nice girl," he said, extending his hand. "Welcome back. I was all over London trying to get a release order for you. Should've known Shiloh would beat me to it. How'd she manage it?"

Justin didn't want to think about that. "I haven't asked her yet. I knocked her on the head with a drainage grate when she came to my cell."

Duff shook his head. "I won't ask for an explanation of that; I'm sure it would take too long. Is she all right?"

"I think so."

"Good. Because we've got to get the hell out of England. There's a ship in Falmouth, the *Cutter's Way*, bound for the States. I'll have to miss that one; I've some business to do. But you and Shiloh had best be aboard it when it sails."

"We can be ready to leave in a few hours," Justin said. "Hire a good coach; I want Shiloh to be comfortable."

Duff nodded. Before he left, he asked, "Was it worth it, Justin?"

For the first time, Justin grinned. "Hell, yes," he said. "Wait till you hear."

As a pair of sleepy-eyed maids worked at packing their things, Justin sat beside Shiloh until she finally gratified him by opening alert, beautifully clear eyes.

He pressed a kiss on her forehead. "How are you feeling?"

"My head feels terrible," she admitted. "What happened?"

Justin squeezed her hand. "You caught me in the midst of attempting an escape. I figured the first person through that door would be a guard. I'm sorry, sweetheart. You don't know how sorry I am."

Shiloh was touched by his sincerity. For perhaps the hundredth time, she regretted her recent behavior toward him. "I'm the one who should apologize. I've been horrible to you about Jessamine. I know now what really happened that night. Can you forgive me?"

"I can forgive anything you do." Even Wilkes, he added silently, vowing that he'd try to forget Jessamine's sly insinuations. "Are you well enough to travel?"

This time she sat up and her head didn't swim. "Of course. Where are we going?"

"To Falmouth, on the Cornish coast. From there, on to Washington, in the District of Columbia."

Shiloh found the town of Washington, rising from the marshes around the Potomac, to be a uniquely interesting place. There was an indolent, somewhat disheveled air about it, an atmosphere of impermanence and unreality, because the town had just one reason for its existence: to house the government of the American people.

Those charged with the task seemed a group of overly serious, self-important men who loved to argue bombastically and air their grievances to any audience.

Her strolls with Justin through the city revealed an amazingly diverse population. There were foreign visitors and government officials, stern judges and pious church ladies clutching Bibles to their bosoms, saucy young belles, Indians, and Negroes. Shiloh found all of them fascinating, unaware that she, too, garnered her share of attention.

"It's that flame-red hair," Justin teased as a young urchin stopped playing at stickball to stare at her. "Or it might be those freckles on your nose."

He left her at their lodgings at Brown's Indian Queen, sometimes called the Wigwam. "You'll have to take dinner alone. I have my first meeting with Mr. Upshur at the State Department."

Shiloh froze, seized by a chill that had nothing to do with the sharp February air. She'd been able to put the nightmare of her last day in London behind her, but now it resurfaced. "Justin," she said, her whisper making little frozen puffs in the air between them. "You mustn't say anything about Judge West's activities in the Caribbean. I promised you wouldn't ruin him. You were in prison and I was desperate. The judge only agreed to help me when I made that promise."

His jaw twitched dangerously. "So you struck a bargain with the judge as well as Krieger Wilkes. Is there anything else I don't know about?" He gave her a last look of disgust and walked away.

A bleak February wind whipped up, scattering the scraps of an old broadside across the road. Shivering, Shiloh tore her eyes away from Justin's tall receding form and went into Brown's. Her appetite gone, she fled to the room they shared and flung herself onto the bed.

The bedding still held Justin's scent, mingling with her own. Punching the pillows, Shiloh cursed. She should have known that her contentment wouldn't last. Instead of being grateful to her for getting him out of prison, he was angry about the methods she'd used. Of course she would have preferred not to deal with West and Wilkes, but what choice did she have?

Wilkes. Shiloh frowned at the pillow. How had Justin known about that? No matter, she decided as she began flinging her things onto the bed. The sooner she got back to Texas, back to a life of her own, the better.

She was interrupted by a knock at the door. A young liveried black boy stood at attention. "Miz Justin McCord." He extended an envelope, clicked his heels, and left.

As she stared at the small engraved invitation, her eyes widened. She could hardly believe what she saw. It was issued by Captain Robert F. Stock-

ton, inviting them to a reception aboard the
Navy's newest steam warship, the *Princeton*.

Shiloh clasped the card to her bosom. President Tyler would be in attendance.

Suddenly, it didn't seem so important to flee
to Texas. Shiloh would wait a day, for not even
Justin's malice could stop her from pleading
Texas's cause to the president in person.

THIRTEEN

Justin's meeting lasted the entire night. He cat-napped in Upshur's office and arrived back at the Wigwam in the early morning chill. He found Shiloh in her robe, sitting at the dressing table while she brushed her hair. With a pang, he saw her narrow back stiffen when she heard him come in. That and the obstinate set of her jaw told him that she hadn't softened.

During a break in his meetings, Justin had spent a long time wandering along the riverside. His initial anger at Shiloh had dissipated. Anything she'd done had been to win his freedom.

"I was wrong, Shiloh." He stood behind her and watched her reflection in the mirror. "I shouldn't have gotten angry at you; I should thank you for getting me out of that scrape."

Still she said nothing. He saw her grip tighten around her hairbrush. Kneeling, Justin pulled her around to face him. "I had no business getting angry," he continued. "But hearing what you promised West, coupled with what you had to go through with Wilkes, just set me off. When I think of that bastard's hands on you—"

"What?" Shiloh broke her silence with loud disbelief. Amazingly, she started to laugh. "Is that what you think, Justin? That I shamed myself with Wilkes to buy your freedom? How could you think for a minute that I'd let that unwashed lout lay a hand on me?"

"Then what—"

"Oh, he tried. But I don't think he counted on my finding his pistol and turning it on him."

"I didn't know," he said.

"Why didn't you ask me? Better yet, why didn't you trust me? Never mind, Justin. Do you know about the reception today?"

He nodded. "Abel Upshur told me to expect an invitation." He placed an oblong velvet box in front of her.

She glanced up at him and then lifted the lid. An array of amethysts, shaped like teardrops, winked out from settings of black onyx.

Shiloh held up the necklace to admire it. Justin fastened it around her neck and enjoyed her pleasure as she put on the matching bracelet and earrings. "Thank you, Justin." Then, suddenly, her lips trembled and he realized that the sparkle in her eyes was put there by tears.

"What's wrong, Shiloh?"

"You're making it very hard for me to say this."

He felt himself grow tense. "What is it?"

"I'm going back to Texas as soon as it can be arranged."

"Damn it, Shiloh, I told you how sorry I am."

"It's not just that. It—it's everything. We simply

aren't compatible. There's no trust between us. I think it's best if we stay out of each other's way."

"The last time you said that, you ended up following me to London."

"I won't do anything like that again. I promise. I'll leave you alone."

At that moment, Justin knew he felt something for Shiloh, because his heart emptied out.

Heads turned to admire the striking young couple as they stepped aboard the *Princeton*. The steam warship was festooned with evergreens and ribbons for the tour up the Potomac. Every inch of wood and steel gleamed with polish. Glancing over at Justin, Shiloh saw none of the strain of their previous conversation on his handsome, smiling face. She hoped that her attempt to conceal her feelings was as successful.

Apparently it was, for when she was presented to President Tyler, the little Virginian complimented Justin on his lovely wife. And many others, including Secretary of State Upshur, were lavish in their admiration of Justin himself.

"Finest agent we've got down in Texas," Upshur proclaimed, lifting his glass. "Thanks to him, we'll have an annexation treaty by year's end. I'm not ashamed to admit it's been a dream of mine for many years. I'm just thankful that I'll live to see this nation made even greater by the addition of Texas."

"Hear, hear," murmured a few of his listeners,

though not too loudly, for the Texas issue was not universally popular.

Miss Julia Gardiner, who was the widowed president's eager companion, took Shiloh's arm and steered her toward a circle of ladies. "Are you enjoying your stay in Washington, dear?"

"Yes. This is my first visit. I'm a native Texan."

Shiloh would have preferred to tour the ship with the gentlemen, for she'd heard that the *Princeton* was the best new fighting ship in the world, but she followed the lady docilely. She made a concerted effort to keep track of names and faces, but there were so many that she had to be content with a great deal of smiling and nodding. She found Dolley Madison utterly delightful and readily answered a barrage of questions about the Texas frontier. She was sure that if she extolled her land's virtues well enough, Texas would win the ladies' favor. After a while, she escaped to the rail for a breath of fresh, cold air and to listen to the band of musicians who had come aboard at Alexandria. It was a flawlessly bright, chilly day, the sky a scintillating blue. Along the shore, tenuous masses of ice were breaking away, being pulled around and around by a lazy current as they drifted downstream.

Every so often, a sailor would yell out, cautioning the illustrious guests to open their mouths and cover their ears in anticipation of the ship's guns firing. Shiloh felt a huge concussion of air as one of the long guns shattered a distant ice floe, which Captain Robert Stockton claimed was three miles away. It was an awesome spectacle as the ice was shattered into a cloud of flurries.

"Amazing, isn't it?" murmured a cultured voice. Shiloh turned to see a striking woman of middle years, swathed in a fur cape, her silvering blond hair glinting with diamond pins. The woman smiled. "I'm Caroline McCord. Justin's mother."

Shiloh didn't know what to say. She considered embracing the woman, but Caroline's eyes had grown cold as they studied her.

"I think—Shiloh, is it?—that we had best get to know each other."

"Justin's here. Don't you want to see him?"

Caroline's nostrils flared. "I haven't made up my mind about that yet. Why don't the two of us talk? When did your family migrate to Texas?"

"Before I was born. My father was one of the earliest followers of Moses and Stephen Austin."

Caroline appeared to relax. "Ah, so he was part of a select group."

It was fast becoming obvious that Caroline McCord was groping for something respectable about the woman her son had married. Shiloh was not about to color the truth to appease the woman. "Actually, my father left Tennessee because he'd been convicted of drunken brawling. He didn't want to serve time and couldn't afford to pay for his freedom."

The older lady was genuinely flustered now.

"Oh, my. Well, I suppose gentlemen do tend to overdo—"

"Mrs. McCord, my father isn't a gentleman; he never was. I wish I could tell you that I come from a fine, wealthy family, but I can't. My father was born to a sod farmer in Ireland. He came here as a boy because his family couldn't afford to feed him. And my mother was born to a serving girl and, unfortunately, had no father to give her a name. She died when I was a child."

Caroline staggered back against the rail, her nostrils working in earnest now. She had gone quite pale.

"I don't mean to shock you," Shiloh said quickly. "But neither will I hide the truth about myself. I'm not ashamed of who I am. Now, don't you think it's time you said hello to your son?"

"Hello, son."

Justin turned from his inspection of the ship's great gun, called the Peacemaker. He was flooded by tidal waves of memories at the sound of his father's voice.

"How are you, sir?" he said, masking all emotion. But as they shook hands, something very warm passed between them and they embraced, briefly, awkwardly.

"By God, it's good to see you, lad," Angus said. "It's been too damned long."

Justin nodded. "That it has." There was still a strain between them, the remembered tension of harsh words and bitter arguments. But Justin could tell that the years had mellowed his father, just as they had tempered his own feelings.

"Your name is on everyone's lips today," said Angus.

Justin secretly wondered whether his father would have welcomed him back if he'd been a failure in Texas. But now was not the time to probe those feelings. The two men found a quiet corner belowdecks to have a cigar and a glass of champagne.

"How are things at the Willows?" Justin asked.

"The tobacco yield just gets better and better, in spite of the depletion problems most folks have had. Your mother has redecorated at least three times. Tell me about Texas, son."

Justin sipped his champagne. "Best thing that ever happened to me."

"Maybe so, but staying on at the Willows wouldn't have given you those scars." He indicated the crescent-shaped mark on Justin's cheekbone and the more recent one on his temple.

"I've had a few scrapes."

"Indians."

"Comanches, Mexicans . . ." He touched the small line on his temple. "And one hell of an ornery filly. I've got a horse ranch near Houston. It's not much of anything yet, but I mean to turn it into something big someday, when my work for the government is done."

"Any chance you'll come back to Virginia?"

"I have a new home now. Hell, I even got married."

"Married!" Angus roared, his rugged face alight with surprise and pleasure. "That's fine, lad. That's just fine. Tell me about her. You had every belle in Loudoun County at your feet, including, I might add, a perfectly charming young lady I myself selected for you. What sort of woman finally snared you?"

They met on the lower deck. Caroline McCord, ever mindful of propriety, kissed Justin lightly on both cheeks, although her eyes were bright with tears.

"What a man you've become, my son," she murmured, marveling at his great height and the breadth of his shoulders.

"I see you two have met." He took Shiloh's hand and drew her closer. "Shiloh, this is my father, Angus."

"How do you do, sir?" Shiloh found herself staring at an older replica of her husband.

"Justin told me you were something special," Angus said. "I'm inclined to agree." He turned to his wife. "I think this calls for a celebration." He signaled a steward, who was passing with a tray of sweet whiskey punch. Raising his cup, he said, "To all the McCords."

Shiloh looked from father to son. They both seemed so happy. Caroline spoke of neighbors

Shiloh had never heard of, and expounded on the merits of a certain family in particular.

"The Grangers bought an adjacent plantation. Do you remember young Conrad, Justin? He's at the university now. It was the greatest disappointment of his life that you didn't marry his sister Ivy."

Justin gave his mother a sharp look, which she ignored. "And speaking of Ivy, she never married. It broke her heart when you left. She went to Paris to study art."

Caroline addressed Shiloh. "Have you ever been to Paris, dear? No, of course you haven't. I imagine your farm life keeps you quite busy. But a trip abroad is *de rigueur* for every young lady of quality. Dear Ivy is *so* accomplished. Why, even when she and Justin were courting—"

"That's enough, Mother," Justin snapped.

"No, Justin," Shiloh interjected. "Let her finish."

Only the slight flaring of nostrils betrayed Caroline's agitation. "Ivy Granger was perfect for Justin. She adored him, saw to his every need. *She* was of his class. As Justin's mother, I want to know that he has married wisely, and not just as an act of defiance against us."

"You're making everyone most uncomfortable, Caroline," said the older man. "Let's talk of something else."

"Excuse me," Shiloh said, tossing her head. "I'm sure you all have a lot of reminiscing to do."

* * *

"What the hell do you think you're doing, Mother?" Justin asked, his voice deadly quiet.

She opened her fan and flipped it in front of her face. "Such language!" she scolded. "But I'll forgive you, son. I'm sure you've been under a lot of strain lately. It can't be easy living with a woman like that." She gave him a sorrowful look. "How could you, Justin? How could you marry that impudent little nobody—"

"You will apologize to Shiloh," he commanded.

Caroline's carefully pruned eyebrows shot up. "I shall do no such thing."

"Then we have nothing more to say to each other." He extended his hand to his father. "It was good to see you again. I'll write." He turned to stride away.

"Justin, wait!" Caroline called. For the first time, he saw his mother's haughty mask fall away, saw the vulnerable, sad woman beneath. "I wanted so much for you, Justin," she whispered. "Perhaps that was where I went wrong. I tried to put my own ambitions before yours." Caroline hung her head. A strand of hair fell down along her cheek. "When I learned about Shiloh, it was the final realization that you were your own person."

Stunned by these revelations, Justin handed his mother a handkerchief and waited while she daubed at her face. "In Shiloh, you've found the one woman who can take my place. You love her deeply, and that is why I attacked her."

Justin tensed. It was the first time anyone had given a name to what he felt for Shiloh. He gathered his weeping mother against him. "There is room in my heart for both of you."

Although the *Princeton*'s master gunner was taking great pains to explain the power of the Peacemaker to his august audience, few were listening. The men clustered around the great cannon had got into a political discussion.

"It's a Southern plot, I tell you," said Peter Shane, a congressman from New England. "They only want Texas to enter their immoral fold as yet another slave state. It's a well-known fact that Texans favor the institution."

"I beg your pardon, Mr. Shane," Shiloh said, "but pray, where do you get your 'facts'?"

"Young lady, this discussion is between knowledgeable men."

"Answer the lady, Shane," said Abel Upshur.

"He doesn't need to," Shiloh replied. "I wouldn't want him to make more of a jackass out of himself than he already has."

"The question of slavery overshadows all other considerations," Shane maintained. "But of course, that is not an issue with you, is it, Mrs. McCord? Why don't you tell these gentlemen just how many slaves you own."

Spots of furious color appeared on her cheeks. "Mr. Shane, I would no more own a slave than you would." Then, remembering something she'd read in a Washington paper, she added, "But perhaps that is not quite true. In your state you work children in cloth-making factories until they drop from exhaustion in front of their looms."

She saw Mr. Thomas Gilmer, the secretary of the Navy, lean over to Upshur and quip, "If this is a Texas woman, what are the men like?"

Shiloh saw Justin and his parents some yards away, at the stern. From their faces, she could tell they'd heard the argument. Justin raised his glass in tribute. His father had a look of amused devilment in his eyes. Although Shiloh expected righteous indignation from Caroline, she was amazed to see a softness in the lady's look.

With a great flourish, the master gunner gave the order and the cannon was loaded, powder and sulphur tamped in place.

"Stand ready to fire!"

"Ready, sir!"

"Fire!"

Sparks flew, and the burn of sulphur filled the deck.

Justin was still thinking about what his mother had said. Love . . . was it possible? As he looked down at Shiloh, her face flushed and expectant as she clasped her hands, something touched him. Her spirit shone like a beacon.

Suddenly, his view was blocked by billows of acrid smoke. A blinding explosion followed, splintering wood and metal, filling the deck with flames.

Justin tore across the planks, instantly aware that the cannon had misfired. He waded through utter chaos to get to Shiloh. Men were screaming, cursing, begging for mercy as sailors rushed to douse the fire. A man ran past, his back in flames.

"The president!" someone shouted. "Where is the president?"

Through thick, eye-stinging smoke, Justin stepped around unspeakable carnage. Bodies lay riddled with debris, some torn and burned beyond recognition. Justin saw Abel Upshur, his friend, his mentor, left with only half his skull, the rest of it blown to pieces. He saw Gilmer's body, face down, a gaping, bloody hole in his back. And beneath, a slim wrist, the onyx-and-amethyst bracelet gleaming.

A cry of anguish tore from his throat as he heaved aside the lifeless body of Thomas Gilmer, who apparently had thrown himself in front of her.

Shiloh's face had been burned and cut by debris. There were several places where fire and hot metal had seared through her gown, and a bloody stain, widening like a macabre blossom, on her skirt.

Heart hammering, Justin gathered up the limp form and bore her away, past a dazed and injured Captain Stockton. The thunderstruck onlookers who had come up from below, including the shaken president, cleared a path for him to the stern.

As the *Princeton* steamed back to Alexandria, from where the injured would be ferried to the hospital in Washington, agonized screams rose above the churn and hiss of the great engines. But Shiloh lay still.

The ship's surgeon worked feverishly, applying bandages and tourniquets. At Angus's insistence, he hastened to Shiloh's side. The gash was wide and long, a piece of metal having ripped through the flesh of Shiloh's leg.

"It'll have to be sewn," the doctor mumbled, "or she'll bleed to death." He thrust a pile of clean linens into Justin's hands. "Here. Stanch the flow as best you can. I'll be around as soon as I can."

"Do it now," Justin snapped.

"I've got to attend to the worst cases first, sir. Perhaps you can find someone else to cleanse and close the wound."

Justin's mother flung aside her elegant cape. "I'll do it."

Angus commandeered a cart of medical supplies as Caroline plucked off her gloves and rolled up the sleeves of her gown. She placed several thicknesses of toweling beneath Shiloh's leg and dipped a bandage into a basin of water. As she daubed gingerly at the torn flesh, she removed several tiny splinters from the wound.

Shiloh moaned again and began to thrash.

"Hold her still, Justin," Caroline said. "That bottle there—it's chloroform."

He held a cloth soaked with the stuff above Shiloh's nose until her lids fluttered shut and she lay still.

There was none of the glittering socialite in Caroline McCord as she began to work in earnest. Justin was confident of her skills; as the mistress of a huge plantation, she'd done more than her share of doctoring, from delivering babies to tending field hands who had been injured. She threaded a small curved needle and began closing the flesh. With every stitch Justin winced, watching Shiloh closely to assure himself that she remained unconscious. The ooze of blood was slowing as a result of his pressing on the artery above the wound, and by the time Caroline was finished, it stopped. The jagged but neatly sewn cut stood out like an ugly black line on the pale perfection of Shiloh's thigh.

Caroline, who had worked steadily and with great concentration and precision, stood up slowly and collapsed against her husband.

"Well done, my dear," he said. "What's this? You're shaking."

Caroline gave Justin an agonized look. "I'm so sorry," she whispered. "So very sorry."

He frowned. "I'm sure you did an excellent job," he assured her.

Tears squeezed from her eyes. "No, it's not that. I just feel so responsible for this. Shiloh never would have gone to the gun deck if I hadn't been so monstrous to her." She crossed to Justin and took his hand. "You must let me make it up to her. Let me bring her to the Willows. I'll tend her myself."

A man approached. "Mrs. McCord?"

She raised her tear-stained face. "Yes?"

"I wonder, could you help me? My brother was injured in the explosion."

Caroline drew herself up. "Of course. Show me to him."

Silence hung like a pall over the shocked passengers. President Tyler moved solicitously among the wounded and the grieving friends of the dead, offering comfort. Women wept quietly and the engines hissed on, until finally the warship, with twenty feet of its bulwark torn away, bumped and jostled its way home.

FOURTEEN

Willow trees, the hallmark of the McCord plantation, were in evidence everywhere, dipping their slender branches into the river, standing protectively above a stone springhouse, bending over a small, high meadow. Evergreen holly bushes surrounded a white gazebo and grew along paths to dozens of neat, regular outbuildings. In the distance were the fields, brown corduroy-plowed earth stretching for what seemed like miles.

At the center of it all was the house. Shiloh had known to expect some measure of wealth from the McCords, but nothing could have prepared her for what she saw.

White columns rose majestically in front of a long, railed verandah. Dozens of windows, covering three stories, looked out over the lawn. The gabled roof made the single structure look endless, like a many-faceted jewel. Even in winter, devoid of the color of flowers, the house sat in stately serenity.

Both Angus and Caroline were watching

Shiloh expectantly. Noticing them, she smiled. "You have a lovely home."

"You're welcome here," Caroline said. "This is your home, as well."

Shiloh looked again at the plantation house and wondered if she could ever call such a place her home.

Justin insisted on carrying her, even when she protested that surely she should be allowed to walk on dry land. "I'm not about to let you undo some of my mother's best stitchery."

"I'll take care," she said, not at all reluctant to remain safe in his arms.

The house servants had lined up in the grand entry to welcome the family. They stood, smiling but decorous, obviously trying to hide their amazement at seeing Justin again.

But he would have none of it. Setting Shiloh gently on the black-and-white marble floor, he said, "Nine years, and this is the welcome I get?" He opened his arms to the slender black woman at the head of the line. "Miranda, my love, you're still a beauty, and I'll bet you've still got the sharpest tongue in Loudoun County!"

They embraced and were quickly joined by the others. There was a great deal of laughter, dozens of questions, sincere embraces.

And then Justin presented Shiloh to the staff. "Ladies and gentlemen," he said grandly, "my wife, Shiloh, from Texas."

Caroline insisted that she was to go to bed at once, and showed her up a long, wide staircase.

"Justin's room is just as he left it," she explained on the way up, past a series of portraits of stern-faced McCord men and women. At the top, she hesitated, staring in wonderment at the last painting.

There was no mistaking Caroline, who had been tall and aristocratic even in her youth. Posing before a blooming garden graced by willow trees, she stood with her hands upon the shoulders of a young boy.

Justin. Shiloh didn't know why she was surprised by his appearance, but she was. A face that was now hard and sculpted had once been sweetly rounded. The piercing eyes of steel had been, in younger years, soft, almost dreamy. The one feature that hadn't changed was Justin's hair. The artist had caught it in a moment when the breeze had lifted silken strands that gleamed in the muted light. It looked so real that Shiloh had the urge to stroke it, to put the strands back in place.

"That's a great favorite of mine," Caroline said, noticing Shiloh's interest. "Justin was eight at the time it was done. You can see why I was so possessive of him." They went down a long paneled hallway and stepped into a bright room.

Again Shiloh was transfixed by the remnants of Justin's past. The wide alcove bed where he'd slept in his youth, had perhaps lain dreaming about the man he would become. The double-doored clerk's desk where perhaps he'd labored with his tutor over his studies. A shelf of books, from schoolboy's primers to agrarian manuals. And on a small seat at the recessed window sat a frayed and faded skin horse, missing one of its button eyes.

Caroline mistook Shiloh's silence as she moved about the room, touching a wooden chest, gazing out the window at a spectacular view of the lawn and river.

"There are other guest rooms, if you'd prefer," Caroline suggested.

"Oh no," Shiloh said quickly. "This will be quite comfortable."

Shiloh seated herself at the window ledge, watching the play of evening light across the river's slow-moving water. A movement off to the side caught her eye. It was Angus and Justin, galloping up the lane on two of the finest-looking horses she'd ever seen. Their black flanks gleamed in the amber light, their hooves thudding on the packed-earth track.

There was something about the two men that touched a tender note in her heart, a deep camaraderie that, even from a distance, she could see. They were so alike, they of the flashing grins and dimpled cheeks, the careless grace with which they moved. Shiloh felt a wave of satisfaction at their reconciliation. As they slowed their horses and came up the curving drive, she couldn't help thinking of her own father.

After an absence of many years, Justin and Angus were closer than she and Nate had ever been. She tried to swallow the lump that rose in her throat, a sharp pain born of all the years of unloved and unloving emptiness she'd shared with her father.

Perhaps if she'd been a better daughter to him, he would have shown her some affection. *Affection.* It was something Shiloh hadn't even known she craved until she had experienced it with Justin.

He'd taught her so much, so many painful lessons. It was no wonder she fought him; every time they got close, she learned more about her own inadequacies. Yet she couldn't hate Justin for what he showed her.

In the drive below, he dismounted and, smiling, tossed the reins to a waiting groom. As Angus did likewise, Justin looked up and saw her in the window. His grin widened as he waved. Shiloh raised her hand to the cold windowpane.

As February slid into March, Shiloh spent her days at the Willows couched in luxury. The passage of time was marked by lazy hours of bed rest, with a book from Angus's vast library in hand.

Bethany's daily visits were something Shiloh looked forward to. The talented healer was full of stories and earthy good humor, always ready with her big-toothed smile.

The day came when Bethany announced the leg wound clean and free of infection. "The worst is over, missy. I was looking for the bad fluids, but they never came."

"You and Caroline have taken such good care of me."

Bethany took out a tiny pair of scissors and removed the black stitches one by one. Shiloh gripped the bolster she was resting against and gritted her teeth.

"Not so different from your husband, are you, missy?" said Bethany without looking up.

"What do you mean."

"Sitting there, grinding your teeth, when you really want to cuss me to high heaven. Mr. Justin was the same way. He wasn't but twelve years old when he broke his arm falling out of a tree. Didn't make a sound as I was setting the dadblamed thing, squeezed his eyes shut so tight that nothing could come out."

"I'm sure this doesn't compare to having a broken arm set."

"He was a good boy," Bethany reminisced, cleansing the cut. "Not a mean streak in him, but jackass-stubborn and so dadblamed honest he'd put a preacher to shame. Boy was just fourteen when he knocked out the overseer for whipping a field hand. I guess that's why he went to fight the Mexicans down in Texas."

He appeared just as Bethany finished her visit. "You're amazing," he said, sitting on the edge of the bed. "You're mending so fast. But I guess that shouldn't surprise me. You're too damned bullheaded to sit still for long."

"This is all so foreign to me," Shiloh said,

"being waited on hand and foot. I haven't lifted a finger since I arrived at the Willows."

Justin sat forward, searching her eyes. "Do you like it here, Shiloh?"

"I—It's lovely. But I feel so useless."

Again he gave her that heart-melting smile. "Idle, maybe, but not useless."

Shiloh found herself wishing, as she had many times lately, that he would pull her into that familiar rough embrace, the one that excited her beyond measure and made her feel wanted and whole. But Justin had been unusually tender with her, his infrequent touches light, almost impersonal. Even when he slept beside her at night, she was aware of a certain restraint.

"What are you thinking?" he asked gently.

"I . . ." A dozen questions popped into her mind, but Shiloh wasn't ready to hear the answers. "I was just thinking I'd like to go out for a walk."

There was a narrow, winding path along the river, where the tight-budded trees bent over in a natural arch. Squirrels trilled and scolded as Justin and Shiloh strolled beneath, savoring the sharp air and sensing, only faintly, the promise of the coming spring. A duck shot up from the reeds at the water's edge, its wings bearing it westward, toward the setting sun.

"Are you glad to be home, Justin?" Shiloh asked, watching the duck's graceful flight.

"This place was my whole world once upon a time."

"Everything is so perfect here, so well ordered and neat. No flooding bayous or Indian raids, no foreigners peddling their influence."

"We're a long way from all that, Shiloh."

They walked on in silence for a while. Justin showed her a tiny, bubbling spring and a pool so clear that the rounded, colorful pebbles were visible in sharp focus. They doubled back past a glade of alders and took a higher path back to the house.

Caroline hurried in from the front parlor to meet them. "We've had an invitation," she said. "The Fairfaxes are hosting a hunt, complete with breakfast and races later."

Justin frowned. "I don't know, Mother. I'm not sure I want everybody gawking at Shiloh all day."

"Don't be silly," Shiloh chided. "Of course people will gawk. After all, I'm your new wife from Texas."

An early morning frost clung to the meadow grasses and hedgerows along the river road. Justin took Shiloh's hand and tucked it into the crook of his elbow as the carriage bounced northward to the Fairfax plantation.

She wore a high-necked blouse with her riding habit, which concealed the still-visible scars on her neck, shoulders, and arms.

To the casual eye, she looked very delicate, but

the dainty exterior concealed a will of pure steel. A lesser woman would be eaten alive by the honey-voiced planters' wives today, but Justin had no such fears for Shiloh.

A half-dozen coaches were already in the circular drive in front of the house. As Justin handed Shiloh down, he caught a waft of her honeysuckle scent. He'd dispatched a rider all the way to Alexandria for that soap, although Shiloh wasn't aware of it. She was a hard woman to buy gifts for, appreciative of jewels and ornaments and clothes, but not sentimental about them. The soap was the only thing Justin knew that she craved.

The hunt was being organized around the back of the house. Hounds bayed and strained at their leashes and were subdued by a pair of heavy-handed slaves. Justin didn't care much for the useless sport but didn't mind a lively morning ride.

Shiloh looked around at all the activity. "You'd think an army was being mustered, all for the sake of pursuing a little fox."

Like a flock of chattering birds, the company descended on them, full of hearty greetings and curious stares. Justin's hand was shaken, his back slapped, his cheek kissed by several women. He tried to keep Shiloh at his side, but she was swept away by the women, already speaking animatedly to a rapt audience.

The hunt began with much fanfare, the blowing of horns, the singing of "John Peel."

* * *

It was like London all over again. Insulated on their elegant plantations from the outside world, the ladies begged for tales of wild Indians, Mexican desperadoes, the rough frontier life of Texas. Shiloh complied, hoping to temper the women's view of her country without detracting from the decided mystique of it. As she spoke of the wild land, trying to find words to describe the dusty plains, the endless prairies, the wide starry sky at night, she was amazed at the longing she heard in her own voice. It had been nearly five months since she'd left the shores of Texas. For all its ruggedness and discomfort, she found herself wishing for the buzzing of cicadas, the sight of a buffalo herd grazing amid bluebonnets in the hill country.

"Imagine," said a girl called Helen, clutching her bodice with exaggerated drama, "living on the very fringe of the civilized world. You must be constantly fearful."

"I'm usually too busy to worry about things I can't do anything about."

"Besides," said another, the Fairfax girl called Virginia, "Shiloh is Justin's wife. What better protection could she ask for?"

Shiloh had taken an immediate dislike to the raven-haired beauty. Just before they were introduced, Virginia had been berating a houseboy, twisting his ear until the lad cried out.

"I don't need a protector; I never have."

Virginia swept her eyes over Shiloh. "I don't guess you would," she said smoothly. "But tell me, my dear, how *did* you come to marry Justin?" She directed a scathing glance at pretty, shy little Ivy Granger. "Lord knows, a number of us tried to snare him."

"If I told you how we wed, you'd never believe me. We were introduced—sort of—by a judge. Soon after, it was apparent that marriage was inevitable." She allowed her listeners to draw whatever titillating conclusions they would from that, and deftly turned the subject.

"These pumpkin cakes are wonderful, Mrs. Fairfax. You must tell me how they are made." She was, of course, a complete stranger to kitchens and cooking, but she listened carefully and let the attention ebb away from herself.

Some time later, the hunters returned on winded, steaming mounts. They had not even a small field mouse to show for all their efforts, but they were in high spirits nonetheless. Coffee laced with brandy was served, and the company sat down to the lavish hunt breakfast.

The meal was a delicious profusion of local specialties. Tender biscuits slathered with fresh white butter, thick slabs of cured ham, mountains of fluffy eggs, and trays of sweets graced every table and were consumed with ravenous good cheer.

Justin and Shiloh were seated at an oval table with an elderly couple, the Boyds, a timid young solicitor called Hamilton Pruitt, Virginia Fairfax

Holmes and her stodgy-looking husband, Emory, and the quiet Ivy Granger. Shiloh guessed that it was no accident that Ivy was included in the group. Virginia tried her best to dredge up old memories.

"It was that ball in Richmond. Surely you remember it, Ivy, dear. You were so afraid that Justin wouldn't ask you to dance, and then when he did, you ran off with a sudden fit of the vapors!"

Ivy blushed down at her plate, and Shiloh directed a look of pure venom at Virginia. Then, pointedly, she turned to Mr. Boyd and asked him about his fine yacht, which was moored down at the docks. His long-winded explanation of the craft's virtues dispelled the tension Virginia had tried to create. Under the table, Shiloh felt Justin's knee press against her. When Mr. Boyd had exhausted the subject of boating, she asked Ivy about fashion, complimenting her on the lovely, understated style of her pink dress. By the time the meal ended, the small group was relaxed. Even the fearful Pruitt did his share of talking and showed unmistakable interest in Ivy.

As the gentlemen went to retire for a while with their pipes and cigars, Justin ran his hand across Shiloh's shoulder. "Well done," he murmured. "You left Virginia flat on her face. But I think she's gone to the powder room to sharpen her claws."

Shiloh moved away. "I'm glad I haven't

shamed you, Justin. But remember, we've the rest of the day ahead of us."

There was a long period of lazy rest after breakfast, the men at their smoking and the ladies discussing needlework in the morning room. Shiloh grew restless and bored and was more than happy to don her cloak and follow the company outside for the races.

A pavilion had been set up and a track marked off in a field. The betting was lively, and Shiloh quickly surmised that Justin, on his excellent midnight stallion, was the clear favorite. No one was surprised when the expertly handled horse won by a length and a half.

"Do the Texans favor racing?" Ivy asked, watching as Justin claimed his prize, a silver cup overflowing with champagne.

Shiloh nodded. "Most holidays are celebrated with riding. There are a lot of stunts and rough games on horseback. The Mexicans have one in which the riders try to capture a greased rooster."

"How positively barbaric," said Virginia. "And silly."

"No sillier than chasing all morning after a single small fox."

Virginia tossed her raven head. "That is a time-honored sport. A sport of kings and nobles."

There was more eating and drinking afterward, and then a shooting match. Markers were set up at various distances, and shot at with dueling pistols. The wagering became more outlandish as more champagne was imbibed.

Finally Malcolm Boyd, a son of Shiloh's breakfast partner, declared that he would destroy six champagne bottles in a row, and defied anyone to dispatch the targets more quickly.

"I'll take you up on your challenge, Mr. Boyd," Shiloh said.

"Ah, our little guest from Texas. Will your husband be your champion?"

"I'll do my own shooting." A murmur rippled through the crowd, and then more wagering started up. The odds were lopsided, favoring Malcolm heavily. Six more bottles were set up on the fence.

Malcolm steadied his two pistols and watched while Shiloh sent the groom to fetch hers.

"What the devil is that?" he demanded, staring.

Shiloh lifted the heavy pistol, loading it as she spoke. "It's a Walker Colt," she explained. "Very new. I believe my husband brought it along to show you gentlemen. I hope he'll forgive me for upstaging him."

Justin leaned indolently against the back of a chair. Shiloh had almost hoped he'd be angry, but he gave her a wink of encouragement.

"This chamber allows for six shots," she continued. "Useful for fighting Indians on horseback, I'm told."

"Just a minute, now," Malcolm began, but a barrage of catcalls silenced his protests.

"Let the lady shoot!" "You gave the challenge, Boyd!" "Get on with it."

Even before Malcolm got off his second shot, Shiloh had laid waste to all six of her targets.

When the Virginians had a celebration, Shiloh learned, they squeezed every bit of amusement they could out of the day. After the shooting there was a light buffet and then an enforced rest period before the evening's festivities.

The ladies retired to a dim guest room where cots and trundle beds had been set up. Shiloh wasn't at all sleepy, but she allowed a maid to help her undress to her shift and reclined on a bed next to Ivy.

The girl was staring openmouthed at the scars on her shoulders and arms. "Oh, Shiloh . . . is that from the *Princeton?*"

"I guess I found myself in the wrong place at the wrong time."

Virginia sniffed, arranging herself on a pillow. "From what I heard, your whole ordeal could have been avoided. Mrs. Benton, who was at the reception, said you behaved outrageously, joining a gentlemen's discussion about politics."

Shiloh gave her a cool stare. "The discussion was about Texas, my home. I wasn't about to stand by and listen to lies about it."

"I don't know why everyone's so keen on Texas, anyway. Who needs a great wilderness overrun by savages and Mexicans?"

Suddenly, Ivy spoke. "I'd be proud to have Shiloh as a fellow citizen."

Virginia gave them both a scathing look and turned her back, pulling the covers up. Shiloh took Ivy's hand and squeezed it, surprised and pleased with her unlikely ally.

"I'm so happy that Justin found you," Ivy confessed in a whisper. "I was always a little afraid of him. He was so intense, so driven. I was relieved—for both of us—when he struck out for Texas. You and Justin have something very rare."

"Rare . . ." Shiloh said wryly. "It is that. But I can't help but wonder if it's right."

The upper veranda offered a spectacular view of the Willows, now starting to bloom with the coming spring. Crocuses were in full blossom, hundreds of small purple and golden heads bursting through rich brown soil. A waft of lilac scent rose as Shiloh turned the page of the newspaper she was reading.

She heard hoofbeats and looked up, spying Justin and Angus as they rode in from the fields, where the spring planting was beginning. Not for the first time, she was struck by how effortlessly Justin had slid back into the role of gentleman planter, fitting in perfectly with his well-bred peers.

She shouldn't have been surprised. It was the life he was born to, steeped in long tradition. According to what Angus had told her, the Willows had been founded by a Scottish adventurer four generations before. It was only natural that Justin would follow in his ancestors' footsteps.

More and more, Shiloh was beginning to think that Justin's nine-year odyssey to Texas had purged him of his restlessness, and now he was ready to settle down. Here, where he belonged and fit in. No mention had been made of returning to Houston.

A maid appeared with a cup of mint tea and a silver tray of biscuits. Shiloh murmured her thanks and sipped the tea. The lazy luxury in which she lived was seductive, but still she wasn't completely comfortable being waited on by slaves, or having nothing better to do than while away the hours.

She glanced down at the paper and an article caught her eye. "Letter from Texas" was the title of the piece. Shiloh savored every phrase praising the stark beauty of the land, the tenacious, hardworking settlers, the untold thousands of fertile, flower-painted acres.

An intense wave of longing swept over her. Texas, for all its unrelenting heat and dust and wildness, was the only place she could truly call home. She was but a visitor at the Willows. The sense of belonging that she lacked created a great void in her life, a sadness she was finding harder and harder to conceal.

She had to tell Justin, but how? How could she explain her burning need to be back in Texas, away from this plantation splendor? Was there a way to explain to him that this life wasn't for her?

She bit her lip. There was only one solution. She had to go back to Texas alone. She couldn't bear to ask him to come with her, knowing that he'd long for the Willows every day. She didn't want to be responsible for his unhappiness.

Justin's mind strayed from the discussion with his father and the overseer, who were talking of the spring planting as if it were a matter of life and death. At first, he'd enjoyed working along-side his father. They were equals now not adversaries, and their feelings ran deep.

But the gratification Justin found in this new relationship with his parents didn't extend itself to other things. He couldn't stop thinking about Texas. With Upshur's untimely death and the Whigs pushing against annexation, statehood was no longer a foregone conclusion. There was still much to be done, and Justin wanted to be part of it.

In his mind, he contrasted the Willows with his own property, Post Oaks. While the plantation shone like a polished gem, the ranch was as rough as an uncut diamond, but just as valuable, waiting to be carved into its potential. Justin wanted his hand to be the one that did it, because although the Willows was the home of his birth, Post Oaks was the home of his heart.

His eyes scanned the upper veranda, where Shiloh sat, reading and sipping tea as she warmed herself in a shaft of golden afternoon sun. By now he knew that the stirring he felt each time he saw her was love, as pure and light and glorious as the sun itself. He also knew that was why he had been holding himself back from her. Justin had never been afraid of anything until now.

He wondered how long he could sustain the facade of contentment for her sake. Although Texas called to him, he could see it was the opposite for Shiloh. Her life at the Willows was effortless, and she deserved every last bit of comfort she got. Was it fair to ask her to go back to Texas with him, to a harsh life and an uncertain future? Or should he stay here for her and let her live as the lady she was?

Justin was stirred from his musings by a sudden silence. The overseer had left, and Angus was looking at him, a question in his eyes. Then he followed Justin's gaze to the upper veranda. "She's settled down here at the Willows like she was born to this life."

Justin nodded.

"But you haven't, have you, son?"

"Am I that transparent?"

Angus smiled. "All the signs I saw years ago are coming back. Something down in Texas must've gotten into your blood."

"But I don't want to disappoint Shiloh. No woman in her right mind would give all this up for the rough frontier."

"Is that the only thing you're worried about, son?" When Justin didn't answer, Angus said,

"Damn it, boy, don't you think I haven't noticed how you've been treating her? You've been walking on eggshells for weeks. She's not some fragile butterfly, so easily crushed. And she's not a mind reader, either."

Angus put a hand on Justin's shoulder. "Go to her, son. Tell her what's in your heart."

FIFTEEN

Shiloh would never forget the view of the placid river slipping by as she and Justin sat together that evening in the garden gazebo. The scent of new growth was in the air, the call of the returning birds celebrating spring's arrival. All was soft and new, gilt-edged by the setting sun, unspeakably lovely. The setting contrasted sharply with the feeling in her heart as she contemplated what she had to say.

"I'm glad you asked me out here," she began. "It seems like a long time since we really talked."

"Too long," said Justin. "Your accident scared me so damned bad that I didn't want to upset you."

"What could you possibly say that would upset me?"

"Used to be, a word or two got your dander up."

She smiled a little, remembering all the bitter clashes and heated arguments. The smile faded when Justin suddenly captured her hands in his. "Shiloh, I have something to tell you. Something that's been on my mind for a long time. I should have said it a long time ago, but I kept fighting it."

Dread curled in her stomach. "I, too, have something to say." She ran her fingers over his hand, choosing her words. "The Willows is a beautiful place, and I couldn't be happier for you and your parents. They've been wonderful, like a real family to me. And I want to thank you, too." She looked up into his questioning eyes. "You've taken me so many places, shown me so many things. But I don't belong here, Justin. I want to go home to Texas. Of course," she added quickly, plunging on, "I wouldn't ask you to come with me, not after you've found your way home after such a long time. I'd like to leave as soon as it can be arranged."

He sat so long in brooding silence that she grew nervous. "Justin," she said at last, "I'm sorry. I know you wanted me to be happy here, but I can't."

"And so you will, since that's what you want."

She breathed a sigh of relief. Yet there was no happiness, only a leaden feeling in the pit of her stomach. "Thank you," she said.

Justin regarded her intently, tasting bitter irony. What he'd planned to say was that he loved her, that he wanted to take her back to Texas. Had she protested leaving, he would have agreed to stay on at the Willows, just to please her.

But none of that mattered now. Like a fool, he'd allowed himself to love this woman, to open himself up to the hurt that only she had the power to impart.

"You won't be going to Texas alone. I'm taking you there."

"Please, you don't have to do that."

"Do you really think I spent the last decade fighting for Texas just so I could come back here and farm tobacco for the rest of my days?"

"You *want* to go back to Texas?"

"Hell, yes, I want to go back. I just had a letter from Calhoun, the new secretary of state in Washington. He wants me down there again."

"So you want to go because of your work, and the ranch." Wild hope leaped in her heart. "Justin, are those your only reasons?"

He looked at her with eyes hard as granite. "What other reason would there be?"

Shiloh knew, from the chill in the bed and the absence of a certain unique scent, that Justin hadn't slept with her that night. She'd spent the evening packing and retired alone, tossing restlessly without the protective circle of his arms. She went to the dressing room and poured water into the basin, shaking her head. She didn't understand why he was so angry. It seemed they both wanted to go back to Texas and make their home there. So why did he seem so bitter toward her?

She looked down and saw their things being loaded into the sailboat. She barely touched the excellent breakfast that had been sent, and hurried down to say good-bye to Justin's parents.

They were already on the porch, waiting for her. Caroline turned a tear-dampened face to her, and the two women embraced. "I can't say I'm surprised," Caroline said. "I think I knew, deep down, that the two of you had a different road to travel."

Shiloh nodded, a lump in her throat. "You've been lovely to me. I've never really had a family before."

Caroline stroked her cheek. "Make one of your own, dear, down in Texas. I was blessed with only one child, but even that one made my life so full. You and Justin have so much to give."

Angus brushed his lips across her forehead. Then, flinging decorum aside, the big man gathered her against him in a great bear hug. "You're quite a girl, Shiloh. A man would be a fool not to follow you to the ends of the earth."

She held fast to Angus, feeling more fatherly affection from him than Nate had ever shown her.

Her last impression of the Willows was poignantly sweet. As the sails filled and drew the boat downriver, Angus and Caroline stood before the grand house, amid all the spring color, their hands raised in farewell.

Post Oaks had fared well over the months of their absence. An able manager, Wylie Stokes had augmented the herd with more mares and fenced a bigger range. With obvious pride, he told Justin how well the newly broken horses had done at auction, how cheaply he'd bought a number of new wild horses from the valley.

"You've done a wonderful job," Shiloh said, her eyes devouring the longed-for sea of grass and the herd in the distance.

"I hope you paid yourself well," Justin added. "If not, you've got a bonus coming."

Wylie colored slightly and his grin widened. "Matter of fact, Justin, I did draw a little extra pay. Needed to. Done got myself hitched, and there's a little one on the way."

Justin clapped him on the back. "Why, you slippery old horse thief. So your bachelor days are over."

"Come on," Wylie said, so full of pride he seemed about to burst. "I want you to meet her."

They crossed the stable yard to the bunkhouse. That building, once a sorry little clapboard structure, had been transformed into a neat white-washed cottage, complete with picket fence and rows of sunny marigolds in the front.

"The hands have been sleeping up over the stables," Wylie explained. "I told them they didn't have to, but they insisted. Besides, Prairie Flower feeds them better than they could ever do for themselves." He leaped to the door and called inside, "Honey? Come on out. There's some folks I want you to meet."

Shiloh staggered back against Justin; his hand steadied her.

"This here's Isabella," Wylie said.

She was as beautiful as ever, even with swelling belly and ponderous breasts. Her moist red mouth curved into a smile as she extended her hand, first to Shiloh and then to Justin.

"Welcome to Post Oaks," Shiloh said.

"And welcome back to you, Shiloh," said Isabella in her husky voice. "Please, you must excuse me. I cannot take the strong sun." She drifted back into the house.

Justin congratulated Wylie again, though not as heartily as before. As they walked up to the main house, his jaw ticked in irritation.

"What's *she* doing here?" Shiloh asked.

"I've got a few ideas. But let's worry about that later."

Ina rushed out to greet them, hugging them both together, not noticing how they stiffened at each other's nearness. "Shame on you for leaving us so long," she scolded happily. "I hope you are home to stay." Ina and Shiloh went to the kitchen to see Prairie Flower. The Indian woman set to preparing an elaborate homecoming supper. She chased Shiloh and Ina out onto the back porch, to sit in the shade and go over all that had happened in the months of separation.

"It was many weeks before we realized you were missing," Ina said. "Your father asked after you, so I decided to visit you at your aunt's. Imagine what an awkward moment that was."

"I really was planning on going to Aunt Sharon's, but then I heard about Justin's trip."

"We assumed he took you along."

"He didn't exactly take me," Shiloh admitted. "But I think, after all, he was glad I was there." She pushed aside the wistful memory of the wild night of love on Antigua, and all that had come after it.

"What was England like?"

"I can hardly describe it. The countryside is beautiful, but London is old and smoky, so crowded you'd hardly believe it. At first we were treated like honored guests. Parties in houses like palaces, opera, the theater, every sort of entertainment. Every street corner, it seemed, had its own little amusement. A dancing dog, a fiddler, a mouse in a small spinning cage . . . We had to leave the country suddenly to avoid the wrath of a very powerful man. We went to Washington, in the District of Columbia."

"Did Justin have business there?"

"Yes. But our stay was brief. Did you hear about the explosion on the steam warship *Princeton?*"

"It was in all the papers. *Dios,* were you there?"

Shiloh closed her eyes, remembering. "It was horrible. I was injured in the blast and went to the home of Justin's parents in Virginia to recuperate. It was a lovely stay, Ina. Justin's parents are wonderful. And everywhere I went, people complimented me on your dresses. A number of ladies demanded to know the name of my *couturier.*"

Ina clasped her hands in delight. "And what did the ladies say when you told them it was an old Mexican woman on a farm in Texas?"

"They declared you must be a genius."

"It is not the dress so much as the wearer that makes an ensemble beautiful. You have been good advertisement for me, though. Mrs. Allen and Mrs. Hanks both wanted me to sew for them after they saw you at the auction house."

Shiloh sipped her lemonade and gazed out at the wavy green prairie, the wide cloudless sky above. "It's so good to be home," she sighed.

"You have been to the capitals of the world, and you still like it best here?"

Shiloh nodded. They sat in amiable silence for a while, listening to the bees buzzing in the ligustrum hedge and savoring the sweet, warm air.

Then Shiloh turned to Ina again. "How is my father?"

"Well, I think. I know there were some lean times for him, but then things picked up. Some of the new arrivals had him searching for their relatives."

"Did he ask about me?" Shiloh didn't know why she was doing this to herself.

But Ina's answer surprised her. "Ask about you, indeed! When it appeared you were missing, he was like a madman. He went to Galveston and practically tore the town apart until he found a Creole woman—one with a shocking reputation, I might add—who confirmed you'd gone aboard the *Falcon.*"

She gave Ina a dubious look. "Perhaps he needed money. He was broke after that cattle raid. Oh, why didn't I leave him some?"

Ina grew stern. "Why do you not admit that the man loves you and was worried about you?"

"My father loves his work and his whiskey bottle."

"He just never knew how to show you his love. Raising children is women's work, and he felt inadequate."

Justin galloped into town, trying out one of the new horses. She handled well, had a smooth gait but a hard mouth. He'd have to speak to the hands about that. But overall, in the week he'd been back, he'd been greatly pleased with the ranch, although there were things that troubled him.

He and Shiloh had come to a sort of fragile truce, working, eating, even sleeping side by side, but they always seemed to be miles apart. Nights were sheer torture, lying so close he could feel her soft warmth, the beating of her heart, but at least he was safe. There were no hotheaded arguments, only cautious conversation here and there. It was better that way, Justin told himself for the hundredth time.

And then there was Isabella. She was like a dark shadow, ever present, but hard as hell to figure. She'd made herself scarce in the past week, yet Justin knew she was watching him. He hoped

Lamar Coulter could shed some light on the problem.

He strode into the solicitor's log-cabin office, extending his hand to the lanky man.

"Glad to see you, Justin," Lamar said. "Congratulations. The U.S. Senate voted in favor of a treaty. Houston's being mighty coy about it, though. He wants the States to beg for Texas."

"That's not such a bad idea. We'll get all the concessions we want if Houston plays his cards right. Have you heard from Duff Green?"

"I have. A bit of an opportunist, I think. He's got this Del Norte land company and hopes to make a bundle off it when Texas is annexed. Will Murphy doesn't like the way Green does business, so there's some tension there."

"What's Harmon West up to?"

"He's been lying mighty low. Our main worry is Captain Elliot."

"I've got a feeling he's put a spy out on my ranch. I came home to find that Isabella Hernandez had married Wylie Stokes."

Coulter whistled. "Be careful, my friend."

Justin strode outside and remounted, and headed for Nate Mulvane's house off Main Street.

Nate didn't bother welcoming him. "How's my girl?"

"Why don't you see for yourself?"

"Just answer the question, McCord."

"She's fine."

Nate exhaled loudly and chewed on his cigar. "Did she have a good time?"

Justin strode into the room. "I didn't come here as a message boy. Shiloh'd like to see you."

"I'm available most days," he answered indolently. "If she has anything to say to me, she'll say it in her own good time. Why the hell are you so all-fired eager to get us together?"

"Because you're family, Nate. There's nothing like being close to your family. It gives a man something to hold on to."

"I'm an old warhorse, and a drunk one at that. I got nothing to offer Shiloh; never have."

"She looks up to you, Nate, no matter what you think of yourself."

Mulvane's meaty fist pounded the table. "Last I saw of Shiloh, she was trying to give me money."

"Because you wouldn't take anything else from her."

"Leave me be, Justin. You know better than I how to keep Shiloh happy."

"She's not happy, Nate. That's why I'm here. Shiloh's put up a wall around herself and there isn't anything I can do about it."

Nate picked up a bit of whittled wood from the mantel and turned it over in his hand. "Sam Houston taught Shiloh how to whittle, back when she was a bright-eyed little firecracker of a girl. Houston was always carving something. Shiloh made this for my birthday one year. She was just about ten years old at the time." He handed the piece to Justin. It was a small horse, roughly done by a childish hand.

"I was drunk when she gave it to me," Nate said, a faraway look on his face. "I remember saying it looked like a deformed armadillo, when I knew it was meant to be a horse." He clenched his fist. "God, I'll never forget the look she gave me; those big green eyes, and her mouth all pressed together so she wouldn't bawl. . . ." He choked out the words and buried his face in his hands.

"It's not too late to make things right," Justin said, thinking of his own father. "Believe me, I know."

The heat of the afternoon sun beat down on Shiloh's bare head as she led one of the new mares around the corral, speaking soft words of encouragement to the skittish animal. She had been adamant about changing the ranch hands' breaking methods. Their way was to blindfold a horse, jam a huge bit into its mouth, and jump onto the bare back wearing six-inch spurs with knife-edged rowels. As the frantic horse was run to exhaustion, the bit tore its mouth to shreds. The wildness had been punished out of it, but the ill-treated beast could—and often did—turn on a rider.

This mare, whom Shiloh had dubbed Belle because of her well-formed shape and beautiful long-lashed eyes, was to be her example. So far, the gentle treatment was working. After she and the mare had done several more turns about the corral, she stopped beneath the branches of a spreading oak for a rest. She gave Belle corn from her own hand and a bucket of water.

Tomás came to sit in the shade with them. "She is a real lady, this one."

"That's because I treat her like one. Whatever kindness and respect I show her, I'll get back tenfold when I'm finished."

"But it is so much faster to ride them to their knees. Leonicio can break a horse in one hour."

"Leonicio can turn a horse into a fearful beast."

"Your husband said we were to do exactly as you told us."

No wonder the men had been so agreeable. She felt a prickle of resentment at his meddling.

"He also said we should feel privileged to work for the finest woman in Texas."

She didn't understand Justin at all. Most of the time he treated her as if she didn't exist, yet he'd praised her to the ranch hands. It was all so maddening, especially since she had no one to confide in.

The mare grunted and raised its head, ears pricking. A few seconds later, Shiloh heard the noise, too.

She ran to the gate to see who was coming up the road. Her hands tightened around a fencepost as she recognized the riders.

Nate spurred his horse and galloped up to her.

His eyes seemed to devour her, and his fingers worked restlessly over the reins.

"Shiloh," he said. "Shiloh, my girl."

Without quite realizing what was happening, Shiloh leaped the gate as Nate dismounted. Then she found herself wrapped in his embrace for the first time in her life.

SIXTEEN

For a long moment, neither of them spoke. Feelings long suppressed passed between them, and Shiloh felt her eyes fill with tears. Stepping back, she saw her own astonished joy reflected in her father's eyes.

"Hello, Papa," she said finally.

"I haven't heard you call me that since you were two years old."

They embraced again as the years of estrangement fell away. Over her father's shoulder, Shiloh saw Justin walking his horse to the stables.

Supper consisted of cornbread, snap beans, and a big ham from the springhouse. Shiloh watched her father closely, noting with great satisfaction that he didn't touch the wine. Ina seemed to know exactly what portions of food to put on his plate, and that he loved plenty of butter on his wedge of cornbread.

Justin seemed to derive real pleasure from Nate's new affection for his daughter. A few times, Shiloh caught his eye and gave him a questioning look, but he only smiled vaguely.

Afterward, they watched the sunset from the porch, enjoying the beauty of the long mare's-tail clouds as they streaked evening color across the sky. They spoke of the ranch and the influx of settlers into Houston and the coming elections in the fall.

"Excuse me," Nate said suddenly. "I'm going to see if Ina could use some help in the kitchen."

Shiloh watched him go. "Justin, do you think my father is courting Ina?"

He grinned. "If you could call washing dishes courting. Would you like them to be?"

"They both need someone to love. Doesn't everybody?"

"You don't seem to need anyone."

"Neither do you, Justin."

"Maybe I don't know any other way." His gaze had grown so intense that Shiloh had to force her eyes away, fearful that he'd discover her longing. She watched the breeze stirring the top of a distant oak.

"We had a bit of a talk. He showed me a little carving you made for him when you were a child."

"The first time I saw General Houston, he was sitting on a fallen tree, whittling a piece of driftwood. I was so fascinated that he showed me how to carve. What does that carving have to do with tonight, anyway?"

"He finally saw it for what it really was. A gift from the heart. A gift of love."

"This is all very confusing to me, Justin." Suddenly she was in his arms. He had stood and pulled her from her chair and wrapped her against him, holding her so tightly that she gasped.

"You really can't stand the thought that someone could love you, Shiloh," he said against her hair. "Long ago you must have convinced yourself of that. You're still that frightened little girl who jumped me at Washington-on-the-Brazos."

She twisted away and went to the porch railing, clutching it tightly. They stood in tense silence, not speaking, not looking at each other. Laughter drifted out from the kitchen, mingling with the rising night sounds.

A shadow crossed the yard between the porch and the side of the house. Leaping down the steps, Justin captured the dark figure. "Evening, Isabella. Is there something I can do for you?"

Her eyes were fierce and searching in the evening light. "No, Justin. I was just out taking some air." She passed on and headed for the cottage.

"Justin, tell me about Isabella."

He pulled out a cheroot and rolled it between his fingers. "I met her back in March of forty-three. 1 was scouting down along the border near Mier. I'd been following Ampudia's contingent. There was a Texan expedition there, and the Mexicans laid waste to them. I took a ball in the shoulder."

Shiloh recalled his crescent-shaped scar.

"Isabella got a doctor for me. She took excellent care of me and I started to trust her. Then she turned me over to the Mexicans. I wasn't able to escape until the Mier executions took place in Saltillo." He lit his cheroot and inhaled deeply. "Later, she turned up in Galveston, and now here."

Nate came out, interrupting them. "I'd best get on my way if I want to make town before dark." He shook hands with Justin and hugged Shiloh close. "I'll see you again, girl. We'll talk some more."

"Good-bye, Papa."

They watched him ride away in the deepening twilight, and then they went their separate ways: Justin to his study, and Shiloh to the comfortable little parlor to sit and think. So much had happened, so much had been said. It was impossible to make sense of it all. The only thing she was certain of was that the two men in her life, Justin and Nate, needed something from her. And she wasn't sure she had the capacity to give it.

Summer passed with all its heat and dust, baking the clay banks of the bayous and searing the long, yellow prairie grasses. Despite a long dry spell, Post Oaks flourished under Justin's expert management. He was constantly supervising new building and adding selectively to the herd. His day began at sunup and didn't finish until after dark. He was away a lot, too, making frequent trips to Galveston and San Antonio, Washington-on-the-Brazos, and the new capital in the hill country called Austin.

Shiloh worked tirelessly with the horses. Her method of saddle-breaking proved successful, and soon the ranch hands adopted her approach of patience and restraint. McCord horses were in great demand that summer, and profits were good.

One September day, as Shiloh was walking a newly tamed young stallion, she reflected on their good fortune. She rode to a small ridge on the eastern boundary of the ranch and looked back at the house. It sat neatly amid the trees and outbuildings, a symbol of the ranch's success.

Everything was perfect on the surface. The promise of the land had been fulfilled. But a great gulf still existed between her and Justin. He held himself aloof, and she responded with a distance of her own. In Houston they were feted as the golden young couple, a symbol of the bounty of Texas. At the auction house and at parties, they garnered admiring stares. It was small comfort during the long, restless nights when even an accidental touch was studiously avoided. And every day, the pattern became more set, more impossible to stray away from.

Isabella was in the small garden plot behind the cottage she shared with Wylie, bending down over a pumpkin vine. There was something not quite right about her movements, or about the fact that she was outside in the full blaze of the afternoon heat. As Shiloh watched, Isabella doubled over and fell to the ground.

Shiloh dug her heels into the stallion's flanks and sent him galloping toward the house.

Isabella lay awkwardly upon the ground amid the ripening pumpkins and squash.

"Is it the baby?" Shiloh asked.

"*Sí.* I think so."

Shiloh placed her hands under Isabella's arms, hauling her to her feet. "We'll get you into bed, and I'll fetch Prairie Flower." Calmly, she helped her into the cottage and to the bed, arranging pillows comfortably around her. She left quickly, but once she was outside, she ran as fast as she could to the kitchen.

"Isabella's baby is coming!" she shouted at Prairie Flower.

With infuriating slowness, Prairie Flower donned a fresh apron and washed her hands in the basin. She gathered herbs and salves from the cupboard and placed them in a basket.

They found Isabella huddled miserably on the bed, her knees drawn up and her fists clenched.

"Do not fight it," Prairie Flower instructed.

Shiloh knelt beside the bed and took Isabella's tightly closed hands, gently stroking them until they opened. She helped Isabella relax her legs and arms, and spoke encouragingly as a pain rose and then passed.

Prairie Flower administered her medicines and draughts while Shiloh bathed Isabella's brow. Isabella slid in and out of moods ranging from pitiful whining to outright hostility. She screamed; she swore; she cried; she babbled Spanish prayers. She cursed her husband and the baby, who were the cause of her pain. As she screamed, Prairie Flower drew back the hem of her dress. "Bear down," she said. "Bear down."

Something like relief appeared in Isabella's eyes. She gripped the side of the bed and did as she was told. Her face grew red and then purple. It was terrifying to watch, but fascinating, too.

The birth happened quickly. First the crown of a tiny head appeared, followed by a wizened face. Then, with a final push, Isabella delivered herself of a girl.

Isabella rolled her eyes and turned her head away. "I need some water. And then I'm going to sleep."

Shiloh called Wylie in, assured him that Isabella was fine, and handed him the baby. Cradling it awkwardly, Wylie grinned from ear to ear. "Bella said I could name her. I'm calling her Cassandra, for my mother."

"That's beautiful," Shiloh said. "Congratulations, Wylie." She took the baby from him while he went to see his wife.

Isabella was more than willing to hand Cassandra over to Shiloh. She was a singularly disinterested mother, suffering the periodic nursings and looking forward to the day when the child was weaned.

The days of November were warm, almost balmy, and Shiloh loved to take the baby walking. Justin had made a small bench beneath one of the post oaks, and Shiloh often went there to sit in dappled shade and hold Cassandra.

Justin found her there one afternoon as he was coming in from the fields.

"I think she likes you," Shiloh declared. "Here, take her." She laughed when Justin recoiled. "Go on; she won't break."

"I'm covered with dust and sweat."

"She's not fussy." Without further ado, Shiloh placed the baby in Justin's arms.

"Well, I'll be," Justin said. "Little lady, I do believe we're going to be friends."

He gave her back to Shiloh reluctantly. "You spend a lot of time with the little mite."

"Isabella doesn't seem to want to have anything to do with her."

"She's not yours, Shiloh. And she's going away."

Dread curled within her. She clutched the baby closer.

"Wylie told me this morning he's thinking of settling in Bastrop, a hundred miles northwest of here. They'll probably go in the spring when Isabella is stronger."

* * *

Houston festooned itself grandly for election day. Banners were strung across the streets, bunting hung from the Capitol Hotel, and speakers shouted from raised platforms along the bayou landings. Excitement vibrated through the air as men clamored to cast their votes.

The results surprised no one. Sam Houston, the hero of San Jacinto and a veteran of two terms, had placed Anson Jones, his secretary of state, in office.

There was a Christmas reception for the victor at the home of Harmon West, who had wasted no time ingratiating himself to the president. Jessamine fancied herself the social equal of Mrs. Allen and made a great show of ordering her servants about.

Captain Charles Elliot was much in evidence at the reception. Shiloh wasn't surprised to see him, since he was a personal friend of Dr. Jones, but his presence made her nervous. She acknowledged his greeting with a nod.

"The belle of Post Oaks," he said. "You've made quite a reputation for yourself."

"If you say so." She started to move away.

"Mrs. McCord, wait. There is no reason why we can't be civil to each other. My work in Texas is nearly over. I still think it's ill-advised, but it seems that Texas will soon join the United States, keep its Negroes in bondage, and go to war with Mexico."

"Why are you telling me this?"

"Because I've seen the way you've been looking at me all evening. You don't trust me."

"Not in the least," she stated. "And I've been wondering what your friend Isabella is doing at my ranch."

"I can't answer that." He bowed slightly and said, "Goodnight, Mrs. McCord. I wish you all the best."

"What was that all about?" asked Justin, coming to her side.

"He wants me—and everyone else—to believe that he's through meddling with Texas. But there's something going on, I know it."

"How do you know it?"

"I haven't been snooping around. It's just a feeling I have. But what about you, Justin? I think you know something, and you're not telling me."

"Let me handle this in my own way."

She folded her arms. "Of course."

Her first impression of the new president was that he seemed a little in awe of his position. His great jowls quivered and his eyes darted nervously. He kept looking to his predecessor, Sam Houston, as if to gather some of the man's forcefulness to himself.

"Mr. President?" Shiloh said.

"Good evening, Mrs. McCord. It's a pleasure to see you."

"I wonder if I could have a word with you."

They retreated to a quiet corner of the room, away from the crowd and the noise of the musicians.

"I'm concerned about Captain Elliot, sir. I'm afraid he will try to prevent a treaty from going through."

"What are you accusing him of?"

"Trying to turn Texas into a British protectorate."

"I don't like the sound of that, Mrs. McCord. Charles is a forthright, honorable man. I trust him implicitly." He moved away, leaving Shiloh to flush in embarrassment. Looking around the room, she saw that a number of people had seen Jones snub her. Gritting her teeth, she went to find Justin.

"You should've known better than to try that," he said once they were on their way home.

"Don't start in on me, Justin. I know I made a mistake." When she went up to retire, however, he followed her. Embarrassed, Shiloh went to the window and opened it to the cold night air. Night sounds filled the silence of the room: the horses nickering and stamping in the stables, the screech of an owl. And, faintly but disturbingly, the cry of a baby.

Shiloh looked troubled. "Isabella leaves the baby to cry too long. It's not good for her."

Justin went and shut the window. "Would it make you happy to have a child of your own?"

She was mesmerized by his nearness, his soft, compelling voice. His suggestion conjured up images of unspeakable bliss. A baby of her own, someone to love and be loved by. And Justin would be so fatherly . . . but then she thought further and saw another aspect of his suggestion.

She searched for the words. "I just don't think it would be right for us to make a child. It—it's too much like breeding the horses, putting a mare and a stud together for just one purpose." She looked at him squarely. "I won't lie to you, Justin. I would love to have a child. But when—if—it happens, I want it to be more than mating. I want it to be a celebration of love, conceived by parents who understand and trust each other. It wouldn't be fair to the child otherwise. We can barely get along with each other, much less raise a child together."

He didn't stay with her that night, or for the next several weeks, as he went out of town. Shiloh found herself lonely for his presence, and she was constantly haunted by the idea he'd put into her head.

SEVENTEEN

Justin dropped a creased, blotted letter onto the desk in his study. A March breeze swept it into the lap of the American chargé d'affaires. William Murphy looked up questioningly. "Where did you get this, Justin?"

"Don't ask. Maybe you'd better remain seated," Justin said.

Lamar Coulter, who had already read the letter, grew livid. "I can't believe my eyes."

Handing Murphy a drink of whiskey, Justin said, "It's from Charles Elliot to his superiors in England. Apparently we were right in thinking he'd have a last-ditch effort up his sleeve. He's going to Mexico to see if he can get President Herrera to recognize Texas as a sovereign nation. He'll be traveling incognito to Vera Cruz as soon as he can get a ship out of Galveston."

Murphy tossed back his whiskey. "Does President Jones know?"

Lamar went to the window. "Jones is sending him, he and Saligny. It's all there in the letter. In a way, I can't blame the man. The presidency of Texas is a mighty powerful position."

"I'm going to Mexico," said Justin. A great weariness swept over him. It was starting all over again: the secrecy, the underhanded dealings. Once it had been exciting, uncovering plots, manipulating things. But by now it had grown old. Justin had no desire to go capering down to Mexico, dressed as a padre or an adventurer. He'd do it only to stop Elliot once and for all.

Shiloh sat beneath the awning of the dry goods store, holding little Cassandra Stokes. Isabella was inside, getting some things for their move to Bastrop. Cassandra grew restless and cried to be let down, to practice her new skill of crawling.

"I guess there's no harm in it," Shiloh said, and set the child down. Cassandra explored a knothole in one of the planks. Then she crawled to the edge of the walk, drawn by a shiny porcelain butter crock that sat there.

"No, you don't." Shiloh hurried over and scooped the baby up. Out of the corner of her eye she caught a flash of movement. There was a long, narrow alley at the side of the dry goods store and a flight of wooden steps leading to some living quarters above. Shiloh looked up just in time to see Isabella disappear into one of the doors. Giving the baby a corner of her blanket to suck, Shiloh mounted the stairs and stopped, listening.

". . . be found out," Isabella was saying urgently. "They know about your Mexico trip. Justin has been writing a lot of letters; he seems to be getting his things in order. Charles, he means to follow you to Mexico."

There was a long silence, and then Charles Elliot laughed. "It's perfect! The ship I'm taking is the *Eurydice*. The *Eurydice*! It's a British warship commanded by my cousin George. Once we're on the high seas, we'll be able to get rid of McCord for good."

Shiloh's first impulse was to tell Justin what she'd heard, to warn him. But that was no good. He would never abandon his plans just because Elliot was plotting his death.

Yet she couldn't let him go. In the stable, she brushed a horse's side. The scent of spring wildflowers drifted in through the windows, mingling with the smell of hay and horses. Again, she vowed that she couldn't let him walk straight into a trap. He was too precious to her to lose.

Shiloh dropped her currycomb and ran to the stable window. The greening meadows shifted in the breeze. Clouds were piled high on the horizon against the sharp blue sky. She put a hand to her racing heart.

It was all so clear to her now. So painfully, wonderfully clear. It had taken the possibility of Justin's death to chase away the fog of numbness that had shrouded her for months, but finally it had happened. A mockingbird alighted on a branch in front of her and cocked its shining eye.

"I love him." Her voice shook, almost beyond recognition as it came from her heart. "God help me, I *love* him." She didn't know when it had started. Perhaps the feeling had been there right from the beginning, when she'd huddled on the saloon floor in Washington-on-the-Brazos, studying him. Nearly two years had passed since then, and Shiloh had fought her emotions, denied them, refused to let them blossom within her. But it was love she felt now, pure and sweet and aching. That was why her heart leaped each time she saw him, each time he smiled her way. That was why Justin's touch, and only his, ignited in her a flame of passion so intense that the world fell away. And that was why she couldn't bear to lose him.

All the dark shadows in her life were burned away by this new, bright flame of feeling. She rushed out to the stable yard, where Tomás was working.

"Where's Justin?" she asked. He pointed down to the western range, where a carpet of bluebonnets rippled up to the tree-fringed bayou. Squinting, Shiloh saw him and his horse as two specks against the cloud-piled horizon.

Lifting the hem of her frock, she ran toward him, her veins pounding with the fever of her newly discovered love. She didn't think, didn't plan. She only knew that Justin was where her heart's destiny lay. She called his name, a shout of gladness, as she raced over the field of bluebonnets.

He straightened up from the fallen tree he was hewing with an ax. Shiloh pitched herself into his arms and stood on tiptoe to cover his astounded face with kisses.

"Oh Justin," she said, savoring the salty taste of him. "I've been so foolish. All these months of denying you . . . please, please say you'll forgive me." She held his face and placed her mouth upon his, giving him a kiss that spoke her heart for her.

Justin returned her kiss that promised a night of passion, then lifted her onto his horse. Mounting in front of her, he walked the horse slowly back to the house.

Shiloh rode in glowing silence, her hands wrapped about his waist, her cheek against his back, her bare legs dangling. Never had she felt so utterly complete. The rest of her life stretched rosy before her, and it seemed nothing could mar her happiness.

Yet the sight of Wylie Stokes's loaded wagon shot her through with a shaft of pain. She jumped from the horse and ran across the yard.

"You're leaving?" she asked.

"Wylie has found a steamer going up the bayou. We leave tonight," Isabella informed her.

Cassandra had been drowsing, but she came awake and greeted Shiloh with a smile. She held the baby to her cheek as if to stamp herself with the impression for years to come.

Wylie cleared his throat and Shiloh looked up.

"Time to go, ma'am," he said regretfully. Only Justin's warm presence behind her kept her from feeling that her world had emptied out.

"It'll be all right, sweetheart," he said. "We'll visit them. When the new capital is built in Austin, we'll be making plenty of trips up that way."

She nodded and turned in his arms, leaning up to kiss his cheek. Hand in hand, they walked to the house.

A snug room in a boardinghouse insulated them from the rollicking noises of the port of Galveston and the rushing sounds of waves on the sandy shore. There had been a bittersweet note in their lovemaking this night, for in the morning they would be separated. Justin expected to be aboard the British *Eurydice,* bound for Vera Cruz. And Shiloh expected to take his place on the vessel.

Shiloh wondered if he'd ever forgive her for what she planned to do. She had purchased a supply of widow's weeds, a shapeless black bombazine, and the all-important concealing bonnet and veil. Then she went to the offices of the Galveston *News* to confer with its editor.

Shiloh's last errand in Galveston that day had been the most difficult of all. She found the handsome Creole woman called Sylvie, who had cautioned her against Christopher St. James.

Sylvie had sold her a sleeping potion.

* * *

Justin dreamed of floating on a warm, shifting sea. The smell of brine was strong, the waves swishing gently as they lapped over him. He heard his name called by a faraway voice, faint at first and then growing louder. Finally, he dragged himself awake and reached for Shiloh.

"Best be going, sweetheart," he mumbled.

"Justin! Are you there."

He recognized Will Murphy's voice. The pounding on the door thudded in his aching head. It felt as heavy as iron when he raised it from the pillow.

He pulled on his trousers and stumbled toward the door, reeling slightly.

Murphy stormed in. "My God, you look terrible. Have you been drinking?"

Justin shook his head. "You shouldn't be here, Will. We don't want anyone to suspect a connection between us."

"What does it matter now? We've lost the *Eurydice,* and the *Electra* as well."

Justin snapped out a curse and grabbed his empty coffee cup. "I was drugged." He set the cup down so hard that it shattered.

"That means someone knew about your plans."

"My wife."

"Shiloh? Why would she do a fool thing like that?"

"I don't know. But she'd better have a damned good explanation."

"We've still got Elliot's letter. I'll see what I can do."

Justin sat down on the bed and held his throbbing head in his hands. A storm was whipping up in the Gulf, the wind shivering the windowpanes. He noticed that Shiloh's carpetbag was missing. With a growing sense of alarm, he went through his own belongings. They were all there, with one notable exception. His billet was missing.

Apparently, she'd never got over her passion for detective work, and wanted to make a name for herself by exposing Elliot's excursion to Mexico.

And that, Justin realized with dull misery, was the reason for her sudden change toward him. He wasn't surprised that he'd swallowed her lies. He was still crazy in love with her.

But no more, came the hard-edged thought. At least she'd freed him of the damnable burden of loving her. When she returned, she'd find herself a divorced woman.

He tried to tell himself that Shiloh deserved whatever she got in Mexico, but the Gulf between Galveston and Vera Cruz was a pirates' haven; the ships that passed through were loaded with Mexican gold and silver, even goods from China via Acapulco. And the Mexican interior was rife with bandits and brigands, desperados hiding in the rocky hills. Elliot himself was a threat, too. There was no telling what the Englishman would do if he found out Shiloh was watching him.

Justin collected his things, hoping to find a ship bound for Vera Cruz in the harbor. Although, even if he found one, the incoming gale would have to pass before they could sail. He opened the door to leave.

And found himself staring down the barrel of a pistol.

"Apparently," said Harmon West, "Captain Elliot's information wasn't quite accurate. I was supposed to come after your wife, Justin. Where is she?"

"Gone to stay with relatives," he said, gauging the distance between himself and the pistol.

"Don't get any crazy notions. I wouldn't mind pulling this trigger. Not at all." Harmon kept the gun pressed to Justin's side as they went out to a small landing where Houston-bound steamers started up the bayou. Murphy was already in the judge's boat, under guard.

The judge pointed the pistol at Justin, his other hand gripping a tree root that rose up out of the mud. "Now, you get into the boat, nice and easy."

A dark, slithering shadow crept down the tree behind Harmon.

"A moccasin," Justin whispered. "Behind you."

The judge only laughed. "Nice try, Justin."

"Damn it, I'm not bluffing."

West lost his footing in the mud and groped wildly with his hand. The snake struck like a bolt of black lightning. With a scream of terror and agony, Harmon dropped his pistol and slid down the bank, the snake whipping wildly, locked to his wrist.

While the guards quailed in the boat, Justin and Murphy went to the judge. The bite mark on Harmon's wrist was growing livid.

"Get him in the boat," Justin ordered.

"It's too late, Justin," Murphy said. Harmon's eyes had glazed over and his breathing had become rapid and shallow. He made no sound. And then the breathing simply stopped.

Justin felt nothing as he scaled to the top of the bank, followed by Murphy.

"Where are you going?" Murphy asked.

"To Mexico," Justin said. "To get my wife."

"He hides beneath the wide brim of a white hat," Shiloh wrote, "his features obscured by shadow. Yet there is no doubt as to the identity of this mysterious stranger. He is none other than Captain Charles Elliot, the British chargé d'affaires in Texas."

Shiloh ended her dispatch with a few remarks and folded it away, putting it in a packet that she intended to send to the Galveston *News*.

The thirteen-day voyage had been abominable, as all sea travel seemed to be for Shiloh. She kept to the cramped mustiness of her cabin, alternately shivering and sweating, tormented by nausea. This did have one fortunate effect, however. She was left completely alone by the crew and passengers. She ventured out only to seek more information about Charles Elliot.

Relief washed over her when the *Eurydice* made port at Vera Cruz. Shiloh made note of the fact that the warship was reported under another name, so she could include that in her dispatches. A packet going to New Orleans took her first set of reports.

She also added a personal letter to the mail. In just two weeks, she'd grown accustomed to putting her thoughts on paper, and she'd written a brief but eloquent message to Justin. In it, she'd explained why she'd had to trick him. It was so much easier to say "I love you," on paper than to his face. There was no danger of rejection from the paper.

Vera Cruz was a colorful melange of humanity, busy and restless, never sleeping. Dark-skinned girls hung out of flower-laden balconies along a narrow street called Independencia, watching the stream of burros and carts below. The town was dominated by the cathedral in the Plaza de la Constitución, and by a fort with rough, flattened battlements, called San Juan de Ulúa, but its true appeal was the vibrancy and energy of the people themselves.

Shiloh rode with Captain George Elliot, Charles in his ridiculous white hat, and a few others, crowded into a poor conveyance. They squeezed through a crowded marketplace, where dark-gold-colored, loud-voiced vendors stood behind their mounds of fruit. There were coconuts, mamey, zapote, oranges, and a dozen other varieties that Shiloh didn't recognize. She nearly swooned at the smell in the fish area, declining the concoction of lime-seasoned raw *huachinango*, called *ceviche*, which the others availed themselves of.

They spent the night in a small *posada*, none too clean, lorded over by an ingratiating proprietor. While the others went out to tour the city, Shiloh stayed in her dank, cell-like room, unable to go because of her guise of mourning. The room's one redeeming quality was that it had an iron-rimmed balcony, which looked out onto the busy *zócalo*. From that vantage point, she sipped a glass of hot, sweet coffee and watched the action in the plaza below. The open-air palm-roofed cantinas overflowed with people. Somewhere a small harp strummed, exhaling sweet sounds in a rippling, roundabout rhythm.

Shiloh sighed, longing for Justin. The dulcet song of the harp touched a chord in her heart. She wanted nothing more than to feel his arms about her, his breath in her ear as he whispered to her.

What was he thinking now? Did he miss her as badly as she did him?

It was a rough three-day journey to Mexico City. The small contingent lumbered through the dusty highlands, which were dominated by the maguey plant standing in straight, gray-green rows. The driver offered Shiloh a flask of *pulque,* which, he explained in broken English, was made from the maguey's *aguamiel.* The sweet-sour taste of the whitish liquid was surprisingly pleasant.

Through her veil, she watched Charles Elliot closely. He conversed in low tones with his cousin, and neither man took any notice of her. The journey passed uncomfortably, through tiny, hill-clinging pueblos, past a few opulent haciendas, until they reached the outskirts of Mexico City.

Evening was coming on, orange against the hills, but the driver promised they could reach their lodgings by nightfall. For the first time, Shiloh was at a loss. Her traveling companions expected to escort her directly to her family, and she had no idea what to tell them. She moved forward in the cart and seated herself next to the driver. He gave her a mustachioed grin and offered her more *pulque,* which she drank sparingly, as it was potent stuff.

She pressed a gold coin into his hand. "I do not know where to go in Mexico City. But I have told these gentlemen that I have family there. Do you understand?"

"*Sí.*"

"I don't want them to question anything I do."

Looking straight ahead, he said, "I know of a place. Quiet, clean, very safe. No one will question you."

As they wound through narrow, flower-hung streets, she looked in wonder at lamp-lit gardens, airy saloons, poverty hidden behind ancient, crumbling walls, and a steady stream of people walking in high-spirited, laughing groups past beggars who huddled in doorways.

Captain Elliot and his white-hatted companion were left at the British consulate, and she went on with the driver.

He took her a few blocks away to a small hotel and carried her bag in for her. Shiloh was shown to a little room in the back of the second floor and served a meal of *pozole*. She spent the remainder of the evening on the terrace, which overlooked a tiled patio. A small fountain surrounded by dahlias and hyacinths bubbled in the middle. Holding her writing in her lap, she wrote out a description of the journey from Vera Cruz, again emphasizing Charles Elliot's amateurish guise and his easy assurance that the Mexican president would prove instantly compliant.

She also started a private journal. In it, she unabashedly wrote everything that was in her heart, including all she felt when she and Justin made love. Somehow, it soothed the ache in her to put the words on paper. The explicitness of what she wrote shocked her, but she knew that no eyes but her own would ever see it.

For the next two weeks, she was like a shadow in Mexico City's streets as she delivered her letters for mailing, then went as close as she dared to the British consulate.

One April day, she saw them leave on horse-back, their bags stuffed with papers. She entered the consulate and struck up a conversation with one of the clerks, who mentioned that Mr. Pack-enham, the British minister, had a meeting at the president's palace in Tacubaya, four miles distant.

Shiloh knew that the negotiations had reached a pivotal point. The British were undoubtedly going to offer all manner of concessions to Mexico in order to get that nation to recognize Texas. Elliot would return from Tacubaya loaded with damning evidence.

And Shiloh meant to get her hands on it.

EIGHTEEN

Shiloh thanked all the stars of heaven the next day that she'd resisted the temptation to shed her widow's garb, because among the passengers in the coach to Vera Cruz was a white-hatted Englishman.

"Mrs. Willows, I'm surprised to see you," he said, addressing her by her assumed name. "I thought you'd planned to stay on in Mexico City."

"It doesn't suit me," she said, her voice studiedly soft and lower in pitch than it normally was. "I'm going back to Texas. And what about you, sir? Your trip was quite short, also."

"Mexico City is an abominable place. I was robbed last night, most brutally. Besides, my business is concluded. I shall spend a little time at Jalapa, awaiting the results. The climate is quite pleasant there."

Outside Mexico City, the road climbed to the maguey fields and pine forests, through the broad lands and clear air of ranch country, and then higher still, to whitish hills that embraced flower-fringed lakes. Finally, the road descended again into pueblos huddled beneath the ice-capped Pico de Orizaba and the brooding extinct volcano called Perote.

The coach stopped to allow a herd of sturdy goats to pass. Shiloh noticed the tattoo of hoof-beats as they waited, but thought nothing of it until the driver, a lad of about fifteen, gave a shout of alarm.

"Brigands!" he cried, and raised his hands in supplication. He was armed with a rusty pistol but didn't think to avail himself of it.

As the other passengers began to shout and scream, Shiloh twisted Justin's willow ring off her finger and dropped it into the bodice of her dress.

The two brigands rode up on tired-looking mounts. The robbers were both painfully thin, trembling from drink, or perhaps the lack of it. In their frayed serapes and ancient boots, they were a sorry sight.

Shiloh bent and took up the driver's pistol. The weapon was unfamiliar and rusty, but loaded. She fired off a shot that knocked the gun from the brigand's hand.

His horse reared, then bolted down into the valley. The other followed close at his heels. The driver and passengers stared in disbelief at the little tejana widow. Shiloh returned the pistol to the driver.

"Let's go," she said as she set the gun down. She suffered their gratitude in silence, looking down at her hands. When one of the passengers insisted on treating her to a meal in Jalapa, she could hardly refuse. They ate a hearty *comida*, served by a barefoot girl in a wide skirt, near the town's ancient public washing place.

At the end of the meal, Shiloh went to avail herself of the facilities. As she was returning through the dusty back dooryard, someone grabbed her from behind. She had no time to cry out. A foul-smelling sack, stiff with dust, was placed over her head, her hands bound behind her back.

She felt herself being lifted up and tossed onto the bed of a cart. Helpless and furious, she was taken a short distance away. Again strong arms lifted her and carried her up a flight of stairs. She was placed upon a mat of some sort, and then her hands were unbound. She clawed the filthy sack from her head, removing her bonnet and veil with it.

The door closed after two fleeing men, but there was still a presence in the room. Charles Elliot stood against a long, iron-barred window. "It frightens me," he said, "when I think how close you came to getting back to Texas. I assume that was you in my room the last night. I didn't suspect a thing though, until you shot at those brigands. Very few women can shoot like that."

Shiloh wiped a hand across her sweat-stained face. "Let me go, Captain. Holding me here will serve nothing."

"Do you think I'm going to let you carry tales back to Texas?"

She smiled in bitter triumph. "You're through, Captain Elliot. Your story is in all the papers. I sent off the last dispatch the day we left Mexico City."

"I don't believe you."

"You'll find out soon enough. I'm afraid your career is over. Of course, this sort of thing goes on all the time in diplomatic circles. But you've committed the cardinal error of being found out. Oh, and if you murder me, you'll hang. The editor of the Galveston *News* has a sealed letter, which is to be opened if I don't return to Texas by June first."

"Damnably clever," he remarked, calming a bit. He turned on his heel and left the room, bolting the stout door from the outside.

There was no hope of escape. The one window had close-set bars and looked out over a small yard, where hens scratched in the dust. Shiloh waited out the night and through the next day, watching for someone to call to, but no one crossed the yard.

Finally, when the second twilight fell and blue fog settled on the mossy mountains, she heard voices outside the door. Fear prickled at her as she heard something familiar in one of the voices. The bolt slid and the door opened.

Shiloh looked up, her head tossed back defiantly. Then her face drained of color.

"*St. James* . . ."

The strikingly handsome man with his lazy, glittering eyes and thin mustache strode into the room. His sensual lips parted, revealing twin rows of ivory teeth.

"So you remember me," he said, seemingly delighted. "But here I do not go by Christopher St. James. I am known as Cristobal Santiago."

He grasped her gown and tore the garment from neck to hem. He studied the scars Shiloh had received on the *Princeton,* but said nothing.

His cold inspection made her furious. "How bold you are, now that my husband is not around."

Santiago looked over at Elliot and laughed. "You did not underestimate her charms."

"I think you'll find she's well worth the price."

They traveled the night through, winding down the hills around Jalapa to the outskirts of Vera Cruz. At a rocky cove where the waves rushed in, Santiago thrust her down a jagged incline. A small boat waited at the shore. Santiago settled Shiloh in the bow and cast off. He set them on an easterly course, secured the rigging, and came toward Shiloh, a knife held between his teeth.

She shrank back.

He laughed at her. "Did I pay for you in gold just so I can kill you?" he asked. "No, my beauty, I will relieve you of your bonds now. These waters are full of hungry sharks. You wouldn't want to try to escape by swimming." He cut the ropes on her wrists and removed the gag.

Shiloh chafed her raw flesh and worked her aching jaw, accepting a canteen of fresh water to relieve the appalling dryness of her mouth. "I am a citizen of Texas. What you're doing is a violation of international law."

Santiago threw back his head and laughed. "I am bound by no law, *cara mia*. I am a citizen of the high seas."

"Where are you taking me?"

"To Sacrificios. A small island not far from here. I have a fine house there, very private. No one ever comes to Sacrificios, so named because of the offerings the Old Ones made to their gods there."

"My husband is a wealthy man," Shiloh said. "He'll reward you handsomely for my safe return."

"Come now, my dear. What kind of man would reward me for buying his wife from an Englishman."

Dawn broke in the east as they approached the tiny island. It rose up out of the dark blue water like a forbidding castle. Anchored some distance away, safe from the jagged shoals, was a tri-masted ship. The *Falcon*.

"Ah, Sacrificios," Santiago said happily. "And that," he added, pointing to the ship, "is my real mistress. She is called *Angélica* now."

He moored the boat in a narrow cove and lifted Shiloh from the bow, carrying her to dry land. "Tiny as the *mitla* bird," he said as he held her. "I think you will make me very happy, my love."

Shiloh bit the inside of her lip until she tasted blood. Then she coughed, convulsing violently, spitting blood onto the rocks.

"What is this?" Santiago demanded. "Are you ill?"

She nodded, spasms still lifting her chest. "Consumption. My mother died of it."

He dropped her so quickly that she fell to the rocks. *"Puta!"* he raged. But then he hesitated. "This is a trick, is it not? You are not really sick."

"I wish that were so," Shiloh said.

"Why did I not see you cough blood before."

"The mountain air of Jalapa agrees with me. But here, at sea level, I am weak."

"I do not believe you."

"Why do you think Captain Elliot was so eager to be rid of me?" Shiloh had another fit of coughing and brought up more blood.

"Get away from me," he ordered. "You will be a slave to slaves, a servant to scullery maids. And if I find that you are lying to me about this wasting disease . . ." He let his voice trail off and his long-fingered hand move to the knife in his belt.

Shiloh stared, unflinching, at her captor. It was far too soon to despair. Santiago was fierce, yes, and darkly dangerous. But she, too, was a fighter.

* * *

Justin slowed his horse to a walk as he entered the dark labyrinth of Mexico City. He searched every face he passed, looked through iron grilles into flower-decked patios, and scanned dozens of markets for a glimpse of Shiloh's fiery curls, the creamy fairness of her skin. But it was useless. He didn't know how she'd disguised herself or where she might have stayed. The only thing he knew with any certainty was that she'd used the alias on his billet, J. Willows. The name meant nothing to the numerous innkeepers he'd asked.

At nightfall he found a good livery for his horse and went to the house of his friend and associate, Hamilton Coffey. Coffey worked for the American consul and had been instrumental in getting the Mier survivors released after a long imprisonment.

The intense, agitated little man gave Justin a cordial welcome, but his concern was evident. A barefoot servant brought food and a bottle of fiery mescal.

"What can I do for you?" Hamilton asked, biting into a tortilla-wrapped *carne asada*.

"I'm looking for my wife. She came here under the name of J. Willows."

"Alone?"

"She—Shiloh—is an unusual woman. She's done some detective work in the past and is damned good at it. She followed Charles Elliot here."

Coffey's astonishment increased. "Elliot is here? What the hell are the English up to now?"

"He made some offers to President Herrera in order to persuade him to recognize Texas's sovereignty."

"So what's your wife's part in it?"

"She wanted to catch Elliot in the act."

"Then your best bet is to find Elliot."

"I intend to do that first thing in the morning." He sipped his mescal, savoring the burn of it.

"Tell me a little about your wife so I can spread the word."

"If you saw her, you'd never forget her. She's petite, I guess you'd call it, with the brightest head of red hair you ever saw. Pretty as a Texas wildflower. Mighty outspoken, especially when she feels strongly about something. She's got a stubborn streak a mile wide, too, and more courage in her than most men."

Hamilton looked at him squarely. "She sounds like she's worth the trouble of finding, Justin."

Lewis Packenham, the British minister, was a harried-looking, sloppy man. He looked up from his papers at the tall, blond American who had entered his office.

"Yes? What is it."

"I'm Stephen Turner." Justin extended his hand. He hoped like sin that Packenham had never met the real Turner, one of Anson Jones's aides. "President Jones sent me," he lied.

"Do you have a dispatch for me?"

Justin shook his head. "I must see Captain Elliot. Can you tell me where he is?"

Packenham looked at him sharply. "How would I know a thing like that? He's assigned to Texas. There was something about his going to South Carolina. . . ."

"Come on, Mr. Packenham. We both know he's in Mexico."

But the man wouldn't budge. Justin fought the urge to lunge across the desk and choke an admission out of the Englishman.

"I'm sorry, but I can't help you. If you had a dispatch, something in writing, I might be able to tell you something useful, Mr. Turner."

Their gazes locked and held for a moment, Justin's fierce and steely, Packenham's stubborn.

"Good day, Mr. Turner," he said quietly.

Justin strode past a Mexican clerk who was bent over a ledger.

"Jalapa," the clerk mumbled.

Justin froze. "What did you say?"

The clerk's pen scratched across the book. Without looking up, he said, "I was just thinking the weather is fine in Jalapa this time of year."

For two days he climbed toward the hilly, high region of Jalapa, stopping only to give his horse a rest and a drink in one of the icy mountain pools. Finally, the chalk-white hills came into view, shrouded by a thin fog that rose up from the valley.

It was time for caution. Before entering town, he dyed his hair and mustache with lampblack and saddlesoap. Then he slouched in the saddle and walked his horse into town. He stopped at a small, dirt-floored cantina near the *zócalo*. A fine, needlelike rain began to fall through a tear in the canvas awning over the table. Justin moved away from the rain to prevent it from removing the coloring in his hair.

"*Chipi-chipi*, we call this rain," said a voice behind him. "Penetrates like needles." The speaker was a stocky little man with several teeth missing and a large silver hunk of a ring on one hand. He was speaking English. Justin tensed, disappointed that his disguise was so inadequate. He squinted at the stocky man, saying nothing.

"You like our little town, Jalapa?" the man asked.

"Just passing through."

The Mexican eyed his saddlebag. "There is much to be had in Jalapa, for a little sum."

"I'm looking for an Anglo, an Englishman. Middle-aged, well-fed. Probably has plenty of money."

The serving girl, barefoot and wearing a wide skirt, approached and said something to the man in rapid Spanish.

The man stroked his grizzled face. "It is possible that I have seen such a man. . . ."

Reaching the end of his patience, Justin shot

to his feet and grabbed the man by his filthy collar. "I don't have time to play games with you. Just name your price and tell me what you know."

"The man you seek calls himself Marshall. He is at a villa in the Calle Morelos, a house with a brass snake on the door."

Leaving his coin on the table, Justin walked his horse up a network of narrow, cobbled alleys, studying the doors of a series of a pastel-painted facades. Near the top of the hill, he found the brass snake knocker. It was the hour of siesta, and the stinging *chipi-chipi* still fell steadily, so no one was about. Justin brought his horse across the alley and tethered it under the shelter of a tiled eave.

Loose plaster crumbled under his fingers as he scaled the wall, pulling himself up with a handhold on the iron grille of a second-story window. From the top of the wall he looked down into a tiny patio surrounded by open hallways on the ground and upper floors. He dropped to the tiles and scanned the three windows, two of them dark. The third glowed with lamplight. He stole toward this one. Through a gap in the fringed curtains he saw a small stove with a fire glowing inside. And the bulky form of Charles Elliot, sitting at a table, writing.

Justin stood in front of the arched wooden door and drew both pistols. His boot splintered the wood as he kicked opened the door.

Elliot shot to his feet, upsetting the table. His heavy face drained of color. He backed away from Justin, toward the glowing stove. Clearly, he saw through the disguise.

"Where is she, Elliot?" Justin demanded.

The man's nervous eyes flicked to the papers that had fallen from the upended table. Justin holstered one of his pistols. He kept the other trained on Elliot as he stooped to gather up the fallen papers.

"Don't move," he warned Elliot, and studied the florid scrawl, glancing up frequently. The first page appeared to be a self-congratulatory summation of the meetings with Herrera, the second a brief letter to Mrs. Elliot. Finally Justin found the passage he was looking for. His eyes darted over the phrases:

". . . *was but a small annoyance, easily dispensed with, and quite profitably, I might add.*" He crumpled the letter and raised hate-filled eyes to the Englishman.

Elliot reached for the oil lamp and hurled it at Justin's head. Justin ducked and nearly pulled the trigger on Elliot. But not yet. The captain still had something to say.

A burning pool formed on the tile floor. "It's getting mighty warm in here," Justin drawled. "You'd better talk fast, Elliot. Now. What have you done with Shiloh?"

"I—she was kidnapped. I had nothing to do with it!"

"Try again, Elliot. The more you lie, the hotter this stove's going to get."

"She was taken by a man called Santiago. He

has some sort of pirate's lair on an island called Sacrificios, off Vera Cruz."

"What was your part in it?"

"Nothing! I did nothing, I—" Elliot screamed as his backside touched the hot iron. "She was going to ruin me! I—I sold her to St. James— Santiago—ah!"

Justin shoved him against the stove. "You're not worth the lead in a single bullet. But if I don't find Shiloh, alive and whole, I'll hunt you down."

Shiloh ached in places she hadn't known she had. From the time she was kicked roughly from her pallet at sunup until she collapsed again after cleaning up from the late dinner hour, she worked. The winding stone halls and stairways of Casa Santiago were spotless from her ceaseless enforced labor. Every wall, every tiny window ledge and nook was cleaned daily. The dark, heavy furniture gleamed.

Shiloh was given every odious task that existed, from emptying chamber pots and spitoons to mucking out the small dog run at the side of the strange, pieced-together house.

Her reward for all of this was that she was left alone by Santiago and his bizarre crew of seasoned pirates and lithe young men. She could stand the taunts and little cruelties of the other maids, but she knew she couldn't have stood being Santiago's whore.

"Get to work," ordered a flat-faced *Indio* woman, stopping to prod Shiloh with her broom.

Shiloh dropped to her bruised knees and resumed her scrubbing. A cough rattled in her throat. She no longer had to pretend illness. The cold, windy nights on a thin pallet, coupled with a poor diet and exhaustion, had weakened her.

When the house settled down for afternoon siesta, Shiloh stole out every day to the beaches, slipping barefoot across the sand and scaling the sharp crags to a hidden, secret cove. Coming and going was easy; Santiago was confident of the security of his sea-moated lair.

Shiloh had spent days gathering driftwood, lashing the smooth white pieces together with the ropelike grass that grew in profusion on the isle. Now her crude raft was finished. Tonight she would climb the wall, drop to the forbidding, ancient ruins of an Olmec sacrificial altar, and dart down to the tiny cove. Her raft wasn't sturdy, but with luck, the ingoing tide would carry her to the mainland.

Shiloh did her usual work and ate rancid, watery *pozole* that evening. It tasted abominable, but she would need all her strength. She stole some corncakes from the detached baking house and ate some of those too, tying a few others into her ragged apron.

Finally, she settled down on her pallet to wait. A small, high window displayed the openness of the night sky, and freedom whispered in on the waves as they crashed against the rocks. By the time the moon rose, Shiloh's nerves were wound taut. She ventured out into the hall, leaning against its cool dampness to will away the trembling of her limbs.

She groped her way along the dark hall and left by a narrow window. A small ledge led up to the walk. Shiloh didn't allow herself to look down; it was a sheer, deadly drop to the crags below. But she had made the climb plenty of times before. Her toughened bare feet knew every foothold and tuft of vegetation to help her along the way.

She reached the upper wall and, as expected, found the watchman snoring under a full moon. She hoisted herself up with a final heave.

Part of the wall crumbled and rocks catapulted fifty feet down. Shiloh froze and hung, legs dangling, watching the guard. Her breathing returned to normal when he didn't stir. She slung her leg over the wall.

Frenzied barking filled the air. *The dogs.* Shiloh had forgotten about the dogs. As she scrambled over the wall, the watchman awoke. She ran the length of the narrow walkway.

The guard shouted to alert the household and dashed after Shiloh. The blood pounded in her veins when she reached the wall, barely touching the jagged stone as she leaped over.

It was a ten-foot drop to the hard-packed ground. Shiloh fell clumsily, pain shooting up her leg. She ignored it and stumbled on toward the Olmec ruins. The moon cast an otherworldly, eerie glow on the ancient temple. But to Shiloh, the crudely cut monoliths offered safe haven from her pursuer, a place to hide.

She delved into the scattered carvings, darting amid huge faces with thick, leering lips rolled back over pronounced jaguar fangs. The creatures from another time, animals given distorted human features, glared in the moonlight. Shiloh crouched behind the jutting chin of some age-old deity, not daring to breathe.

The underbrush rustled nearby. Finally, the footsteps receded and Shiloh dared to creep to the far edge of the cliffs. Like a shadow, she stooped low and scuttled from one rock to the next.

The waves rushed ceaselessly; the salt-scented wind rustled the grass. There was no human sound. She burst from her hiding place, astounding herself at her own speed. Never had she run so fast, so desperately. The brink loomed closer, closer. . . .

And then it was all over. Her ankles were grabbed by a diving, cursing figure. She hit the ground with a jarring thud that knocked the breath from her. It was not the lumbering guard who had caught her, but Santiago.

She raked her broken, uneven nails across his eyes.

Santiago bellowed a curse, clutching at his eye. "Blind!" he screamed. "I'm blinded!"

Shiloh scrambled, half crawling, away from him. But despite his screams, he picked her up and slung her over his shoulder. He went back to the ruins, where a central stone had been crudely cut into a wide-based, bowl-shaped altar. He lay Shiloh on the rough, unyielding rock, straddling her, placing his knees upon her hands, grinding them into the stone.

Shiloh struggled, beating her bare feet against the stone. "The consumption—"

"No more lies!" he shouted. "A woman who is wasting away could never run like you did." Roughly he grabbed a handful of her matted curls. "Do you know what this place is, *diabla tejana?* It is where the ancients fed their hungry gods." He jerked her head to one side and she found herself staring at an obscene goddess, with breasts jutting, the tip of her tongue pointing.

"She is the love goddess. You find her repulsive, but she is the elemental woman: frank, lustful. You will be my love goddess, Shiloh." His dagger gleamed. Shiloh felt the cords of her neck tighten. But the knife didn't touch her. Santiago slipped the point under first one button and then the next. "The ancients had many ways of offering sacrifice. Some victims had their throats slit; others had their hearts cut out before their living eyes." He fumbled at the top of his trousers. "The time has come. The Old Ones will wait no longer."

"No!" Shiloh screamed, writhing beneath him.

She stopped, sure that terror played a cruel trick with her mind. As graceful and catlike as the jaguar deity, a tall form dropped into view. Dripping wet, the moonlight carving shadows in the muscles of his bare chest, he was himself a god, as strong and fierce as the feline sculpture.

She breathed his name like a prayer.

NINETEEN

With a snarl of animal rage, Justin leaped at Santiago, the two falling to the ground beside the altar.

Santiago was beneath Justin, cursing and struggling. The hand that held the dagger was locked between them, quivering in midair, edging first toward one man, then the other.

A bitter, incomprehensible curse leaped from Santiago's mouth. His muscles gave out and the knife, held by his own hand, drove down into his neck.

Blood pulsated from the wound. Incredibly, Santiago dragged himself up, holding the edge of the stone altar. He collapsed onto it, gurgling his life out into the bowl.

Shiloh turned to Justin, unable to speak. She was filled with such a profusion of emotions—horror, relief, love, disbelief—that no words could say what she felt. Justin stood tall and straight with the moon at his back. Shiloh took a step toward him, then another, and then tumbled into his arms. "Justin. I thought I would die tonight. I—"

"Shh. Don't talk. Are you all right?"

Her feet were raw and bleeding, her hands scraped, her jaw already beginning to swell from Santiago's blows. "I'm all right," she said.

He took her hand and led her down to the water. "I left my boat about a hundred yards out," he said. "Can you swim it?"

Shiloh didn't hesitate. More than anything, she wanted to be away from the horror of Sacrificios. She shed the ragged remains of her dress and walked down the sandy beach wearing only her shift. The salt water stung her myriad small wounds, but it was a cleansing sensation and she welcomed it.

They struck out together, Justin staying close in case Shiloh weakened. Both were aware that sharks circulated in the inky night waters, but neither voiced the fear.

Justin pulled himself into the small shallop, helped Shiloh up after him, and began rowing swiftly toward the distant winking lights of the harbor of Vera Cruz.

An hour later, they boarded a French brig of war, called the *Céline*. Justin shielded Shiloh from the stares of the crew and passengers, taking her to a private cabin. A young boy brought fresh water and towels and a meal on a tray.

"Shall I get the ship's doctor?" Justin asked.

"No. I just need to get cleaned up."

Looking at her thin, battered body, he felt a wave of pity.

"How long were you on the island?" he asked. As he spoke, he wetted a towel and began daubing at the lacerations on Shiloh's legs and feet.

"I don't know. Maybe three weeks. I lost track of the time."

There were bruises everywhere in various stages of healing. Her ribs showed plainly and there were shadows beneath her eyes, giving her face an ethereal, hollowed-out look.

"What the hell did he do to you?"

"They were trying to work me to death."

He gave her one of his white broadcloth shirts to wear as a bed gown.

She ate ravenously, devouring the thick fish soup and a quantity of white cheese and bread. Then, as abruptly as a candle flame going out, her eyes closed.

Justin washed himself and lay down, but sleep would not come. He couldn't stop thinking about how close he'd come to losing her.

The usual sickness plagued Shiloh during the voyage home. Yet it was even worse this time. A constant hunger induced her to eat, although most of it was rejected by her protesting body.

Justin was gentle and solicitous, yet strangely distant. While she was in Mexico, Shiloh had imagined their reunion a hundred times. The reality was a far cry from that daydream.

After a brief reunion in Houston with her father, who was now installed in the cottage at Post Oaks to take Wylie's place, they shared a meal and went up to retire for the night. Shiloh bathed in the dressing room, glorying in the feeling of being completely clean for the first time in weeks. She slipped on a white cotton gown and went out to the bedroom. Justin was gone.

Pursing her lips, she went to find him. He was in his study, standing at the open window, looking at the spray of stars across the sky. Shiloh padded over to him on bare feet and wrapped her arms about his waist. She laid her cheek against his back.

"You feel so good to me," she murmured, breathing his scent.

He removed her hands and set her away from him. "You've had a long ordeal, Shiloh. Go upstairs and get some rest."

Her spirits plummeted. "But Justin, we're home at last. Don't you at least want to—"

"No. I have work to do."

"Justin, why are you treating me like this?"

"Perhaps you've had a lapse of memory. Don't you recall drugging me and stealing my billet in Galveston."

"I had to do it. It was the only way."

"You never give up, do you, Shiloh? You had to do it all on your own, to prove your worth as an international spy."

She froze. "Is that what you think?"

"Of course. I'm tired of it, Shiloh. All your

tricks, your lies . . . You really had me fooled
back in March when you threw yourself at me.
I thought we finally had a chance together. But
it was just a way to follow me to Galveston and
take my place on the Mexico mission."

Slowly, she backed away. "You're so wrong."

"Go to bed, Shiloh. I've got things to do."

She fled, slamming the door behind her.

Justin went to his desk and sat down. The idea
of divorce pushed its way back into his mind
again. He'd ask Lamar Coulter about it in the
morning.

For now, he needed something else to occupy
his mind. Nearly two months' worth of correspondence was stacked on his desk. The night
might not seem so long and lonely with the mail
to occupy him.

He shuffled through letters from various
places: Washington, the new capital of Austin,
a thick envelope from the Willows, copies of
newspapers with pieces about the "man in the
white hat" by S. Mulvane. He picked up one of
the letters, creased and smudged, with Mexican markings and his name penned in Shiloh's
tight, neat hand.

"My dearest Justin," he read, his hands tightening on the paper.

*By the time you read this I shall be in Mexico in
pursuit of our acquaintance Capt. E_____. I know
you consider it your place to be here, but I had to come
in your stead. You see, your careful plans were dis-*

*covered by Mrs. S_____, who relayed them to your en-
emies. You would not have been allowed to reach
Mexico alive. It was a cruel deception I played on
you, my darling, but a necessary one. Having so recently discovered my great love for you, I could not
bear the thought of losing you. So forgive me, my heart,
and look to the day when this business is concluded
and we are reunited. Until then, and forever after, I
remain your loving wife, S.*

The words swam before his disbelieving eyes.
She loved him. She *loved* him. Everything she
had endured in Mexico had been for his sake.
His heart filled as he jumped up and climbed
the stairs, taking them two at a time.

He threw open the bedroom door and stood,
clutching the letter in his hand.

Shiloh was at the window. In the moonlight,
tears gleamed on her cheeks.

He lifted the letter. "I didn't know," he said,
his voice rough with emotion.

"I thought you had all the answers."

He winced. "I never knew how you felt about
me, sweetheart. I thought you went to Mexico
just to prove how clever you are."

"You're a fool, Justin. A blind, proud fool.
Didn't you understand what I was saying to you
last March? I was giving myself to you; I don't
know how I could have made myself any
clearer."

"But you never said it, Shiloh."

"I was afraid you'd reject me. Besides, you should have trusted me."

The space between them was wide. The moonlight slid across the floor, emphasizing the distance.

"Is it too late now?" he asked.

She studied his face for a long, searching moment. "No, Justin. I can no more stop loving you than I can stop my heart from beating."

"Girl, you're glowing like the Texas sun," Nate proclaimed, opening the door to his cottage the next morning. "Never saw the likes of it before."

Shiloh leaned up and kissed her father's cheek. His face was tanned and healthy-looking, a great contrast with the dissipated way he used to look. "Ranch life seems to agree with you."

"Oh, it does, believe me. Come on into the kitchen and have something to eat."

She was surprised to see Ina there, frying bacon and setting out a plate of biscuits.

Shiloh was suddenly ravenous. Eagerly she accepted a mug of coffee and sat down. Nate brought an extra stool and seated himself across from her. "Have I told you how proud I am of you?"

She felt a little thrill of pleasure. "No, Papa."

"Well, I am. You pulled off that bit in Mexico like nothing I've ever seen before. Those articles you wrote were the talk of the town. Elliot didn't have a prayer."

She sipped her coffee. "I'm glad it's over. The legislature has voted for annexation and now it's just a matter of time."

"We'll be at war with Mexico soon," Nate said, tempering her gladness.

Ina set down plates heaped with food. Shiloh stared at the bacon and fluffy eggs, her appetite leaving as abruptly as it had come. The smell reviled her and she turned her head away. Not wanting to offend Ina, she nibbled at a biscuit and sipped her coffee. But she saw the bright dark eyes looking pointedly at her plate.

Nate seemed preoccupied as he ate. Shiloh looked at him quizzically. "Are you still thinking about war?"

Nate glanced up, and then at Ina, and burst out laughing. "It's something much closer to home." One of his broad hands reached for hers; the other closed around Ina's. "You're not going to believe this, Shiloh, but this lovely lady has agreed to be my wife."

Ina looked slightly apologetic. "I know I can never replace the mother you lost, Shiloh, but we can be friends if you will allow it."

"Allow it!" Shiloh cried, jumping up. She threw her arms around Ina, her heart bursting with happiness. "Nothing could please me more. When are you getting married?"

"As soon as it can be arranged. Telling you was the last formality."

* * *

In the two weeks that followed, the days were filled with the fun and anticipation of preparing for the wedding, and the nights were soft with tender lovemaking. It was a golden time, aglow with love and kinship.

The weather was perfect on the day of the wedding. The ranch hands had raised an octagonal gazebo in the yard. Shiloh and Prairie Flower festooned it with ribbons and golden marigolds, dark-pink crepe myrtle, and the laceweed that grew wild in the meadows.

Nate and Justin were setting up benches for the guests as Shiloh arrived with still more wildflowers. Nate gestured to her and she came to his side.

"I wanted to tell you together," he said, looking from one to the other. "Ina and I will be making a wedding trip. We're leaving tonight on the late steamer. I'm taking her to Mexico to find her family."

"Are you sure that's wise, Nate?" Justin asked.

"We'll be all right. War's still a long way off."

Shiloh kissed his cheek. "I think it's a lovely idea. How long will you be gone?"

"Months. Maybe a year." He turned to Justin. "I've asked Eb to take my place around here while I'm gone. He's an old coot, but he works damned hard."

"Thank you, Nate." Justin shook his father-in-law's hand. "And good luck."

Shiloh placed her flowers in a large crock and went upstairs to find Ina. At Shiloh's insistence, Ina had agreed to dress in an upper guest room, her own quarters off the kitchen being far too small.

"All this fuss," Ina scolded. *"Dios,* I am not a young bride of eighteen."

Shiloh laughed and hugged her. "Every bride is special, Ina."

The handsome face softened. "I have a present for you."

"But this is *your* day," Shiloh protested. She broke off and gasped when Ina opened a box and moved aside the tissue. Proudly she held up the most beautiful dress Shiloh had ever seen.

It was a gown of muslin, its lines simple, but it was embroidered so lavishly that it stunned the senses. Tiny, varicolored stitches depicted every field flower known in Texas: the intense color of spring bluebonnets, the deep reds of Indian paintbrush, lavender wisteria, and yellow jessamine, all united by twining green vines.

"I started it a long time ago, when you left. It was for your birthday in May, so it's a little late."

Shiloh hugged the gown to her. Digging deeper into the box, Ina took out a circlet of dried flowers, woven together.

"For your hair," Ina said.

"But it's your wedding day, not mine, Ina."

"Don't worry," Ina said, smiling. "I managed

to make something quite acceptable for myself from that yellow silk you insisted on buying me."

The minute Ina held up the dress for her to see, Shiloh knew she wouldn't outshine the bride. The yellow dress had been cunningly pleated and gathered, the skirt drawn up on one side with a subtly Latin flare.

Prairie Flower arrived with a tray of food to tide them over until the barbecue after the wedding. Shiloh attacked the cornbread and pickle-preserved vegetables.

Almost immediately, she regretted it. The now-familiar nausea rose, and she ran for the chamber pot. When she returned, she looked slightly sheepish. "I guess I've had a nervous stomach lately," she said. "I don't understand it, I've always been so—" She broke off, seeing the curious way the other two women were looking at her.

"What is it?" she demanded. "Why are you laughing?"

Prairie Flower circled Shiloh slowly, speculatively, lifting her chin, examining the lines of her torso from breasts to hips. "Six moons," she said. "Maybe five and a half. Then the baby comes."

"A *baby*?" Shiloh whispered, hardly daring to breathe the word. Then she gave an overjoyed whoop, hugging Prairie Flower and then Ina. "A baby of my very own! I can hardly believe it." She ran for the door. "I've got to tell Justin." She leaped down the stairs and out into the garden. "Justin!" she cried, running across the lawn to him. "Justin, I have something to tell you!" She collided with him.

He caught her in his arms and pulled her against his sweat-damp chest. "Slow down, sweetheart. Now, what's on your mind?"

"Justin," she panted, "I—I'm—" She broke off, looking around. The ranch hands were watching her, openly amused by her display. Suddenly, she knew the time wasn't right. Something so important demanded privacy, intimacy, a special moment.

"Well?" Justin asked, grinning.

"I love you," she said simply, and leaned up to kiss him. Then she was gone, leaving him to smile, bemused, behind her.

Birdsong and the gentle strumming of Leonicio's guitar provided wedding music of incomparable sweetness. Rows of smiling guests from Houston—the Allens and the Hankses, Lamar Coulter and Mr. Murphy, even two Texas Rangers—graced the benches beneath a spreading oak tree. Nate Mulvane stood, stiff and nervous and glowing with pride, awaiting his bride. Shiloh caught his eye and smiled encouragingly.

Ina arrived shortly, blushing, clutching Justin's arm. Justin placed Ina's hand in Nate's, bent and kissed her, and stepped back to stand beside Shiloh as the ceremony began.

His hand stole out and found hers, squeezing it as Nate and Ina repeated their vows. Shiloh looked up at him. The two of them had never spoken such words to each other, but now, hearing them, it was as if they had. Silently they promised a lifetime of love and faithfulness, erasing all the bitterness that had gone before.

Shiloh had never felt so full. Tears of happiness rolled down her cheeks as she contemplated their bright future, with her loving husband, her father and Ina nearby, and soon, a baby. . . . She almost sobbed for joy.

The wedding celebration was glorious. A fiddler from town scratched out happy melodies, and food was consumed in huge quantities. Everyone was full of good wishes, toasting the newlyweds until shadows crept long and the sun began to set. The guests trickled homeward, and Shiloh and Justin stood beneath the flower-decked gazebo, smiling at each other.

"People say there's nothing more beautiful than a bride," he murmured, "but I think I've found someone who is."

It was time to tell him about the baby. The moment was perfect, shining with rose-gold light, alive with the sounds of birds and fragrant with the perfume of flowers.

Shiloh brought both of Justin's hands to her lips and kissed them. "Justin —"

"Oh, my," interrupted a familiar voice. "Aren't they the happy couple?" Jessamine West, escorted by Charles Elliot, came up the walk.

"This silly little wedding has turned out to be the social event of the summer," she said. "I'm quite miffed that I wasn't included. And poor Charles here has been treated like an outcast ever since those terrible articles came out in the paper."

"You both got what you deserved," Shiloh said.

Jessamine's yellow ringlets bobbed in agitation as she began to pace. "Nothing in my life has been right since you came into it, Shiloh. First you robbed me of the man I was supposed to marry, and then you ruined my father with your meddling. He was killed because of you, too. Both of you!"

Shiloh felt an unexpected wave of pity for the girl. She had a twisted sense of logic, but beneath the anger she was truly agonizing.

"Jessamine, I'm sorry about your father."

"Shut up! I don't want your sympathy. I think it's time Justin learned exactly what went on down in Mexico."

"He already knows everything," Shiloh snapped.

"Does he know you and the captain were lovers in Mexico?"

Justin's face hardened; Shiloh's hand went to her mouth. "Oh, my God," she whispered, shaking her head in denial. "Oh, my God."

Justin had gone rigid. He spoke in a deadly calm voice to Charles Elliot. "Is this true?"

Elliot produced a crumpled sheet of paper, holding it out as if it were a distasteful thing.

Shiloh gasped as she recognized a page from the journal she'd kept in Mexico, where she'd recorded her most private and intimate thoughts. "You have no right," she stormed. "That journal is private!"

Justin snatched the paper and scanned it with his eyes. Shiloh knew with one glance that it was the page she'd written about their lovemaking, one soft night when the music of harps had set her to longing. She saw a small flower which she'd idly drawn in the margin.

"I can tell you other things about your wife that only a lover would know," Elliot suggested. "The scar, for instance. Pity such a lovely thigh had to be marred like that."

Justin's fist shot out and smashed into the leering face. Elliot reeled and fell, blood spurting from his nose.

"Get out of here," Justin said. "If I ever see you again, I'll kill you."

When they had gone, Shiloh collapsed against Justin's chest. "I hope I've seen the last of them." She put her arms around him to try to recapture the tender moment that had been so unpleasantly interrupted. But his body was stiff and unyielding and his arms hung at his sides.

She looked up. "Justin?"

His fist crumpled the page he was holding. "Is it true?"

She took a step back. "I can't believe you're

asking me that. Doesn't my word mean anything to you?"

"You didn't give me your word about anything. Did you go to his room?"

"How dare you interrogate me!" She snatched the paper away. "Yes, damn it, I did go to Elliot's room. But it was to get evidence!"

"And did you show him your scar while you performed your patriotic duty? How far did you go to prove yourself a master spy, Shiloh?"

Fury burst from her and she slapped his face, all the rage she felt putting great force into the blow.

Justin gave her a last hard look and turned sharply. He strode off into the evening light.

TWENTY

Houston swarmed with immigrants eager to settle the nation's newest state. Cotton factors, jubilant after sending off a record crop, celebrated in the grog shops and hotels. There was an air of newness about the town, anticipation of good things to come.

Justin hunched over his beer in a saloon, listening to the talk and laughter around him. Now and then a woman sidled up, her painted face issuing a clear invitation. Justin only shook his head and looked away, and signaled the barkeep for more beer.

A pair of traders came in, their fringed and beaded buckskins greasy and stained, probably from weeks on the trail. One of them had a copy of the *Morning Star.*

"What month is this, Jake?" one of them asked.

"You kind of lose track out on the frontier, don't you, Mason?" He glanced down at the papers. "October ninth."

"What's been going on?"

"One of these days I'm going to learn you to read, Mason. Let's see here . . . seems we'll be joining the Union officially early next year. Oh, and here's another article by S. Mulvane. I hear tell she coaxed the secrets out of Captain Elliot in the boudoir, so to speak."

Slamming his beer down, Justin stalked out of the saloon. At first, he'd challenged everyone who dared repeat the rumor, laying the men flat and leaving the women gasping at his language. But now he realized that there was little he could do to stop the gossip that had been perpetuated by Jessamine West.

He didn't go to town much. He couldn't stand the knowing looks, the pitying glances. Thanks to Jessamine, half of Houston knew his wife had left him after a confrontation with Charles Elliot. The Englishman had fled north, pleading ill health, and Shiloh was away at her aunt's.

He went to the auction house and did some horse trading, making a good profit for himself. He got no satisfaction from the deal; he never did anymore. His life was hollow, joyless. He lived haphazardly from day to day, trying—and failing— to forget the red-haired girl who had, for one golden, fleeting moment, captured his heart.

He stopped on the rise in front of Post Oaks. The ranch was the picture of prosperity, a land tamed. Horses grazed on autumn grasses and drank from a placid, newly dug tank. The fencing was finished, straight outlines stretching for miles across the acres. Tomás, growing tall and straight into adolescence, was working with a horse in the corral.

Browning leaves blew across the path as Justin rode up to the house. He tried to ignore the gnawing at his gut. This should have been a triumphal year for him and Shiloh. Statehood was imminent; the ranch was a success. The culmination of all they'd worked for should have made their happiness complete.

But she'd left without speaking another word to him that night in June.

Months later, he was still haunted by her, hearing her laughter in the rustle of the wind, seeing her smile in the opening flowers in the morning. And then there were those articles, dozens of them, published by the *Morning Star*. She wrote political opinions, supported abolition, or merely described a pastoral Texas scene. Justin tortured himself by reading all that she wrote. It was like hearing her speak again: impassioned, witty, full of conviction.

He knew that something would give soon. Perhaps he'd sell the ranch, hook up with the Texas Rangers, and leave for the frontier.

A flock of geese wheeled overhead, flying to the sun-warmed regions below Matagorda. Shiloh watched them from her rocking chair on the porch, feeling as bleak as the iron-gray November sky. There was a pronounced stirring in her belly. The tiny, secret presence there was as restless as Shiloh herself.

Sharon appeared with a tray. She poured two cups of tea and leaned on the railing, the strands of her graying hair lifted by a cool breeze. "I finished putting up the late squash."

"You should have let me help you."

"Nonsense. You were busy with your writing. Did you finish with the piece?"

Shiloh nodded. "I wrote about a barn cat making a nest in the hay for her kittens. I seem to be preoccupied with nest-making these days."

"It's only natural. Your time's getting close."

"The weeks seem to drag by. I can't wait to make this little person's acquaintance."

Sharon reached into her apron pocket. "A letter from your father. He tells me they've located Ina's family in San Miguel de Allende."

"That's wonderful."

"Nate's not going to like it when he finds out you're here, Shiloh."

"I'll deal with that when he gets back from Mexico. Was there anything else in the post?"

Sharon produced another envelope, pursing her lips. Shiloh immediately recognized the scrawling handwriting. As always, she peered inside. And as always, there was a sum of money without a word of explanation. "Send it back," she said, handing Sharon the envelope.

"Shiloh, he wants to help."

"I won't accept a penny from him. I'm surprised he hasn't gotten the message by now. I must have sent back a dozen of these." She winced slightly as the baby moved.

Noticing, Sharon shook her head. "We're going to be so helpless, you and I. Neither of us has ever been a mother before."

"We'll manage," Shiloh assured her. "There was a baby at Post Oaks for a while. Cassandra. I think we all fell a little bit in love with her. Even Justin used to—" She broke off and swallowed, angry at herself for blundering into the unwelcome thought of him.

"Shiloh," Sharon said gently, "hasn't this gone on long enough?"

"I'm not going back there."

"The man has a right to know about the baby."

"No. I won't have him pitying me, or trying to reconcile with me for the sake of the baby."

"This is all just an awful misunderstanding. If you simply went to him and explained, I know he'd forgive you."

"There's nothing to forgive. Don't you see, Aunt Sharon, he didn't trust me. He believed all those lies—"

"Only because you allowed him to. You're two proud, stubborn people. Foolish people. Living in misery when, with a word or two, you could be happy together."

"I could never be happy with a man who doesn't trust me."

Sharon looked up, spying a small figure coming up the path in a mule cart. "Here's Mrs. Mimms, come to check on the baby."

Mrs. Mimms was a "granny lady," an ex-slave who claimed to have delivered some three hundred babies. She lived with a family a few miles distant.

Sharon brought her some tea, and she examined Shiloh and questioned her closely about her diet and activities. "Four weeks, girl," she proclaimed. "Not a day more."

Shiloh felt a thrill of excitement. "Thank you, Mrs. Mimms." She pressed a silver coin into the woman's hand.

Afterward she stood on the porch, watching the evening color streak the horizon and the first winking star in the sky. Her hand strayed to her middle.

"It won't be long now," she whispered.

A chill wind rolled in off the plains. Shivering, Shiloh turned and went into the house.

"Are you sure you want to do this, Justin?" Lamar Coulter asked, looking across his paper-strewn desk

He shrugged. "It won't raise any more of a scandal than we already have."

"I've never handled a divorcing before."

Justin indicated a shelf that sagged with numerous fat tomes. "You've got all those law books. You should be able to figure it out."

Lamar sighed "I just don't feel right about this."

He looked dubious, but promised to get the papers ready and present them to Shiloh.

Justin walked out into the muddy street. The penetrating, bone-chilling iciness of a blue norther whipped down the alleys of Houston. The weather matched his mood. It was raw and inhumanly cold. An appropriate setting in which to end a chapter of his life.

Shiloh could have the ranch; with Nate's help, she'd do all right. Justin would satisfy his bitter restlessness somewhere on the frontier, riding with the Rangers in the Comanchería, on the very fringes of civilized society.

The rough life would suit him, just as scouting had suited him when he'd first come to Texas. He'd come full circle, experiencing many things before learning where he belonged. Yet in spite of all the pain and bitterness, he wouldn't have traded a minute of it.

Sleet lashed against the windowpanes of Sharon Bledsoe's house, and the wind penetrated even the smallest cracks in the walls. Shiloh shifted her position on the settee, where she lay before a large, crackling fire. She couldn't seem to get comfortable today, nor could she concentrate on her writing. The baby, too, was restless, writhing within its increasingly cramped space.

Mrs. Mimms had been staying with them, since the weather had been bad and Shiloh was so close to her time. The baby had dropped two days earlier. It was the week before Christmas, and Mrs. Mimms clearly expected the birth soon.

Above the hiss of the wind and the rattle of the windows, an insistent rapping sounded.

"My goodness," Sharon murmured, "who can that be?"

The voice Shiloh heard was vaguely familiar. Frowning, she tried to remember. And then it came to her: Lamar Coulter. In sudden alarm, she drew her knees up and pulled the quilt up to her chin, concealing the rounded swell of her pregnancy. She didn't want Coulter to go running to Justin with her secret.

"Sit down, Mr. Coulter," Sharon was saying. "I'll bring you something warm to drink."

His eyes took in the small cozy room and the aging black woman sitting in the corner with a bit of knitting to occupy her hands. Shiloh held her breath as he looked about. There wasn't a proper cradle for the baby, but Sharon had lined a small wooden crate with blankets. It stood near the hearth.

"What brings you here, Lamar?" she asked.

He hung his hat and cape by the fire to dry out and pulled a stool up next to her. Looking distinctly uncomfortable, he drew out a sheaf of folded papers. "Justin asked me to go over this with you."

"Oh? Is it something concerning the ranch? I figure it would be clear that I lay no claim to Post Oaks."

He handed her the papers. "This is a bill of divorcement. Believe me, I tried to get the marriage annulled, but couldn't come up with sufficient cause. However, we've managed to avoid any mention of you and El—er—that is, it's a simple case of abandonment."

Shiloh's heart turned to stone. Only when she felt a light snuffed out within her did she realize that, all these months, she'd harbored and nourished a faint flicker of hope that Justin would come for her. The papers she held in her hand dealt that tiny flame a suffocating blow. She knew she shouldn't be surprised. Justin was a young man. He could marry again. . . . She forced aside the agonizing thought and picked up a pen from the table beside the settee. "Where do I sign?"

Lamar suddenly took the papers from her. "Shiloh, maybe you shouldn't. This is all a big mistake."

"No," she said, reclaiming the papers. "If this is what he wants, I'll sign."

"It's not what he wants. The man doesn't even know himself anymore. You should see him; he's like a hollowed-out shell. He needs you, Shiloh."

Her pen scratched resolutely across the bottom of the paper. "If Justin's confused, I'm not."

"Breathe out, girl. Don't be holding your breath," said Mrs. Mimms, allowing Shiloh to clutch at her hand. "You've got to send that baby some air."

Shiloh let out her breath in a huge puff. Her labor was passing in a thick haze of pain, punctuated by the sharp, iron-banded agony of her contractions. She endured it in silence, concentrating on the star pattern of a quilt that hung from a rack at the end of the bed.

But now the pains were coming fast, thundering through her, battering her spirit. A pressure began building deep within her, pounding, demanding release. Shiloh heard herself calling Justin's name, but she was in too much pain to chide herself for it.

"Bear down," said Mrs. Mimms.

Shiloh strained with all her might until her ears rang, and her hands grew raw as she clutched at the bed frame. The baby burst from her in a great rush. Sharon sobbed and Shiloh grew rigid. Then a high wail filled the room.

"A boy," Mrs. Mimms said. "A fine boy-child."

There was one last, convulsing pain, the afterbirth, and Shiloh's body returned to her control. She reached for the hastily swaddled bundle.

He was a miracle, pure and simple. Blotched and wizened, dark, colorless eyes unseeing, tiny mouth opening to cry, yet he was the most awesomely beautiful thing Shiloh had ever beheld.

"Hello, baby," she whispered, already full of love for the tiny creature. At the sound of her voice, the child quieted and seemed to stare into his mother's face. He grimaced slightly, appearing to smile.

Shiloh's heart caught in her throat. The little

red cheek was creased with a dimple, one that echoed his father's so precisely that she began to cry.

"Damn it, Lamar, it's been eight weeks since Shiloh signed that paper."

"Be patient, Justin," said Lamar Coulter. "These things take time. All the legal cases have been slowed down by the transition from republic to statehood."

Justin had the distinct impression that Lamar was evading him. He turned to watch Tomás in the corral. The boy was working with Dawn, the little filly Justin and Shiloh had brought into the world together nearly three years ago.

It seemed like only yesterday when a young girl, feisty and full of bravado, had accosted him in Washington-on-the-Brazos. Every memory was crystal clear, as if it had just happened. Justin had hoped that the years would dim the remembrances, but it hadn't worked that way. He wouldn't rest until it was all over, and he was deep into the open grasslands of the Comanchería.

A dog barked in the distance, a little cur pup Justin had given Tomás at Christmastime. He looked up to see the dog running down the road toward an approaching wagon. Justin recognized Nate and Ina Mulvane returning at last from their wedding trip.

Nate jumped down from the cart. "Damn, but

it's good to see you," he said. "And the ranch looking so fine. Here, I think my wife needs a little help getting down."

Justin grinned from ear to ear as he beheld Ina. The woman blushed furiously under his delighted scrutiny of her pregnant belly. He kissed the flaming cheek and turned to Nate.

"Why, you old coot," he said, pumping Nate's hand.

Nate swelled visibly with pride. "This time, there'll be no mistakes, no foolishness. Where's Shiloh?" he asked. "Where's my girl?"

"She's staying with your sister." Keeping his voice flat, holding back all emotion, Justin explained.

"You ought to be horsewhipped," Nate growled when he'd finished. "She loved you, you dadblamed fool. She wanted to protect you. Have you bothered to think about what it was like for her in Mexico? She was alone, desperate. She did the best she could. And you threw her out because of it."

"She left of her own accord. I think she was secretly glad that we ended it. I've been sending her money regularly, but she always returns it. Apparently, the paper's paying her enough to get by on."

Nate shot him a hard look. Then he called over his shoulder to Tomás. "Saddle me a horse, lad. I'm going to see my girl."

* * *

"I'm glad we decided to make this trip to Austin," Shiloh declared to Sharon. The big coach bounced and she clutched the sleeping baby more firmly to her bosom. "I think it's important for little Nathaniel to witness the birth of his state. When he's older I'll tell him all about it, so he can be a proud son of Texas."

"Don't forget to tell him of your part in all this. Texas owes you a debt of gratitude."

Shiloh knew she'd never be able to speak of those years of her life, for those were the years she'd spent with Justin.

She glanced down at the baby. He was the center of her life now. So sweet, so beautiful. Nathaniel almost filled the cold emptiness in her heart. Almost.

When he grew older and inevitably noticed the absence of a father, she didn't know what she would tell him. She'd given him the McCord name, even though she wasn't sure whether or not she was divorced at the time of his birth. But it was the only thing she'd allow Justin to give, unknowingly, to the boy.

One of the riders ahead of the coach shouted. Leaning out, Shiloh saw the new capital city far in the distance. A cluster of log buildings, and little more. But she'd already decided that this would be her home.

She hadn't told Sharon yet, but her mind was made up. Her editor at the *Morning Star* had agreed to let her be the Austin correspondent and had generously given her enough money to set up housekeeping. In Austin she wouldn't have to hide. Her son would be a hundred miles away from the father he'd never know.

Austin, Texas
February 19, 1846

"Look, we're not too late," Nate said, pointing to the crowd in the distant capital city. He made sure that Justin spurred his horse faster, and then followed.

Nate had convinced Justin that this February day in 1846 was not to be missed. That was the first hurdle. His next task was much more difficult, but the rewards would make it all worthwhile.

Nate knew that the reunion he was forcing on the unsuspecting Justin and Shiloh might end in disaster. But better that than never to know. He would merely bring them together; the rest was up to them.

They tethered their horses at the foot of newly cleared Congress Avenue and made their way through a noisy, celebrating throng clustered around the pine-timbered capitol building. President Anson Jones was on the porch, surrounded by other officials, including Mr. Henderson, who would become the new state's first governor. Overhead, the lone-star flag flapped its farewell to the wind.

"Come on, Nate," Justin chided. "You don't have to push."

"I just want to get a closer look. There. There's a space, just to the right of the steps."

Justin stood stock-still while the crowd around him surged and swayed.

There was Shiloh, not ten feet away, her red-gold curls blowing against her beautiful face, her eyes contemplative as she lifted them to the flag.

Justin groped for his voice. "Damn you, Nate."

"Go to her, Justin."

His eyes left Shiloh for a fraction of a second. He noticed Sharon Bledsoe, a few paces back. Seeing him, she lifted a swaddled bundle to reveal the sleeping face of a blond-headed baby—*his* baby.

His heart began to race. But he stood rooted to the spot.

And then Shiloh's gaze locked with Justin's. He could see from the rapid rise and fall of her chest that she was as shocked as he.

The crowd blurred into the background. Everything except Shiloh ceased to exist.

All around, the crowd hushed, and Anson Jones began to speak. A few of his words penetrated the thundering in Justin's ears.

"The lone star of Texas, which rose over fields of carnage, and obscurely shone for a while, has culminated . . ."

Shiloh took a tiny step backward. Justin's fists clenched and sweat broke out on his brow.

". . . and become fixed forever in that glorious constellation . . ."

The baby woke and whimpered a little, the sound a miracle to Justin's ears.

Finally, his leaden feet began to come to life. He took one step, slowly. He wouldn't be able to stand it if she ran away.

". . . the American Union. The final act in this great drama is now performed," Jones continued. "The Republic of Texas is no more."

The crowd stamped and hooted wildly, mostly for joy, although there were a few protesting catcalls. Then silence reigned as the lone-star flag was lowered and the Union banner rose in its place.

Justin crossed the distance between him and Shiloh, his heart so full of adoration that he almost soared to her.

Suddenly, they were clinging to each other, desperate with love. Caught together in the aching sweetness of their embrace, the small baby in view behind them, their two shattered hearts became whole again, became one.